S0-BOB-570

HANK STEINBERG

OUT OF RANGE

HARPER

An Imprint of HarperCollinsPublishers

HARPER

An Imprint of HarperCollins*Publishers*
195 Broadway
New York, New York 10007

First Harper premium printing: July 2014
First William Morrow hardcover printing: June 2013

HarperCollins® and Harper® are registered trademarks of Harper-Collins Publishers.

Printed in the United States of America

Visit Harper paperbacks on the World Wide Web at
www.harpercollins.com

10 9 8 7 6 5 4 3 2 1

*For my K, who gave me L and V
and everything else*

ACKNOWLEDGMENTS

This book would never have been written without the prodding and support of Richard Abate, Erwin Stoff and Walter Sorrells. To my wife, who reads every draft of everything I write, I owe a debt of gratitude for her invaluable feedback and her constancy. To my parents, thank you for engendering in me a love of stories and for always being such unabashedly biased readers of my material. I also must thank my editor, David Highfill, for his patience, optimism and guidance throughout this process. And to all the fans of *Without a Trace*, whose enthusiasm and support gave me the opportunity to hone my craft, I really hope you enjoy reading this. . . .

OUT
OF
RANGE

PART I

ORIGINS

Charlie Davis lit the day's umpteenth cigarette as he pressed the brake on his battered Toyota Land Cruiser, slowing down to address the heavily armed men in gray uniforms.

It was the fourth military checkpoint he and his guide had to contend with in the last hundred miles. For Faruz, this was a routine matter, an inconvenient repression like many others he had to endure as an involuntary citizen of the Republic of Uzbekistan. For Charlie, an American who'd spent the better part of two years here, the presence of these soldiers continued to be a source of unchecked outrage.

"Papers!" demanded the sullen young private, negligently pointing his AK-47 at Charlie's chest.

Charlie handed over his documentation—U.S. passport, press identification, forged interprovince visa (thanks to his resourceful friend Faruz).

The soldier examined the papers for longer than seemed necessary, then finally grunted, "You are journalist." The young man spoke in accented English, but in any language, the tone was clear. This was an accusation more than a question.

"You can read," Charlie quipped, hoping the hostility in his eyes complemented his sarcasm.

"What you doing in Fergana Valley?"

"Meeting some friends for *plov*."

Charlie felt his travel mate shift in the passenger

seat. Faruz hated it when he did this—made things harder than they needed to be—but Charlie didn't care. He stared defiantly at the soldier. "Would you like me to call the American consulate and have someone speak to you? I can do that."

The soldier assessed Charlie. This was not a headache he needed. He handed back the documentation and reluctantly waved them through.

Charlie put the car in drive and sped away, kicking up dirt in his wake.

"Cowboy," Faruz noted dryly, and lit a cigarette of his own.

Half an hour later, Charlie steered the Land Cruiser up a steep slope and into the tiny border town of Ragdovir.

"I don't like this place," Faruz said, his accent an odd amalgam of Uzbek, Russian and American. "I don't like one bit."

Charlie didn't like it either. But there was no way in hell he was turning back now. It had taken three days just to get here. Three days following the ancient path of the Silk Road from the Uzbek capital of Tashkent, up increasingly pitted and dangerous roads, through at least a dozen hostile checkpoints, and into a mountainous region whose inhabitants seemed poorer and more sullen with every kilometer he drove.

Three decades ago Uzbekistan had been a thriving province of the Soviet Union, famed for its cotton and silk production, a mining and manufacturing center. But after the Soviet Union collapsed, its captive markets and special privileges had collapsed, too. Now Uzbekistan was a ragtag fiefdom ruled by one man, Islam Karimov, a former Soviet apparatchik who had used the fall of the USSR as a chance to seize an entire country, running it into the ground for the benefit of himself and a small group of cronies. Ragdovir had once been a way station on the Silk Road, a major stopping point between Samarkand and the high passes of the Hindu Kush. Of course, the Silk Road had died centuries ago, even before the coming of the Russians, and now Ragdovir was just an insignificant little dot on the Kazakh border, an insular haven for smugglers and thieves.

It was a risk even driving in here, but Charlie knew that if he didn't find the woman they were looking for, he would lose a golden opportunity to expose the Uzbek government for what it was. And that was something he'd been determined to do since the first week he'd set foot in this godforsaken country.

As they neared the center of the town, the screechy wail of the muezzin called the people to prayer, his voice amplified by speakers hanging from a tilted minaret that seemed to loom over everything.

"Left here," Faruz said, squinting at a wrinkled old Soviet-era military map.

Charlie squeezed the Toyota between two houses into a narrow gap that barely qualified as an alley, much less a street. A collection of undernourished children were playing war with plastic guns, shooting each other and dying extravagantly. Seeing the oncoming car, the children scattered.

The alley—so narrow that Charlie's mirrors scraped occasionally on the walls—traced a serpentine path through a collection of houses that looked to have been in decline for centuries.

"Stop here," Faruz said, pointing to a reddish door.

Charlie parked and climbed slowly out of the car, his legs aching from the long, tense drive, and his guide banged on the scarred maroon door with his fist.

A minute passed.

"I thought they were supposed to be here," Charlie said.

Before Faruz could respond, the door opened. A young boy with one milky white eye and one startling green eye stood in the doorway, aiming an old shotgun at them.

"Hey!" Faruz shouted. "Get that out of my face!"

Charlie quickly read the boy's age as twelve or thirteen and knew that despite the scowl, he had to be terrified. "Your mother asked us to come," Charlie reassured him in impeccable Russian. "We're here to see your brother."

A staccato female voice broke the stalemate.

The boy stood aside silently, allowing Charlie and Faruz to enter the courtyard. In the center of the small enclosed space was a fountain of cracked tile, burbling with clear water. A crooked fig tree stood at the far end. Underneath it sat a small, weary figure. Eyes dark and guarded, her wrinkled face lit by the last glowing rays of the sun, she looked to be about sixty. Charlie knew, in this country, that would put her much closer to forty.

"*Asalaam alaikum*, Palonchi Ursalov," Charlie greeted her, hand over his heart.

"You said you would be here yesterday." She spoke in Uzbek and she spoke directly to Faruz.

Charlie knew that if he was going to get through to her, to break the barrier of distrust, he would have to be the one to respond. He also knew that it would go a long way if he could converse with her in her native tongue, even though she would surely be fluent in Russian, as he was.

"I'm sorry," Charlie said in his halting Uzbek. "As I'm sure you know, the journey from Tashkent can be a rigorous one."

The woman looked at him oddly and Charlie instantly realized his faux pas. This woman had never been to Tashkent. No one in this part of the country had. She would have no idea what the journey would be like or how long it would take. Thankfully, she was too proud to admit this and let him off the hook with a fatalistic shrug, turning to the boy and ordering him to bring tea.

The boy went inside the tiny house and shouted at someone else. As the last echoes of the muezzin's call died out, Charlie's eyes began adjusting to the fading evening light and he grew conscious of a faint, unpleasant odor emanating from behind him. He realized it came from something he'd only glanced at briefly as he entered, something draped in a white sheet that lay in the shadows of the darkest corner of the courtyard. He looked at Faruz. They both knew what must lie beneath it.

A small girl, no more than four years old, came out with a warped tin platter. Perched on it were a small plate of almonds and dates, along with two chipped glasses containing dark, steaming tea.

Charlie slowly sipped the offering, burning his tongue. In Uzbekistan it was never wise to stampede to your point, but finally he set the tea down and said, "Tell me about your son."

The woman glanced at Faruz. The guide nodded his reassurance and she began: "Two weeks ago, they took him away. When they gave him back to me . . ." Her eyes flicked briefly to the shroud in the corner. "When they gave him back to me, they told me that he had fallen off a stool in his prison cell."

"What really happened?" Charlie asked.

She hesitated, peering at the boy squatting in the doorway to the house.

"I have two sons. I don't want Salim to fall off a stool, too."

"I understand that." Charlie leaned forward. "But we have a chance to do something. To give some meaning to this tragedy. If someone doesn't try to make this country better, nothing will ever change."

Palonchi Ursalov studied her surviving boy, lip quivering briefly, emotions threatening to spill out. But then her face became a mask. She rose, walked to the dark corner, knelt next to the white-covered form, and put her hand on the shroud.

The woman hesitated, then turned, her eyes pinned on Charlie as though he were the one responsible for what lay beneath it. With one hard, angry tug, she yanked the cloth off.

Faruz instantly turned away and made a sound as if he'd been punched in the throat. Charlie had been a foreign correspondent for a decade, and had seen a lot of terrible things. Somalia, Afghanistan, Burundi, Yemen . . . but this was about as bad as it got.

A young man, barely more than a boy, lay on a

board. He appeared to have been torn apart. His genitals were gone. A rib protruded like a blackened stump from his chest. One leg was twisted at the knee, the foot rotated backward. The other lay separated from the body, tendons hanging limply around the glistening ball of the hip joint. An ear had been removed, perhaps ripped off with pliers. His face was an unrecognizable mess.

"Jesus," Charlie whispered.

"He was an engineering student at the university," she said. "He never hurt anybody. He never agitated against the government. He never caused trouble."

Charlie cleared his throat. "Do you know why he was arrested then?"

"Some of his friends at school. They are the ones who agitate. But not my boy. Not my boy."

When things got ugly like this, Charlie fell back on his professionalism to maintain composure, so he tried to remain clinical, to keep careful tabs on the appearance of the body, on all the little physical details. But finally the horror of it overwhelmed him and he had to look away.

Faruz was squatting on the far side of the courtyard, holding his head in his hands, visibly shaking. The brother, Salim, stood in the doorway, jaw clenched with anger and grief, tears running down the side of his nose.

Charlie looked once again at the dead boy's grieving mother.

"You understand I'll need pictures," he said gently.

For Muslims, any depiction of the human form was fraught with difficulties. Traditionally, art in the Islamic world was forbidden from representing the human body at all. To take photographs of her son this way was more than just a violation of his privacy. It was an act of profound impiety.

Palonchi Ursalov rose slowly to her feet, glaring at Charlie. There was naked disgust in her eyes. Maybe even hatred. But for all her anger, she knew what had to be done.

With her head held erect and her face composed, she walked silently back into the house and softly closed the door. After a moment, Faruz rose from his fetal crouch and scuttled out into the alley.

Charlie was left alone with the younger boy, who continued to squat on the other side of the courtyard, his one good eye watching Charlie's every move.

Slowly, gravely, Charlie pulled out his camera and began to photograph the ruined young man on the ground.

Three weeks later

The protest in Babur Square, in the heart of the provincial capital of Andijan, had been building for hours and Julie Davis had been handing out placards since midmorning. The event had been organized hastily—the day before—in order to stave off restrictive action from the hypervigilant government, but the crowd was growing far beyond what anybody could have expected. As she watched the thousands of angry, inspired people pour into the square, Julie realized the event was taking on a heady—maybe even frightening—momentum, and with her baby due in less than five weeks, she wanted to be with her husband.

She checked her watch and searched for him again in the crowd. With his sandy hair, broad shoulders and indefinable American-ness, Charlie would be easy to pick out. Finally, she spotted him and Faruz making their way through the throng of protesters. When Charlie saw her, he waved and ambled over, greeting her with an impassioned kiss on the lips.

"What'd I miss?" he asked with a grin.

"Only the beginning of a revolution," she said proudly.

He marveled as he took in the scene. "There must be ten thousand people here."

In the center of the square stood a statue of a turbaned man on horseback—a famous Uzbek sultan named Babur—portrayed in a slightly jarring Soviet-realist style. A young man stood on the pink granite pedestal, shouting into a bullhorn in strident Uzbek.

Julie saw Faruz's eyes open wide as he watched with a combination of hope and fear. She couldn't help but try to allay his anxiety. "It's all right, Faruz. It's just a peaceful protest."

Faruz looked at her skeptically. "You shouldn't be here." He noted her protruding stomach. "Not with your boy coming."

She felt Charlie look at her and knew he was thinking roughly the same thing.

"If the government was going to stop it, they would've done it by now," she said confidently.

Faruz looked at Charlie. "My cousins supposed to be here. I'm going to try to find them." Charlie clapped Faruz's shoulder and his friend disappeared into the burgeoning crowd.

Julie squeezed Charlie's hand as he looked around

with an expression of concentration, his blue eyes scanning for details that would fill out his latest story. For her, being at the rally was simply an opportunity to be part of a growing democratic movement in a country which sorely needed to reclaim freedoms for its people.

Julie had come here four years earlier on what had been a bit of a lark. A product of England's elite, she had decided early on that she didn't want to live as her parents had, sitting smugly on top of the English heap. There was a chance to make a difference here in a country that was overdue for change and she'd taken it: helping small artisans earn a decent living through microlending, shuttling from the capital to the villages where she ran several aid projects for an international charity based in London. Over time, she found not only a sense of fulfillment here, but had also come to love the country, to feel invested in its people, its culture and the possibilities for its future. Plus, this was where she'd met and fallen in love with the kindred spirit who was now her husband.

She peered at Charlie adoringly, considering for a moment just how fortunate they were. To have each other, to have this beautiful boy growing inside her, to be able to live the kind of life where they felt they could make an impact on the world.

Julie felt a palpable shift in the energy of the crowd, as if someone very important and famous was arriving. Then she saw Alisher Byko moving through the throng, surrounded by his usual coterie of assistants and bodyguards.

Julie and Byko had attended Cambridge together, where he was renowned as the flamboyant son of one of the richest men in Central Asia. But it wasn't just Byko's wealth and confidence that made him such a charismatic figure. He had an innate sense of his own power, a command of his surroundings, and a presence that seemed to suggest he could be a leader of men. At university, Julie had always found there to be more substance to him than others gave him credit for and they'd fallen into an unlikely romance. As an impressionable twenty-year-old she'd often felt sucked into the vortex of his captivating, larger-than-life personality but ultimately she knew their relationship couldn't last and after eighteen tumultuous months, she'd managed, just before graduation, to gracefully extricate herself from his clutches. Now, after all of these years, she'd come to his country and they'd become erstwhile partners in a growing movement to liberate the Uzbek people from decades of darkness.

Byko's handsome face was flushed with excitement as he approached Julie and kissed her on the cheek, then pumped Charlie's hand, brazenly demanding, "See what you started?"

"Me?" Charlie responded implausibly.

"This is all because of your article," Byko insisted. "I took the liberty of translating it and printing up samizdat copies. They've been circulating for days. Very powerful work, Charlie."

"I'm surprised you're here, Alisher. This could be risky for you."

Byko smiled. "Karimov and his cronies don't give a shit about anything but their Swiss bank accounts. The U.S. and Britain only care about basing troops here to support the war in Afghanistan. I simply had to decide whether I stood with my countrymen or not. At any rate, I want to thank you. Your story has made quite a stir here."

"So far it hasn't made much difference in the States, I'm afraid."

"Just the fact that it was published in a major magazine shows that someone finally cares. Someone other than Julie, that is." This Byko said with a flirtatious wink and Julie could feel Charlie shift on his heels, a hint of jealousy that ushered Charlie's hand onto the small of her back. The jealousy didn't bother her in the least. As a matter of fact, she had to admit she enjoyed it. Especially now that, in her eighth month of pregnancy, she was tipping the scales at 150 pounds, her husband's proprietary energy was a boon to her hormonally imbalanced ego.

Someone shouted and beckoned toward Byko from a few yards away and he excused himself with a flourish.

"He still has a thing for you," Charlie noted.

"It was a million years ago," Julie sighed. "He's married now, and so am I . . ." She leaned in and kissed him. "Thank God."

A few minutes later, Charlie was snapping photographs of the crowd. As a seasoned journalist, he normally kept a certain detachment from the events he was covering, but today he was flooded with anticipation. He'd witnessed popular uprisings before, in countries even more repressed than this, but there was something in the spirit of the people here that gave him hope this could be more than just a one-time expression of pent-up fury. Today could be the beginning of something historic. And as Byko himself had said, Charlie was very much a part of what was happening here.

That idea—that he might actually be influencing and not merely reporting on events—filled him with pride and excitement. And there was no one he would rather have at his side in a moment like this than Julie. He was nearly thirty-eight now, and in all of his years of travel, he'd never met anyone quite like her. He lowered his camera and watched her handing out placards to the locals, laughing and bantering in her fluent Uzbek. She might have been raised with a silver spoon in her mouth, but she had the common touch, an ability to immediately connect with people on their own terms.

Just for fun, Charlie turned his camera on her and snapped a few candids. An old Uzbek woman was rubbing her pregnant belly. Julie threw back her head and laughed in that unbridled, carefree way that had slayed him the first time they met. It was as if her joy—her very life force—was contagious. In her presence, he could recognize and approach his best self, and in reaching for that self, he could then be worthy of her. Of course, the flip side of her unmitigated optimism and faith in humanity was a stubborn resolve that could be impenetrable, and the old woman's hands on Julie's belly only served to remind him of this.

He and Julie were in the midst of an ongoing argument—she wanted to stay here for the birth, he wanted to go to London where they could be sure they were getting the best medical care. To Julie, it had become almost a moral issue. Leaving here for the safety of London would be, in her words, "a callous repudiation of our solidarity with these people." For Charlie, it was merely a question of self-preservation. It was one thing to advocate for a third world country, it was another thing to risk having his first child there.

He watched Julie accept a homemade necklace from the woman and recognized it as a traditional token of luck for expectant mothers. Julie smiled gratefully and put her hand to her heart. He noticed a tear glistening in the corner of her eye and it reminded him that her maternal instincts were kicking in. In the end, he thought those instincts might just override any of her moral or political objections and he would win the argument yet. At any rate, he still had a few weeks to convince her and he had a feeling that if today went well it might soften her up.

A growing buzz in the crowd diverted Charlie's attention and he soon realized what was happening. Byko was getting on the statue. Charlie moved quickly toward Julie. "Is he really doing what I think he's doing?"

"It bloody well looks like it," she replied, eyes widening.

Charlie knew there was lingering affection between them and he'd tried not to let it bother him, but after all, there were many places in the world Julie could have gone to do her "good works" and she'd chosen to come here.

As for Byko, he was something of a conundrum to Charlie. His father had been a Soviet official and a friend of President Karimov. After the split from the Soviet Union, the elder Byko had ruthlessly amassed a fortune in the mining and energy sectors and had become a billionaire by the time he died, leaving the entire empire in his son's hands.

But the younger Byko had been cut from a different cloth. Educated at Cambridge, Westernized in almost every way, Alisher hadn't fought the regime outwardly, but in his own quiet fashion he'd done much to improve the lot of his countrymen.

The thing was, you didn't hold on to your billions in Uzbekistan by rocking the boat. Byko had been canny about understanding his limits, where he could press and where he couldn't. So his mere presence at the rally was a departure from his established approach. Now it seemed as though he was about to take a public stand—an extraordinarily risky, some might say reckless step.

Sure enough, the young man who had been speaking embraced the billionaire, then jumped down into the crowd as Byko took the megaphone. For a moment, everyone went silent.

"My name," he yelled into the bullhorn, "is Alisher Byko!"

The crowd responded with a roar. Byko was one of the best-known men in Uzbekistan, about as close to a rock star as the country had. If he was publicly putting his stamp on the nascent rebellion, then surely success had to be in the offing.

Charlie aimed his powerful telephoto at the statue of Babur, and snapped off a few photographs of the billionaire.

"Many of you know that my father was one of the richest men in this country. When he died, I inherited everything that was his. I tried to make changes, to bring fairness to my companies, to bring *real* elections to the provinces where I have support, to reform the standards in my gold mines, to provide decent working conditions for all my employees. But every step of the way, our government has tried to stop me.

"Time and again, we hear promises for reform but only see more of the same. This is not the country that I want to live in. This is not the country that I want my own son to grow up in."

The crowd erupted in applause as Byko indicated someone in the crowd. He was pointing to an attractive young woman standing on the curb, a boy of three in her arms. She wore a head scarf but otherwise was dressed in fashionable Western clothes. Charlie recognized her as Daniella, Byko's wife.

As the applause died down, a throaty, roaring sound cut through the air.

Charlie craned his neck. Byko, too, turned to look.

A row of armored tanks rolled slowly toward the square. Each one carried a machine gun on the turret, manned by a soldier.

Charlie wheeled on Julie, his heart pounding: "You've got to get out of here." Before she could stammer out an argument, he cut her off. "Don't be stupid, Jules." He gestured toward the nearby municipal building. "Over there. Go. Now."

Julie was stubborn but knew enough not to contradict him when he had that tone in his voice. Still, she wasn't leaving without a word of her own and grabbed him hard, forcing him to look into her eyes. "*You* don't do anything stupid."

"I won't," he promised. "Now go!"

Her hand slipped from his shoulder, fingertips brushing against his, as if she wanted to clasp his hand one more time. But Charlie was already turning away, intent on what he had to do.

* * *

Julie pushed through the last few feet of the crowd and ducked into the municipal building at the edge of the square. She looked around and found herself in the corner of a dim, high-ceilinged lobby. The big space was entirely empty of people.

In the silence, she couldn't help but notice the huge murals on the wall—muscular women in head scarves picking cotton and heroic men in overalls driving tractors. The images were a cartoonish homage to the hard work of a robust people. It was a common form of grotesque propaganda and it made Julie sick.

But it wasn't her moral outrage that accounted for the sudden pain shooting through her abdomen. It was the baby.

She hadn't wanted to say anything to Charlie earlier, but she'd been feeling twinges all morning, like fishhooks snagging briefly in her flesh.

And this one doubled her over.

Braxton Hicks. Early labor pains. But nothing to be concerned about. There was no way it was happening today. She was sure of that.

When the pain finally eased, she straightened up and looked out the door. Charlie was shimmying up a light pole. She realized, as he wielded his camera, that he'd climbed up there to get a better vantage point. He steadied himself and began snapping photographs of the scene below.

She felt a glow of pride. Most Western reporters in the Middle East had ignored the things that had been going on in Uzbekistan. And the ones who were in Tashkent, they were too chickenshit—an apt American expression she had learned from Charlie—to come out into the hinterlands and report on what was really going on here. Despite the distance that separated her from Charlie now, a deep sense of connection warmed her. They were going to have an extraordinary life together.

Another wave of pain swept through her. This time, she felt something wet on her leg. For a moment she couldn't figure out what had caused the large stain on her pants. Then she realized . . . her water had just broken.

The baby was coming today. He was coming right now.

She tried moving toward the door, but doubled over in pain.

"Charlie!" she cried, hands on her knees.

And then she collapsed.

A chopper—Charlie recognized it as an Mi-24 Hind—thundered over the roof of a hotel across from the square. A man with a scoped rifle sat in the open bay of the chopper, legs dangling in the air. Charlie squeezed off several more photographs, then returned his attention to Byko. He seemed to be reveling in the tension, pointing at the oncoming troops. "Well, I see we now have the attention of our great leader, President Karimov."

Charlie watched the approaching tanks. Several armored personnel carriers followed, filled with soldiers. A tall young officer with an enormous hat leaped from the lead vehicle to the ground and began pointing his arms, ordering men from the vehicles. The troops poured out, but they weren't carrying riot shields or batons, as Charlie expected. They were carrying submachine guns.

Charlie felt a twinge of fear. Surely they weren't planning—

Before he could even finish the thought, the officer shouted a command and the soldiers loaded and cocked their weapons. Charlie zoomed in tighter on one young soldier, his face grim with determination as he racked a live round into the chamber of his weapon and pointed it at the crowd.

Time seemed to slow. Could this really be happening? Without so much as a warning, they were going to fire on unarmed civilians?

The hubbub of the crowd died down as they seemed to sense what was about to happen. For a moment, there was no sound at all but the idling of the tanks.

Then the cry of the officer rang out. "Fire!"

Framed in the powerful lens of Charlie's camera, the young soldier squinted down the sight of his weapon and pulled the trigger.

Bang!

The young man's eyes widened as though the sound of the gun had surprised him.

Charlie tried to keep his focus on this soldier, to capture in the intimacy of this poignant vignette the entirety of what was about to happen. But the cacophony of the onslaught was too much to bear and Charlie lowered his camera to take in the full scene, clinging to a brief hope that maybe the soldiers were firing rubber bullets or some other non-lethal form of crowd control.

The screams of fear and agony batted away that hope and confirmed the sickening truth.

All of the soldiers opened fire at once until the shooting became a deafening rattle of death. From Charlie's vantage point on the lamp post, he saw pure chaos. The crowd, unsure which way to flee, facing gunfire from snipers on every side of the square, swirled and surged frantically in all directions.

Charlie knew he had maybe ten more seconds before he'd have to run for his own life. He also knew that he was the only Western journalist here and therefore had to grab as many photos as he could—something to document today's tragic events for the rest of the world. He popped off a few shots of the frantic crowd, then zoomed in, framing a close-up of a bloody woman dragging a lifeless man, her face crazed with disbelief and horror. Next, it was a child—knocked down, disappearing in the melee. Next, an old man in a turban, blasted in the chest, falling like a puppet whose strings had just been cut.

And then he picked up Byko, pushing his way through the crush of the masses. Even through the lens, Charlie could feel Byko's furious intensity and force of will as he desperately tried to get to his wife and son.

Charlie panned, trying to find them as well. Somehow, his eye caught a glimpse of Daniella's steel blue scarf and he was able to lock on to her. She was huddling her son into her chest, her face twisted in fear, screaming, "Alisher! Alisher!"

Suddenly, she dropped out of Charlie's frame.

He quickly adjusted and found her again. She was on the ground and seemed to have been folded, her torso oddly twisted, like a paper doll that had been bent at some anatomically impossible angle. Charlie detected no sign of a bullet wound, but there was no sign of life either. She simply lay motionless, drained of all animation.

Then Charlie saw the boy. Byko's son lay underneath his mother, eyes open, mouth wide, staring at the sky.

Charlie stopped shooting, looking through the lens merely as a way to understand what was happening.

When Byko's agonized face came into the frame, it was clear. He grabbed his wife and his son, scooping them into his arms. Now, Charlie could see blood, all over Byko's white shirt. It was the blood of his family. Clutching them to his chest, Byko's mouth opened as he roared, "Nooo!"

It was too intimate, too grotesque, too haunting for Charlie to bear. He lowered the camera in a daze, thinking of his own wife. Of his own unborn son.

He had to get out of there. Now.

He slid down the pole as the soldiers marched across the square, firing relentlessly at the crowd. They were approaching fast.

Charlie turned and saw the doorway of the municipal building where Julie had disappeared. It was fifty yards to that door, if he could navigate his way through the panicked crowd, which was now trampling each other in a frenzy to find shelter.

He shouldered his camera and bulled into the blurry mass of humanity, trying to create a path for himself. Suddenly, there was a huge push from his right, a survivors' stampede that knocked him to the ground. Someone's knee smacked him in the chin. A stray elbow stabbed his temple. Charlie fell to all fours, his camera dangling from his neck.

It wasn't the soldiers who were going to get him. It was the terrified crowd, moments earlier united in their hatred of the regime now reduced by that regime to its lowest form of humanity, an every-man-for-himself battle for survival. As Charlie tried to gather himself and find a way out, he noticed a girl lying on the ground, trapped as he was.

Somehow, amid all of the chaos, their eyes locked.

"Help me!" hers seemed to say.

On his hands and knees, bumped and jostled and kicked by those fleeing past him, Charlie found his way to her.

When he lifted her into his arms, she screamed and clawed at him, her large brown eyes wide with bewilderment. She was a beautiful child of eight or nine, old enough to wear a head scarf. But the bright blue scarf—now stained with a discordant splotch of red—had slipped from her head, her long black hair spilling out. It was only then that Charlie realized she'd been shot in the chest. The child's mouth opened and closed as though she wanted to say something, but no sound came out.

"It's going to be okay, sweetheart," he said in Uzbek.

The crowd was parting just enough that he could catch a glimpse of the municipal building. The door was still open, beckoning to him.

He rose, the wounded girl in his arms, the day's testimony inside the camera which now dangled over his shoulder, determined to make it to that door.

He got only three steps before an impact jarred him from behind. He turned and saw a small fire-plug of a soldier brandishing an assault rifle. Only then did he realize he'd been slammed in the kidney with the butt of the gun. The soldier swung at him again. Instinctively, Charlie curled up to protect the girl and dodged to the side. Instead of hitting him full in the head, the gun grazed his face. Still, the impact was enough to make him see stars.

Charlie fell to his knees, trying to shelter the girl from the blows.

But there were no blows coming. Miraculously, it seemed, the soldier moved on.

The building was only forty yards away now. It had been a long time since he'd graced the gridiron at Ohio State, but Charlie could still move, in spite of the once-ruptured knee that had ended his football career. If he'd done the forty then in 4.6 seconds, how long could it take him now, even with this girl in his arms? Ten seconds? Maybe twelve?

He cradled the girl and barreled toward safety. If he could just make it into the welcoming darkness of that door . . .

Three seconds.

Five.

The dark rectangle swelled larger and larger as he pounded ever closer.

Six seconds.

Halfway now. At least.

Seven. Eight.

Nearly . . .

Crack.

At first, Charlie thought he must have sprained a ligament in that bum knee of his. But then, as he felt the searing pain shoot through the right side of his back, he realized he'd been shot.

For a second or two, his adrenaline disguised the stinging pain and he continued forward, a laser beam of purpose, focused on that door. He was ten yards away, maybe fifteen, before he felt the searing, white-hot fire ignite inside his body.

Feet pounding across the big flagstones, he refused to acknowledge the import of this fire, convincing himself it was something that could be dealt with later, once he was inside the building.

That was when the second shot hit him.

His leg, penetrated just below his injured knee, gave out underneath him, as though it had been chopped off, and he slammed to the ground, still cradling the girl as he absorbed the impact of the fall.

A wave of nausea overcame him and his eyes hazed. He was only three or four feet from that door, but he knew his leg had been completely shattered. The only way now was to crawl.

He dragged the wounded girl with him, reaching the building in just a few seconds. It took nearly every ounce of strength to reach for the door, but he managed to pull it open.

He was greeted by a hailstorm of wailing and screaming and as he pulled himself and the girl inside, he saw nearly a dozen wounded people.

Dizzy and disoriented, his consciousness slipping away, he had the vague sense that there were people here to help the wounded. He let go of the girl, intent now on finding Julie.

And then he heard her voice cutting through the bedlam.

"Charlie! Charlie!"

But it wasn't recognition that he heard in her voice, it was desperation. She was in trouble. And she was screaming for her man.

On his hands and knees, he struggled toward her voice, pushing and crawling past everyone in his path.

When he came upon her at first, he couldn't register what she was doing. She was lying on her back, face twisted in agony. And then he saw that her knees were raised, her legs spread far apart. The floor beneath her was soaking wet and stained with crimson.

She might have been giving birth. But she was surely hemorrhaging.

"Doctor," Charlie tried to say, though the words came out as barely a whisper.

"Charlie," he heard her say. This time, there was gratitude in her cadence. She had seen him. He had made it.

He reached for her hand, hoping that if he could simply grasp her, they would all somehow survive this. But as their fingers touched, everything slipped into a white fog.

And faded away.

PART II

RETURN

CHAPTER ONE

Santa Monica, California, six years later

The sizzle of frying bacon and the burble of childish laughter filled the air as six-year-old Ollie darted into the kitchen, followed by his three-year-old sister Meagan, nearly colliding with Charlie as he cooked breakfast.

"Hey, guys!" Charlie warned cheerfully. "Daddy's working the grill here. Elbow room, huh?"

"Daddy, why aren't you coming to Disneyland?" asked Meagan.

"Because your mother just got home from New York and she hasn't seen you all week, so this is going to be a special time for you and Ollie to be with her."

"And you have to work!" Meagan reminded him proudly.

"And I have to work," Charlie confirmed, returning his attention to the grill.

Julie had only been away four days, but for Charlie it had felt like an eternity. They'd moved to Santa Monica nearly six years ago, with Charlie taking a job covering local politics for the *LA Times* and Julie

forgoing her work in favor of raising the children.
They had traded their lives of adventure for a cushy,
suburban existence, but even so, any time he was
separated from Julie or the kids for more than a day
or two, Charlie's worry would overtake him. He had
never forgiven himself for allowing Julie to leave the
Square that day without him, for not being by her
side when she and Oliver nearly died as she gave
birth. And from the moment that he recovered from
his own wounds, he swore that he would never place
his family in that kind of jeopardy again. Besides,
what had he managed to accomplish in Uzbekistan? Next to nothing. In the wake of the tragedy
in Babur Square, life for the people there had only
gotten worse. And so he'd told himself that it was
time to grow up: that he was done trying to change
the world, that his world now had to be his family.

Julie knew that Charlie would always be haunted
by what had happened to them in Uzbekistan and
she'd willingly sacrificed her loftier ambitions to
make a more "sensible" life in California, but as she
lay here in their bed, staring at the snaking cracks
in their ceiling, she found herself blaming him for
the chasm that had grown between them. Of course
she knew that wasn't fair. It takes two to tango and
at this point, she had done more than her fair share
to create the distance.

But how would they even begin to come together
again? The task seemed so daunting that rather than
search for the solution, Julie tried to pinpoint when
exactly they'd started drifting from each other.

Had the seeds been sown that day in Babur

Square? No. Those first few weeks in London, when he was recuperating from his injuries and she was recovering from Oliver's traumatic birth, they had never been closer.

And when Charlie had suggested that they fly to Los Angeles, she hadn't blanched. At the time they were, in effect, homeless. They couldn't go back to Uzbekistan yet, and neither had a place in the U.S. or the UK. She had no family to speak of in London—her father had died a year earlier and her mother was dwindling away in a rest home in Sussex—so when Charlie's old college buddy Sal Peretti extended an invitation for them to "come out to the coast" for a few weeks, it had seemed like a perfect place for them both to clear their heads.

In short order, Sal had offered Charlie a coveted, well-paid gig at the *LA Times* and Julie had to agree that making a life for themselves in Southern California made a world of sense.

But as she rose now from their bed and gazed out the window at the palm trees in their yard, she realized it was that first concession which had started them on this path. At the time, she thought Los Angeles was going to be merely a pit stop, assuming that at some point they would resume their old careers abroad.

She had tried at various moments to broach the subject with Charlie, but he was always adamant. He would not subject Julie or the children to any kind of danger just to serve their adventurous inclinations or overdeveloped sense of heroism. Julie thought that he was being unfair—to both of them—but she understood his position. And she told herself that he wanted to stay more than she wanted to leave.

So she had let it go. Because she wanted to make him happy and she knew she had little to complain about. Charlie was a devoted father and loving husband—smart and funny, sweet and giving with the kids yet tough when he needed to be. More important, she felt grateful every day that they'd all survived that brutal day in Andijan, that they'd become a family. It so easily could have gone the other way. Of course, it was precisely this cocktail of compassion, gratitude and guilt that kept her from confronting the simmering resentments that had been building in their marriage.

And now she had betrayed his trust.

Out of the shower now, she lifted her suitcase onto the bed and began to unpack her clothes when she saw that she'd forgotten to remove the baggage claim ticket.

It was a stunningly careless mistake. Or had she subconsciously left it there, hoping that Charlie would notice it and catch her in the lie?

She caught a glance of herself in the mirror and rolled her eyes. Here she was, wearing a pink Mickey Mouse sweatshirt, preparing for a day at Disneyland. If any of them downstairs only knew where she'd been the past four days.

She grabbed hold of the sticky ticket and ripped it off her luggage.

Charlie put the childrens' food on their plates, turned off the stove and checked his watch. He knew Julie had gotten in late and wanted to let her sleep, but the kids would be getting antsy soon enough and he had to be at work by nine.

"Jules, are you up? Breakfast is ready!"

As if on cue, Julie bustled into the room with an exuberant rallying cry. "Is everybody ready for the Magic Kingdom?"

Meagan assaulted her mother, wrapping her arms around her neck. "We missed you!"

"Oh, and I missed you guys so much!" Julie cooed, smothering her with kisses, then setting her back on her feet.

"I didn't," Ollie announced with the straightest of faces. Charlie knew this was his son's way of saying he wasn't particularly thrilled with his mother's recent excursion to the Big Apple.

"Well, did you miss . . . Derek Jeter?" Julie winked at Charlie and whipped out an autographed baseball.

Ollie's eyes widened. He had started playing t-ball the year before and now considered himself the world's biggest baseball fan. "Wow!" He grabbed the ball and studied the signature. "That's *really* Derek Jeter's autograph?"

Julie laughed. "It's really Derek Jeter's autograph."

"Does this count as a birthday present?"

"I don't know," Julie teased. "What do you think?"

"No!"

"What about me?" Meagan demanded, tugging at her mother's sweatshirt. "Did you get something for me?"

Julie bent down and put her arm around her daughter. "For you, I got a promise. Anything you want from the Disneyland store."

"I want Donald Duck!" Meagan's favorite cartoon character.

"A stuffed animal or an action figure?"

"Both!" she shouted.

"We'll see. Maybe we'll even let Ollie pick out something."

"If he's nice," Meagan added with the utmost seriousness.

Watching his wife with their children, Charlie felt a burst of happiness and relief. She was home. The planets were realigned. All was right again.

"Okay, who's hungry?" Charlie called cheerfully.

"Me! Me!" The kids waved their hands, beaming at him.

"And here we go," Charlie said, setting down the plates, "one French toast slightly-burnt-so-you-don't-see-the-egg for Prince Ollie; one blueberry pancake, maple syrup, light on the butter for Princess Meagan; and one English porridge, warm skim milk, for my queen."

"You're too kind, my liege," Julie quipped as the kids dug in noisily.

"You should've woke me last night," he whispered, kissing her on the lips.

Charlie felt her body stiffen, her tone become defensive: "The flight was delayed, then there was a foul-up with my car service. I didn't even get home until three."

He regarded her for a moment as if he barely knew her. What was meant to be a sweet gesture of longing had been received as an accusation. This was unlike Julie, but Charlie wasn't about to deal with it in front of the children. And maybe she was just tired after the long flight.

"Well, I'm glad you're home," he said. "Now sit and eat your breakfast."

* * *

After cleaning up the kitchen, Charlie helped Julie bundle the kids into the back of her Prius, warning them as always about the perils of public adventure.

"All right, guys, now remember, there's lots of people there and it's easy to get lost. You remember the buddy system, right?"

Ollie wasn't paying any attention, but Meagan, ever eager for favor, raised her hand and cried, "Always keep Ollie in sight."

"That's my girl!" Charlie kissed her, buckled her into her car seat, and gently closed the door. He leaned into Julie's window to find her texting feverishly on her BlackBerry.

"My sister," she explained.

"Do me a favor?" he heard himself say.

"No calls from the car . . . ?"

He ignored what he could have sworn was a slight roll of her eyes and pressed on. "I checked Sigalert. The 5's going to be a mess. Drive carefully." And then to take the edge off his command, he managed to add, "Please."

He smiled self-consciously, a Cheshire grin which seemed to disarm her for an instant, and he leaned into the car for a kiss.

"Love you," he said as half apology.

"Love you, too," she rejoined in a more perfunctory spirit than he would have liked.

She made an ostentatious show of putting away her BlackBerry, flipped him a wave, and backed rapidly into the street.

As they disappeared around the corner, Charlie

felt a thin reed of anxiety rising slowly up his chest. Unconsciously, he touched the scar on his back where he'd been shot. Every year around the anniversary of Andijan he'd get twinges of pain there, twinges accompanied by a feeling of just how fragile the life he and Julie had built together was.

He rolled his eyes, irritated at himself, trying to shake off his fears. Everything was fine. They were just going to Disneyland.

CHAPTER TWO

John Quinn felt a little naked. Normally he wore his .45-caliber bobtailed Les Baer 1911 beneath his photographer's vest, concealed in an inside-the-waistband holster. A lot of firepower, very inconspicuous. But Disneyland had too much security and the laws in California were too draconian to take the chance of going armed here. So he contented himself with following the happy little family around the park.

It was noon and they had worked their way through Adventureland to Frontierland. Quinn watched them carefully but couldn't help notice the dumb ass dressed in a Goofy costume standing by the gift shop, posing for pictures, making hokey effeminate gestures with his three fingered hands. You had to wonder what kind of guy would do something that pathetic and humiliating for a living. God, he hated this place. The screaming children, the overweight people, the incessant jingles and jangles. It was enough to make you sick.

He happened to catch a glimpse of himself reflected in the window behind Goofy and regarded himself objectively, assessing his disguise as much as anything. He was a fireplug of a man with the build of a collegiate wrestler, his balding head hidden under a baseball cap with a picture of Winnie-the-Pooh on the crown. He knew there was something menacing about his eyes, so he kept them covered with a pair of mirrored Oakleys.

Acting the part of a dad waiting for his kids, Quinn waved at some random family on Thunder Mountain, as though little Quinn Junior was up there having a jolly old time on the jolly old ride.

There was, of course, no little Quinn Junior. Not here, not anywhere.

He homed in on the woman again. She was watching her son shoot a toy gun at an arcade right next to Thunder Mountain. Her daughter tugged on her ridiculous Mickey Mouse sweatshirt, whining to be taken somewhere. Quinn couldn't make out what the mother's response was but it looked like there were gestures of reassurance and pleas for patience.

Thank God he'd never had children. What a colossal waste of time and energy.

The woman's son blasted away his last few shots with the air gun, then she grabbed his hand and led both kids past Goofy into the gift shop. Quinn had to approach the shop's entrance a little closer than he liked in order to make sure he didn't lose her going through the door on the other side.

Of course, cell phones were God's gift to surveillance operators. You could hide your entire face behind a Droid and nobody would make you—especially if you changed an occasional article of clothing. So he tossed the Winnie cap in the trash and pulled on a drab fishing hat that he kept rolled up in one of his vest pockets.

For a split second, the woman turned in his direction and he thought that perhaps she'd caught on to him. He turned his back on her casually, examining some of the overpriced souvenirs and waited a solid ten count before turning around again.

She was exiting in what looked like a hurry through the opposite door.

Afraid she might have spotted him, Quinn chose to retreat through the door he'd entered and pick them up again outside.

For a moment he thought he'd lost them in the sea of obese, ridiculously dressed tourists, but then spotted them again. She was pulling a point-and-shoot camera from her voluminous purse and setting up the kids for an all-important photo op.

"Come on guys, stay still," she beckoned. "Say cheese!"

It was a pathetic shot: the boy was cross-eyed and sticking out his tongue while the little girl was waving her Donald Duck in front of her face.

"Oh, forget it," the woman said, laughing and grabbing the girl's hand. "Come on, Ollie. Meagan wants to go see 'It's a Small World.'"

As Quinn followed them, trading his olive fishing hat for an auburn golf visor, he couldn't help but smile.

Indeed, he thought. *It is a very small world.*

CHAPTER THREE

Charlie threaded through the bullpen, nodding to his colleagues as he arrived for the day. There had been a time when he'd managed to convince himself that the *LA Times* would be an exciting place to work. Going to a zoning board meeting in Encino wasn't the same as bombing around western Afghanistan in a Range Rover, but in the beginning the job still held its challenges. The first couple of years, he'd had to build up his network of contacts, learn the city, and absorb the breakneck rhythms of daily journalism. For better or for worse, those days were long gone and Charlie could now sleepwalk through most assignments.

Today, though, he was feeling a bit more enthused. He'd been chasing down a lead on corrupt spending in the L.A. public school district and the spiky-haired young computer jockey named Mac had apparently come up with something juicy for him.

Fingering his earring and staring at the computer as Charlie approached, Mac grabbed a stack of papers and tossed them toward Charlie without missing a beat. "Got that background you were looking for," he added with false modesty.

Mac was a smart kid with good instincts but more than that he was something like a genius when it came to digging up information in cyber-space. Charlie was reluctant to use the word in front of anyone at the paper, but Mac was essentially a hacker. A hacker who should have been working for the NSA or Wikileaks, but somehow didn't realize how much his talents were being wasted here.

Charlie flipped through the dense pages and marveled, "This is the actual public schools budget?"

"Every line item in the entire county. You want to know what Beverly Hills High spent on toilet paper, it's in there."

"How'd you—" Charlie shook his head and smiled. "Never mind, I don't even want to know. Just be discreet, huh?"

"That's why they call me Deep Throat."

Charlie managed a chuckle and headed for his own cubicle.

"Oh, hey," Mac called after him. "Sal was looking for you."

Charlie felt a catch in his chest. The recession and a declining readership had been slowly strangling the paper for years now. Only last summer, twenty-six people had been laid off and for several months Sal had been hinting that Charlie might need to show some "flexibility" if he was going to avoid the next round of cuts. He knew that Sal had been angling at those cuts for the early spring, and lo and behold, April had now passed into May.

Was today the day the shit hit the fan?

Charlie dropped his bag off at his cubicle and headed for Sal's office. When he got there, Sal held up a finger, indicating that Charlie should wait for him while he wrapped up his phone call.

Charlie sat down on Sal's beat-up leather sofa and found himself gazing at the framed photos on the wall. One in particular caught his eye: *Charlie and Sal in Tibet*, fresh out of journalism school. They had been there as freelancers to cover the Workers' Hunger Strike and had somehow found a way to grab the first and only interview with Zhou Yong, its organizer. It was a major coup for two twenty-four-year-old guys and only confirmed for Charlie that they were on the path to greatness. Together they had planned to be the last of the gonzo journalists, searching out the toughest stories in the most out-of-the-way places, righting society's wrongs, shining the light of truth on falsehood and abusive power. But when they'd returned from Tibet, Sal had shocked Charlie by taking a staff writer's job at the *Chicago Sun-Times*. Within a few years, he'd worked his way up the managerial ladder inside the Tribune papers—a fact which Charlie had ribbed him about on every possible occasion. Of course, after Uzbekistan, Charlie had to admit he was grateful to have such a close ally in such a conventional place. And even though he was now Charlie's editor and boss, Sal had gone out of his way never to treat Charlie like an underling. They were friends and friendship meant everything.

Sal hung up the phone, looked up from his paper-strewn desk, and sighed. He was a big bear of a man with a thick shock of close-cropped black hair and a gut that was one size larger than his waistband. "Close the door, would you?"

Charlie knew what was coming. "You spoke to the board?"

Sal nodded. "They're digging in their heels on this one. Unless you start taking on long lead assignments internationally, there's no way to justify your salary."

"So they want to fire me."

"You know the kind of cutbacks we've been making. I can hire three smart kids straight out of J school for the money we're paying you."

"You think some kids out of J school can do what I do here?"

Sal's face took on an evasive expression. "Look, Wallace was supposed to be covering the economic summit in Shanghai, but he's getting bogged down on this Libya thing. I thought it would be a perfect opportunity for you to get out there again. It's an analysis piece. Two weeks, maybe three, you're home again."

When Charlie didn't respond, Sal spread his hands impatiently and warned, "Charlie, you need to get out in the field again. You're overqualified for what you're doing."

"We agreed when I came here—"

"That was six years ago—"

"We *agreed* that I could stay in town and work domestic. That was the deal."

Sal leaned forward, rested his chin on his hand and gave Charlie a long, skeptical look. "What does Julie say about all this?"

Charlie picked up a stray paper clip off Sal's desk and flicked it toward the trash can.

Sal kept after him: "Two months this has been brewing and you haven't mentioned it to her?"

"I didn't think it was real until today," Charlie replied. Even before he spoke the words, he knew how lame that was going to sound.

Sal leaned back in his chair, his body retreating. "Look," he said, "I know what you all went through, but don't you think it's time you put it behind you and got back out into the world? I really don't think Julie would have a problem with it."

"She said something to you?" Charlie read Sal's hesitation—clearly he didn't want to sell her out. "What did she say, Sal?"

Sal leaned forward, trying to calm the tenor of this. "Come on, kid, when you met Julie, you were both tearing up the world. She's not a soccer mom . . ." He waved his hand around the cramped, paper-strewn office. "And you're not *this*."

"What did she say?" Charlie demanded.

"She's suffocating, Charlie."

"She told you this?"

"She told Laura. Laura told me."

Laura was Sal's wife and had become a good friend to Julie, so this hearsay evidence, as galling as it was, had an air of credibility. And Sal was anything but a shit-stirrer.

Searching for confirmation, Charlie's mind drifted back to that morning . . .

Julie's defensiveness, the way she'd acted with him at the car. The cursory "Love you, too," her tearing out of the driveway like she couldn't wait to get out of there.

Suffocating. I'm suffocating my wife.

Sal wasn't through. He apparently had a lot to

say, and one way or another, he was going to get it off his chest.

"You can tell me to go jump off a bridge if you want, but I'm gonna give you some of my pearls of wisdom about marriage. I'm on my second go-round here and I can tell you what screwed it up the first time. It wasn't that we were fighting. We should have been fighting. Instead we were so damn polite with each other we ended up strangers. Strangers with secrets. I don't want to see you go down that road."

Charlie sat silently for a moment. He knew if he stayed in Sal's office, he would say something to fracture their friendship or cost him his job. Without a word, he rose and jerked the door open.

He strode through the bullpen, averting his eyes from his colleagues, and made his way to the elevators. He hit the call button and waited, but he had no idea where he was going.

CHAPTER FOUR

Julie sat in the boat with Meagan and Ollie, bobbing slowly through "It's a Small World." The trippy 1950s-style animatronics, the almost hypnotically repetitive song and the slow, rocking motion of the ride seemed uniquely suited to the turbulent state of her mind.

One hates what one wrongs, she thought. It was her favorite line from her favorite film. Richard Burton explaining to Peter O'Toole in *Becket* that O'Toole's King Henry "hated" the commoners precisely because he treated them so badly.

The phrase had caught her fancy as a teenager the first time she'd seen the film and had always stuck with her because she felt it explained so much of human nature. And it helped her understand now why she had treated Charlie so shabbily this morning. She had *wronged* him—and rather than admit it, she had been edgy, intolerant, and passive-aggressive, preying on his weaknesses while refusing to show any of her own.

It made her sick that it had come to this. Particularly because she still loved him deeply and still respected so much of who he was, even if the man she'd fallen in love with had in some ways retreated from the world. But how could she possibly explain her lies to him now? Part of her wished he *had* seen the baggage claim ticket on her suitcase, or that she'd had the audacity to leave it there for him to find. At least that would be a way to begin the conversation.

"Mommy, look!" Meagan cried, tugging on Julie's sleeve and snapping her out of her introspection. She was pointing at the kaffiyehed Arabic dolls. "Why do they wear those scarves on their faces?"

"It's part of their religion," Julie tried to explain. "Like some Jewish people wear black hats and coats. It's almost like a uniform."

"Like Santa Claus?"

Julie couldn't help but smile. "Sort of, yeah."

The answer seemed to satisfy Meagan and she resumed watching in wonder at the spectacle around her.

For a moment, Julie was able to see the ride through Meagan's innocent eyes, appreciating the fantasy that all peoples and cultures could somehow exist side by side.

Her work for World Vision had taught her, sadly, that people were essentially tribal, that by nature they almost always needed some kind of Boogeyman to align themselves against and that choosing one's particular Boogeyman inevitably became a central and inescapable part of one's identity.

It occurred to her that in some ways she had unconsciously made Charlie her Boogeyman. The source of her unhappiness, the person she blamed for whatever was lacking in her life. It wasn't fair and she knew it couldn't go on this way.

She gripped the safety bar at the front of the boat. It had to be tonight. She would come clean with him and let the chips fall where they may. For the first time in a long time, she breathed a full, deep breath. Though she was buzzing with anticipation and fear, she felt as though a weight had been lifted from her shoulders.

The boat emerged from the dark tunnel, shimmying along the rail, delivering them into the afternoon sun. As it came to a stop, she took the hands of both her children and led them up the ramp into Fantasyland.

She felt free.

CHAPTER FIVE

Charlie found himself driving aimlessly down Olympic Boulevard, swirling and blending Sal's incendiary words in his mind. Was Julie really *suffocating*? Keeping *secrets*? Had they, in the process of tiptoeing around each other, become *strangers*?

One moment, he was sure that Sal was being melodramatic—possibly as a way to shake Charlie into action. The next, he had the sinking feeling that Sal was not only on the right track, but that he only knew the half of it.

But there was no denying the central fact: over the past year, he and Julie had drifted apart. The usual banter and humor that existed between them had largely dissipated, replaced instead by methodical, almost clinical, conversations about the banal details of their domestic life. Who was taking which kid to which class, what couple they might be having dinner with on which night, who was going to call the gardener or plumber . . . And their sexual encounters—which had always been dogged and feverish—had become tepid and infrequent. Even discussions about the children, always an animating and uniting force between them, had begun to feel lackadaisical and rote.

Before today, he'd understood all of this to be a unique phase, a downward rhythm in the natural parabola of any marriage. But if what Sal said was true—and his own gut was confirming this—they were in real trouble.

The sound of an incessant, droning car horn startled Charlie. It took a moment for him to realize that he was sitting idly at a green light, cars whizzing past him on the left while the frustrated driver behind him waved furiously for him to get moving.

As Charlie put his foot to the accelerator and continued west, it occurred to him that he should probably choose a destination. He supposed that he had been unconsciously driving home, but sitting alone in the house staring at the family photos, wondering where the love had gone, didn't exactly feel like the choice. Then again, what was he supposed to do? Hit the driving range at Rancho Park? Grab a latte at Starbucks and watch all of the wannabes work on their screenplays?

When he stepped into the house, Charlie put down his laptop and grabbed himself a cold beer. He sat at the kitchen table and looked around— the French pots and pans oh so carefully chosen from Williams-Sonoma, the table and chairs from Restoration Hardware, the Riedel wineglasses, the Wüsthof knives . . . what exactly was this life they had constructed?

He had grown up in the blue-collar confines of Youngstown, Ohio, and had spent most of those seventeen years desperate to escape it. He'd wanted to play on a bigger field for higher stakes. He'd wanted to get out into the world and make a difference. The night before he'd left for college, he'd gotten drunk and scaled a rusting iron ladder to the top of the tallest chimney at Republic Steel and yelled down toward the feeble lights of his dying hometown: "Go to hell, Youngstown!"

Was the narrow little existence he'd created here in Los Angeles any less stifling? How had he let it come to this?

He opened his computer and checked his email. Sal had sent him a bunch of material on the Shanghai conference with a succinct note: "Time to get back in the saddle."

Charlie downloaded the material and thought about what it would mean to be flying all over the world again. He knew that his worries for his family were largely irrational, that there were countless investment bankers, marketing execs, sales reps from every business sector who traveled the globe three-quarters of the year without contemplating the idea that they were leaving their families unprotected. But they hadn't been through what he had. They hadn't seen their wives hooked up to a breathing tube in the ICU or their premature babies poked and prodded for weeks in an incubator.

Charlie perused the documents for a few minutes, trying to picture himself on that plane, in that hotel, calling home and Skyping every night; to imagine how the physical distance from Julie and the kids would gnaw at him, how his worries about them would begin to take its toll. And even if he took all of that concern out of the equation, what would it be like to miss all those days of their lives? To miss their Little League games and their dance recitals? And how was he supposed to repair whatever was damaged in his relationship with Julie if he was suddenly away from home for huge chunks of time?

He pushed the computer away. None of it could really be considered until Julie got home and he was able to talk it out with her. He hopped up from the table and began making dinner. Assuming Julie didn't let them go crazy with cotton candy and other junk, the kids would be ravenous when they walked through the door. He'd greet them with their favorite—spaghetti with Charlie's famous marinara sauce—and then, after the kids went to bed, he would begin the soul-searching conversation that would set him and Julie on a course of reparation.

He sautéed a couple of onions and garlic in olive oil, added some fresh tomatoes and spices, then let it simmer. He turned on the sink, filled a pot with water, then put it on the stove and ignited the flame under it. It would take fifteen minutes for the water to boil, another twelve for the pasta to cook. Hopefully they would be home by then.

He flicked on the TV, looking for a ball game when his cell phone rang. It was Julie.

He answered with a chipper hello.

"Calling from the greatest place on earth!" Julie shouted, her voice sunny.

"You're still there?"

"Just got in the car," Julie said on her Bluetooth. "We had an amazing time, didn't we, kids?"

Charlie heard Meagan and Ollie shouting joyfully in the background.

"Oh, that's great!" he said.

"So how was your day?" Julie asked.

"Fine. The usual. How soon before you're home?"

"Looks like traffic's jammed on the 5." Charlie heard a loud honk and then Julie shouted, "Oh, bloody hell!"

Charlie felt his blood pressure rise. "You okay?"

"Yeah, just some a-hole driver."

Charlie stifled the urge to caution her and waited for her to make the next move.

"Maybe I could speed things up going that fancy way you told me about," she said.

"It's like six different freeways," Charlie said. "Why don't I stay on with you till you get to the 405?"

"I thought you didn't want me on the phone when I was driving," she said.

Charlie wasn't just being paranoid. L.A.'s freeways were a maze that sometimes confused even people who had spent their lives in the city and Julie had a notoriously terrible sense of direction. Nevertheless, he forced himself to keep his voice calm. "I know what I said, but there's a lot of merging. It would really be easier if—"

"Fine, fine. I'm coming up on the 91 now. Is that what I'm taking?"

"You want to get over to the right and take it west."

"Got it," Julie said. "Looks a lot better here. What's next?"

Charlie stirred the sauce. Two minutes earlier it had smelled great. Now it seemed off, like he'd burned the garlic or something. "You'll hit the 605 in about ten minutes."

"Stooooop it!" a high voice whined in the background.

"Meagan, what happened? Ollie! Are you pinching your sister?"

Shit. Charlie hoped Julie was paying attention to the road and not the kids.

"Owww!"

"Ollie! Answer me. Did you pinch your sister again?"

"I don't know," came Ollie's distant, sullen voice.

"Meagan, stop kicking the seat!" Julie's voice rose in Charlie's ear as he gripped the phone tightly. "Meagan, honey! Stop it."

"She's been doing this all week," Charlie chimed in. "She'll settle down after a—"

"Sweetheart, it's all right!" Julie called. "Tell Mommy what's wrong."

"She's turning all red, Mom!" Ollie shouted.

"Okay, honey," Julie said, raising her voice over the crying, "Mommy's going to pull over now."

"Julie, don't pull over on the side of the freeway!"

"I'm not pulling off on the freeway," she said testily. "There's an exit. I'm going to jump off here and calm her down. I'll call you back in five minutes."

"I don't know if that's such a great—"

The phone clicked dead.

Charlie set it down gingerly on the counter.

She would call back in five minutes.

CHAPTER SIX

Charlie looked at the clock: 7:04 P.M.

It had been thirty-one minutes. What could she possibly be doing? Why would she not have called him back yet?

He wanted to believe this was just another case of his being wound too tight, but for the life of him, he couldn't imagine any reason why Julie would hang out for half an hour on some dark exit off the freeway. As soon as Meagan calmed down—which shouldn't have taken more than a few minutes—she should have been on the road again.

He picked up his phone and dialed her cell.

"You've reached Julie Davis. Please leave a number."

He hung up without leaving a message and turned his attention to the television, trying to distract himself with the ninth inning of the Dodgers game. The Braves' closer, a kid who looked like he was barely out of Little League, struck out the last three batters on eleven pitches, mowing them down with ninety-seven-mile-an-hour fastballs. He switched off the TV and looked at the clock: 7:11.

Thirty-eight minutes.

He went to the front door and scanned the street for Julie's car. This was nonsensical, of course. There was no way she could be home by now.

He called again. "You've reached Julie Davis. Please leave a—"

Charlie went back inside to find the water boiling hard and the sauce bubbling on the stove. He turned down the flame and put the lid on the pot.

Forty-three minutes. Maybe Meagan had peed on herself and needed to be changed? Maybe Ollie had to go to the bathroom? Maybe Julie needed to fill her tank? Could any or all of that eat up forty-three minutes?

He called her again. Straight to voice mail.

He checked his texts and emails. Nothing.

He paced. He compulsively straightened up the kitchen and den.

Fifty-one minutes.

He grabbed his laptop, logged on to MapQuest and found a detailed map of Anaheim. She'd gotten on the 91 West and then what? How long had they been on the phone before she jumped off the exit? Two minutes, maybe three? He double-clicked on the map, zooming in for more detail.

If his calculations were correct, she would have gotten off at either Pioneer or Norwalk Avenue. A quick search found him the two closest hospitals. Norwalk Community to the east, St. John's to the north.

He dialed St. John's first. An automated answering service greeted him. It was another three minutes before someone in the emergency room answered.

"My name's Charlie Davis. I'm calling to see

if . . ." He trailed off for a second. Just articulating the words was giving him a knot in his stomach. "I'm calling to see if my wife or children were admitted there in the last hour."

"Their names please?" answered the nurse matter-of-factly. Charlie thought he could hear her clicking away at a computer.

"Julie Davis, that's my wife. Oliver and Meagan are my children. They're six and three."

"One moment please."

Muzak. Bad elevator Beatles.

Charlie glanced at the clock again: 7:33.

The nurse came back on the line, more quickly than Charlie would have expected. "I'm sorry, sir. No Julie Davis. No Oliver or Meagan."

"Okay," Charlie sighed. "Thank you."

As he hung up the phone, he wasn't sure if he should be relieved or more worried.

He quickly called Norwalk Community and got the same result. No Julie. No Oliver. No Meagan.

Seven thirty-seven. Over an hour.

He tried to tell himself that her BlackBerry must have run out of power, but that didn't make any sense. She had a charger built into her glove compartment. And even if she had somehow lost her phone when she got out of the car, she would have borrowed someone else's. Or used a pay phone. She said she would call back in five minutes. And she had to know that he'd be concerned. No matter how irritated or frustrated she was with him, this would not be the tactic, to punish him like this. That would be cruel. And there wasn't a cruel bone in Julie's body.

The kitchen clock ticked to 7:42.

He turned off the flame and looked at his keys on the granite countertop.

He knew what he was thinking was crazy, that he was allowing himself to succumb to his greatest, most irrational fears. But what good was he doing anyone here? Sitting around his kitchen?

He grabbed the keys and ran out to his Pathfinder. Ten minutes later he was speeding down the 405.

CHAPTER SEVEN

An airplane glided gently over the horizon, headed for a safe touchdown at LAX as Charlie barreled toward the 105 at eighty-six miles an hour. He'd been in such a hurry as he bolted out of the house that he hadn't taken the time to punch his destination into his navigation system, so there were no computerized predictions as to his time of arrival, but he calculated that at this rate he'd be approaching Pioneer Avenue in about half an hour.

He tried to convince himself that it wouldn't come to that. That he'd surely hear from Julie before then. She'd call and he'd have to turn around. Meet them at home. Explain why the kids' favorite dinner had gotten so cold and caked. This whole episode would simply be an embarrassing admission that he was holding on too tight, that he needed to let go.

He dialed Julie again.

"You've reached—"

He hung up and merged onto the 105, heading east.

. . .

The mini-malls whizzed by as he veered onto the 605 South. Only a mile and a half to the 91. He glanced at the clock on the dashboard: 8:08. Nearly an hour and a half since she'd pulled off the road.

He called her cell one more time. Straight to voice mail.

He tried the home line. Just in case. No answer.

Streaking down the 91 now. Almost there. It was either Pioneer or Norwalk. He felt confident about that. Pioneer Avenue was first and he took it.

The exit ramp spilled almost directly into a Mobil station, but Julie would have been coming from the other direction and he had to retrace the steps she would have taken. He turned left and crossed under the freeway. There was a Denny's on his left, right next to the Quality Inn. Eyeing the northbound ramp, he saw that Julie's easiest course of action would be to drive directly into the 76 station. He pulled in, looking around for her Prius. Across the street was a Chevron. Beyond that, an El Pollo Loco. A busy area. And still quite a bit of activity at 8:14.

Charlie got out of his vehicle, eyes darting around. No sign of them anywhere. He whipped out his phone as he entered the mini-mart.

"Have you seen these people?" he asked the attendant, showing a photo of his family on the tiny screen. "Did they come in here tonight?"

The customers ahead of him glanced backward: *who the hell do you think you are?* Charlie ignored them.

"Tonight! Within the last couple of hours. Were they here?"

A disinterested shrug was all he got.

Charlie barreled out the door and rushed to the Chevron, gazing down the dimly lit residential street as he crossed it.

Again, no sign of them. He looked for an attendant but here the mini-mart was already closed. Self-serve only.

Back on the 91, Charlie headed for Norwalk Boulevard. If there was no sign of them here, he had no idea what his next move would be. He pulled off the freeway, once again crossing under the overpass, once again attempting to retrace what might have been her steps. At the stop sign, he looked in both directions. But there was no need. Right in front of him was the only feature of the exit that Julie would have paid any attention to—a lone gas station. He crossed the road and pulled in.

Unlike Pioneer Avenue, Norwalk was quiet. Eerily quiet. Across the small street was a plumbing-supply office. Down the road, a drab industrial office complex lay partially hidden behind a row of scruffy trees. At this time of day, everyone would be long gone. As he stood there, the wispy wind shuddering against him, watching the cars cruise by on the freeway overpass, he suddenly noticed a gas nozzle dangling off its holster, dripping fuel onto the pavement.

He walked toward it, noting the way it was splayed out in a serpentine figure. Something about that felt ominous. Next to the rubbery tube was a small lump of gray on the ground. He approached it with growing anticipation as he realized what it was . . .

Donald Duck.

A brand-new Donald Duck, the fuzzy material soft and clean, a tag on the bottom from a Disneyland gift shop.

Adrenaline coursed through Charlie's body. For a moment, he felt exultant. But then a thought struck him with a sudden gloomy force: the doll could have fallen out of the car innocently enough, but the flailing gas nozzle right next to it . . . together the evidence spelled trouble.

Charlie scanned the area. There was no one here. No Prius parked behind the building, no—

Suddenly, he heard the high-pitched wail of an approaching siren.

The first black-and-white whizzed by at what Charlie figured had to be seventy miles an hour. Four seconds later, another one followed. Then another.

Everything in Charlie's bones told him these cops were headed for his family.

He sprinted back to his car and tore out onto Norwalk. The black-and-whites had a sizable lead on him and Charlie pushed the pedal all the way to the floor, the needle creeping toward eighty.

A half mile later, the lights in front of him slowed and turned left onto a residential street.

He followed. Two streets down, another left turn. Then a right. Then another left, past a yellow sign: DEAD END.

Charlie watched the squad car slow at the end of the cul-de-sac, trying unsuccessfully to turn off the terrifying thoughts that were buzzing through his brain. There were five other squad cars already here, red and blue lights puncturing the soft night sky.

They surrounded a gray Prius.

CHAPTER EIGHT

Charlie felt an inarticulate howl erupt from his chest as he slammed his car to a halt in the middle of the cul-de-sac. He tried to think of a benign explanation for the scene unfolding in front of him. But you didn't send a half-dozen police cars to a lonely residential neighborhood just because some nice lady had taken a wrong turn and blown a head gasket.

Charlie bolted out of his SUV and rushed toward the knot of policemen surrounding Julie's car.

"Let me see them!" he shouted. "Where are they? Let me see them!"

"Please step back, sir."

Charlie sensed someone to his left and managed to focus on a trim young cop but it wasn't until she was wrapping her arms around him that he even realized it was a woman.

"Sir! You have to—"

"I have to see them!"

"Do you live here, sir?"

"No, I—"

"Then you need to stay back."

He was nearly dragging the small police officer off her feet.

"Assistance!" she shouted. "Goddamnit, I need assistance *now*!"

Charlie kept plowing forward as blue uniforms rapidly converged on him.

"Get his arms! Get his arms!"

But Charlie was not going to be stopped. Because he'd seen something that breathed hope into him for the first time since he'd hit the freeway . . .

It was the hair. The auburn hair of a tiny girl.

Clinging to the neck of a large African-American policeman, she was rubbing her eyes with her chubby fist. A motion he had seen a thousand times.

"That's my daughter!" Charlie shouted as two more cops slammed into him, pinning him against one of the squad cars. They grunted and cursed, heaving on him as he struggled. Charlie fought back, blinded by the red and blue flashing lights.

"That's my daughter!"

They pinned his face against a squad car and he felt the cold steel of cuffs touching his wrists.

"Daddy, Daddy!" he heard Meagan squeal.

Then an authoritative, booming voice over hers. "Let him go! I said let the man go!"

Charlie felt three sets of hands release him. As he righted himself and regained his vision, he saw that the booming voice belonged to the big black cop. "Let him see his girl."

"Sorry, sir," the female cop said. "We thought—"

Charlie didn't care what she thought. He pushed through the knot of policemen and weaved toward Meagan.

"Daddy!"

He grabbed her from the sergeant, holding her tight, his mind jumping rapid fire to the next question: *Ollie and Julie. Ollie and Julie?*

He ran toward Julie's car, his daughter's legs bouncing against his ribs.

"Daddydaddydaddy!"

The Prius was parked ten yards from the wall at the end of the cul-de-sac. No crumpled fenders, no buckled doors, no obvious damage. Charlie's heartbeat began to slow. There'd been no accident. And it occurred to him that there were no paramedics or ambulances here. That had to be a good sign.

Then he saw them, poking out into the street. A pair of Nike sneakers. Red and black. Size nine, boys'. Above the sneakers was a pair of knees, the left one covered by a Band-Aid with a picture of Mickey Mouse on it. Ollie's face was blocked by the hood of the Prius, but Charlie was quite sure now that he must be all right.

Maybe the car *had* just broken down. Maybe Julie *had* taken a wrong turn and gotten lost and maybe the head gasket *had* blown. Maybe her phone had stopped working when the car died and she'd freaked out a little, scaring the neighbors, who'd called 911. Maybe it was a slow day for the cops in Norwalk. Maybe . . .

Charlie felt a burst of elation as he rounded the front of Julie's car and saw Ollie looking up at him. The boy was holding the hand of a tall, beefy man in a blue LAPD uniform.

Then Charlie saw the tears. Streaming down Ollie's face. But it was the eyes that arrested him. Pure terror. Whatever had just happened here, it wasn't a blown head gasket or a wrong turn.

That was when Charlie noticed the broken glass next to the car. The driver's-side window had been shattered.

"Who are you, sir?" asked one of the cops.

"Dad!" Ollie whimpered, reaching toward Charlie.

A cold sensation clamped around Charlie's chest as he grabbed his son.

"I'm their father," Charlie whispered. "I'm their father." Then his eyes found the big policeman's face. The officer looked at Charlie with the cool, contained expression of a man who knew how to keep his distance from other people's pain.

Charlie's pulse roared in his ears as the question barely escaped his mouth:

"Where's my wife?"

CHAPTER NINE

The central bureau of the LAPD was a window-less bunker of a building with an unattractive mural painted on the front.

Charlie and the kids had been sitting in a waiting area outside the detectives' bullpen for nearly three hours and it was well after midnight. The children were exhausted, and Charlie wanted answers, but nothing indicated that they were getting out of here anytime soon.

"What's taking so long?" Oliver asked.

"I don't know," Charlie answered.

"Do you want me to tell you again?"

Charlie's heart nearly melted as he regarded his son and gently brushed back his hair. "That's all right, kiddo. I think we've got it now."

Ollie had told his tale so many times to the patrol officers at the scene, but when they first got to the police station, Charlie had wanted to go over it one last time—to see if he remembered anything new. In a slow, halting voice, the boy had recounted the nightmare . . .

Julie had pulled off the freeway as soon as she had hung up the phone with Charlie. At the gas station,

Julie had taken a thrashing Meagan out of her car seat and walked her around until she had calmed down. Julie had then started gassing up the car. Suddenly she got back in the car and tore away. Ollie said they drove "really fast and the tires screeched a bunch" until the car came to a stop. Julie then told Ollie she was going to get out of the car and lock the door behind her. No matter what Ollie did, he was not to open the door for anyone.

Finally, Ollie said he heard some voices outside the car—angry male voices—but he couldn't make out any of the words.

"Did Mom scream or yell?" Charlie had asked.

Ollie shook his head. He heard doors slam, then a car drove off and then everything was quiet. After that, he just waited. "Mom told me not to open the door for anyone. That's why the police had to break the window. But I swear that's what Mom told me to do, Dad."

"You did great, son," Charlie had reassured him. "You did great."

Meagan was stirring now and rubbing her eyes. "I wanna go home, Daddy."

"I know you do, sweetie. Soon."

Charlie's mind was whirling. What had Julie seen at the gas station that made her want to flee like that? And once somebody started chasing her, why would she have stopped and gotten out of the car? Was she protecting the kids? But from whom? And why didn't she call 911? Or Charlie, for that matter? None of it made any sense.

The arrival of three people he took to be detectives offered some hope for clarity.

"Mr. Davis, I'm Detective Gerry Albez and this

is Detective Reamer." The one who spoke was a Hispanic man of about thirty-five, wearing a neatly pressed white shirt, a beige tie and khakis, his wavy black hair frozen into submission with hair gel.

"Cathy Ann Reamer," the second detective said, shaking hands. She was older than Albez, with close-cropped prematurely white hair that gave her a somewhat grandmotherly quality.

Detective Reamer gestured toward the third person, a frumpily dressed black woman with pinched features and very long fingernails. "This is Jessica Mitchell from Social Services. She's going to keep an eye on the kids for you."

Charlie looked sharply at Detective Reamer.

"Standard procedure," Reamer said. "We may get into some issues you wouldn't want the children to hear."

Charlie got a frigid feeling from Mitchell, particularly given the circumstances. Unlike the detectives, she had neither offered her hand nor met his eyes. But Charlie knew that the detectives were correct. This was standard procedure and there was going to be plenty to discuss that the children shouldn't hear.

"It'll just be a few minutes," Charlie told his kids. "Give me a hug, huh, then go with this nice lady."

Charlie watched them walk slowly away then disappear into a room at the end of the hallway. Collecting himself, he turned to the detectives.

"So what have you found out so far?"

"Unfortunately, we don't have any forensic evidence at this point," Albez said.

"And there are no witnesses at the cul-de-sac or the gas station?"

"Afraid not." Albez gestured toward a door leading into a drab interview room. "If you wouldn't mind . . ."

It was only as he stood that Charlie noticed the sign on the wall next to the interview room:

HOMICIDE UNIT.

Charlie knew that, like taking the children away, it was standard procedure for homicide detectives to follow up on disappearances. It was precautionary and bureaucratic: if a disappearance turned into a murder, there would be no need to shift to a new set of detectives. But that was hardly a consolation.

As Charlie walked toward the door, Reamer stood at the entrance to the room, holding it open. A simple enough gesture, but Charlie immediately read it for what it was: a command masquerading as a courtesy.

Albez patted the back of an uncushioned metal chair—"Have a seat"—and waited until Charlie obeyed. He crossed to the other side of the bolted-down desk and sat down opposite Charlie.

Detective Reamer did not sit. Instead she crossed her arms and leaned against the wall, studying Charlie's face. Her expression was pleasant enough, but there was a slightly unnerving quality to her gaze.

Albez fussed around with a notebook, crossed his legs, uncrossed his legs, clicked his pen and asked a few housekeeping questions—Julie's full name, age, date of birth. Charlie did his best to remain patient, watching Albez dutifully record the data in his notebook. Jotting down the information in small, obscenely neat handwriting, Albez seemed very satisfied with his fastidiousness. "Now then . . ."

He leaned forward, for the first time taking his eyes off the notebook. "You told one of the patrolmen that your wife just returned from New York."

"That's right."

"Where she was visiting her sister?"

"Yes."

"Rebecca."

"Becca, yes. Rebecca Wingate-Rees."

"Occupation?"

"She's a real estate broker in Manhattan. Do you need her contact information?"

Albez hesitated, then slid a piece of paper toward Charlie. "Sure. That would be great."

Charlie took a deep breath and gazed at Reamer. Her bland eyes held his. Charlie took Albez's ballpoint pen, scribbled down Becca's essentials, and handed the paper and pen back to Albez.

There was a long silence. Albez scooted his chair back, the legs screeching loudly on the tile floor, then crossed his hands over his chest.

"What?" Charlie said sharply.

Albez reached into his breast pocket and took out a folded piece of paper, which he set on the table. "Yeah . . . see we checked with the FAA. Your wife wasn't in New York. She was in London."

Charlie unfolded the paper and stared at it. It was a printed ticket record showing that Julie Davis had flown on a direct flight, British Airways 293, Heathrow to LAX, arriving last night at 10:05 P.M. For a moment he imagined that maybe it was a case of mistaken identity, some other woman with the relatively generic name of Julie Davis. But it only took another second to disabuse himself of that appealing fantasy: all of Julie's contact information was on the ticket record—street address, home phone, the whole bit.

Charlie felt the blood drain from his face. He'd called Becca's apartment yesterday morning looking for Julie and Becca had told him point-blank that he'd barely missed her. Not only had Julie lied to him, but she'd apparently enlisted her sister as an alibi.

"Any idea what she was doing in London?" Albez asked.

Charlie pushed the paper back across the table, his fingers shaking slightly. "None."

"Did you know your wife was lying to you?"

Charlie's temper flashed. "Obviously, I wouldn't have told you she was in New York if I knew she was in London!"

The room was silent.

After a moment, Reamer shifted almost imperceptibly and in a light, conversational tone, as if she was offering him a cup of coffee, asked, "She sleeping with somebody, Charlie?"

Charlie kept his voice even and soft. "No."

Reamer shrugged apologetically. "Because we find that's usually what's going on when husbands and wives lie to each other."

"Well that's not what's happening here," Charlie insisted.

"Then how do you explain your wife jetting off to her old stomping grounds and using her sister to lie to you about it?"

Charlie searched for a reason that made any sense. But rather than offer some half-baked hypothesis that would only make him look more suspicious, he stuck to the truth. "I can't," he said.

"We already spoke to Rebecca in New York. She confirmed for us that your wife was seeing somebody. In London."

Charlie felt his stomach drop.

"She said you called her apartment yesterday morning looking for your wife. She said you sounded suspicious."

Charlie looked from one to the other. Was this just a bluff? Or was it possible Becca had actually told them that?

Albez glanced at Reamer.

"Seems as good a time as any," she said, then hit the play button on a VCR. "This is off the security camera from the gas station on Norwalk."

A grainy black-and-white image appeared on the television screen. It was a view from inside the mini-mart, several gas pumps visible through the front door.

After a moment a car drives up and stops. A woman gets out.

Even with the graininess of the video, Charlie instantly recognized her—

—the slim body, the way she brushes back a lock of her long black hair, the graceful economy of her motion. Unruffled as she opens the back door and takes Meagan out of the car.

The only sound as they watched was the soft hiss of the air conditioner. But the tiny black hole of Meagan's mouth made it clear she was screaming.

Julie cradles her, walks her up and down, disappears from the frame, then comes back. Meagan's fit has passed. She's in a dead sleep, limbs draped around Julie's neck, head nestled deep into Julie's thick hair. Clutching her Donald Duck.

Charlie's breath caught. It was so entirely normal, so peaceful, so unmarred by any sense of impending trouble that it seemed impossible anything could have gone wrong after that.

Julie lifts Meagan into the car. The Donald Duck falls from her hand. Julie doesn't see it. She grabs the pump. Leans one hip against the car, motionless, as the tank fills.

Charlie shifted in his seat, knowing from Ollie's account what would be coming next.

A flare of light on the camera lens—headlights pulling into the station. Julie's face turns, tracking the car as it crosses the lot. But the approaching vehicle is ominously out of frame. Her body stiffens. She scrambles back into the car. And tears away. The gas nozzle sprays fuel everywhere then lies limp on the asphalt.

Reamer paused the tape. "Somebody was following her."

Charlie read her expression. "And you think that somebody was me."

Reamer looked at him briefly, one eyebrow raised, as if to say, "You said it, not me."

Charlie couldn't believe this was happening—they were treating him as the prime suspect.

"Jesus Christ," he said, "can't you get an angle off the security cam? You can grab a license plate."

"Whoever it was, they managed to avoid the cameras," Albez said.

"Which means they were really smart," added Reamer.

"Or really lucky," chimed in Albez. They really had their Abbott and Costello thing working now.

"Of course," Reamer added, "they might not have realized how lucky they were. Which is how the do-er usually gets tripped up—trying to cover his tracks."

She hit the fast-forward button. The counter scrolled forward, then suddenly the detective jabbed the play button again. For a moment the screen was empty. Then a car pulled up. It was Charlie's white Pathfinder.

He felt himself flush as his image moved around the screen.

"Looking to see if there was a security camera?" Albez asked blithely.

Charlie finds the Donald Duck.

"Ohh. You found your kid's doll. Better take that with you. If you're lucky, maybe nobody'll realize she was ever at the gas station."

"I told you." Charlie gritted his teeth. "I was looking for them. When she hadn't called me back, I thought something had happened to them."

"If you were so concerned, why didn't you call 911?"

"And what would I have said? My wife hasn't called me back for an hour, send out the SWAT team?"

"Exactly our point, Mr. Davis." This was Albez at his most condescending. "You don't hear from your wife for an hour, so you jump in the car and go chasing after her forty miles from your house. And then by some giant stroke of luck you manage to find them at some gas station in the middle of nowhere."

"I told you, I was navigating her home. I knew where she got off the freeway."

Albez gave him an ironic smile. "We understand you left work early today. Decided to take a half day?"

Charlie was reeling. They'd already talked to Sal?

"I had a disagreement with my boss," he told them.

"And where'd you go?"

"Home."

"Anywhere else?"

"No."

"Anybody see you there?"

"Look . . . ," Charlie said, taking a deep breath, trying to reason with them. "I get it. Ninety percent of the time wife goes missing, husband did something to her. You're playing the odds and I'll admit there's some circumstantial evidence here, but look at me. Do I look like a man who did something to my wife, or do I look like a man who's desperately wanting to find her?"

Charlie searched their eyes, trying to form a human connection.

And for the first time, Albez connected with him. But now, the glib, sarcastic artifice fell away. Instead, the man was dripping with anger and certitude. "You found out that she went to London and not New York. You knew she must have been running around on you, so you bolted from work, ready to tear her head off. Your office is downtown, only twenty minutes from Disneyland, why not head over there and confront her? You get there, maybe you realize this is not the best forum for it, so you follow them. When they head home, she calls you, not even knowing that you're right behind her on the freeway. Now, you can't resist. You start arguing. Maybe she figures out you're stalking her, maybe not. Either way, your daughter melts down, your wife pulls over. You tear into the gas station.

Maybe to continue the argument, maybe to beat the crap out of her. The second you pull in, she recognizes your vehicle. She drops the gas nozzle, hops in her car and hightails it out of there. You chase her. She makes a wrong turn, winds up at a dead end street. She knows it's going to get ugly so she tells the kids to sit tight, don't open the door for anyone, not even Dad."

"She never said that. That is not what Oliver told anyone."

"It was implied," Albez continued, unruffled. "She didn't want to freak the kids out about their daddy. So she says 'not anyone.' She gets out of the car to confront you. Oliver hears an angry male voice."

"Voices," Charlie insisted.

"Maybe. With a six-year-old, it's hard to tell. At any rate, you and she brawl out there. Only question is, what happened next? I think you lost your cool, hurt her in a way you never really intended. Now it's panic time. You got to get rid of the body and do it fast. You're also going to need an alibi and an explanation for why you're not home, what you're doing in that area. You start calling every fifteen minutes or so—make it seem like you're a concerned guy. But you never leave a message 'cause you're not sure you can sell it." Albez pointed at the video screen. "Then you realize maybe that camera there picked up your car going into the gas station. You doubleback to check it out, find the doll, and now we're back to where we started."

"You're wrong." Charlie was seething. "Dead wrong. And while you're in here pointing the finger at me, someone out there's got my wife. Doing God knows what to her."

Charlie looked from Reamer to Albez. Their vacant, cynical expressions said it all.

"You know what I do for a living? You think I won't have your names splattered all over the front page of my paper when all this goes south? When I prove you rushed to judgment—against a man with no record of violent behavior?"

Reamer stepped forward with concern, her voice gentle. "Mr. Davis . . . when did you find out that your wife was cheating on you?"

Charlie knew it was over—that there was no convincing them.

"You charging me with something?"

Reamer and Albez exchanged a look. "Not yet," she offered brightly.

"Then I'm going home."

Charlie stormed out and hurried down the hallway, searching for the room where the Social Services lady had taken his children.

He found them in a grungy office, half asleep on a weary old couch.

"Come on, angels," he whispered, leaning down to them. "We're going home."

CHAPTER TEN

Holding one sleepy child in each arm, Charlie shook with anger as he strode through the precinct parking lot at almost two thirty in the morning. He passed a trio of cops, standing by a squad car, drinking coffee and cackling about the wacky events of their graveyard shift. He was sure they had no idea who he was, or why he was here, but their laughter felt personally directed toward him. He wanted to grab them. To shake them. To order them to put away their French fries and get out there and find Julie. Instead he climbed into his car, phone clutched in his hand. The moment the door was closed, he dialed Julie's sister.

The phone rang and rang before finally going to voice mail. Becca's clipped English voice answered, "You've reached Becca. Do what you do. Cheers."

"Becca, it's Charlie." He cleared his throat, struggling to keep his voice under control. "I know you spoke to the police. And I know Julie wasn't in New York. You better have some goddamn answers for me. Call me back."

• • • •

Forty-five minutes later, Charlie arrived at home, carried the children up the stairs, gently removed their socks and shoes and tucked them into their beds.

He barreled downstairs and hurried into Julie's office. The first thing he needed to do was check her computer. If she was carrying on some kind of affair in London—and that was somehow related to her disappearance—there might be some evidence of it in her emails.

He opened her computer. Normally her screen saver brandished a photo of the kids, but now it was just a pale blue screen. Had the power gone off and caused it to reboot? No, that didn't make sense. It had a battery backup. He typed in the codes for system check. It didn't take him more than a few moments of key tapping to realize there was nothing there at all. Her computer was empty. No files, no software, not even an operating system. It had been wiped clean. Had Julie done that? To hide something from him?

Charlie hurried toward the kitchen. He could access her email from his own computer, assuming she hadn't changed the passwords. But when he got there, and he saw his laptop, he was faced with the same blank blue screen. His computer had been wiped too?

He felt the hairs stand up on the back of his neck and remembered that he hadn't set the alarm before he'd rushed out the door. Could someone have broken into the house?

He opened a drawer and grabbed for the longest, sharpest knife he could find. But before he could venture a step, his cell phone rang.

At three in the morning?

He grabbed the phone from his pocket and looked at the screen.

It read—JULIE.

He held the phone for longer than he might have expected, then stabbed the button.

"Jules?" he implored.

"Not quite." The voice was husky and male.

"Who are you? Where's my wife?"

"If you ever want to see her again, you'll come down to the basement. Now."

Charlie glanced upstairs. Where the kids were.

"Your children won't be harmed," the voice assured him. "We only want to talk to you."

Charlie gripped his weapon, looking down at the blade.

"And leave the knife," the voice said.

Charlie spotted a man standing in the shadows of his front yard, staring blankly at him through the kitchen window, muttering into what appeared to be a Bluetooth as he raised a gun toward him.

Charlie considered his options—he could make a run for it, dash upstairs, grab the children, and try to get away. Or lock himself and the children in his bedroom and call for help. But for all he knew, there was another man already upstairs. Standing guard.

Whoever these people were—they were professionals.

Charlie set the knife down on the counter, moved to an interior kitchen door and opened it. At the bottom of the stairs was the basement. It was pitch-black down there. Charlie felt for the light switch and turned it on. Nothing happened. Had they shorted the circuit? Taken out the bulbs?

Slowly, Charlie descended the stairs, the wood boards creaking beneath his feet. Even in the darkness, he could make out the shadow of a man down below.

Charlie paused in the middle of the staircase, wondering if he was walking placidly toward his own death.

"Keep coming," the bland, husky voice told him.

Behind him, at the top of the stairs, Charlie heard the door close and lock from inside the kitchen. He was trapped.

Charlie took three more steps. As his eyes adjusted to the darkness, he thought he spotted another figure to his right. He paused again.

"Keep coming, Charlie. If we wanted to kill you, you'd be dead already."

Charlie took the last two steps and felt his feet arrive on the hard stucco floor.

"How about turning on some—"

Charlie's request was interrupted by a nasty zapping sound from behind him.

He felt a jolt of electricity course through his entire body and everything went to black.

When the veil of pain had parted sufficiently for Charlie to be aware of his surroundings again, he found himself seated and restrained, his body still buzzing from whatever it was they'd done to him. He would have asked what they wanted but there was a rolled-up sock in his mouth.

The lights were on now, which was of very little comfort. He was in his own basement—cheesy Formica wet bar (inherited from the previous owner), paneled dark brown walls, baseball bats, hockey sticks and football helmets strewn around, the last vestiges of his days as a star athlete.

To Charlie's left stood two very large men wearing leather jackets. But from the deferential way they eyed him, it was clear the guy in the photographer's vest was in charge. He looked to be about fifty, a bull of a man, with hard eyes and a bald head. As Bull pulled one of the signed bats off the wall, his vest gapped open, revealing a shoulder holster underneath. He slapped the bat in his palm and nodded at one of the goons, who took out Charlie's gag.

"Before you do anything stupid," Bull began, "just recognize that if you scream and fuss and freak out the neighbors, I'll have no choice but to kill you and your children."

Charlie's heart was pounding, but he needed to maintain control.

"You have my wife?"

Bull took a couple of practice swings, the bat passing so close to Charlie that he could feel the wind of it on his face.

"I think I'll be asking the questions," Bull said.

"Who are you?"

Bull aimed his cold smile at one of his men, then shrugged—"I guess he didn't hear me"—and drove the knob of the bat into Charlie's solar plexus.

Charlie's body tried unsuccessfully to wretch, but his diaphragm was so paralyzed that all he could do was double over in his chair and gasp. When he finally managed to sit up, Bull asked, "Who does your wife work for?"

"She doesn't work for anybody," Charlie gasped. "I have no idea what you're talking about."

Bull walked to the wet bar, set down the bat and picked up a small plastic first-aid kit, white with a red cross on top. He made a show of opening it, inviting Charlie to have a peek. Inside the kit lay a row of syringes on a bed of foam egg-crate material. Bull rolled up the sleeves of his button-down shirt and Charlie noticed a tattoo on his forearm—five stars on a blue field surrounding a red diamond with the Marine Corps logo in the middle.

Bull pulled out two syringes and held them up, one in each hand. "You have two choices. Red. Or green." He held up the syringes in turn, then approached Charlie. "Red?"

But before Charlie could even begin to respond, Bull slammed the syringe into his neck. He felt a brief impact then a burning sensation running up the side of his face and head. Sweat poured from him, his heart began racing and his entire body began to tremble.

"Your heart should be clocking about 250 beats per minute right now. That's the norepinephrine. Pretty potent stimulant, don't you think?"

"I don't *know* anything," Charlie said, gritting his teeth.

Bull just stared at him. Convinced he was going to die, Charlie thrashed wildly, trying to free himself from the chair.

"You ever drop acid, Charlie? We got a new substance now—salvinoran A—it's like acid on steroids if you can forgive the mixed metaphor. The thing we found is, if you mix it with norepinephrine, man, the whole cocktail's like a giant fear amplifier. You got the fight or flight impulse combined with the hallucinogen, all I have to do now is mention your kids and boom! The thoughts you're going to have about what I might do to them . . . Did you ever see that movie *Saw*?"

Images flitted through Charlie's mind, graphic and horrible. He clawed at the air, trying to reach out and touch his children, their eyes wide with terror, their mouths screaming . . .

Bull held up a second syringe, this one containing the green fluid. He plunged it into Charlie's neck. It burned even worse than the red one. But his heart rate slowed to a normal rhythm and his skin stopped pouring sweat. And the fear . . . the fear disappeared entirely, replaced by a strange emotional hollowness. He felt almost nothing, as though his mind was a tooth deadened by novocaine.

"Who does your wife work for?" Bull asked again.

But all Charlie could focus on was that tattoo on Bull's forearm. Because he had seen it before—at the Marine Corps Special Operations Regiment at Camp Lejeune. It was the kind of elite unit from which operators often graduated to black ops work, the kind of work that was too sensitive to be performed by men in military uniforms.

And it dawned on Charlie—the tattoo, the power of these drugs, the way Bull was talking about "we" . . . these men had to be working for the American government. CIA, NSA, Special Ops, some other shadow group. What the hell had Julie gotten herself involved in that she'd inspired the wrath of men like this?

"I'll ask you again, Charlie . . ."

"I don't know!" Charlie growled. "I thought she was in New York. I have no idea what she was doing or where she was."

Bull smiled, then leaned forward, studying Charlie's face from only inches away. "You expect me to believe that?"

"She told me she was going to New York. She even brought back a baseball with Derek Jeter's autograph on it. It's in the living room. On the mantel."

Bull nodded to one of his goons, who headed upstairs, apparently to check on the ball.

Charlie was about to tell them the truth, that Julie had used Becca to lie for her, but quickly realized—if he told them that, they might soon be paying her a visit. He had to hold on—to keep Becca out of this somehow. Because if Bull was going to kill him, if he'd already killed Julie, Becca was the one they wanted to raise their kids. They'd already decided that—six years ago when they'd left Uzbekistan and drawn up their wills.

"I swear to God," Charlie implored. "She told me she was going to New York. That's all I know."

"And where was she supposed to be staying there?" Bull asked.

"The Mercer Hotel," Charlie insisted. "She likes to be downtown. She has some friends who live there."

"And did you call her at the hotel?"

"No. I was only calling her cell. I never had any idea she wasn't in New York."

"Wow," Bull exhaled. "Pretty elaborate lie, huh?"

"Yeah," Charlie admitted. "Pretty elaborate."

Bull sighed sadly. "Doesn't say much about your marriage, does it?"

Charlie stared at the floor. For the first time since receiving the hit of green, he felt something—the sting of Julie's betrayal and what it was costing all of them.

"You know, Charlie . . . my instincts say that you're telling me the truth. Unfortunately in this case, I don't have the luxury of being able to simply trust my instincts."

Bull pulled out a second syringe of the Red.

"No!" Charlie screamed, swirling his neck around in a futile attempt to avoid the shot. "No. Please, no . . ."

The syringe bit into his neck, and once again, he began to shake. Once again, the fear blazed through his mind like an inferno of doom.

"Please, no! I don't know anything. I swear I don't know anything."

Bull looked at Charlie, entirely unmoved, almost as though he was bored.

"Well," he said, "that's what we're going to find out."

CHAPTER ELEVEN

harlie? Charlie?"

He awoke with a start, his pulse racing. He was lying on the floor. In the living room of his house, he felt sure of that. But he wasn't sure how he'd gotten there. He tried to sit up but fell back against the couch. His head was pounding and his brain felt muddled and slow.

"Charlie?" It was a woman's voice, calling to him from the other room. A woman with an English accent.

It was Julie. This whole thing had been a terrible dream, a drunken nightmare after his meeting with Sal.

"Charlie?"

"In here. In the living room."

He glanced at a clock—it was almost 9:00 am—and tried to steady himself, get a handle on what had happened. The only problem was that he didn't remember going to a bar. Or drinking at home. Or the last time he'd gotten drunk for any reason.

The woman entered from the kitchen, obscured ever so slightly by the morning light shimmering through the tall windows.

"Charlie, are you all right?"

Charlie rubbed his eyes. It wasn't Julie. It was her sister Becca. What in the hell was *she* doing here?

Becca walked toward him with concern. "The police called me last night. I took the first plane I could this morning. I didn't even get your message until I landed. I just got here, the door was open."

Then it all started to flood back to him. The cul-de-sac. The cops. Bull.

The kids.

Charlie brushed past her and sprinted up the stairs. If Bull had done anything to them . . .

Charlie tripped over Oliver's PlasmaCar in the hallway, stumbled toward their bedroom and burst inside.

The first thing he saw was a lump under Meagan's blanket. His eyes darted toward Oliver's bed. A mat of his hair and half his face poked out beneath his covers. Meagan was closer so he moved to her first, ripping away the blanket. And there she was, her chest moving slowly up and down as she quietly took in breath. Charlie bent down to Oliver's bed and lowered the covers. His boy—his sweet, precious boy—was sleeping soundly.

Unharmed. They were both unharmed.

Charlie sat on the floor and quietly wept.

A moment later, Becca appeared in the doorway. Charlie rose quickly, wiped his eyes and headed out of the room, closing the door behind him.

"They must be so tired," Becca said softly.

But Charlie was in no mood for commiseration. He was furious and he wanted answers.

"She said she was going to New York and you lied for her. Now what the hell has she gotten herself into?"

Becca looked disconsolately at the floor. "I don't know."

"Well, what did she say to you? Why did she have you lie for her?"

"She wouldn't tell me. I assumed she was having an affair." Becca wiped away a tear. "I'm sorry, Charlie. I'm so sorry."

"You told the police that I was suspicious of her?"

"No," she protested. "I didn't say that. I never said anything like that."

"Well, somehow they've got me lined up as the number one suspect. She was seeing somebody in London?"

"I told you I don't know. She called me last week, she said she had to go out of the country, she said she needed me to cover for her, to say she was visiting me in New York. When I asked her if it was about another man, she said she couldn't get into it. I told her I was uncomfortable with all of it, but she kept begging me. She kept saying this was something she had to do. So I agreed."

Charlie marched down the stairs again, Becca on his heels. "Well, I just had three spooks in here shooting me full of psychedelic speed, demanding to know who Julie's working for."

"Spooks?"

"Special Operations, black ops, American military intelligence of some kind."

"Oh my God."

Charlie hurried through the kitchen and barreled

downstairs to the basement. "They kept asking me who she was working for. Is it possible she was meeting someone involved with her old work? Someone at World Vision?"

"I don't know. I guess so."

He turned on the lights and studied the basement. Everything was perfectly in place. Not the slightest sign that Bull and his men were here last night.

Charlie headed back upstairs, Becca following him once again.

"Why don't you call the police?" she asked.

"They're not going to believe a word I say."

"But if these guys were in the house . . ."

Charlie paused, examining the kitchen. His famous marinara sauce (now burned and cold), the pot of overboiled water, the box of spaghetti on the counter—a poetic tapestry of the life they'd shared together. A life he thought he'd understood.

"Charlie," Becca pushed, "if they broke into your house—"

"There's no sign of forced entry. Nothing's been left out of place. They wore gloves, so there won't be any prints. The kids are perfectly unharmed and can't vouch for my story. These guys were professionals. If anything, the cops will just assume I'm creating a smoke screen."

"But isn't it at least worth having the police take a look? To tell them what you suspect?"

"I'd rather have them spending their time canvassing the area where Julie was taken, even if they're looking for evidence against me. Maybe they'll stumble upon something useful. Besides, you don't want to call the LAPD to take on the CIA or the NSA. I can tell you that."

"The CIA?" Becca pleaded. "Why would the CIA want to kidnap Julie?"

CHAPTER TWELVE

Quinn stood inside a shipping container, a ten-foot-tall corrugated steel box lit by a dim drop-light hanging from a hook in the center of the space. A cot lay in the far corner. In the other corner sat a chemical toilet and a small refrigerator containing various medical supplies—IV bags, saline, glucose, hypodermics.

A medic and a guard were by the door, looking apprehensively at Quinn.

The medic was a fat, sweaty little guy, a former Iraqi Army doctor with a sizable heroin problem. The guard—a large, intimidating Uzbek with a gun—had several grams of pharmaceutical grade smack in a bag inside his shirt. The medic would do exactly what the guard told him, no problem there.

"Tell it to me again," Quinn said as he closed the door.

"Me?" the medic said, holding a pudgy hand over his chest.

"Who the hell else you think I'm talking to?" Quinn snapped.

"Yes, yes, of course, sir!" The medic swallowed

hard. "I keep the woman on the IV the whole time. Glucose, saline, vitamins. She will be fully sedated yet every eight hours I'm to let her come out of sedation just enough that she can stand and do her necessaries. As you say, letting her stand up and move around minimizes the likelihood of medical complications." He hesitated and leaned forward in an insinuating way. "I presume, sir, your expectation is that once we reach our destination, she will not remember anything about the journey?"

Quinn gave the medic a cold smile. "You presume correctly, Doc."

"Might I presume, also, to ask what our destination will be, sir?"

"Sure. And I might presume to tell you to shut your goddamn mouth and concentrate your meager attention on doing what I goddamn tell you."

The medic's head bobbed rapidly and he smiled a broad, please-don't-hit-me smile.

"All righty then," Quinn said, clapping his hands together. "Bring her in."

The guard opened the door and waved to the van that stood outside the container. They were on Pier J at the Port of Long Beach, California, hidden in the middle of a giant tangle of semitrailers used for hauling containers.

At the other end of the pier, Quinn could see a tramp steamer peeping over the trailers. That steamer would take this container to Juneau. From there the rest of the trip would be by air.

Quinn watched as two of his men hauled Julie Davis out of the van. He'd given her a jab of something to knock her out earlier, so she was limp and essentially unconscious. As far as he was concerned, all of this was a needless complication. If it had been up to him, he would have had her in an abandoned warehouse outside Chino and been running the whole "red-green" drill on her right now, but the man calling the shots wanted her brought to him and there was nothing Quinn could do about it.

Quinn's men dropped the woman roughly on the cot, her head thumping as it hit the thin foam mattress.

"What are you, morons?" Quinn shouted. "We didn't go to all this trouble so she'd get there with a goddamn subdural hematoma."

The men filed sullenly out of the container.

"Listen up," Quinn said to the guard and the medic. "She's a beautiful woman. You might be tempted to have some fun on the way. If she gets there and there's a scratch, a bruise, a blemish, her hair's messed up—swear to Christ, guys, I'm gonna put a bullet in both your goddamn brains. Got it?"

The medic and the guard nodded.

"Good," Quinn said. "See you there then."

Quinn closed the door and watched as the port inspector crimped the customs seal onto the door.

"What I'm giving you?" the inspector said. "This here's a high-security bolt seal, more or less tamper proof, color coded, imprinted with a unique number so you can track it from shipper to destination. High-security seals receive faster customs clearance than standard, what we call 'indicative,' seals. Faster's better, am I right?"

"You are indeed."

The inspector looked up nervously at Quinn as he pocketed the crimping tool. "So, ah . . . now'd be a good time to take care of the other half . . . ?"

Quinn looked at him blandly, watching the man squirm.

"The five thousand," said the inspector.

"Actually, I've been thinking about that . . ." Quinn looked around. "And my feeling is . . . now's not such a good time."

In a flash, Quinn pulled out his telescoping baton and hit the man four times in the head. His skull was cracked by the third blow. But Quinn always gave himself that one extra lick. Because a life that was all business was no kind of life at all.

CHAPTER THIRTEEN

Charlie let the hot water run over his weary body, though right now he couldn't care less about getting clean. This shower was about knocking the cobwebs out of his brain so he could concentrate on what had happened last night. There were so many gaps in his memory, no doubt the effect of all the drugs, but he tried to piece it together . . .

The repetitive questions about whom Julie worked for and what she knew. Was there a safe in the house? Where did she keep her computer? On and on it went. Charlie with nearly nothing to give them. Except Becca. And he'd managed to hold on to that. To keep her out of it. Safe.

Who was Julie working for? That was the main one. The one they kept harping on.

Charlie and Becca had already called all of her old contacts at World Vision, but none of them had heard from Julie in months or had any idea that Julie was coming to London.

Then what was she doing there? Who was she seeing? How had it led to all of this?

Charlie forced himself to return to the interrogation, to try to put himself back in that basement.

He remembered now—that he was sitting in the chair, slumped over and depleted. There was a sharp prick in his arm and then a soft buzzing noise. The world began to grow shaky and dim, like a fade in some black-and-white movie from a hundred years ago. Later—he had no idea how much later—he felt hands pulling him out of the chair. Then the carpet against his cheek and a pair of boots walking in front of him. Then someone speaking in a foreign language.

Suddenly it dawned on him—it was Russian they were speaking.

One of the goons said, "Are we taking him to Tashkent?" He'd meant Charlie. And what did Bull say . . . ? Charlie opened his eyes and looked out the shower door, as if the memories might drift up here from the basement. What did Bull say?! He called the other guy *"durak"*—an idiot—and then he said, "We're going to have a hard enough time getting the woman there."

Charlie's eyes widened.

Julie was alive. And they were taking her to Uzbekistan.

Charlie hustled out of the shower, toweled himself off quickly and made a beeline for his cell phone. Many of his old contacts were still programmed into the phone and he would begin there. First on his list was Faruz: the most resourceful, most connected of them all. He only hoped Faruz hadn't changed his phone number—six years was a long time. He dialed and waited. Uzbekistan must be one of the few places in the world where one still got an echoey faraway ring on a long-distance call.

Two rings, three . . .

Charlie glanced at his watch. It was after midnight in Tashkent but he certainly wouldn't be waking Faruz. Finally, he heard a click and then an outgoing message in Russian: "You reach Faruz, tell me what you need."

After a few seconds the beep kicked in and Charlie left a message: "Faruz, it's your old friend Charlie. Charlie Davis. I need your help. Badly. Call me as soon as you can." He left his cell and home numbers and hung up.

He was about to make the next call when he noticed Oliver standing in the doorway, bleary-eyed and disheveled and still wearing yesterday's clothes.

"Dad?"

"Hey buddy."

"Who were you talking to?"

"Oh, that was just . . . that was just an old friend. Someone who can help us find Mommy."

But Charlie had a queasy feeling in his stomach. Because speaking the words aloud to Oliver made what he was saying naked and plain. He was phoning people ten thousand miles away, people he hadn't spoken to in six years, people who no longer owed him much loyalty, people who may or may not have any resources whatsoever to help . . .

And in that moment, he knew that finding Julie was not going to happen from his armchair in Los Angeles. It was going to have to happen with his boots on the ground. It was going to mean leaving his children.

"Do you know where she is?" Oliver asked.

"I have some idea," Charlie said.

"Are you going there?"

Charlie stepped toward his son and got down on a knee. "You know if I do that, you and your sister will have to stay here."

"So?"

Charlie looked at him.

"You need to find her, Dad."

Charlie searched his son's eyes. These were not the eyes of a young boy demanding an extra birthday present or some ice cream. These were the eyes of a fully formed person, utterly serious, intuitively aware of the gravity of the situation.

"Find her," Oliver said again, as if he suspected his father needed a final push.

Charlie brushed aside Ollie's hair and touched his face.

"I will."

CHAPTER FOURTEEN

There was only one set of connecting flights that would get Charlie to Tashkent that day and the outbound from LAX didn't leave for another ninety-two minutes. Which left him just enough time to get to his bank. The one thing he knew he would need in Uzbekistan was money. Cash on hand for bribes and payoffs. It was a way of life there, and without it he would barely make it out of the airport.

Inside the Wells Fargo on Montana Avenue, he was ushered into an office by the assistant manager, a chatty Rubenesque young woman in a suit that was about one size too small. "Hi, Mr. Davis. Read your piece last week in the *Times* about that budget thing. Amazing, isn't it, how these crooks think you can—"

"I'm in a bit of a rush," he said, cutting her off. "If you don't mind?"

Her smile faded. "Sure, sure, of course."

Charlie slid a legal pad across the table. "I need to move some money around. It's all written down right there."

"Okay, yeah, sure," she said. "Now has anybody

talked to you about the tax implications of taking money out of a Roth IRA and moving it to—"

She caught the gleam of impatience in his eye and this time cut herself off.

"I'll just be a minute," she said, hopping up from the desk.

The instant she stepped away and he had a moment to himself, his mind turned to Becca and the children. Clearly, there was no one he would rather have left them with, no one he and Julie felt more comfortable with, but still—he already felt a physical ache at being separated from them. During their good-byes, he'd hugged each of them so tightly that he feared he might actually crush them. But Oliver was resolute as ever, without an ounce of sentiment that Charlie should stay. And Meagan had given him a small drawing she'd recently made in preschool—"for Mommy," she'd said. He'd caught Becca's eye in that moment and they both nearly lost it. But she'd rebounded quickly and whisked the kids into the playroom for a game of Chutes and Ladders. That was the last he'd seen of them before he left the house.

He'd considered having Becca take the kids somewhere else—to be safer—but he was quite sure that Bull was done with all of them. Most important, he'd overheard Bull saying, "We're going to have a hard enough time getting the woman" to Tashkent, which meant that Bull and his goons were probably already out of the country and on their way to Uzbekistan with Julie. How he was planning on taking her there—and why—was the question that was plaguing Charlie. But as his mind turned to that question, the assistant manager returned, chipper as ever.

"Okay, super, so we've got the IRA and 401(K) funds moved into checking. Was there anything else?"

"Now I'd like to make a withdrawal in this amount." He wrote the amount on the legal pad.

$9,900.

"Would that be a cashier's check?"

"Cash."

The assistant bank manager adjusted her blouse over her substantial bosom, a nervous little smile on her face. Banks were supposed to report any cash transaction over $10,000. United States customs made you report it when you took anything greater than $10,000 outside the borders of the country.

The only people who moved cash around in $9,900 increments were people doing something outside the law.

Charlie flashed her an impish smile. "If you wouldn't mind . . . ?"

"How would you like that then?"

"Twenties, fifties and hundreds," Charlie said evenly.

She got up, ducked behind one of the cashiers and soon returned with the money. As she slowly counted it out on her desk, Charlie looked at his watch. It was getting tight.

". . . and ninety-nine hundred." Charlie grabbed the money and headed out.

"Mr. Davis?" she called to him. "Your receipt . . . ?"

She held it aloft, as if this was what he had really come here for.

"You keep it," he replied and bolted out the door.

*　*　*

Back in his car, he stuffed the cash into a money belt and started the engine. The flight to London left in seventy-nine minutes. Traffic permitting, he'd have barely enough time.

As he raced down the 405, trying not to think of his harrowing journey from the night before, Charlie forced himself to concentrate. To put himself in journalistic mode. To be an investigator. How would Bull, being ex–Special Forces, possibly working for the CIA or some other government agency, smuggle Julie from Los Angeles to Uzbekistan? Some years ago, Charlie had written an explosive story about extraordinary rendition, the process by which American prisoners were flown to foreign jurisdictions where local authorities didn't feel particularly burdened by the Geneva Convention's prohibition on torture. Uzbekistan was one of the major destinations for this practice. That might explain why Bull's men were speaking Russian. He was most likely using Uzbek mercenaries to minimize exposure—particularly in a covert and risky play like the rendition of an American citizen to a foreign country.

But even with the tacit approval of foreign governments like Uzbekistan, a covert agency still had to be careful about how they transported a prisoner. To avoid any paper trail that might lead back to the American government, they were often taken out of the country using shell companies. There had been much political backlash in the past few years against the use of rendition, but Charlie suspected these front companies might still be in existence.

He picked up his phone and dialed Mac at the *Times*. "Hey, bud, I need a favor."

"Name it."

"I need you to track down an international shipment . . . It was probably sent out of the Port of Los Angeles. But I suppose it could have gone out of anyplace on the West Coast. Ultimate destination Uzbekistan."

"That's all you got? West Coast to Uzbekistan?"

"Start with a couple of freight forwarders. One's called Global Reach Logistics and the other is called . . ." Charlie probed his memory. "Corrigan Brothers."

"What story is this for?"

"It's an . . ." Charlie tried to think of something plausible. "It's in the realm of an extradition-type thing. The package would need to be in something big enough to hold at least one person."

"A dude in a box—that sounds a lot more like extraordinary rendition to me . . ." Mac's voice trailed off nervously. "I mean, if I'm going to be getting a visit from Homeland Security in the middle of the night I'd like to at least have—"

"It's nothing like that."

"Because Sal didn't mention you were working on anything—"

"Mac, I said it's nothing like that," Charlie said sharply. "Now I'll need everything you can find. The shipper, destination, identifying numbers on the container . . ."

"Uh-huh." The kid sounded skittish.

Charlie felt a bit sordid about the possibility—however distant it might be—of exposing Mac to the same people who had invaded his house. But Charlie simply didn't have the expertise to track something like this down on his own.

"One last thing," Charlie added, "I need to get into Julie's email. Her account seems to have been wiped. Is there any way to recover emails in an account that's been erased like that?"

"Is she in some kind of trouble?"

"The less I tell you the better," was all Charlie said, but he knew it would convey the urgency. And the risks. There was a long pause at the other end of the line. "Mac?"

"Depending on the mail provider, there's probably a way, but Jesus, Charlie—"

"This is very important to me, Mac. Life and death important."

Again, there was a long pause. Was he losing the kid?

Finally a frightened, halfhearted voice answered him. "Okay, Charlie, I'll try."

As he hung up the phone, Charlie pulled off the 405 at Century Boulevard. One mile from LAX. He still had fifty-three minutes to catch his plane.

CHAPTER FIFTEEN

Charlie hadn't slept on the flight over from L.A., not for even a minute, and exhaustion only contributed to his feelings of unease as he made his way through Heathrow and arrived at his gate. Three cheap cardboard posters on the wall indicated the gate was shared by Uzbek Air, National Airlines of Tajikistan and an airline with the optimistic name of Air! Line! Armenia!

Charlie surveyed the people around him. He could still look at the faces and gauge what ethnic groups they were from—Russians with their dyed-blond wives, Uzbeks, Tajiks, Kyrgyz. Some wore the blocky polyester suits of the post-Soviet republics while others donned the traditional flowing shirts and baggy pants of the region. The last time he'd seen this many people dressed like this was in Babur Square six years ago.

Charlie took out his phone and dialed Faruz again. This was his third call and he'd still heard nothing back. He left another message—this time leaving his flight details and arrival time. As he hung up, Charlie was hit with a stab of shame. Over all these years, he'd never once reached out to his old friend. For all Charlie knew, Faruz could be dead.

A thick accent crackled over the PA system, "Please, attention, is now boarding first class. Is now boarding, first-class passengers only."

The message was repeated in Russian, Uzbek, Tajik, and Urdu, but the Uzbeks all ignored it, crowding around the door, pushing and shoving, tripping each other with their bags. A characteristic series of shouting matches and semisurreptitious exchanges of bribery ensued as the attendants at the gate tried to deal with the crush of people surging forward.

Andijan. That's all Charlie could think about. Andijan.

And then his phone rang. Faruz? No—it was Mac.

"Tell me you have something," Charlie said as he stepped away from the crowd.

"Nothing on the container yet. There's a lot of security on these things now. It's taking me a while."

"Well, how about Julie's emails?"

"I got into her account, but it's been wiped totally clean. No backups, nothing in the cloud, it's just gone."

"Damnit," Charlie muttered.

"Hold your horses. I didn't come up totally dry. I was able to access her computer remotely and I found some cookies on there that led to a second account."

"What do you mean, second account?"

"She opened a second email account back in June."

"And can you access her correspondence?"

"I can and I did."

"Well, send it to me then."

"I'm doing it now."

"And have you read them?"

Mac hesitated. "Not all of them, no." As Charlie pressed, he could feel a hint of embarrassment creeping into Mac's voice. "The thing is . . . there's eighty-six emails and they're all from or to the same guy."

Charlie's heart sank. He knew he'd be able to read them soon enough, but he had to know. "Who's the guy?"

"Somebody named Alisher," Mac said.

Alisher Byko?

She'd been corresponding with Byko for almost a year from a secret account? With an ever-expanding pit in his stomach, Charlie thanked Mac, urged him to keep working on the container and found a place to sit.

It couldn't be a coincidence, could it? Julie starts a secret email correspondence with Alisher Byko and now Special Forces guys are kidnapping her and taking her to Tashkent? Byko must have been the man she met in London.

Charlie opened his computer, logged on to his email and found the message from Mac. There was an attachment labeled "Julie's recovered mail." He clicked on it and found an extremely long text file, email after email jammed together without a break. As much as he wanted to know how their correspondence had started, to pore over every detail of every letter between them, he scanned down to the most recent email. If Byko was mixed up in her disappearance, this was the logical place to begin

his research. The email had been sent last Sunday—
May 5. Only six days ago:

To: abyko@global.net
From: Julie17@julie.com
Subject: Visit

Alisher, I have some very good news. After all of our
conversations, I've decided that I should, in fact, consider coming out of "retirement." My old company has
agreed to fly me to several locations in Central Asia, including Tashkent, to explore the possibilities. I arrive in
Uzbekistan on Thursday for two days and I'd obviously
love to take you up on your offer to meet for a drink.
I should have enough time to come to Samarkand if
that makes things more convenient for you. Sorry for
the short notice, but hopefully you can make it work. I
really would love to see you again after all of this time.

J

Charlie froze. She'd gone to see Byko? In Uzbekistan? But the LAPD had checked with the FAA
and located her flight to London—and there was no
connecting flight to Tashkent. Maybe she'd stopped
for a layover in London on the way? Maybe she'd
bought separate tickets back and forth to Tashkent?
But why? Was it for Charlie's benefit? In case he
started snooping, all he'd find was the round-trip to
London? If she was going to bother with that, why
didn't she just tell Charlie she was going to London
in the first place? Why create the alibi with her
sister in New York?

For a moment, the fact that she'd been kidnapped

receded and Charlie felt himself in a jealous rage. *His wife had flown ten thousand miles from home to visit with an old lover? Who she'd been secretly corresponding with for almost a year?*

He read Byko's response to her.

To: Julie17@julie.com
From: abyko@global.net
Subject: Visit

My dear girl,
    I cannot tell you how much it means to me that we will see each other again at long last. I will phone your mobile first thing on Thursday and we'll make all the arrangements.

As ever yours,
Alisher

My dear girl. As ever yours. It was enough to make Charlie vomit. And clearly, Byko already had her cell number, which meant they must have been speaking on the phone as well as by email. Charlie took a deep breath, realizing that his jealousy would only cloud his judgment and decision making.

As he calmed, he realized that she'd clearly misled Byko as well. She was only gone for four days, yet she'd told Byko she was on a weeklong tour of the region. Charlie jumped online and immediately accessed his and Julie's joint accounts for their American Express and Visa cards. He scrolled through the recent activity, but there was nothing there. No charges to British Airways, no charges to any airline for that matter. He'd already confirmed that she'd had no contact with World Vision. Who had paid for her ticket to Tashkent?

There were no answers, but then the reality of the situation was clear: she'd gone to see Byko and now she'd been absconded by Special Forces Bull, who was secreting her back to Tashkent. The only reasonable explanation was that she had mistakenly gotten caught up with something dangerous in Byko's world. Or that someone in that world believed Julie knew something very important about Byko.

And then it occurred to Charlie: what if Bull wasn't working for American intel? Was it possible that he was working for the Uzbek government? That kidnapping Julie was merely an insane extension of Karimov's paranoid, repressive regime? Charlie remembered that Byko's sister had been arrested and tortured last year. Was it possible that anyone close to Byko was now a target? That Karimov's reach could extend all the way into the United States? That he would apprehend an American citizen on American soil?

At first, it seemed preposterous, but then Charlie considered who Julie was. Who he, Charlie Davis, was. To Karimov and his cronies, they were instigators. Outspoken critics of the regime. It was Charlie's series of articles which had prompted the rally at Andijan. It was Julie who'd been handing out placards in Babur Square.

Charlie took out his phone to call someone at the State Department. But what if his theory was wrong? Or only half right? What if American intel was working with Karimov on this? After all, Uzbekistan was an important ally in the "war on terror" and Karimov provided the U.S. a military base in Karshi-Khanabad, which gave American troops an access point and supply line for the Afghan campaign.

There were too many things Charlie didn't know and if there was one seminal lesson he'd learned as a journalist it was this: don't ask the wrong people questions if you don't have an idea what the story is.

Hungry to understand how all of this had developed between Julie and Byko, Charlie scrolled back to the beginning, scanning to Julie's first email, dated June 22 of last year.

To: abyko@global.net
From: Julie17@julie.com

Alisher, It's so good to hear about many of the things that you're doing over there. I'm especially encouraged with what you're managing in Namangan. I know that you always treated your employees at the gold mine fairly, but to hear the expansiveness of your vision for the region is really commendable. Have to run out now and pick up the kids from school, but just wanted to say a quick hello. By the way, I've opened up a new email account, so please delete my old email address and use this one from here on in.

J

There was no way to tell when or how their correspondence had begun, but clearly their first few exchanges must have taken place on her gmail account—the one that Charlie knew about—and evidently, she'd decided that it was too risky to continue without Charlie catching wind of it. In spite of the blithely casual way that she'd mentioned her change of address—*By the way, I've opened a new email account*—it was a painfully thin disguise for her deception. And it would have been as obvious to Byko then as it was to Charlie now. It was an admission that they were carrying on something illicit, and it couldn't help but being read by the other man as a form of encouragement.

Charlie's blood began to boil but he hungrily devoured the next emails.

At first they were relatively businesslike—particularly on Julie's end. Quickly they became more personal. Any pretense—if that's what it had been—of this being purely a friendly business correspondence quickly evaporated. There were small observations on daily life, an occasional bared emotion, philosophical musings—a slow corkscrewing increase of intimacy and trust.

Byko shared his feelings of anguish about his sister's death, his weariness with the constant wrangle to keep himself on the straight and narrow in the midst of Uzbek corruption, oblique references to "personal demons." And all the while Julie was becoming more confessional. She spoke of missing the times in Uzbekistan when she felt she was doing something important and complained, however gently, about the humdrum life of car pools and t-ball practice and laundry. At times, she protested a little too stridently about how they'd made the right decision to settle in Los Angeles, as if to paper over the sadder truth. She never said anything overt, but there was a strong implication that things weren't right in their marriage.

Meanwhile Byko was slowly planting seeds in Julie's mind: she would find more fulfillment if she was working, wouldn't she? She had so many gifts to offer the world. She had barely scratched the surface of her talents. He had projects in Uzbekistan *begging* for people of her natural ability, judgment and charisma. Slowly his finely tuned references to her wonderful personal qualities and his need for managerial talent in his development projects began to converge. It was a seduction. And a very good one.

When Charlie had finished deciphering the emails, he simply stared at the screen. As if gazing at the words long enough might somehow change them.

Grasping at straws, he noted that there were no emails between Julie and Byko since she'd gotten back to Los Angeles. Perhaps the sparks weren't there after all. Perhaps she'd had second thoughts about throwing their marriage under the bus.

Was it possible there was some other explanation altogether? That she genuinely wanted to return to Uzbekistan? That she really wanted to work for Byko in some capacity? That she wanted to get all her ducks in a row before broaching the idea with Charlie?

It seemed ludicrous that any of that would require such deception on her part and he felt like a sap for even trying to convince himself that this was not what it seemed.

Apparently, Julie had become a bored housewife, restless with her suburban life, tired of her husband, seeking adventure in old places with old lovers. She'd gotten herself into a world of trouble and now here he was, chasing her down the rabbit hole.

Charlie shook his head, trying desperately to exorcise the image of her and Byko together. The issue of her infidelity—and how they would deal with that—would wait until he found her. For now, all that mattered was that he figure out how to save her. Even if their marriage couldn't be repaired, he would deliver her back to Oliver and Meagan.

And then he had the awkward and humiliating realization that the one person he needed to get hold of right now was Alisher Byko. Byko would be infuriated to hear that Julie had potentially paid such a price for their rendezvous and he would undoubtedly have some insight into what might have happened to her. Most important, Charlie had to admit that Byko might in fact be more equipped to find his wife than he was.

Back in the day, Charlie had used Byko for background on a number of stories and he still had Byko's old cell phone number in his contacts list. He dialed it, but almost immediately heard the irritating singsongy chimes that told him he'd reached an inactive phone number.

Charlie muttered under his breath, but at least Byko had an active email account. He typed in Byko's address and a message:

Julie's been kidnapped. I think she's in Tashkent. I'm on my way. We need to talk. Charlie Davis

He tapped in his own email address and cell phone number then pressed send. As he did, he heard the announcement for the final boarding call.

Charlie packed up his computer and headed for the gate. He'd be out of range for the next thirteen hours. By the time he touched down in Tashkent, there would surely be a reply from Byko.

CHAPTER SIXTEEN

Alisher Byko walked up the long stretch of waving green grass toward the simple stone structure. The hill was long and steep, but this didn't trouble him. In fact, he enjoyed the exertion and the solitude. From the top of his private oasis, the grim city and its problems seemed very far away.

This was one of the largest tracts of undeveloped land in Tashkent and Byko had purchased it for the graves of his family. He could have built a monument as elaborate as the Taj Mahal if he'd wanted, but that would not have suited him. The large but unadorned mausoleum was enough. Flanking the mausoleum where his wife, son, and sister were buried were a handful of additional gravestones marking the resting places of friends who had died in Babur Square, their simple inscriptions all carved in Uzbek.

Byko stopped when he reached the graves, his mind drifting back to the time just after the massacre. If he had not been as rich and powerful as he was, he probably would have died in prison six years ago. Instead, after his wife and son had been killed, he had visited President Karimov and begged forgiveness.

The tyrant had sat at his huge and grotesquely carved desk in his gymnasium-size office, the walls covered with vast, ugly murals depicting various scenes of invented Uzbek history, and listened in silence as Byko humbled himself. Byko had said that he was sorry, that his opposition to the regime had been a youthful indiscretion, and that Karimov would see: Byko would become his biggest supporter.

Byko had walked out of Karimov's palace with his life, but he'd left a piece of his soul there. In the weeks and months that followed, he had stumbled around in a haze of humiliation, rage and pain, a choking cloud that had kept him from being able to concentrate, to think, to act. He neglected his businesses, instead holing up in rented villas in Bangkok or Abu Dhabi or Gstaad, drinking and banging a virtual United Nations of socialites, debutantes and whores. Gradually, the humiliation dissipated and the anger turned inward. Yes, Karimov was a ruthless and brutal dictator. But it was he—Byko—who'd been the fool to try to play revolutionary. It was, in fact, his own hubris that had killed his wife and son.

The self-loathing only made the pain more dear. And all the drinking and women and skiing and Ferraris couldn't dull it. Couldn't even begin to touch it. Then one day at a club, a girl handed him an opium pipe. It was the sort of thing that the old Byko, even the partying Byko of his college days, would have rejected out of hand. But he had come to feel by then that doing one thing was hardly different from another. Any distraction was a worthy distraction. And so he'd taken a hit.

Instantly, there was a shift. The opium filtered out the noise that had been threatening to overwhelm him for nearly every instant of his life since the bullets had taken his wife and son. The pain didn't go away, but he was able to pack it neatly into a little box in the back of his brain. And as soon as he did that, he was able to see the world with startling clarity. Like a snapshot caught in the brilliant flare of a camera flash, he saw that it was not he who was to blame. Or even Karimov. It was the larger political system—the inheritance of a corrupt Russian autocracy mixed with the financial backing and tacit approval of the West. Yes, the opium allowed him to see all of this. See it clearly.

Of course, every drug has its cost. As he quickly came to find out, opium sapped your will, your drive, your energy. And so there had been cocaine. Which required a certain delicacy of application—and, for want of a better word, management. That "management" had taken the form of various other mood enhancers, stabilizers and modifiers, both legal and illegal.

But it was all carefully administered, neatly titrated, scientifically applied. The drugs didn't control him. Quite the contrary. All the drugs were in the service of keeping Alisher Byko—the purest, most crystalline version of Alisher Byko—focused like a laser beam on his plan of action.

That plan, originated in an opium den in the hills of Thailand, began as a way to take back his country. The assassination of Karimov and his cabinet, a military coup, the installation of himself and a handful of respected tribal and sectarian leaders in a transition government. He would spend the next four years scrupulously calculating how it might be done. Gradually, after hundreds of clandestine meetings feeling out generals, clerics, and strongmen, Byko felt confident that he saw a path.

And then his sister was taken.

The revelations which followed her death would change how he saw everything. With that change in vision came a change in plan. A plan that was now, at long last, about to come to fruition.

Byko knelt before the graves of his family, the soft wind stirring his hair. He kissed each one in turn. "You will be avenged," he promised. "All of you."

CHAPTER SEVENTEEN

As Frank Hopkins made his way down the hallway toward the War Room in MI6's headquarters in Vauxhall Cross, he had a queasy feeling about the impending operation. Apparently he wasn't the only one. Eyes probed him watchfully from the offices that lined the hallway and he knew there was talk going around. Something to the effect that perhaps he didn't have the magic anymore.

Hopkins had been an MI6 field man since leaving the British Army twenty-seven years ago. He had been a Sandhurst-educated infantry officer and spent his career working in the Middle East with a reputation as one of the best in the business. But one's reputation, he reflected as he put his eye to the retinal scanner at the door of the War Room, was only as good as one's last successful assignment.

And this one wasn't going well.

The door opened and everyone in the room looked up.

"Everything sorted?" he asked.

"Comms online, sir," the communications officer said. He hit a few buttons as Hopkins picked up the headset.

"Bird's online," a technician said. As he spoke, the feed from the MI6's TopSat-II spy satellite appeared on the big screen at the front of the War Room. It was an infrared image from seventeen miles above Samarkand, Uzbekistan, the picture composed of a series of greenish blobs that were not easy to make sense of. Then a greenish-white blob moved, revealing itself as a human figure.

It was Osprey—real name Marcus Vaughan—the sole MI6 agent operating under diplomatic cover at the British Embassy in Uzbekistan.

"How's my level, Osprey?" Hopkins asked. A second screen blinked to life. This one monitored a microcamera in Marcus's glasses.

"Five by five," Marcus responded.

"Give me a sitrep," Hopkins said.

"I don't bloody like it, that's my situation report. Two big abandoned factories to my left and right. In between we've got a big space about the size of a bloody football pitch. And it's full of machinery. Gantries, locomotive parts, cranes, can't even make them all out. They could be hiding an army in there, I'd never see it."

"Looks clear," Hopkins said. "No heat signatures."

"What about in the factories?" Marcus asked, the fuzzy outline of his head moving from side to side as he attempted to track activity in the adjacent buildings.

"You know how it works," Hopkins replied. "The bird can't see through walls."

"Right. Just thought I'd ask," Marcus said. "I'm heading in, recon a bit, see if I've got company."

Through the minicam, Hopkins saw a pair of

headlights swing around the far corner of the factory.

"Too late," he told his agent. "Visitors. Vehicle incoming."

Marcus muttered something under his breath. He was frightened and Hopkins didn't blame him. To do this right, they ought to have an eight-man team in there. But Marcus was there by his lonesome on the most important piece of intelligence Hopkins had worked in years.

As Marcus began walking between the two buildings, Hopkins stood at the shoulder of an expert video analyst. "Mercedes S-Class," the analyst said matter-of-factly, pointing at the image on the big screen. Two men climbed out of the car. Even here, at a two-thousand-mile remove, Hopkins could feel his agent's palms sweating.

"Two subjects leaving the vehicle," Hopkins said.

Marcus began walking silently toward the Mercedes. He carried a small, cheap briefcase with twenty thousand dollars inside.

That would be a small price to pay if it led to information on how to find Alisher Byko.

Marcus had been working overtime on the project for months and this was his first concrete lead, but Hopkins still hadn't told Marcus why London wanted to find Byko so badly. It was part of the trade that Hopkins had never liked, men going into harm's way for things they didn't even understand.

There had been an attempt to take Byko down three days earlier—based on intel to which Marcus had not been privy. Much to Hopkins's chagrin, the takedown had been a total cock-up and Byko had gotten clean away.

All of which made it that much more important that Marcus successfully complete this transaction. Marcus had gotten a tip from one of his trusted sources that he could put him together with someone in Byko's organization, someone who could give Marcus an exact time and place where the billionaire would be within the next twenty-four hours. The source knew enough details about Byko's security and traveling arrangements to make his story sound plausible. And the price, twenty thousand U.S., was cheap under the circumstances.

As Marcus approached the car, Hopkins thought he saw a tiny flash of greenish white, peeking out from under one of the big pieces of machinery in front of his agent. He put his hand over the mic and turned to the video analyst. "What's that?" he barked, pointing at the screen.

"What's what?"

But by then it was gone.

"Bloody lights," Marcus muttered. "Can't see shite now."

His wobbly green image pointed in the direction of the Mercedes.

"Turn off your lights!" Marcus shouted in Russian.

The man on the passenger side of the Mercedes waved languidly. "Come over this way."

"No!" Marcus called back. "Not till you turn off the bloody lights."

"We're friends! Come on."

"Turn off the lights or I'm leaving."

"What's wrong?" the man called, switching to English—Uzbek accented with a sprinkling of American vowels. "We're friends, bro. Friends!"

Hopkins had debriefed Marcus extensively and knew that he'd never identified himself as an Englishman, much less as an agent of the British government. From the beginning, Marcus had played the false flag game, claiming to be a Pole freelancing for the Russians, never using his diplomatic car or his embassy phone. So how did this man know to speak English to Marcus?

"I'm leaving," Marcus shouted.

Hopkins picked up the distant voice of the man by the Mercedes. "Okay, my friend. You don't like lights, no problem."

The car's lights went out.

Marcus picked up the briefcase and started walking toward the men. Hopkins could see the jaunty confidence of his walk, even from the satellite. And he knew just what an act of will it was for Marcus to keep calm under the circumstances.

When Marcus got halfway to the Merc, he looked toward one of the factory windows and nodded, as though signaling to a shooter hidden in overwatch. If this was a simple rip-off, the hope was that a little crumb of humbuggery like that might be enough to make these men think twice.

"Base, do you see anything on my ten?" Marcus whispered furtively.

Hopkins scanned the screen. "Nothing," he answered. "You're clear."

Marcus began moving again, his right hand inside his jacket. No doubt gripping the butt of the SIG under his jacket as he approached the two men.

"Stop there, Osprey," Hopkins said as Marcus reached a point about forty feet from the Mercedes.

Again Hopkins saw the briefest flash of white next to one of the fallen cranes.

"Was that us?" Hopkins said urgently to the video analyst, cupping his hand over the mic so that Marcus couldn't hear.

The analyst's eyes widened slightly. "I saw it too. I don't like it, sir."

"Come on!" Hopkins said. "Is that a hostile or not?"

The analyst shrugged. "How bad do you need what these men have?"

"Bloody well badly."

The analyst sighed. "Then I'm telling you I don't know if that was a video artifact or a hostile."

"Watch your nine, Osprey," Hopkins hissed into his mike.

But Marcus must have already sensed something, too. The Minicam scanned from side to side as he eyed various piles of machinery. All Hopkins could see was a blur.

The driver came out from behind the open door of the Mercedes and began walking cautiously toward Marcus.

"That's close enough, mate," Marcus said.

"You got the money, bro?"

"You don't see a penny until I know something."

"I don't tell you nothing till I see the Benjamins."

"You've been watching too much bloody American TV."

The man crossed his arms and shrugged. "Hey, bro, we do it or we don't."

"Who's behind that pile of rubbish?" Marcus demanded, cocking his head toward the pile of equipment to his left.

"What! Dude! There's nobody here but me and my boy Vladislav," the man said, teeth flashing.

Hopkins's heart was slamming in his chest. This didn't feel right.

But Marcus was already opening the briefcase, tossing a small stack of money onto the ground in front of the car. "That's a taste," Marcus said. "The rest when you talk."

The guy from the car didn't even bend over to look at the money.

And Hopkins knew this had all gone sideways.

"Abort, Osprey," Hopkins said, his voice rising louder than he wanted it to. "Abort, abort."

A flash of white by the crane. Then gone.

Another, up in the window of the factory.

"Oh, shit," gasped the analyst.

"Abort!" Hopkins shouted. "Shooters at nine and three o'clock high. Repeat, shooters at nine and three high!"

The SIG appeared in Marcus's hand.

And then there were shapes moving all around him, greenish-white blobs disconnecting themselves from the dark piles of machinery.

Marcus got off two shots, perfectly composed masterpieces of combat shooting, the two men by the Mercedes crumpling to the ground.

Then Marcus was running.

Hopkins could hear the tiny *pop-pop-pops* of automatic fire and then a grunt.

"Marcus! Marcus, are you all right?" Blatant violation of radio discipline, calling his agent by his name rather than his radio code.

"Cheers," Marcus said. "Getting a bit sporty right now. I've taken two I think."

Another grunt.

"Bollocks. That one was bad."

Then Marcus fell, the view from the Minicam taking a whirling tumble.

The figures who had come out of cover were advancing now, firing and firing and firing.

"Christ," Hopkins muttered, forcing himself to keep watching.

It was the professionalism in their movements, the telltale signatures of experienced men at arms, moving briskly but unhurriedly—firing, reloading, firing—that told Hopkins the story. These were not cheap gun thugs, but highly trained, disciplined fighters.

One of the assassins leaned down toward the camera.

"He's wired," the assassin said in perfect English. "Switch it off."

There was a burst of static then the monitor went dead.

And Hopkins knew. Knew by the way it had all gone down.

This was the handiwork of John Quinn.

CHAPTER EIGHTEEN

Charlie felt something bump and slam against his back. He awoke with a jerk—heart pounding—to find the Soviet-era Tupolev Tu-154 descending toward Tashkent like a punch-drunk fighter, veering from side to side as though the pilot were landing it with his eyes closed.

Uzbek Air certainly did not inspire great confidence. The pilot was a haggard-looking man with strange staring eyes, and the careless, surly flight attendants wore toothpaste green polyester pantsuits that might have seemed vaguely fashionable in the early 1970s. The plane itself was a wreck: strips of peeling wallpaper dangled off the ceiling like streamers at a parade, there was chewing gum under the seats, graffiti carved into the tray table and a missing armrest on Charlie's chair where his white-knuckled hand should have been.

Sitting near the rear of the plane, the howl of the aging Russian turbines assaulting his ears, Charlie diverted himself by looking out the window. Finally the plane touched down on the runway.

He breathed a sigh of relief and saw that nothing had changed since he left—the same grungy little airport, the same ugly collection of hangars, the same arid terrain, the same low and unremarkable skyline.

Tashkent.

Charlie took out his cell and checked his voice mail. There were three new messages. The first one greeted him rudely: "Hey there, Mr. Davis, Detective Albez here. We see that you happened to have left the country. Doesn't look too good for you, you know? Not if you ever want to see your kids again. I were you, I'd rethink this going-on-the-lam strategy and get your ass on the next flight back—" Charlie deleted the prick.

The next was from Sal. He was beginning an awkward apology about overstepping his bounds when Charlie deleted that, too. At this point, he could care less.

The last message was from Mac. "Okay, Charlie, don't ask me how, but I did it. The freight forwarder was Corrigan Brothers, like you thought. The container, serial number A427-HXQ, left Port of Long Beach, Pier J in a Liberian-flagged steamer, SS *Albert J. Mott* to Port of Sitka in Alaska. Transferred there to a Russian air freight outfit called AeroTrade, which flew through Petrapavlovsk and Kazakhstan en route to Tashkent. The flight is scheduled to arrive at Tashkent International at 7:58 this morning. I'm emailing you all the relevant info, but—" Mac hesitated, voice lowering gravely, "I don't know what you're into, Charlie, but be goddamn careful."

The line went dead.

Charlie looked at his watch: 7:06. He had fifty-two minutes to deplane, hurry through customs, and get to the freight terminal.

He quickly checked his texts and emails. There was one from Faruz—he had no idea what was going on but he would be at the airport to pick Charlie up; one from Becca—the kids were doing just fine; and another from Mac with the serial numbers and info on the container. But there was nothing from Byko. Surely a man like him didn't allow eleven hours to pass without checking his email. Why would he not respond? Was it possible he, too, had already been taken?

Finally, Charlie heard the forward cabin door thumping open. He jumped up, grabbed his things and forced his way through a group of Russian businessmen, all of them smelling of cologne and vodka. "*Prastitye*," he said. "Emergency." The Russians, and everyone else for that matter, swore at Charlie as he pushed, elbowed, and cajoled his way to the front of the plane.

Four minutes later, Charlie was clumping down the old-fashioned aluminum stairway—shades of 1963—and across the tarmac, squinting against the sunlight.

As he rushed through the terminal, he was greeted by a huge portrait of Uzbek President Islam Karimov, looking down at him with beady, calculating eyes. At passport control, he soon found himself at the end of a long single-file line. Usually there was a separate queue for foreign nationals, but he couldn't see where it was.

A couple of shoddily uniformed soldiers slouched near the line, both carrying AK-47s.

The sight of them made Charlie's heart pound, but he forced himself to step out of line and approach them. "*Izvineetye*," he said. "Is there a separate line for—"

"Back in the line!" The young soldier brandished his weapon as though he'd like to whack Charlie in the face.

Charlie had no choice but to retreat, falling in line once again.

The young soldier eyeballed him for what seemed like a lifetime then finally resumed his playful banter with his comrades. Charlie exhaled and checked his watch.

7:21.

He looked at the line. It was moving—but slowly. *Come on!* he thought. *Damnit, come on!*

At 7:32, he reached passport control. The official, a short man with a wispy beard, stared long and hard at Charlie's documents then took them to an ancient computer in a booth located at another officer's desk. He pecked slowly at the keys, typing in Charlie's name with the eraser of his pencil.

"Is this going to take long?" Charlie called.

The man turned, eyeballed him briefly, then continued typing—if that was even the right word for this glacial activity.

The bearded man dinged what appeared to be the last key, hit enter and waited. And waited. And waited. Charlie's entire body was vibrating with impatience until something popped up on the screen.

The officer motioned to his superior, who sat on a chair in a high booth, staring out at the arriving passengers through enormously thick glasses. The supervisor grunted and sighed, then pointed languidly to a red door on the far side of the room.

"What's this?" Charlie demanded.

"You're being detained," said the officer with the beard.

"What do you mean, detained?"

"Detained."

Charlie had been afraid this might happen. His articles about life here had never put him in high favor with the government. No doubt his name was on some kind of list of undesirables.

But making a scene out here in the open would do him no good. If there was a deal to be made, it would have to be made in the room behind the red door. He raised his hands in surrender and walked as quickly as he could to that door. He entered, followed by the passport-control officer and his supervisor.

The only thing in the room was a table with a handcuff attached to it. Charlie set his bag on the table, turned to the two men and began the proceedings. "Just name me a price."

The supervisor's eyes widened, magnified to the size of boiled eggs behind his glasses. "Are you attempting to *bribe* me?"

Charlie reached into his pocket, took out three hundred dollars in twenties, which he kept in a roll with a rubber band around it. It would be cheaper if he pretended that these weren't bribes but fees, if he talked in code about it, if he flattered and cajoled. But to hell with that. There was no time.

"Here," he said, counting out his opening offer: two piles, a hundred each.

The supervisor laughed. The passport-control officer laughed.

"Okay, okay," Charlie said, splitting another eighty between the two piles. It left only a twenty in his hand. "I have to keep something for the cab," he said.

The supervisor blinked. "You insult us . . . then you speak about *cab fare*? You won't need cab fare when we put you on the next plane back to London."

Charlie sighed heavily and put the last twenty on the table. "It's everything I have."

The supervisor waddled around him in a slow circle, smiling cynically. Finally he reached out and poked Charlie's stomach. "Everything?"

Charlie backed away from him.

The supervisor snapped his finger at the passport-control officer, who walked out of the room, closed the door, then came back moments later with the soldiers. One of the uniformed young men grabbed Charlie and pushed him against the wall while the other yanked up his shirt and jerked the money belt off Charlie's midsection.

"Please!" Charlie begged. "I need that!"

The supervisor stood with his hands folded over his chest while the passport-control officer zipped open the money belt and dumped the contents on the table.

"I thought you said you only had three hundred?" The supervisor waved at the bills on the table. "We may be forced to seize this as evidence of a possible crime."

"What crime?" Charlie asked indignantly.

The passport-control officer splayed the money out, licked his finger and began counting. The only sound in the room was the rapid *shick-shick-shick-shick* of money.

"Take it," Charlie said with abject resignation. "Take it all. I don't care. Just please let me go. I'm in a hurry."

The supervisor took a small fleck of tobacco from between his teeth and flicked it into the air. "Will you require a receipt?"

"Just give me the belt back," Charlie said.

The supervisor shrugged, then tossed him the empty belt. "Enjoy your stay in Uzbekistan, Mr. Davis."

Charlie grabbed his bag and walked as swiftly as he could out the door.

He permitted himself a brief smile as he paused behind a potted plant, reached into his pants and pulled nine thousand dollars out of his underwear. He'd expected there might be a shakedown and knew the money belt would be their first target, so the underwear was his fallback position. It seemed silly, but even extortionists don't like sticking their hands into other men's boxer shorts.

He shoved the money back into the belt, secured it underneath his shirt and sprinted for the exit, looking at his watch.

He had fourteen minutes.

CHAPTER NINETEEN

Charlie exited the terminal and scanned the area. There was no Faruz.

And the taxi stand was a mob scene—Uzbeks yelling and waving money, Russian mobsters shouting at their flunkies, a couple of muscular Englishmen who had the look of military contractors shoving their way through throngs of drivers. Cabs were parked higgledy-piggledy, blocking one another, the drivers honking and swearing.

It could take half an hour just to get out of this mess.

As Charlie pushed his way through the crowd, he heard a loud screech of tires. The mobsters all looked up—alarmed—hands reaching under coats as they ducked behind their cars.

To Charlie's relief, it was his old friend, waving out the window and pounding on the horn, a wide grin splitting his roguish features. He was parked in the middle of the road but seemed not to notice the inconvenience he was causing the other drivers.

Charlie scrambled toward him, escorted by a chorus of honking horns and epithets from the Russian mobsters. Faruz hopped out of the car, shouting, "Holy shit! I never thought you come back this fucked-up place." Before Charlie could reply, he found himself locked in a bear hug and enduring Faruz's traditional slobbering double kiss on the cheeks.

Charlie couldn't be bothered with pleasantries. "We need to get to the air freight terminal. Now."

Faruz squinted curiously as Charlie got in the car, then circled around his side and returned to the driver's seat of his old BMW. "The air freight terminal?"

"I need to see something that's being delivered there. Seriously, I mean *now*."

"Still the cowboy, huh?"

Faruz smiled, put the car in drive and navigated his way out of the terminal. He pulled a pack of Marlboros out of his leather coat, whacked them on his palm, held out a cigarette for Charlie.

"I quit," Charlie said.

"Look at you! Cut your hair, dressing like an old man. You pretending to be a grown-up now?"

"Julie's in trouble," Charlie told him. "She was kidnapped in Los Angeles and taken here." Faruz looked at him incredulously. "She's in a shipping container arriving at the freight terminal in twelve minutes. I'll need to get onto the tarmac."

Faruz lit his cigarette with a gold lighter, steering the car with his knees as he monkeyed around with the pack of Marlboros. "You're joking, right?"

"I'm dead serious."

"Whoa, whoa, whoa. We gonna have to back up a little. Flesh this out, what we up against. I mean, air freight terminal is like Fort Knox."

"Faruz—"

Faruz held up one hand. "Look, brother, I understand you got a serious situation. Believe me, we ain't gonna just drive up, say, 'hey let me in air freight terminal.' Not gonna happen."

"We've got to find a way."

"Okay. Just give me a second to think."

Charlie nodded and examined his old friend for a moment. There was a hint of a potbelly under his handmade silk shirt, and a thin line of gray had appeared in his mane of thick brown hair. But he still exhibited the youthful charm and enthusiasm that had helped him move easily between the interlocking worlds of the democratic movement, the arts, and the fuzzy edges of the underworld. Charlie had missed him more than he'd anticipated and it was a comfort to have him as his wingman.

"Okay, look," Faruz said, "what I can do is get you up someplace you can watch incoming flights, movement on tarmac, whatever. At least we see if this container is even there. If it's down there, we figure out what next to do, okay?" Charlie looked at him. "I'm telling you, kid, there's no way we get in there. No way."

Charlie realized it was the best he could hope for right now and soon they were speeding down a one-lane road beside a chain-link fence topped with razor wire.

"Let's try this," Faruz said, steering the BMW off the road. It bounded and bounced up a hill. At the top was a large cluster of boulders, shattered with age and covered with lichen. "Perfect. Nobody see us here."

He stomped on the brake and the car skidded to a stop on the bone-dry grass, throwing up an immense cloud of dust.

Faruz climbed out of the car, looked around nervously and walked to the boulders. "Behold," he said. Sprawled out in front of them was a collection of warehouses and hangars.

Charlie found a crevice in which he could survey the entire freight terminal, but his stomach twisted with disappointment. There were literally thousands of containers stacked up in long rows from one side to the other. Charlie glanced at his watch. It was 7:56.

"What time it supposed to come?" Faruz asked.

"Two minutes," Charlie replied, pulling out his Nikon. He screwed in a powerful 500-millimeter lens and began a slow, careful scan of the facility. Faruz wasn't kidding about the security in the freight terminal. Roving teams of three and four armed men—some of them with German shepherds—moved throughout the facility and guard towers rose from each corner of the fence.

With the magnification of his big lens, Charlie was able to barely make out numbers on the sides of the shipping containers, but there were so many he almost didn't know where to begin.

"You know," Faruz reminded him, "there's no such thing as 'ahead of schedule' in the U-stan. If it's supposed get here in two minutes there's no way it's here yet. Nothing ever come early here. Now how's about you tell me what fuck going on with Julie."

Charlie glanced back at his friend. "I don't know exactly. Except that she came here to see Byko last week and somehow got herself into trouble. She was grabbed in L.A., and whoever took her is bringing her back here. That's your next assignment: help me find Byko."

"No way. Nobody seen that guy for months."

"What are you talking about?"

"Byko, man! I'm talking about Byko. Speculation, the guy got in some kind of beef with Karimov. All I know, everybody's like, hey, Byko's gone to the mattresses."

Charlie considered this. If Byko had gone underground months ago, then how would he have been able to meet Julie in Samarkand or Tashkent? Then again, Charlie remembered Byko's final email to Julie: *I'll call you on your mobile and we'll make arrangements.* At first, it seemed innocent enough. Hearing what Faruz was telling him now, Charlie figured that Byko didn't want to give away his comings and goings online. Whatever the scenario, it seemed clear that Byko had risked his own safety and come out of hiding just to meet Julie. Or perhaps Byko had sent his men to escort Julie to one of his many outposts in the Fergana Valley. Either way, Charlie was convinced more than ever that her disappearance had to be connected to him.

Charlie looked into Faruz's dark eyes. "If anybody can find the guy, it's you, Faruz."

Faruz looked out thoughtfully toward the cluster of warehouses and stacks of containers below them, then whipped out his phone and began a series of conversations, carried on in a rapid mixture of Uzbek, Tajik, Russian and English. He was putting out a net for Byko.

Meanwhile, Charlie directed his camera at the distant steel structure. A small fleet of wheeled containers sat on the tarmac behind it. Unfortunately, not only was it at the farthest point from their little promontory, but his view of many of the containers was blocked by the massive warehouse.

Suddenly, Charlie saw Faruz flattening himself against the rock.

"Get down, get down!" he hissed, switching off his phone in mid-conversation.

As Charlie ducked behind the rock, he saw why Faruz was panicking. A Jeep Cherokee was driving slowly by on the road below. Inside were several heavily armed men. And they would not look kindly on an American journalist snooping around up here.

Charlie lay flat against the cool rock, listening to their approach. He thought that he heard them slow but then realized it was the sound of the motor receding into the distance.

Faruz rose and stared at the receding plume of dust. "Goddamnit, I hate those people," he said. Then he began talking on the phone again— laughing, wheedling, chiding, flattering—as though nothing had happened.

Satisfied that the security patrol was gone, Charlie rose slightly and stared through his lens again. As he tried to reorient his camera, a very large multiengine turboprop taxied slowly toward the warehouse, cutting off his view.

The airplane stopped. It appeared to be some kind of military transport—its markings on the side read AEROTRADE in bold Cyrillic letters. After a moment, the entire tail began to rise, opening a giant maw in the rear of the plane. Down came a big steel ramp and a low, trucklike towing vehicle crawled slowly up it.

Could this be the flight she was supposed to come in on?

Charlie zoomed the camera in on the plane. The towing vehicle was bumping down off the ramp—behind it was a container on a little flatbed trailer. As he racked focus, something in the viewfinder caught his attention. Four white letters flashing in front of him: A427. Those were the first four digits of the serial number he was looking for. He tracked across the container and found the last three: HXQ.

A wave of excitement ran through him. That was it.

Suddenly, with a horrific clatter of rotors, a helicopter burst over the hill. Faruz threw himself to the ground and Charlie thought for sure the chopper was part of a security detail sent to apprehend them. But it screamed right past and thundered toward the forest of containers on the other side of the fence.

"I'm getting too old for this shit," Faruz muttered. "How much longer?"

Charlie ignored him, fixated on the tarmac.

Down by the big transport aircraft, the towing vehicle slowly pulled the container into the middle of a large clearing and stopped.

"Oh shit!" Faruz said.

"What?"

Faruz merely pointed.

The Jeep that had been patrolling the perimeter road was back again. But this time it was driving across an open field, heading for the back side of the hummock on which they were situated. And it was hauling ass.

Faruz ran toward his car.

"Wait!" Charlie yelled.

"We gotta go! These guys don't fuck around."

"Just wait, goddamnit!"

Charlie raised his camera a little and saw the chopper lowering itself toward the container. Four slim steel cables slid from its belly, unspooling downward.

Charlie watched two men spring up onto the container and attach hooks to the ends of the cable, connecting the chopper to the four corners of the big steel box. The task completed, they jumped down to the towing vehicle and unhitched the container from the tow bar.

Faruz revved the engine. "Charlie! Don't be fool! Come on!"

But Charlie kept snapping photos as fast as he could. A man appeared in the hatchway of the chopper. He was wearing sunglasses and a baseball cap, and carried an M4 carbine on a sling across his chest. He shouted something to the others, then tossed a duffle bag down to them.

The bag hit the tarmac and broke open, spilling stacks of banknotes onto the ground.

Charlie popped off a few shots of the payoff then swiveled the camera up to the chopper again, snapping one last picture. As he did, the man in the hatchway turned his head and looked out toward Charlie. That was when Charlie recognized him.

It was Bull.

Charlie felt a mixture of triumph and terror. Bull's presence confirmed beyond any doubt that Julie was in the container. It also confirmed what Julie would soon be facing.

The panicked Faruz fishtailed around in a half

circle, preparing to head back down the hill. "You don't come right now, I leave without you!"

"I'm coming!" Charlie sprinted alongside the car, grabbed the open door and dove into the passenger seat.

Faruz thumped and bumped and slid down the hill, threatening to turn over at any second. The vehicle behind them was gaining rapidly, the Jeep so close that Charlie could see the individual security guards' faces, their jaws set, weapons ready.

But Faruz made it to the road at the bottom of the hill. Back on its native territory, the BMW surged forward with a screech of tires and was soon easily outdistancing the slower all-terrain vehicle. Charlie looked back to see the Jeep slowing down and apparently giving up. Maybe they were writing off Charlie and Faruz as a couple of dumb tourists.

Faruz was sweating profusely and he gave Charlie a look as if to say, "Don't pull that shit again!" but a roar overhead brought Charlie's attention back to the chopper.

As he watched it fly east and disappear over the horizon, he tried not to imagine where they were taking Julie and what Bull would do to her once they got there.

CHAPTER TWENTY

As they put a little distance between themselves and the air freight terminal, Faruz set his phone in one of the cup holders. "I got lines out to everybody I can think of. Now we gotta wait."

"Thanks, Faruz. You know I'm going to make this worth your while." Charlie stuffed five hundred bucks into the cup holder next to the phone.

Faruz eyed the money. "You don't need to do that, Charlie."

"Yeah I do," Charlie said. "You're taking a big risk for me."

Faruz hesitated, then reluctantly pocketed the money—as if it was medicine prescribed by a doctor. Charlie pulled out his Nikon and scrolled through the photos he'd shot at the freight terminal. The 500-millimeter lens hadn't let him down. Bull's face was clear as a bell. He zoomed in a little tighter, then held the camera display out toward Faruz.

"You know this guy?"

Faruz glanced at the face briefly. "Nope. Who is he?"

"That's what I need to find out. Is Russell Garman still around?"

"Yeah, he's around, but frankly? That guy scare the shit out of me."

"Yeah, I know," Charlie conceded. "Let's go see him."

Faruz nodded unenthusiastically. They were reaching the outskirts of Tashkent now. Everything was drab, dusty, slapped together, ill-maintained. It felt strange to be back—that odd mixture of alienness and familiarity that you felt returning to any place that had been important to you once, but wasn't anymore.

Charlie wondered if Julie had experienced those same conflicting emotions when she'd returned here to see Byko. Or if there was something else entirely going through her head. He still couldn't fathom how she'd managed to pull off that kind of deception, that she'd come here to explore a romantic interlude with Byko. But in the back of his mind he kept wondering, kept hoping, that there could possibly be some other explanation.

Charlie found Russell Garman seated in his neat office on the third floor of a nondescript building in downtown Tashkent. Charlie felt pretty sure that no one in this office had ever taught any languages to anyone, but screwed to the wall next to the door was a very small sign that read: LANGUAGE TRAINING INTERNATIONAL, LTD.

And Garman certainly looked the part. He had the air of a certain kind of down-at-the-heels international teacher—his thinning brown hair was longish and poorly cut, floating away from his face in soft waves. He wore a button-down shirt, wide-wale corduroy pants and a lemon yellow Gore-Tex windbreaker. His expression was genial but distant, as though his mind was still occupied with the book of poetry, *Spoon River Anthology* by Edgar Lee Masters, lying open on the desk in front of him.

To look at the man you'd never know that six years ago, Garman was one of the most dangerous men in the region. Marine recon, sniper, black belt in this or that, executive-protection trainer at Blackwater's semisecret facility in North Carolina, almost certainly eight or ten years in the CIA's Operations Directorate—the kind of guy who could tell you with a straight face that he couldn't show you his resumé unless you had top-secret clearance.

As Charlie entered Garman's lair and greeted him, the military man exuberantly popped out of his chair.

"Charlie! My goodness, how have you been?" Garman half-cooed, raising one eyebrow. His voice had a flat midwestern tinge—Missouri, Kansas, someplace like that—and the careful enunciation of a man who cared about words. "We lost track of you after your little set-to at Andijan. Sit, sit!"

Charlie quickly gave Garman the abbreviated version of the last six years of his life, but it was clear enough that he was here on business and didn't have time to waste on pleasantries.

Sensing this, Garman gave Charlie his mild little smile. "Before we get started, may I remind you of my usual ground rules for journalists? As you may recall, I never talk on record. Anything I utter is strictly on background."

"Understood," Charlie said, taking out his Nikon. On the ride over here, Charlie had considered how he wanted to approach Garman. The thing about a guy like him was that you never knew whom he talked to or whom he worked for. For all Charlie knew, Bull could have been on *his* payroll. It was a risk even to go down this road with a snake like him, but Charlie didn't have many options.

He pulled up his photograph of Bull and passed the camera across the desk. "I'm wondering if you can ID this guy for me."

Garman's smile faded and the first hint of some other, deeper figure behind the history teacher pose began to emerge. He looked at the camera for a moment then picked it up and scrutinized the photo on the camera's display.

"I think he works for the CIA," Charlie said nervously.

When Garman finally looked up, his eyes were cagey and guarded. Garman assessed Charlie for a long beat, then pushed the camera back across the desk. "You're half right," he said.

"Meaning what?"

"He was never a CIA operative, per se. But he *was* an independent contractor they used for a long time."

"And now?"

"The Company gave him the boot a few years back. At which time, he came to me. Looking for work."

Charlie watched the man closely. Was he testing him?

Garman folded his arms, leaned back in his chair. "Of course, we give all our potential hires a psych eval. Let's just say there are reasons why he's not working for us."

Charlie tried not to reveal how relieved he was, but apparently it showed, because Garman laughed. "Oh my goodness, Charlie, you look like you just dodged a bullet."

"We both know I took a chance walking in here," Charlie said flatly.

To his credit, Garman didn't bother denying it. "Yes, well . . . might I ask where this picture was taken?"

The affect was pleasant but Charlie knew that Garman's generosity was reaching an end. If Charlie was going to get any more, he was going to have to give. "The cargo area at Tashkent Airport. Twenty-five minutes ago."

"Bold, Charlie. Bold."

"What's his name?" Charlie asked.

"John Quinn."

"You have a history on him? Anything I can use?"

"He's got pretty much the standard resumé. Spent his whole career in Spec Ops. Ranger school, airborne, sniper training, all the usual tactical training. He retired under duress as a major after some kind of incident that no one ever talks about."

"Any ideas?"

"Probably involved a bunch of dead civilians with brown skin. But that's only a guess. After that, he worked for some contractors to contractors to the Company. He's one of those plausible deniability type guys that the Company uses as sparely as possible for particularly hairy operations. But after a while, even at that tertiary distance, the Company couldn't stand the stink coming off him."

"So who does he work for now?"

"Your guess is as good as mine."

"Karimov?"

"I wouldn't speculate. All I can say is that he was still looking for work last year, then he dropped out of sight."

"But it's possible?"

"Karimov's always been enamored with the cool professionalism and effectiveness of American intel, so yes, it's possible. Now how about telling me what the deal is with that photo?"

Charlie was still unsure if he could trust him. But if there was anyone in the country who might be able to help him—for a price—it was Garman.

"I'm not here on a job," Charlie conceded.

"Oh?"

"It's Julie. She's been snatched."

Charlie thought he saw a glint of surprise in the man's eyes. "Snatched? By whom, Charlie? For what purpose?"

"By Quinn. For what purpose I don't know."

"But it's not for ransom? It's political."

"Can you help?"

"I'll need more information first."

"Apparently, she came here last week to see Alisher Byko. The day after she flew back to the U.S., Quinn kidnapped her. The image I just showed you was her arriving here in a cargo container."

"How can you be sure?"

"The guy tortured me in my goddamn basement. I tracked that container from the port in Los Angeles. All of the timing lines up."

Garman leaned forward. "Tortured you?"

"He was looking for answers," Charlie explained. "Answers I didn't have. About Julie."

"And you said Julie actually *met* with Byko?"

Charlie nodded. "I believe so."

Garman studied Charlie for a moment, then stood and looked out the window as though scanning the street to see if Charlie had been followed.

"You haven't been back here since Andijan, am I right?"

"Right."

"Well, things change. Byko's not the guy you knew."

"How so?"

Garman sat down again, took out a knife and started cleaning his fingernails.

"He's into all kinds of sinister things now. Drugs, guns, you name it."

"And he's still a threat to the regime?"

"Oh, more than ever."

Charlie knew his history. When the English barons started giving King John grief, he couldn't just throw the Earl of Leicester in prison. Not without consequences. In Uzbekistan, Byko was like the Earl of Leicester. Not just a rich man, he also represented a region, a clan, an ethnic group, a whole nest of interests in the Fergana Valley. As powerful as Karimov was, he still had to tread very carefully about going after someone like Byko. The fact that he'd let Byko return to his life after the uprising in Andijan was testament to that. But now, it seemed as though Karimov must have lost his patience.

"So it's come to a tipping point," Charlie said. "Karimov's finally had enough."

"The subtleties of power politics here are enough to confuse a Byzantine emperor. All I can say is that Byko more or less dropped off the map a few months ago. This is a very public man. Poof. Gone."

"You think he's planning a coup?"

Garman gave him a corroborative look. "You heard about Byko's sister?"

"I know that she was arrested last year and tortured at Jaslyk."

"She came home and hanged herself three days later. And now that I've heard what you're telling me, it wouldn't surprise me if Quinn *was* working for Karimov. That business with Byko's sister sounds like exactly the kind of thing that would be up Quinn's alley."

"Of course," Charlie added, "it's also possible Quinn's been subcontracted again by the CIA. That the Company's working in conjunction with Karimov."

"As long as American interests ally with the regime, that is always a possibility," Garman said dryly. "You want to tell me what Julie was doing here, seeing Byko?"

Charlie shifted in his seat. "She was thinking about getting back into some of her work here. They'd been communicating by email. Byko said he might have some opportunities for her."

Garman's eyes pierced through Charlie. "And they used to go together. Back in the day."

"There is that, yes."

Garman raised his eyebrow just enough to irk Charlie, but this was no time to worry about looking like a cuckold. Instead, he dipped into his money belt and tossed five thousand dollars on the desk.

"I need your help. And if we can locate her, I'll need men."

Garman cautiously eyed the stack of cash on the desk.

"I know it's not much," Charlie conceded, "but I can get you more later."

"Look, Charlie." Garman sighed, his face suddenly relaxing into professorial softness. "I knew Julie, and I thought she . . . she lit up a room, you know? I wouldn't want any harm coming to her. But here's the thing. What I do now is mostly petty stuff. Basic security detail for VIPs. The big game? Not my scene anymore. And I'm afraid this sounds an awful lot like the big game."

Charlie suspected this was total bullshit. But he didn't know for sure. And one glance at Garman's empty eyes convinced him that the mercenary was unlikely to change his story.

"Then at least ask around for me. Find out who Quinn works for."

Garman picked up the stack of money and tossed it into Charlie's lap. "People get shot for asking around in this country."

Charlie's eyes bored into the man. "So that's it? Good-bye and good luck?"

Garman picked up the book of poems on his desk and glanced at the page he'd been reading. "You know I write a few verses from time to time," he mused. "Kind of my dirty little secret. Julie said some very kind things about something I wrote once. Not just, *Hey, good job, pal*. Thoughtful, you know? She actually read the damn poem and thought about it, and maybe felt something." He slipped his finger between the pages of the book, then looked up again. "You're going to need that money down the line."

So Garman *would* ask around. And he would forsake even the smallest of fees for his services. Charlie searched the man's eyes. Julie clearly had her charms but was it possible she'd made that much of an impression on him?

"Go do whatever else you have to do," Garman said. "I'll be in touch."

Charlie exited the building, head still swirling as he tried to determine whether or not he could trust Garman. At this point, he figured he had almost no choice. He approached Faruz, who was waiting at the curb, engine idling.

"Good news," the Uzbek said. "My cousin Nirmal used to know this guy who was a falconer for this rich Tajik guy. The Tajik guy was in a sort of hunting club with this other joker who—"

"I don't need all the details," Charlie said as he got into the car. "Did you find Byko?"

Faruz looked at him resentfully. "Why gotta trample all over my story?"

"Because every minute that goes by is a minute closer to some asshole throwing my wife's dead body in a ditch."

"Fair enough," Faruz said. Then he put the BMW in gear and peeled out.

"So you found him?"

Faruz smiled triumphantly. "I found him. And he wants to talk."

CHAPTER TWENTY-ONE

The container sat in the middle of a bare field next to a cluster of large stone buildings. The buildings had the stolid, grim look of an old Soviet military encampment—which, in fact, was what they were.

Quinn threw open the door of the container. Attempting to ignore the smell of unwashed bodies, turmeric, and cigarettes, he walked past the guard and the medic and knelt next to the cot where Julie Davis lay motionless, hair splayed out on the pillow, an IV drip connected to her arm. He checked the pulse in her neck. Nice and strong.

"Wake her up," Quinn said to the medic.

"We do like you say, Mr. Quinn," the guard said, his voice high and urgent. "Everything perfect. Lady in perfect shape."

"Wake her up!" Quinn barked. It put him in a bad mood, people explaining instead of doing.

The medic came over and injected a mild stimulant into the IV bag then squeezed it, pushing the fluids. Julie immediately reacted, sitting up and looking around with a confused expression on her face.

"Good work," Quinn said to the guard and the medic. "Go out and talk to the guy in the blue hat. He'll take care of your pay."

"Thank you, sir! Thank you, sir!"

And the two men, apparently relieved that it was all over, scurried out of the container.

Quinn leaned toward Julie to see how cognizant she was. She blinked at him in a half daze. "Where am I?" she asked.

Quinn stepped forward and backhanded her across the face. "You're in Shut-the-fuck-up. Any more questions?"

Julie held her face, staring at him in shock.

Quinn heard a gunshot from outside the container, then a scream of fear. "We do like Mr. Quinn say! Please! Lady in perfect—"

A second gunshot cut off the guard's plaintive cries.

Quinn walked out of the container, stepping over the bodies of the two dead men. "Get her inside the compound," he said to Mikael, a monster of a man wearing a red baseball cap with a Nike swoosh on the front.

Mikael was just holstering his SIG. "Right away, sir," he said.

Quinn began striding away. He was feeling so much better now that the woman was on the ground.

ordon Bryce was well known in the Service for his calm and apparently dispassionate demeanor. But just now, he was clearly angry.

"Do you know, Hopkins, the last time we lost an officer of the Service?"

Hopkins assumed this to be a rhetorical question. But when the time stretched out and Bryce continued to stare silently at Hopkins through his thick glasses, he decided he better answer the question.

"Seven years ago, sir. Benson. In Pakistan."

"Seven years ago." There was another interminable silence.

Bryce brushed back a lock of hair from his forehead. In a time where everyone in England seemed to cut their hair like Americans, Bryce continued to wear what his detractors in the Service referred to as Empire Hair—parted on the left side and rising up in a strange bristling tangle to the right. "Empire Hair" because it harkened back to the days of the British Empire when a gentleman spent a thousand pounds on his suit and thirty-five pence on his haircut. Now if you didn't spend fifty pounds on your coif no one took you seriously.

Unless you were the Chief of MI6.

"Seven years, Hopkins. Meaning that the last time a sworn officer died in the service of the Queen for this institution, my dearly departed predecessor was seated in this chair. Now I recognize that what we do is not without risk. But the reason my people have been safe under my aegis is that I have forsworn cowboying."

There were those, Hopkins reflected, who argued that under Bryce's aegis, MI6, out of caution, had forsworn doing its job.

"The days of Lawrence of Arabia are well behind us. 'Ready, fire, aim' is no longer accepted modus operandi in this house. Marcus Vaughan is dead because his operation was poorly planned, poorly executed and foolish."

"Agreed, sir."

Bryce's left eyebrow twitched slightly. "You take full responsibility then."

Hopkins gritted his teeth. "You will find, sir, that the dossiers of this operation are crammed full of uncharacteristically shrill appeals under my signature for more staff, more latitude and more resources in country. I was given instructions—as I was told—'from the high-most authority in the realm' that I was to leave no stone unturned. But when I requested a simple eight-man fire team on the ground in Uzbekistan to—"

"We are subject, Hopkins, to political limitations. Incalculable political consequences arising from—"

Hopkins's hands clenched into fists. He struggled to keep his voice low. "Sir, you asked the question. I should like to reply in full. Perhaps out of the wound to my pride, but I rather think more because our missteps heretofore bear on our ongoing prosecution of this operation."

Bryce eyed him unblinkingly—giving him enough rope to hang himself, Hopkins supposed. But right now, Hopkins didn't care.

"Seven days ago we received hard intelligence as to the future location of Alisher Byko. A fixed place and a fixed time. A meeting with a person about whom we had very clear and accurate information. I requested a tactical team to seize Byko. My request was denied on political grounds, my hard-earned intelligence handed to the Uzbek government. The Uzbek government then tasked a small unit from its 'elite' Twenty-seventh Air Assault Regiment for the takedown." Hopkins wrapped his voice in as much sarcasm as he could muster. "The Twenty-seventh, as is well known, is a sinecure for some of the dimmer members of the Uzbek President's extended family. They are corrupt, inefficient, poorly trained and underfunded."

Bryce let a slow breath trail noisily out of his long nose, as though he had become bored with the course of this conversation. "I made a terribly forceful case to the Foreign Office for sending in an SAS team. But they simply couldn't sell it to the Karimov regime."

Not forceful enough, Hopkins felt like saying. But instead he stuck to the facts. "Sir, as you're well aware, the Twenty-seventh blew the raid. Did someone tip off Byko's people? Was it pure incompetence? I really don't know. Perhaps a combination of the two. But what I *can* tell you is that it was entirely predictable."

"I've read your report," Bryce snapped.

"Marcus Vaughan contacted me two days later saying he had information and all he needed was tactical support. If not a full team of trained intelligence operators, then at least a handful of SAS lads. And I had to tell him, 'It's come down from the highest levels that we need desperately to find Byko, but as regards support . . . sorry, old man, you're on your own, Whitehall have ordained there shall be no hard operations in Uzbekistan except by officers acting under credentialed diplomatic cover—of which, dear Marcus, I may remind you, there is only one. To wit, you.'"

"You should have bloody called me."

"With all due respect, sir, would you have bucked Whitehall on this? If you wouldn't do it to catch Byko himself, would you have done it to protect a single agent?"

The black eyes continued to watch him unblinkingly. "I should watch your tone, were I you."

Frank Hopkins considered himself to be a man of great self-control. But the simmering heat of his anger was threatening to burst out of him in a career-ending explosion. He forced himself to take a deep breath. "I recruited Marcus. I brought him along. He had a few personal problems that led him to his rather undistinguished assignment in Uzbekistan. But he was a fine field man and a decent human being. I sweated through several jungles, a handful of deserts and more than a few inhospitable cities in his company, and he dragged my arse out of more than a few rather tight spots. He was a friend."

"Look, Hopkins, we're all damned sorry about Marcus Vaughan. *Damned* sorry." Bryce paused for a moment, hands prayerfully clasped in front of the knot of his tie. Then, having made his show of compassion, he recomposed his face in its usual grave lines. "That said, if you wish to have a future in this organization, I suggest we put an end to this sort of finger-pointing and set our sights on finding Byko."

Hopkins gazed at the man incredulously.

"I know I don't need to remind you that the clock is ticking, Hopkins."

"No, sir. You certainly don't."

And with that, Hopkins turned and headed out of the room, all too aware that one hand was still tied behind his back.

CHAPTER TWENTY-THREE

Charlie and Faruz were bombing down the highway outside Tashkent in Faruz's beat-up BMW. Faruz had assured Charlie that while the Beemer might look tired, the engine had been reconstituted and was more than ready for prime time. Thus far, Faruz had been a man of his word. The car was humming along at ninety-two miles per hour with only the gentlest of purrs.

"So where exactly are we heading?" Charlie asked.

"The way this works, my cousin gonna call me, various steps along way. Byko very particular about who he talk to these days. People gonna be watching us for tails. Right now we heading to a checkpoint east of Samarkand." He pointed at the mountains. "We get up there, my cousin gonna call, give us directions to next checkpoint. Eventually we gonna reach Byko."

"So you have no idea."

Faruz shrugged. He was normally hard to shut up, but it was clear he was nervous and they drove mostly in silence, Faruz pushing the speed, passing trucks and slower cars with his horn blaring, chain-smoking Marlboros.

The low, drab outskirts of Tashkent gradually gave way to the arid countryside and then to a low, purple range of mountains, the first upwellings of the great spine of rock that ran eastward across Asia all the way to the Himalayas. In the foothills of the mountains near the Kirghiz border, they came upon a cell tower extending up from the hard, bare earth like some alien artifact in the midst of a moonscape of barren rock.

"This is it," Faruz said, climbing out of the car and whipping out his cell. "It's me," he said into the phone. "Where to next?"

While Faruz was hashing out the details for their next checkpoint, Charlie noticed a car parked across the highway. Two young men sat in the vehicle staring at him through mirrored sunglasses.

Charlie heard Faruz sign off, then watched him return to the car. As he opened the door and got in, the young men put their car in gear and took off.

"Who were those guys?" Charlie said.

"Watchers," Faruz replied and threw his phone onto the dash. "Let's go."

The Fergana Valley had been strategically carved up by Stalin and now lay divided between Uzbekistan, Tajikistan and Kyrgyzstan. It was devoted almost entirely to agriculture, with long strip-shaped cotton fields lining the sides of the A273 highway for mile after mile after mile. As the most fertile area in Uzbekistan—in fact, in all of Central Asia—the Valley should have been prosperous and lively.

That was hardly the case and Charlie was reminded of it as he and Faruz sped past what appeared to be a graveyard of ancient Russian tractors sitting in an empty field, their paint bleached and rusted, tires pirated, picked clean of extra parts. In the succeeding field, women in colorful head scarves plodded listlessly through a vast field, backs bent, hacking ineffectually at the ground with primitive hoes.

In the Soviet era, cotton picking had been largely mechanized, but the Karimov regime had avoided investing in new machinery or novel agricultural techniques. This was the best way to squeeze the resources out of the region while keeping the people mired in poverty.

During the cotton harvest, schools and universities were shut down and entire towns and cities depopulated, their inhabitants forcibly removed to the Valley, where they picked cotton until the fields were stripped clean. For every dollar earned by the cotton crop, 25 percent went straight into the pocket of the President and his children. Another huge chunk went to Karimov's various cronies and oligarchs. The rest went to the military and national infrastructure. Nothing but a few pennies came back to the people who toiled in those fields. As far as Charlie was concerned—and this was a point he'd argued many times in his stories and columns back in the day—this was a system that closely resembled the American South of a century and a half earlier, and the cotton pickers were essentially slaves of the regime.

Still, the land was green and the mountainous backdrop was breathtaking. As anxious and wired as Charlie was, he couldn't help but notice this and he felt mournful about how he'd left this place.

"I'd forgotten how beautiful this country is," Charlie said wistfully.

Faruz seemed to perk up. "There were a lot of people who didn't want you to leave."

"I had no choice," Charlie said, as much to himself as to his friend.

Faruz just looked at him. This was a conversation that had been sitting between them, unspoken, since they'd liaised in Tashkent and Charlie felt more defensive than he'd anticipated. "Julie almost died, I almost lost my son."

Faruz shrugged infinitesimally. "I was there. I lost people."

Charlie felt a flash of anger. "I'm a journalist. Not a freedom fighter."

"Julie didn't want to leave. She still send packages to the villages she worked in. She still send email."

"Well, I guess she's stronger than me," Charlie said heavily. "Because I needed to forget."

"You never even say good-bye."

"I know," Charlie said softly. "I'm sorry."

"So is it better for you in California? With the palm trees and yoga and blond girls in bikini?"

Charlie snorted an ironic laugh. Both men, it seemed, were happy to return to the safer terrain of cynical banter. But as Faruz flicked ash out the window and futzed with his iPod, Charlie thought about what Faruz had said about Julie—that she'd stayed in touch with her old friends here, that she'd sent emails and care packages. Not really a surprising revelation, given who Julie was, but what struck Charlie was this: she'd never spoken to him about any of it. Why had she felt it necessary to hide this from him? Did she believe he'd be angry with her?

That he couldn't handle hearing about anything relating to Uzbekistan? Perhaps she thought it would humiliate him, that it would shove in his face precisely what he'd just said to Faruz: that she was stronger than him, that he needed to forget while she still wanted to remember.

What if it was something even more difficult to swallow? What if she'd hidden it from him because she was afraid if he knew, then she would be exposed? That healthy gestures of her lingering affection for the Uzbek people would actually indicate something deeper: that she'd never *accepted* their choice to live in Los Angeles, that she was unhappy with the life they'd made there, that she yearned for a return to the time before the safe and rational compromise that landed them in suburbia? If that was the case, then she had spent the last six years living a life of dutiful obligation? Spurred by some kind of misguided sense of what? Loyalty? Guilt?

Charlie was spinning. He knew that Julie had never felt a part of Los Angeles, that its affected Hollywood players and superficial culture were anathema to her. Of course, they were to him, too. But he'd grown to appreciate the sunshine, the mountains, the ocean, and he'd found a great many friends through the paper—people outside the entertainment business who were intelligent, erudite, conscientious citizens of the world. Julie used to joke that people came to L.A. for a "lifestyle" not a "life," but she'd always said it with a wry smile, and he genuinely thought that she'd come to enjoy all that it had to offer.

Had he misread her so badly? He kept hearkening back to what Sal had told him. How could

Charlie have been so blind to what was happening in his own marriage? And if she was so unhappy, so restless and unfulfilled, why had she never come to him? Yes, she had raised the idea of going overseas again—of resuming their old way of life—but had she ever laid it all on the line? Then again, had he ever gone out of his way to ask her what she really thought of the life he'd foisted upon them? Or had he mostly avoided the subject, afraid of what her response might be?

A part of Charlie told himself this was not what he needed to take on right now. Autopsying their marriage, beating himself up over what he did and did not do or say over the last six years . . . ? How was that going to be helpful? But there was another side of him—the morbid, unsentimental side—which reminded him that if he didn't save her, this was what would be left of their marriage. A slew of unanswered questions, a score of issues never to be resolved. He would go to his grave wondering what had happened between them and what her lies meant.

Charlie stared out the window, the cotton fields streaming by in slow, endless procession.

How had they become such strangers?

CHAPTER TWENTY-FOUR

Julie had the oddest feeling, as though she were swimming into her own life from some distant watery place. It was sort of like an experience she'd had years earlier when she had gone snorkeling in the massive kelp beds off the coast of California, weaving in and out of the giant strings of greenery, shafts of sunlight penetrating fitfully into the depths from the surface, no sense of distance or space or location—never quite lost, but never quite sure where she was either.

And then, finally, she found herself in a white room, seated in a sleek white chair. The walls were white too, with tiny black cameras installed in each corner. Her head was hurting, her mouth was dry, and one side of her face stung, as though she had been slapped or punched. But who had hit her? She had no recollection at all.

And then, slowly, the memories began clicking into place.

Night. Meagan crying unceasingly. A Cadillac Escalade parked across a street, a face half hidden in the darkness. Headlights turning toward her. Tearing through the streets. The children in the backseat. Slamming on her brakes. Cornered. Dark shapes erupting from the Escalade. Her thought at the time: *If I leave here, draw them away from the children, maybe they won't hurt them.* Running.

The children! Jesus Christ! Were the children okay?

Suddenly she was seized with panic. She tried to stand, but there were bands made of heavy seat belt material Velcroed around her wrists. What kind of chair had restraints built into it?

She thrashed and screamed. But nothing happened.

Finally she gave up and slumped back into the chair.

How had she gotten herself into this? How had she come this far, hiding everything from Charlie? Her heart broke as she thought about what he must be going through. Was he aware by now of the dimensions of her betrayal? Or was he still muddling around in the dark, wondering why his wife had abandoned their children in a residential cul-de-sac?

She began to weep, her body shuddering. But after a few moments, it occurred to her that they were watching her—whoever *they* were. And she had to pull herself together. To deny them the satisfaction. She took a deep breath and steeled herself for whatever came next.

Then there was a metallic clunk—a key turning in a heavy lock. A door opened slowly and a man walked in, staring at her without expression.

It took a moment to make sense of who he was.

When she did, she knew that she should be terrified. But she also knew if she showed him any fear, he would never let her survive.

CHAPTER TWENTY-FIVE

We're here," Faruz announced.

They had climbed out of the lush Fergana Valley and into the barren, forbidding mountains near the Khazakh border to arrive at their destination.

Charlie peered through the windshield, trying to make out exactly where they were. There was an old stone wall, interrupted only by a large pair of guard towers with a rusting, twisted steel gate between them. A large sign with Cyrillic writing on it was so faded it was nearly illegible. Charlie was able to make out just enough of the letters to realize that they were entering what had once been some kind of Soviet military base. At first glance, the facility appeared to be deserted. A closer look revealed very modern surveillance equipment posted along the walls.

After a moment, the gate moved, opening smoothly on large steel hinges. The neglected appearance of the place was a sham. This was a carefully guarded and well-equipped facility.

"Shit," Faruz muttered. "I'm not liking this, Charlie."

"You want to stay here," Charlie said, "I understand. But I'm going in."

Faruz took a deep breath, then eased off the brake and began driving slowly down a long gravel road between two rows of planted hawthorn trees. As they passed the guard towers and the big steel gate slid shut behind them, Charlie saw that the guard towers were indeed occupied. Several armed men stood on both sides of the road, in the shadow of the guard towers, all of them geared up in the most current Western military gear—BDUs, plate carriers, M4 carbines with fancy optics and lasers.

Faruz drove about a quarter of a mile, creeping along at the same slow pace, when Charlie's phone rang. The number was blocked, but he answered it anyway.

"It's Garman," the voice said. "I've been trying to reach you for an hour."

"We're in the boonies," Charlie said. "No cell service."

"Anyway, I told you I'd heard that Byko had gone into a dark place, right? Some drug issues, all that stuff? Well, here's the bizarro thing . . ."

But then Garman's staticky voice cut out.

"Garman? Garman?" Charlie checked the phone to see if he had a signal. One bar. He spoke again. "Garman, are you there?"

Faruz was driving a little faster now, the BMW bumping and rolling on the pitted gravel drive as they approached the end of the road. In the distance, Charlie could see the line of trees disappearing and the road widening into the parking lot of some sort of large compound. Beyond the lot lay a building covered with blue tile in a vaguely Arabic style, surrounded by several barracks. A wide variety of late-model cars were parked in the broad, recently paved lot. Armed men ringed the area.

Charlie looked at the phone again and saw an incoming call on the other line. Garman trying him back. Charlie answered.

"Is that you?"

"Did you get anything that I said?" Garman replied.

"You lost me at the bizarro thing."

"Oh Jesus."

"What is it?"

"Charlie. Quinn is working for—"

Again, Garman's voice broke up in midsentence.

"Say that again," Charlie said.

"Quinn . . . ," Garman repeated, his voice crackling and echoing, " . . . is working for Byko."

Charlie felt a cold sensation run down his neck. "Are you sure?"

Garman's voice dropped out, but Charlie was able to hear, " . . . confirmed from my most reliable sources . . ."

"What is it?" Faruz barked. "What's happening?"

Charlie saw the armed men coming toward their car. "We just walked into a trap."

"Where are you?" Garman asked.

"Somewhere up near Khazakstan. We're about to see Byko."

"Jesus, Charlie, you gotta get out of—"

The voice dropped out once more.

"Garman? Garman?" But he was gone. The phone dead. "Goddamnit."

"What is it?" Faruz demanded.

Charlie looked gravely at his friend. "Quinn works for Byko. He's the one who has Julie."

Faruz turned around to see if they could reverse out of there. Four armed guards stood a hundred yards back, watching them intently. Faruz's face was sheet white and dripping with sweat.

"I make a run, I don't think we get out of here."

"No," Charlie admitted. "It's too late."

A thousand questions raced through his mind, but the first one Charlie needed to answer was: had Byko brought him here to kill him?

If that was what Byko wanted, he could have done so at any of the checkpoints along the way. For that matter, Byko had left Charlie alive in L.A. when Quinn could have easily killed him in his basement. Charlie quickly concluded that he'd been brought here because Byko needed to ascertain what Charlie knew. Of course, Charlie knew next to nothing. About any of this.

"What fuck we gonna do?" Faruz asked, his voice shaking.

Charlie grabbed for his camera. The evidence against Quinn. Could he use that in some way? He popped out the disc and stashed it in his pocket.

"Stay here," Charlie said, then bounded out of the BMW. To his dismay, Faruz climbed out, too. "Back in the car," Charlie hissed. "You could still make a break for it if things go sideways."

Faruz gave Charlie an infinitesimal shake of his head. "I'm not letting you go in there alone, Charlie."

Charlie felt a burst of gratitude. And there was no time to argue. The security guards were almost within earshot and it wouldn't look right for them to be bickering.

"Hi, there!" Charlie called out, waving to the guards and forcing a broad smile. "Charlie Davis. I'm here to see my friend Alisher Byko."

CHAPTER TWENTY-SIX

Lying back against the warm stone and letting the scorching air envelop him, Byko felt as though his entire body was vibrating to the lowest note in a huge pipe organ. A very lovely and very naked girl crouched beside him on her knees, an opium pipe clutched in one hand, a gold lighter in the other. He nodded and she played the flame underneath the bowl.

When a few tendrils of smoke rose from the small black pearl of opium, the naked girl held the pipe to his lips. He inhaled deeply, relishing the onslaught of the smoke.

He could still smell the scent of Julie Davis in his nostrils. And it almost paralyzed him.

Julie had begged him, had pleaded for her life, had protested her innocence in all of the expected ways, and yet, as much as he ached to believe her, he simply could not.

She was Julie Wingate-Rees when he'd met her thirteen years ago at Cambridge. Fiery, committed, beautiful—she had represented everything that seemed good about the West. Her family had been rich and powerful members of the British ruling class for generations, Tories all. But she had forsworn that stuffy old British Empire nonsense, believing that a world of justice and freedom was around the corner if everyone was just willing to make it so.

She probably never realized how important she had been to him. A turning point in his life, really. He had been smitten with her. And she with him, as far as he could tell.

Their passion had been blinding, relentless.

But then, just before she left Cambridge, she had called it off. He had begged her to continue the relationship, to figure out a way to make it work. But in the end—she had never really articulated it, but this was his impression—she had rejected his privilege, rejected what she saw as his essential frivolity, rejected his willingness to ignore the pain and suffering that all his privileges rested on. On the evening of her graduation, he had made some sort of half-drunken, half-humorous suggestion that he would always love her—and she had laughed uproariously.

But she had never understood him, had she? She had failed to recognize that his partying and carousing and cocktail philosophizing was a mask to cover up his essentially romantic and serious nature. He'd dreamed of great things, but had felt trapped in his role as the son of a man who wielded great power in a place of utterly no consequence. He had always felt that if he'd just had more time, he could have shown her his true face. He even thought of going after her—to Africa, where she'd joined an international aid organization—but then his father died and he was forced to return to Uzbekistan.

Somewhat to his surprise, he found that running

a sprawling business empire agreed with him. There was so much to do, and no time to gad around the world chasing after Julie. And so marriage and fatherhood had followed. His wife had been part of the ruling elite of Uzbekistan, the daughter of one of his father's cronies, and so by all rights it should have been a marriage of convenience, a strategic alliance of mutually interested parties. But it wasn't. He had great affection for Daniella, had even, in some way, loved her. And she had loved him.

But Julie's laugh had continued to haunt him. How many times had he been sitting at his desk, facing a business decision, and thought: "What would Julie think of the choice I'm about to make?"

When he raised the pay of his miners, when he improved safety procedures, when he built the school in Dartak or the clinic in Pakhtakor—it was her voice in the back of his head that had driven him.

He hated to admit it, but much of what he had done to support democracy in his country had been a sort of adolescent Gatsbyesque attempt to impress her. It was absurd when you framed it that way. She wasn't an important scholar or a famous statesman or a great writer. And yet she hovered constantly in his mind, a figure of conscience.

And then, eight years ago, nearly four years after he'd bade her farewell at Cambridge, she'd arrived in Tashkent as an emissary of an NGO called World Vision. When she'd first phoned him and announced that she'd moved to Uzbekistan, his heart had sunk. Because he was already married, already had a son by that marriage and now here was Julie. Had she come here for him? Was it possible she didn't know that he was now a husband and father? Had he blown it by not pursuing her more, by not waiting for her to come around? She had insisted that it was a coincidence, that World Vision had offered her the assignment because of her proficiency in Russian. But he'd always wondered.

Almost immediately, they began working together on microfinance projects as well as the building of schools and hospitals in the Fergana Valley, though they were all too often frustrated at the intransigence of the Karimov regime. For a time, they grew close again, closer in a way than they ever had been at university when all of the embroiled passions of lust and youth cluttered the mind and spirit.

And then Charlie Davis entered the picture. Byko had heard about the new American journalist who'd been poking around some of the more fragile subject matters in the region, and was already curious about him when Julie walked into the Samarkand bazaar on his arm. The American and Brit had met, Byko was told, at an English pub in Tashkent, a dive that happened to be the favorite watering hole for European freelancers and members of BBC News stationed in the capital. It was clear from the moment that Byko laid eyes on the pair that they were steadfastly in love and, even more disheartening, that they were incredibly well-suited for each other. "Kindred spirits" was how he heard them describe it and, as sick as it made him to admit, it was hard to argue with that assessment.

That was how he'd lost Julie Wingate-Rees for the second time.

They had been courteous enough to invite Byko to their impromptu wedding in the dazzling Aral desert, but Byko had contrived an excuse. He simply couldn't stand to watch it happen.

Over the next few months, as he watched Julie's protruding belly blossom, Byko tried in earnest to let go of his jealousy and to be a friend to them both. In fact, he came to respect Charlie Davis more than he ever could have imagined. The man was committed to the cause of exposing Karimov's tyranny and he had the resources, the savvy and the mettle to do just that. It was Charlie's article about the torture of a young man at the infamous Jaslyk Prison that helped launch the protest movement.

Unfortunately for all of them, their hopes and dreams had been smashed that day in Andijan. In the aftermath of the tragedy, Charlie and Julie had shuttled off quickly to London and then to Los Angeles and Byko had counted on never seeing either of them again.

Since then, Byko had walled off his feelings, kept them at bay with opium, coke, single malt scotch, whores, scheming and responsibilities.

But when Julie emailed him last year after his sister's death, the wall came down. It was a simple, emotional, yet elegantly worded note of sympathy for his grief—a breath of fresh air in the stifling desert of his life. The emails they'd exchanged since then had led Byko to believe that she was his for the taking again—so long as he bided his time and allowed it to happen naturally and without pressure.

By slow degrees it had all led to their first meeting in six years.

Sitting there at Padishah in the heart of Samarkand's café district, she had seemed so glad to see him, fixing her warm brown eyes on him as though he were the answer to some great question in her own life. She had been radiant as ever but with a maturity and gravity that shone even brighter than the youthful intensity he had loved about her before. Just seeing her had nearly buckled his knees, and for a moment, he'd even considered putting a hold on his plans for revenge, as if a union with Julie might heal everything.

But it had all gone wrong. Forty-five minutes into their leisurely meal, he'd gotten the call saying that elements from Karimov's Twenty-seventh Air Assault Brigade were converging on his location. He'd left her there without explanation and had barely escaped with his life.

Of course, Quinn, who saw threats behind every bush, was convinced that Julie had been sent, that she was a honey trap controlled by a Western intelligence agency. Byko had resisted at first, but Quinn had made a convincing case. Her inconvenient stopover in London the night before she flew to Tashkent, her quick return to Los Angeles after their rendezvous, her lies about visiting other countries in the region and, most crushing of all, the all-too-reasonable argument that Julie's original condolence email was in fact the insidious beginning of the trap. And so he'd allowed Quinn to snatch her—on the condition that he brought her here so that Byko could talk to her himself.

And now that he'd spent a few hours with her, Byko was certain that she was hiding something. She hadn't cracked, hadn't budged an inch on her story. And yet, somehow, her reactions seemed too pitch perfect, too smooth, too clean—as though she had anticipated this moment and prepared for it.

And so, with some misgivings, he had handed her over to Quinn.

The initial tidal wave of the opium began to ebb away and Byko could feel his hands start to tremble. Once again his darkest suspicions began firming into a sense of outraged certitude. Because in his heart he knew what Quinn would find.

The lying bitch. All these years he had idealized her. And now she had turned out to be nothing but a willing tool for the same hypocritical monsters who ran the world as their private plantation.

He felt his teeth grinding, the rage threatening to explode, and opened his eyes. The lovely girl, no more than sixteen or seventeen, her skin flawless, her breasts soft and buoyant, sat expectantly on the stone shelf next to him, opium pipe still clutched in her hand. Waiting to serve him. He leaned back against the warm, moist wood and wordlessly closed his eyes. She knew her job well enough and she began to fumble with his belt.

A soft tap at the door interrupted them. He looked up see to his bodyguard Hasan enter, his eyes conspicuously ignoring Byko's condition.

"Davis is here," Hasan said.

"Make him wait," Byko replied sourly. "I'll be out in ten minutes."

As Hasan exited, the girl took Byko's flaccidness into her mouth but now the mood was ruined.

He felt a flash of anger accompanied by a brief urge to do something terrible to the girl, to bite her or rip her hair out or pound her with his fists until he heard bones shatter. But instead he simply slapped her in the face.

"Out," he said.

She sat up, stared emptily at him, then padded out the door, seemingly unconscious of the blood running out of her nose. Byko closed his eyes, trying to find that meditative calm, that center where he was at one with himself. A few slow deep breaths and he was there. It was a matter of will, he told himself.

Close your eyes. Just close your eyes and let it come.

And finally it did, a consoling vision he'd turned to in his darkest moments since he'd learned the truth about his sister. In his mind an image formed, an image of a fire spreading across a nearly infinite expanse of city. At first it was just a thin line of red on the horizon. But soon the flames strengthened. And as they grew, they moved faster, racing toward him, growing higher with each approaching meter. Accompanying them was a roaring, rushing sound. The wall of fire grew closer and closer and closer, warming his entire body with a feverish heat. He could feel a smile on his face. It was coming.

By this time tomorrow, the destruction would be unleashed and for the first time in years the feeling of impotence that had invaded his every moment since Andijan would fade away. The heat grew and grew and grew, blotting out everything, enveloping him, transforming him.

It was coming soon. The fire.

CHAPTER TWENTY-SEVEN

Four armed men escorted Charlie and Faruz into the large building through a heavy wooden door that looked like something out of a medieval castle. Inside, the walls were blue tile and the vaulted ceiling was held up by thick stone columns. The air was unusually warm, musty and humid—almost to the point of being steamy—and their footsteps echoed eerily in the silence of the strange building.

"What is this place?" Charlie asked.

"Ancient bathhouse," Faruz said. "My guess, it go back to at least sixteenth century. I hear Byko brings his buddies here to—"

"Shut your mouth," one of the men said, goosing Faruz in the back with the muzzle of his carbine.

They were marched down a hallway. An open archway to one side revealed another vaulted space, this one so full of steam that Charlie almost couldn't make out the intricate tile work on the far side of the room. In the center of the room was a small stone pool in which several unclothed women— very beautiful and very young—were lounging. The young women stared at them blankly, their eyes dull and resentful.

To the right was another steam room, this one containing several bearded men, one of them in the throes of a massage by a half-naked girl who couldn't have been more than thirteen.

Disgust rippled through Charlie's insides. But there was something else there, too. The sinking feeling that he had absolutely no idea what he was walking into. Byko had been a playboy in his heyday but what was going on here was something close to pedophilia. What had Alisher Byko become?

Back in the car, the first thought that ran through Charlie's mind was that Byko must be a deranged lunatic. A drug-addled, lonely, love-struck guy who'd thought he had a chance at seducing Julie. That he'd lured her to Uzbekistan under false pretenses and then when it hadn't gone the way he'd planned, he'd sent John Quinn to America to kidnap her and bring her back to his lair. If he couldn't woo her, Charlie figured, he'd take her by force. The old-fashioned, medieval way. And these girls here were certainly proof that Byko had forsaken any modern, Westernized view of women.

But Charlie quickly remembered Quinn and those questions in his basement: Who was Julie working for? Who had she seen in London? Clearly, this wasn't just some lovesick bully demanding to have the woman he desired. Quinn, and by proxy Byko, wrongly believed that Julie was somehow out to get Byko, that she had set him up in some fashion. This was why they'd taken her and now it was Charlie's job to convince them they were crazy. But there is no way to prove a negative. If someone is paranoid enough, any denial that you give will only reinforce their suspicions. There had to be another way out of this.

And then the idea hit him. The one way he might be able to outmaneuver Byko. To use Byko's greatest fear against him. He'd gone underground, after all. If Charlie could convince Byko that he could expose his location . . .

He took out his cell phone and turned it off, but he kept it in the palm of his left hand. If it came down to it, it would be a bluff of the highest order. But it just might work.

The guards led Charlie and Faruz through two more sets of doors. The next room was much cooler, and—after the mugginess of the steam rooms—the air felt bone dry. It had the look of a library in an English gentlemen's club—except for the books, whose spines all bore Russian script.

There were half a dozen people in the room, large silent men in dark suits who were not going to a great deal of trouble to hide the pistols under their coats.

A man rose from a leather chair in the corner, a broad smile on his face.

It was Alisher Byko.

He was a little thinner than he had once been, with some gray in his mane of fashionably cropped black hair, but there was nothing to indicate that anything fundamental had changed about him as his arms spread wide, calling out in his flawless Etonian diction, "Charlie, my friend, how long has it been?"

Byko kissed him on each cheek then pushed Charlie away, holding him by the shoulders and staring at him with intent black eyes.

"You Americans, always with the weights and the gym. Rude good health personified!" He gestured at one of the heavy leather upholstered chairs next to him. "Sit! Sit! I must know what brings you here. Our old friend Faruz told my people it was very important."

This was not what Charlie had expected. He'd assumed that Byko would either play the heavy right out of the gate or the concerned friend devastated by Julie's disappearance. Instead, he was feigning ignorance. The chess match was under way and Charlie had only one move.

"You didn't get my email?" he asked.

"I'm afraid not," Byko replied with the utmost interest. "What did it say?"

"It said that Julie was kidnapped. And that she'd been brought to Uzbekistan."

Byko cupped a hand over his mouth. "But why?"

"I thought maybe you could help me with that."

"Me?"

"I know that you and she have been corresponding, Alisher. I know that she opened up a second email account to keep it from me. I read all of the emails. I know that you begged her to come here and last week she finally did. You met, I take it, in either Tashkent or Samarkand. What happened there, I have no idea. But she came home two days ago and the next night she was kidnapped. Presumably by your enemies. Because they believe she has valuable information about you."

Byko's face grew deadly serious. "And how do you know that she's in Uzbekistan?"

"Because the same nice folks who took Julie broke

into my house and tortured me for six hours to find out if I knew anything. Which I don't."

"Knew anything about what?"

This was starting to go as Charlie had hoped. Him confiding in his old friend, asking for help, protesting innocence and ignorance. And it was all sounding eminently believable.

"They kept asking me who she worked for, what she knew, who she stopped to see in London on her way. It's crazy, Alisher."

"What do you think they could have meant?" Byko said, fishing. "When they asked who she worked for?"

"I haven't the faintest idea. All I know is that something led her to reach out to you. And then you took advantage of that. Eleven months of seduction, Alisher. I read it all. And then she lied to me. Told me she was going to New York. She flew halfway around the world to get laid and now somebody's got her in a warehouse somewhere, probably torturing her to death to find out how to get to you. You never should have had her come, Alisher. Not when there's this much heat on you."

"You think it is Karimov's people who have her?" Byko asked gravely.

"I would assume. Or maybe CIA."

"And how do you know that they've brought her to Uzbekistan? Why not just interrogate her in Los Angeles somewhere?"

"The men who came to my house—I overheard them speaking. I know she's here."

"And who else have you told about this?" Byko asked.

Now Charlie began to see what Byko was after. "No one. Besides you and Faruz."

"Because you trust us."

"I know that you love her," Charlie said. "It's not a thrilling idea as a husband, but as the man who needs to get her back, I figured it counts for something."

"As a matter of fact, it does count. It counts for a great deal in this matter."

"Then help me find her."

Charlie searched Byko's eyes and could have sworn he saw a flicker of compassion or empathy. And the complete scenario flashed in Charlie's head, a prayer for how the rest of this might go: Byko tells Charlie to sit tight, that he'll put out feelers for Julie, a few hours go by and Byko's men miraculously produce her. Byko emerges as the hero who saved her, Charlie and Julie thank Byko immensely for all that he's done and head home, allowing Byko to feel like Humphrey Bogart in *Casablanca*. It seemed plausible enough, if Charlie had only managed to convince Byko of Julie's innocence.

Then Hasan stepped forward, Bluetooth in his ear, and approached Byko. Byko leaned forward eagerly as Hasan whispered something to him. The debriefing couldn't have lasted more than ten seconds, but as Hasan backed away, Charlie felt an enormous shift in Byko's energy and body language. His adversary seemed to be steeling himself for battle, any remnants of their past friendship drifting away.

"Something wrong?" Charlie felt obliged to ask.

The tiniest hint of a smile curled on Byko's lips. "You haven't asked me if we slept together."

Charlie clenched his teeth. "That's not something I need to know."

"You're not curious?"

"She's the mother of my children. I need to bring her home. That's all that matters right now."

"She told me that she was coming here for some business meetings in Tashkent," Byko began, his voice cold. "That she had meetings arranged in several other countries in the region. That all turned out to be untrue."

Charlie could feel Byko's drug-addled bloodshot eyes boring into him, his suspicion and paranoia practically seeping out. Whatever Hasan had just told him, it had turned things against Julie.

"She lied to you because she was embarrassed," Charlie reasoned. "She couldn't admit that she was coming here only to see you."

"And you know this how? Given that she lied to you as well?"

"Because I know how she thinks," Charlie said, though half of him didn't quite believe that.

"I think," Byko replied, "that you know a great deal. A great deal more than you're saying."

Byko nodded to someone standing behind Charlie. Before Charlie could turn to see who it was, a lean man in an ugly taupe suit stepped forward. Carrying Charlie's camera.

Byko's eyes found Charlie's for an instant and then he grabbed for the Nikon. He turned it on and tried to scroll through the stored photographs. After a moment, he looked up.

"Where is the disc?"

Charlie just stared at him.

"I had you followed at the airport," Byko conceded. "I know you photographed the tarmac. Now where is the disc?"

Charlie reached into his pocket and held it up. "You're more than welcome to it," Charlie said, tossing it at Byko's feet. "But I've already downloaded the photos and sent them to Michael Vance at the American Embassy."

Byko eyed the disc, but refused to pick it up. For such a large man, Hasan moved like a cat. In an instant, he had the disc between his meaty fingers and began loading it into the camera.

"So . . . ," Byko said, exhaling, "Michael Vance?"

"That's right," Charlie bluffed. "And everything's completely documented. The route of the container. Every payment, every manifest, every customs form. The entire file is sitting on the ambassador's desk as we speak."

Byko remained motionless, eyes hooded.

Charlie held up his hand, finally exposing the phone in his left palm. "Right now, all I have to do is turn on my phone and the Foreign Office will instantly know where I am. How long do you think it'll take for the NSA to get one of their satellites homed in on this very spot?"

Hasan handed Byko the camera, but he no longer seemed interested in its contents. Charlie had his attention.

"I don't know what she did to you, Alisher. Maybe she rejected you, maybe she found out something about you that you didn't want the world to know . . . It doesn't matter to me. As far as I'm concerned, the whole thing is one big misunderstanding. No harm no foul. You give me Julie, we walk out of here, you never see or hear about us again."

"And how do I know you won't just turn on your phone when you get out of here? Or tell them where I am when you get to safety?"

"Mutual deterrence."

"Mutual deterrence?"

"You were able to get to us in Los Angeles. I know that you could do it again with a snap of your fingers. Even from prison. All I want is to get out of here. All I care about is Julie."

"And yourself," Byko said. "That you made perfectly clear when you left here six years ago. You had so much 'passion' when it was easy, but as soon as there was something at risk for you, you fled with your tail between your legs. You're a hypocrite and a coward, just like the country you live in."

"If that's what you want to believe," Charlie said, "I won't argue with you. Give me Julie and you have my word, I will drive away from here and never look back."

Byko seemed to seriously consider Charlie's proposal, but then he looked past Charlie to someone by the door.

"Is it true?" Byko asked. "What he says about Michael Vance and the phone?"

Charlie turned to see Faruz framed in the doorway, the barest glimmer of a smile on his lips. "He only found out Quinn works for you ten minutes ago," Faruz said coolly. "The Americans know nothing."

A sluice of nausea rushed through Charlie as he absorbed the betrayal. "You sold me out? You fucking sold me out?"

"What? You think I am suppose be loyal to you? Only reason you ever came here to begin with was so you get your Pulitzer! So you can have stories for cocktail party in L.A."

Charlie rushed at Faruz, but Hasan shoved Charlie back.

"How much did he pay you?" Charlie shouted. "For Julie's life? For mine?"

Faruz wagged a finger at him. "I can feed my mother's whole town for a year with what he paid me today. I have to watch out for *my* family now."

Charlie's head was spinning. He couldn't fathom when and how this had happened.

"So . . . this whole time? At the tarmac? All of that driving around?"

Faruz shrugged. "Selling the con, Charlie. Just like democracy and free speech and the rights of man."

"Hasan," Byko barked, cutting off the conversation. It was one word, but everyone in the room knew it was an order.

The big slab-faced bodyguard drew his pistol. Charlie thought for sure that his life was over. But then the hulking man pointed his gun at Faruz. The betrayer's face registered shock, realizing what was about to happen.

"Mr. Byko, I—"

The bullet caught him in the side of the face. A cloud of dark liquid exploded in the air and Faruz fell with a thud.

"The thing I've always detested about Faruz," Byko said, "is that he's merely an opportunist. No sense of loyalty whatsoever."

Charlie stared at Hasan's pistol, certain that he was next. But Hasan holstered the gun and buttoned his coat, expressionless as a man who'd just polished off some routine household chore.

With that, Byko rose and beckoned to Charlie. "Come. There's something I'd like you to see."

CHAPTER TWENTY-EIGHT

T his way," Byko urged.

He smiled and motioned to Charlie, heading up a dark flight of stone steps and through a doorway. With Hasan right behind him, and three other bodyguards ten yards down the hall, Charlie had no choice but to follow, joining Byko in what was a much smaller room than Charlie was expecting.

Unlike the rest of the building—which was decorated with ancient tile work—this room was brightly lit and antiseptic, with banks of computers, video monitors and communications equipment, all manned by a young Uzbek dressed in Western geek fashion—baggy jeans, trucker hat, a black T-shirt complete with a picture of Homer Simpson.

"Pull up the first interview," Byko ordered.

Homer hit a few buttons and cued up Byko's request. A high-quality video feed appeared on the largest monitor. Charlie could tell the video was taken by a wide-angle surveillance camera. The room in the video had white walls, a white tile floor and was lit with banks of fluorescent lights. Occupying the majority of the screen was a man with his back to the camera. Charlie could immediately tell it was Byko, but the person beyond him, the person Byko was talking to on-screen, was blocked from view.

"This was recorded several hours ago," Byko informed Charlie, crossing his arms.

On-screen, Byko stepped aside, revealing Julie.

Her hands and feet were manacled, she looked strung out and haggard and desperate, but at least she was alive.

Cuffs, Alisher?" Julie growled, jerking her wrists. "Come on!"

"You must understand," Byko said. "Things are very delicate for me right now. I can't afford even the tiniest mistake."

Julie looked down at her lap, her long dark hair momentarily obscuring her face.

Charlie gave Byko a brief glance. He was staring fixedly, almost greedily, at the screen.

Julie's shoulders began to quake. She made no sound, but it was obvious she was crying. Byko said nothing. Finally Julie looked up, her face streaked with tears. "Don't you understand, Alisher?" she said softly. "I love you!"

The words cut through Charlie like a swath of napalm. But it wasn't just the words. It was the way she said them, filled with such ferocious conviction.

Byko did not speak.

"I've always loved you." Julie strained toward him. "Don't you know that? Don't you remember how hard it was for me to escape from you at Cambridge?"

"And why did you?" Byko asked.

"*Because I was afraid you were going to swallow me alive! It was too intense, what we had. You know that!*"

"*Then why did you come back here again?*"

"*Because I couldn't fight it. Because I never stopped loving you, even after I married Charlie.*"

Charlie felt Byko's eyes on him and realized what a fool he'd been. Leaving Oliver and Meagan in Los Angeles, flying out here pretending he was James Bond, ready to save his damsel in distress when in fact she was no longer his damsel to save.

"*Then why now?*" Byko asked. "*After all of these years?*"

"*Because I realized that I can't sacrifice my whole life to be with a man I don't love. He's a good man, but he's a shadow of himself and I just couldn't do it anymore.*"

Byko was sitting next to her now, his profile visible, his face betraying the depth of his conflict. "*You think I don't want to believe you? You think I don't burn to believe these things you say?*"

Julie slumped back, her head flopping in resignation. She stared up at the ceiling. Finally she sighed and locked eyes with Byko.

"*I love you, Alisher,*" *she said softly.*

"*Then why did two hundred handpicked members of the Twenty-seventh Air Assault Brigade decide to join us for tea the other day?*"

Julie shook her head wearily. "*We've been corresponding for a year. Maybe the regime is tapping your phones or your email. Maybe you've got a mole in your organization. Maybe one of the waiters at the restaurant recognized you and ratted you out. Maybe the CIA located you with a spy satellite. I still don't know who you're hiding from or why. It could have been a million things. For God's sake, Alisher, you have to believe me!*"

Byko leaned forward and hit the keyboard, pausing the image on the screen. "Well?" he drawled, his face deadpan. "Do you think she's telling the truth?"

Charlie couldn't speak.

"Answer me, Charlie. Do you think she's telling the truth?"

Charlie looked at the floor. "I do."

Byko studied his face for several seconds, then smiled without warmth. "Unfortunately, I didn't. So I let your friend Quinn take a crack at her. I was only just informed of the results." He looked down at the young man in the Homer Simpson shirt. "Cue up what Quinn wants me to see."

The tech hit the fast-forward button. The screen went blue and empty, nothing left but a digital clock in the upper-right-hand corner. Several hours scrolled by before Julie appeared again. When she did, Charlie could barely recognize her. Hollow-eyed and gaunt, her entire body shaking, she was a broken woman. And Charlie knew all too well what had done that to her. It was the red.

However angry Charlie had been toward her only moments earlier, however betrayed he'd felt, it all washed away, replaced by a tenderness he couldn't have imagined possible. She was still the mother of his children and the love of his life—and to see her this way, reduced to this, was nearly unbearable.

Quinn walked slowly to a small table by the door, set down his syringe, then returned and squatted down in front of Julie, like a kind teacher about to console a child who'd skinned her knee.

"It's okay, sweetheart," Quinn said softly. He reached forward and brushed the hair back from her face, tucking

it behind her ear. "Just tell me the truth and we're home free. Then all of this goes away."

Julie looked up at Quinn, her eyes hopeless and empty. "I'm with MI6," she said.

"MI6?" Quinn nodded. "You're a spy for the British."

Julie shrugged with defeat. "I wasn't a trained agent. Somehow they found out about my correspondence with Alisher. They said that Alisher had gone into hiding and that they needed to locate him. Just to have a talk. In person. They wanted me to help them with that one thing."

"Just to have a talk," Quinn said dubiously.

"They said it was important. Very, very important. And I believed them."

Quinn continued to grill her, but Charlie could no longer hear it. Because he was putting it all together now. Why she'd lied to him, why she'd been acting so strangely the last few weeks, why she'd run so quickly when Quinn tried to grab her at the gas station, why there were no charges on her credit cards for her flights—it all made sense. She'd been recruited by MI6 and they must have convinced her to hide everything from him.

Quinn leaned in close to Julie. "And they never told you why they needed to speak to Alisher?"

"They said that he'd gotten involved with some dangerous people. That they thought they could help him."

Byko switched off the video.

"What do you say about that, Charlie?"

Charlie took one look at Byko's unforgiving eyes and understood the shift that had occurred just a few minutes ago, when Hasan had interrupted their meeting and whispered that Quinn had finally broken her. He knew that with this admission Julie had signed her own death warrant—unless Charlie could turn things around.

"She's making it up!" Charlie said. "For godsake, that son of a bitch doped me up with that red shit, too. After about five minutes, you'd sell him your mother just to make him stop."

Byko dismissed Homer with a flick of his wrist, took out his phone and hit two buttons. Charlie heard a semidistorted ring, then a voice on the speaker—"Yeah?"

Byko spoke into the phone. "I'm standing here right now with Charlie Davis."

"Wow Charlie," said the tinny voice. "I never figured you'd find your way out to our neck of the woods."

It was Quinn.

"You lay another hand on her," Charlie warned, "I swear to God I'll rip your heart out."

There was a brief delay then a burst of laughter from the phone. "He certainly has the American bravado," Byko said to the speaker, one eye on Charlie. "Now how do we know his wife wasn't just making up all that business about MI6?"

"Too many details," Quinn replied. "Who recruited her, when and how. Information about her debriefings before and after Tashkent. She's given most of it up, as far as I can tell. Though I can't say I'm convinced she was drawing you out just so you could 'talk' to them. She's even gone so far as trying to convince me that she was doing it for your own good, to protect you."

"If that was the case," Byko said, "she would have told me that when I first talked to her."

"Agreed," Quinn said.

"Okay, keep working on her."

And just like that, Byko hung up.

"You know," he said to Charlie, "for all we know, her NGO work was a cover. Maybe she's been a professional spy all along. Even back in the day, was she using you to plant those stories about the regime?"

"You're out of your mind," Charlie snapped.

"You do realize that MI6 recruits over half of their agents from Oxford and Cambridge. I'm beginning to think that's why she left me when university came to an end. Because she was heading off for her training. Of course, she ended up in Uzbekistan anyway when it was time to spy on me."

"So she was spying on you and using me at the same time? That's your theory?"

"She was sent here to investigate the potential for an uprising and possibly to help foment one. I suspect the Brits were just trying to put pressure on Karimov for more strategic concessions by stirring up the people. Then when it went too far, when we were ten thousand strong that day in Andijan and it looked like we might really create some instability, even topple the regime, they panicked and tipped off Karimov."

Charlie looked at Byko incredulously.

"Haven't you ever wondered how Karimov managed to mobilize his southern regiments to the square that day? I happen to know that it was MI6 who alerted the regime. Just as I know that it was the CIA who kidnapped and tortured my sister for eight days at Jaslyk. Not only is Julie a user and a liar, but she's working for the wrong side. Has been all along. She helped kill my wife and son," Byko said. "And she might as well have been the one who shot you in the back."

"You're wrong," Charlie said, refusing to accept this. "If she was ever working for MI6, she was merely an asset like she said—recruited in the last few weeks because she knew you. They played her, Alisher. Isn't that the more plausible scenario? That they told her she would be helping you and she bought it?"

"Come on, Charlie," Byko said. "Does that sound like her? If she is who she led us to believe she was, would she ever have been so naive as to accept something like that? Coming from MI6?"

Byko shrugged and pulled out a .45. "Well, my friend, it should hardly matter now to you. Seeing as I have to kill you."

"Alisher . . ."

"I spared you in Los Angeles. But now that you've come here, I really have no choice in the matter."

Charlie held up his hands. "Alisher, listen to me." Charlie was stalling, tap dancing, grasping at straws. "I know you're a man of conviction. Of inherent decency. And you know that I have no love for the Western intelligence agencies. If you're working against them, chances are that you're doing something good. If it's toppling this regime, you know you'd have no stronger advocate for that than me. I respect your . . ." Charlie didn't want to overdo it. But instinctively he felt sure that there was no underestimating the man's vanity. "I respect your purity, Alisher. Your rigor. I'm even a little in awe, I guess. It must take enormous will to do whatever it is you're doing." He paused, forcing himself to maintain a sincere expression as he delivered this absurd flattery. "But if you still feel a scrap of friendship for me—or any feeling for Julie for that matter—

give me a chance to say good-bye to her. Give us a chance to speak whatever needs to be spoken. Let us go to our graves knowing that there's nothing left unsaid between us."

"You need to know who she really is," Byko added.

"I do," Charlie agreed. "Give me that before I die."

CHAPTER TWENTY-NINE

Charlie was sitting in the back of a Cadillac Escalade, hands secured tightly behind him with plastic flex cuffs. Two of Byko's paramilitary goons accompanied him, one driving, the other seated in the back, a tricked-out AK-47 pointed at Charlie's chest.

The SUV was tearing down a road leading toward a small range of hills to the north. Presumably it was all part of the same former Soviet military complex where the bathhouse was located. Infested with massive potholes and gaps in the tarmac, there was no indication that the paving had been improved in at least twenty-five years. But this didn't stop the driver from keeping up a steady pace of close to 90 miles per hour.

"How far?" Charlie asked the man sitting next to him.

But the mercenary or guard or whatever he was stared at Charlie in stony silence.

Left to his own thoughts, Charlie reflected on his strange send-off by Byko. The man had shaken his hand gravely and said, "Well, I'm genuinely sorry it worked out like this, Charlie. I do hope you will be able to find some consolation in the fact that your sacrifice will be part of a greater movement, one that will propel us toward a better world."

A better world? The overthrow of Uzbekistan would almost certainly be good for the people of this country, but it was grandiose, to say the least, to think that anyone outside this region would ever feel the impact of it. It made Charlie wonder—was there something else Byko had planned? Something less obvious than a coup? He was clearly angry with the West. Was it possible Byko's plan was something on a grander scale?

As the car whipped around a hairpin turn, Charlie pushed all of these thoughts aside and tried to focus on coming up with a way to escape. He knew that wherever Julie was being held, it would be indoors, heavily guarded, probably fortified. Quinn would be there. And Quinn was not a guy who'd be bamboozled or outmaneuvered.

No, if he was going to get away, he had to do it now. Before they reached Quinn.

Charlie surveyed the interior of the Caddy with clinical interest.

The cabin was utilitarian. No weapons, no communication devices, nothing that would be of use. He studied the man next to him. Typical mercenary chic. Olive drab cargo pants, military boots, baseball cap, wraparound Oakley knockoffs, nylon rigger's belt, Glock in a thigh holster and of course the ever-present load-bearing bulletproof vest that soldiers call a "plate carrier." The plate carrier's desert tan skin was covered with myriad pockets containing spare mags, med kit, flashlight, and a large fixed-blade knife in a Kydex sheath.

The man was slight and fit, with the barest tinge of the sadist showing through his impassive expression. Charlie guessed he was probably former Uzbek military. But in subtle ways Charlie could see the marks of Western training—the way he held his gun, the pistol grip of the carbine high on his chest, wrist cocked, trigger finger resting lightly on the frame of the weapon. Uzbek soldiers didn't carry that way. They brandished their guns heedlessly, as though they were fishing rods or planks of wood. Odds were strong that this man had been trained by Quinn.

As the car bucked and slammed over the broken pavement, the first thought that entered Charlie's mind was bribery. Byko's men had frisked him back at the house but hadn't bothered with his money belt. But eight grand and change? Split between the two of them? That would never be enough.

Next, he considered running. If he told them he needed to take a whiz and they pulled over, he could try making a break for it through the fields. But with his hands tied behind him, he figured he'd make it about ten yards before Quinn's guy blew him away.

So bribery and flight were out of the question. The only option left was to somehow fight his way out of this. Which meant he needed his hands free and he needed a weapon. He made a subtle attempt to slide his cuffed wrists under his butt in order to pull them in front of his body, but realized that he was neither long armed nor flexible enough to accomplish the task. What then? Throw himself on the mercenary and *bite* the guy to death?

It was hopeless.

He'd have his five or ten minutes with Julie and that would be that. Call it a life.

He tried to imagine what those minutes would be like, how much needed to be accomplished. Demanding from her the truth, working through the anger and guilt, doling out apologies and forgiveness, coming to a reckoning and hopefully some kind of peace. Having one final chance to pull back her hair, to touch her skin, to kiss her lips.

On the face of it, the whole thing might be something out of a Shakespearean tragedy. Romantic and poignant and fraught. But Charlie knew that it would most likely end in pathetic fashion—them begging Quinn for more time only to find that he wasn't feeling so generous; or in clumsy, brutal bloodshed, with Charlie forcing a confrontation he would inevitably lose, all the while knowing that he was leaving Julie behind to more torture and anguish and his children to a lifetime of loneliness and grief.

The children. Beautiful sweet Oliver. Mercurial luminescent Meagan.

Was this really it? Would he never see their faces again? Read them another bedtime story? Teach them baseball? Take them to the beach? Piggy-back them in the sand?

No. He would not allow his mind to go there any further. There had to be a way out of this. As long as he had breath, he could not give up. If he was going down, he was going down fighting. He assessed the situation again. The mercenary three feet to his right, gripping his bull-pup carbine, the hulk of a driver commandeering the Escalade faster than it had any right to be going on such a road.

The car hit an especially big pothole, shocks bottoming out as Charlie flew up, his head banging on the ceiling, his legs lifting up so far that his toes almost smacked into the driver's headrest. As his body slammed back into the seat, a thought came to him . . .

The car. The car itself was a weapon. If he could somehow find a way to harness it.

A sense of calculating calm settled over Charlie's entire body. He remembered the same feeling sometimes when he played football, when the entire field seemed made of crystal—every player, every formation, every blade of grass sharply formed in his mind. And when he fell into that state of clarity, he had always known exactly where he needed to cut or spin, where to shuck a block, where to hit a man with every ounce of his strength.

He slid over slightly so he could see out the front of the vehicle. The road was climbing into a small mountain range and began winding in and out of the hills. At the highest point, the road followed the ridgeline for at least a mile, then took a hard jog to the left as it passed onto a bridge leading across what was likely a wild mountain river.

In an instant, a plan came into his mind, fully formed. A bit of distraction, split-second timing, perfect execution—if he played it all right, he had a chance. Maybe one chance in a hundred, but still . . . a chance.

The car rolled slowly through a series of hairpin turns, then accelerated sharply as it reached the straightaway running along the ridge. Charlie could see the speedometer climbing: 50 miles an hour, 60, 70.

The bridge was getting closer and closer, but still the car rolled on at full speed.

Charlie's heart pounded in his ears. He turned toward the mercenary and gave him a knowing grin.

The mercenary's eyes narrowed suspiciously.

Charlie leaned back in his seat. He had to sell it perfectly. Not too quick, not too strong. One beat, two, three—still with the expression of amusement on his face. Then he eased himself forward in his seat—just the tiniest bit—and sneaked a quick I-can't-help-myself glance out the window on the other side of the mercenary.

With all his gear, the mercenary would have to swivel his entire body around in the seat to look out the window, to see what it was that Charlie thought was so damn interesting out in the cotton fields.

They were almost to the bridge. But would the man take the bait?

Just as the driver hit the brakes so he could make the turn onto the bridge, the merc turned. And in that crystalline moment, Charlie knew he had it. He bucked his hips upward and thrust his back against the seat, jumping so hard that his feet cleared the top of the driver's seat back. He looped his right leg around the driver's neck, hooking his left leg over his own right foot in a tight triangle of muscle. And squeezed with all his strength.

As the moment slowed—the driver shouting and clawing at Charlie's leg, the merc whirling back around and fumbling with the safety on his AK, the car braking with a juddering of antilock-brakes-assisted traction—he felt the driver lose his grip on the steering wheel.

The Cadillac swung right, fishtailed . . .

And then they were rolling, once, twice, three times . . .

Impact.

CHAPTER THIRTY

There was no sound but the ticking of the radiator and something like static. The car was lying on its side, water visible halfway up the windshield, and Charlie realized they had catapulted over the side of the road and into the river. Through the side window—which was now directly above him— he could see they had fallen down a very steep and rocky ravine. And that staticky sound was actually the rush of the rapids.

But Charlie felt curiously stupefied, as if he'd had his bell rung. From his vantage point, he could see the driver lying sideways in an unmoving heap in the front seat, the air bag deflating in front of him. He seemed to be unconscious, though there was no blood or any indication that he'd been seriously wounded.

The mercenary, on the other hand, was done for. He lay on his side next to Charlie. His face was now strangely flattened, its features wiped away, like an orange that had been hit with a hammer. Blood was pouring out of the single gaping hole that had once been his nose and mouth, leaking onto the slick surface of the window in enormous quantities.

And then water began flowing into the vehicle. The SUV was wallowing deeper in the river, showing signs that it might be swept away at any moment. If Charlie didn't get out soon, he would drown in here. But he was pinned to his seat by a heavy canvas bag that had bounced out of the rear of the vehicle, and with his hands behind him, he had a very hard time maneuvering.

From the front of the car, the driver grunted softly—an Uzbek curse—and shifted around in his seat, sloshing water around the cabin. As he began to make sense of what was happening around him, his eyes widened. "You!" he yelled. "What are you doing?"

Charlie pushed himself to his knees and clawed at the door handle, struggling to find the latch. He yanked but it felt limp and dead in his hand. The lock switch must have shorted out.

The driver pulled out his gun. He'd have a hard time turning around to get a good look at his prey, but that gave Charlie only a few seconds.

In desperation, Charlie slid around and inverted himself, his entire torso underwater, and kicked the window.

Nothing happened.

The frigid water was up to his shoulders now and he could feel it robbing his body of oxygen. He kicked again. Once, twice, three times. The water was at his chin. In moments, it would cover his face. He kicked again with all the force he could muster and finally the window gave way.

Before he could even register that he'd penetrated the window, a cascade of water twisted and flipped him inside the car. Gasping and spluttering, he sucked hungrily for air, struggling against the current, trying to find an exit through the broken window. But it was no use. He held his breath and stayed as still as possible, trying to conserve his energy until the rush died down.

When the water finally reached equilibrium, he found a small pocket of air. Pressing his head against the roof, he contorted his neck and managed to suck in a few gasps of oxygen, then pushed himself upward through the window.

As he did, Charlie heard the sound of two gunshots. The driver firing at him somewhat haphazardly. And too late.

Charlie foisted himself on top of the wrecked SUV and stood on the battered door, gazing at the roaring rapids beneath him. It would certainly be no picnic diving into that with his hands cuffed behind his back.

As he hesitated, he heard the driver bellowing inside the car, then saw the front door open. Charlie stomped on it and heard a rewarding yelp of pain. But he knew he couldn't hold him off like this for very long. And as hairy as those rapids looked, if the big man got out while Charlie was still standing on the vehicle, it would be no contest.

The moment Charlie hit the water, he lost all control, all sense of up and down, all sense of direction, the current grabbing him and sucking him beneath the surface of the river. As he spun helplessly, he saw light above him, appearing and disappearing with each rotation of his body.

He kicked and thrashed wildly, trying to get his legs in front of him. Light, dark, light, dark. But none of his feverish activity seemed to have any effect on his relationship to the river. And then suddenly his head broke the surface and air surged into his burning lungs.

That brief glimmer of hope was quickly shattered as he was sucked in again. Propelled by the furious current, his entire body battered and scraped by the jutting rocks, he struggled desperately for another surge of air, only to find himself slammed into something hard. The current flipped him up and he found himself lying atop a smooth black boulder, his lungs screaming. He sucked in another desperate breath, then was swept away again.

All of the muscles in his abdomen, his shoulders, his neck burned as he fought to hold his head above the surface. He didn't know how long he could keep this up, but right now anything was better than being underwater in those rapids.

Floating on his back, his feet downriver ahead of his body, Charlie could see the ravine and the jagged rock walls rising steeply around him. As he passed under the bridge, he saw sunlight piercing through its joints and seams and thought he felt the current letting up.

As he emerged on the other side, he knew it for sure. The water was slowing.

The ravine was widening. And the ominous jagged boulders were replaced by a fringe of benign reeds.

Charlie managed to flip over and look back. The Cadillac was surprisingly far away. But where was the driver? Had he drowned?

Suddenly, Charlie noticed a sound like thunder.

He turned to see what it was. Not fifty yards in front of him, the placid surface of the water seemed to disappear, as though the river had been sawed in half. His brain couldn't make sense of it at first. And then it hit him. That sound.

It was a waterfall.

Charlie kicked as hard as he could. The reeds grew closer and closer. But so did the roar. He sneaked a glance and saw clouds of mist spraying up from the falls. The speed of the current was picking up again as he got closer to the edge. And the rocks themselves seemed to be transmitting the shock of the falls into the water.

Faster, faster. Propelling himself forward with his legs, his arms nothing but dead weight, the water pulling at him, clinging to his limbs.

And then he felt his toes graze the bottom.

Salvation.

Plunging his feet deep into the water, he groped for the earth. But just as quickly it was gone. And the effort to reach it lost him a critical two or three yards. The thrumming deepened, the sound of the falls grew louder, a wave of fine mist began to roll over the top of the falls onto his face.

He panted, trying somehow to kick harder. But the sheared-off wall of water was growing closer. He wasn't going to make it.

Then there it was again.

The bottom.

He planted his right foot in it. And this time, it held. Fighting the inexorable tug of water, his left foot found it, too. And now he was walking. One foot. Then another, then another, gasping and spluttering. Slipping in the silt, regaining, holding again.

With only a dozen feet to spare, he reached the reeds.

Flipping over in the muck, he pulled himself up onto the bank, lying on his back, greedily sucking in air, staring upward. Above him was a steep, rocky bank that rose a good two hundred feet to the top of the small mountain. And higher still, a cloudless blue sky.

Revived, he turned and surveyed upriver.

The driver was alive. Spluttering and coughing, pawing awkwardly at the water, but very much alive. And coming for him.

Charlie staggered to his feet and began trudging through the mud and reeds. The bank soon turned steep, its surface cluttered with rubble and boulders. Not only was the ground uneven and slippery, but the rocks felt unstable, as though every pebble was ready to plunge down the hillside. And without the use of his hands to balance himself, every footstep felt uncertain.

"You're a dead man!"

Charlie turned and looked back. The driver was splashing wildly toward the shore, eyes blazing. Despite his adversary's pathetic swimming skills, Charlie could see that with the use of his hands he would easily make it to the reeds well before the waterfall.

This would be a chase. And Charlie barely had a head start.

Charlie tried running up the steep hill, but in his haste, he slipped and fell, slamming his face against a rock. He scrambled gracelessly to his feet and began forging upward again, working more methodically this time.

Behind him, the driver hit the shore and began plowing through the reeds toward him. Charlie was only halfway up the hill, a hundred feet ahead of his stalker. Looking down, he saw the man pull out his pistol.

Two rounds snapped and clattered off the rocks at Charlie's feet.

"You're wasting your time, dead man!"

Another shot rang out, this one passing close to Charlie's head.

Above him, Charlie spotted a boulder—big enough to offer him some cover—and he hurtled toward it as another near miss slapped into the rocks in front of him. Reaching the huge rock, he paused, bracing himself against it and staring over his shoulder. He was still at least a hundred feet from the crest of the hill.

But even if he made it to the ridgeline—what then? It wasn't like he was going to be able to outrun this guy. Charlie eased his head around the side of the big rock. The bodyguard had stripped off both his coat and his shirt. Grunting and heaving with each footstep, the man's muscles rippled beneath his pale skin as he pushed relentlessly upward.

How the hell am I going to fight this guy? Charlie thought. *With my hands behind my back?*

His pursuer paused, rested one hand on the mountainside to support himself and, raising his gun, took a slow, careful bead on Charlie's face.

Charlie ducked behind the boulder just in time to avoid the shot. The bullet hit a rock. As the shards of shrapnel flew sideways and began bouncing slowly down the hill, something came to Charlie. A play that might work. He braced his back against the mountainside and shoved the massive rock with his feet.

It didn't budge.

The Uzbek below him began laughing. "You gonna hide behind that rock all day, little boy?"

Charlie pushed again. He thought maybe he felt something this time, a miniscule shifting of weight beneath his feet. But still the rock was there. Charlie took two deep breaths, closed his eyes and summoned images of Ollie and Meagan. Anger filled him like a furious red fire. He took one more deep breath, then screamed, pushing with all his might.

Slowly, slowly, slowly, it began to move—at first propelled only by the strength of his muscles—then, suddenly, the boulder lightened as its own momentum took over.

And it began to fall.

It seemed to go in slow motion at first. But then it hit another rock, bounced a little, and began to accelerate, sweeping dozens of smaller rocks in front of it. Those rocks drove another hundred into motion and soon the entire hillside was moving.

The landslide made a curious, horrifying noise, like some mythic giant grinding its teeth, and suddenly the bodyguard, who had looked so intimidating and huge, appeared as insignificant as a gnat before the vast carpet of earth and stone.

For a few terrifying seconds, Charlie was sure the entire hillside would collapse, sucking him down with it. But then the terrible noise of the landslide subsided, replaced once more by the rush of the waterfall. As the dust began to settle, Charlie walked over to the edge of the hill and looked down at where the big man had been. He was barely recognizable now, just a heap of twisted limbs, one arm trailing in the river.

For a moment it seemed unthinkable. Unreal.

Charlie had been in many situations over the course of his career where he thought he might have to defend himself, or someone he cared about. And he had always assumed that if the time came, he would do what needed to be done.

But as he peered down the hill at his adversary's corpse, he was shocked by his own reaction. There was no revulsion at the act, or even fear of the line he'd just crossed. Instead, he was filled with a wheeling sense of triumph. A desire to stick out his chest, point at the dead man and laugh.

And then, as quickly as that feeling came, it was replaced by a wave of nausea. That nausea was a reaction not to what he'd done, but to the primal relish which had just overtaken him.

Charlie shook his head, pushing away the self-analysis. He had no time for introspection or guilt now.

It wouldn't take long for Quinn and his men to figure out that he'd escaped. And he had to get through to MI6 before they did.

CHAPTER THIRTY-ONE

Charlie ran in an awkward trot, his hands still cuffed behind him. He knew the moment Byko learned of his escape, he'd be on the move and Charlie would lose any chance of finding Julie.

From the ridge running along the small river, Charlie could see the ribbon of concrete in the distance, the A217 highway running back to Tashkent. It was probably about two or three miles away if he went cross-country, but the problem was that once he got down off the ridge, he was liable to lose his way.

As he jogged unsteadily past a bend, he spotted a small track diverging from the little road. It was barely more than a cow path, unpaved and weedy, with two deep ruts that probably had been made by tractor wheels, but it seemed to lead off in the direction of the main highway.

He headed down the path, which led up and down a series of small hills and then out into the valley below. Still shivering from the cold water, he crested the final hill and looked down into the valley, spotting a small farmhouse flanked by a ramshackle barn and a livestock pen. The track on which he was running headed straight across the cotton fields toward it.

He had been planning to flag down a ride on the A217 and convince someone to lend him a phone, but this was a much better option.

When he grew closer, he saw two cars parked in front of the farmhouse. He moved faster at first, anxious to see what was going on here, then slowed as he discovered what those cars were.

A blue Toyota van and a sleek red Mercedes SEL. Outside a farmhouse?

Had he stumbled upon one of Byko's outposts?

He scanned the surrounding fields and realized where he was. The characteristic maroon flowers in the fields had faded, but each waist-high plant was still topped with the bulbous capsule that remained after the flower disappeared—a feature that gave the crop a comical air, as though it might have been invented by Dr. Seuss. This was opium.

And even if this property didn't belong to Byko, even if Charlie had just stumbled upon the property of a local drug dealer, getting any help here was a dubious proposition. In fact, merely cutting through the property to get down to the highway was a perilous idea.

The problem was that the fields were very large. If he went all the way around them, he would double the distance to the highway and waste precious time. But if he kept the barn between himself and the main house, he might just be able to scoot through the area unseen. A quick dash past the farmhouse and he'd be no more than a couple of hundred yards from the tree line on the other side of the fields. And then he'd be home free.

When he got within earshot of the house, he slowed. He could hear a steady thump from the building and crept toward the barn, easing his way around the corner. He peered through the open back door and saw two men, wearing identical Adidas hoodies, bright colored warm-up pants and a great deal of gold.

They were dancing. Gyrating to the noise of the horrible electronic music coming from a primitive boom box. Clearly they were partaking of the bounty in the field. How else to explain the sight of this?

Suddenly, a buxom young woman with dyed blond hair and thick black eyebrows moved out the door, wearing nothing but a half-buttoned man's shirt and a pair of thigh-high leather boots. Mumbling and cursing as she moved drunkenly toward the cars, she fumbled with a set of keys and managed to unlock the trunk of the red Mercedes. It was a case of vodka she was looking for.

But as she pulled it out of the trunk, it slipped from her hand and fell on the dirt with a clatter of glass.

She swore in Russian, though somehow the bottles managed not to shatter.

Charlie tried to back quietly away, but it was no use. She saw him.

"Who the hell are you?" she demanded.

"I got picked up by the Internal Security Police," Charlie improvised, swiveling to show her his cuffs. "Have you got a knife or something?"

She stared at him as if he'd dropped in from outer space. "Where did you come from?"

"I don't know exactly. Somewhere in the hills."

He gestured in the direction opposite Byko's compound. "They had me for a couple of days, but I managed to escape. If they find me here with you guys, it's not gonna be good for you. For your own sake, the best thing you can do is cut these cuffs off and let me get the hell out of here."

"I don't know." The woman winced nervously, looking back at the house. "Maybe one of the guys has a knife."

"No," Charlie said. "I'm sure we don't want to bother them." He glanced inside again. "They seem pretty busy with what they're doing in there. Maybe we can find something out here to do the trick."

Charlie quickly scanned the car for something she could use. There was nothing inside the cabin of the Mercedes, so he moved back toward the rear of the car. Lying inside the trunk, next to a loose jack, was a small pallet knife. "See that?" he said. "You can just cut them off yourself."

The drunk girl rubbed her face, smearing her heavy eyeliner. This was too much thinking for her. "I don't know," she said. "I better go grab—"

"Wait!" Charlie barked, immediately regretting how much he'd raised his voice. He peeked inside the house again but the blinged-out dealers were still rapping away. "Wait," Charlie said again, voice softer now. "Five hundred dollars, cash American, if you help me."

"Five hundred?" She appraised him skeptically. "You got it on you?"

"Uncuff me first."

She sneaked a glance at the house, then grabbed the knife and came toward him.

Charlie turned around to expose his cuffed

hands. But freeing him turned out not to be the first thing on her mind. Instead, she lifted the back of his shirt and touched the blade to his skin.

"Don't move," she said.

"What are you doing?" Charlie asked, though he already had a pretty good idea.

She ripped off his money belt, unzipped the flap and pulled out the cash.

Charlie wheeled around to face her. "You don't want to do that," he warned, combing his mind for something that might coerce or scare her. And then it came to him. "I work for Slavik Omarich. You screw with me, you're screwing with him."

Six years earlier Slavik Omarich had been one of the biggest drug smugglers in Uzbekistan, a man unparalleled in reputation for violence and ruthlessness.

The woman stopped, eyes widening, mouth opening slightly. Apparently Slavik was still alive. Good for him and good for Charlie.

"Now get the cuffs off me or your head's gonna end up on a pole."

With trembling fingers, she took the pallet knife out of the trunk and cut off the plastic flex cuffs.

He eyeballed her with menace. "Okay, you stupid cow, my money."

"What about my five hundred?"

He grabbed the girl by the shirt, pulled her toward him and snatched the cash. "You already blew your shot at that. Now your cell phone."

When she hesitated, Charlie got in her face, playing the part. "Your phone, wench! I know you got one on you."

She reached into her boot and handed him a pink,

diamond-studded Nokia. Charlie looked at it—no signal. Not up here.

He grabbed the keys from the trunk of the red Mercedes, hopped in the driver's seat and cranked on the engine. Before he pulled away, he leaned out the window.

"You tell those assholes in the house about me, I'll come back here and kill you myself."

But as he floored it and tore out of there, he heard the girl shouting. By the time he made it to the trees, he could see the men boiling out of the house, shooting wildly toward him, then piling into the blue van.

Charlie thought there were only a few hundred yards of trees separating the fields from the highway beyond, and that escape would merely be a matter of zipping down the dirt track and up onto the A217.

But the reality was not so simple.

The track was rutted and full of potholes deep enough to swallow an axle—if he just floored it and flew down the road, he was likely to bottom out and rip a wheel off the Mercedes.

So he slowed as much as he dared. The little road meandered through the woods, looping around gnarled trees and boulders, then suddenly took a hard left into a small dry creek bed. Charlie poured on the gas and the powerful Mercedes quickly gained speed, but suddenly the dry wash divided in half, creating a fork. Which way?

He knew that left was east. And east was where the highway was.

He went left.

Thirty seconds later, the path narrowed and the

drab brown walls closed in on the Mercedes until he was unable to squeeze through any farther.

He'd chosen wrong.

Charlie turned off the engine, put his head out the window, and listened for the sound of the van.

Nothing.

Were they lying in wait, ready for an ambush as soon as Charlie backed up? Or were they going to wait for him by the highway, expecting Charlie to jump out of the Mercedes and try to make his way on foot?

It was a fifty-fifty proposition and either way there wasn't much time for deliberation.

Charlie threw the car in reverse and backed slowly up the dry wash. As soon as he saw the fork again, he stopped and listened for the van. But he couldn't hear anything over the sound of his own engine. He eased his foot off the brake and continued creeping backward, hoping the drug dealers couldn't hear him.

And then he saw them in his rearview. Backing up from the other fork, no more than fifty feet behind him. Point-blank range.

Charlie floored it.

The big Mercedes flung itself backward so hard that he nearly banged his face into the steering wheel. Within seconds, he was doing almost forty miles per hour.

One of the dealers was hanging out the window looking for Charlie, nothing but his legs inside the van. His eyes widened as he saw the Mercedes hurtling toward him and he swiveled around, trying desperately to bring his AK-47 to bear before impact.

But he was too late.

With a metallic thud and a ripping of metal, the Mercedes smashed into the van. Charlie heard a skittering thud, saw the would-be shooter pinwheel over the top of the Mercedes and disappear below the line of the hood, arms flailing wildly at the air.

Pulse racing, Charlie dropped the Mercedes into drive and stomped on the gas again. The big German V8 responded with a throaty roar and the car jumped forward as he shot down the other fork.

He glanced one more time in his rearview. There was no sign of the driver trying to get out of the car. He must have been crushed by the impact.

As for the Mercedes, its legendary engineering had proved its mettle here. The trunk lid was completely buckled and the cover on the rear bumper fell off after dragging behind the vehicle for a few hundred yards—but there was no sign that the car had sustained any mission-critical damage.

Charlie gripped the wheel tightly and poured on the gas.

He soon crested the incline and found himself on the edge of the highway. Bumping and slaloming onto the A217, Charlie picked up speed then checked his watch—it had been just thirty-six minutes since he'd left Byko's compound in that Escalade.

He pulled out the girl's diamond-studded phone. The moment he got into range, he dialed the British Embassy.

After three rings, he was greeted by a pleasant female voice.

"My name is Charlie Davis," he said. "I need to talk to somebody at MI6. Tell them it's about my wife. Julie Davis."

CHAPTER THIRTY-TWO

Julie sat in a heavy wooden chair, soaking wet and shivering uncontrollably—so exhausted and wrung out that if she had not been duct-taped to the arms and legs of the chair, she would have simply collapsed and fallen to the floor.

"So let's go over that first meeting again," Quinn said for at least the hundredth time. His voice was patient, measured, maybe a little bored. "Where was it again?"

"Santa Monica. The promenade. I *told* you. His name was . . . ." For a moment, her mind skittered out of the room. Why couldn't she just go home and be with her children? Ollie and Meagan needed her. Charlie needed her. Why didn't Quinn understand that?

"The *name*," Quinn said.

"Hopkins. Frank Hopkins." Each syllable seemed an overwhelming effort. "He's an officer. With MI6."

Quinn had been asking the same questions over and over in different ways for what seemed like days. Of course, the tactics that accompanied these questions kept changing. After using the combination of red and green drugs, Quinn had switched gears and played the father confessor for a while. But he soon tired of that tactic and turned to what seemed like his natural home: waterboarding. Which turned out to be even worse than the drugs.

The chair was attached to the floor with hinged rear legs so that it could be tipped backward. Then one of Quinn's henchmen held a towel firmly over her mouth while a second man poured water over the towel until it was so soaked that breathing became impossible. And then, inexorably, as she kicked and thrashed, the water began leaking into her nose and mouth and she began to drown.

Uncannily, Quinn seemed to know precisely the moment at which she would lose consciousness and just before that moment, he would let her breathe again. As the drowning continued, with brief pauses to let her cough out the water in her lungs or occasionally to vomit, the sensation grew more and more hideous. By now, she felt as though she were falling down a dark path that could end only with her own death and her mind was starting to play tricks on her, as though it were slipping through the cracks of time and space, wending its way back to Los Angeles . . .

She had been warming up for her daily run when a short rumpled man wearing an unambiguously English bespoke suit had risen from a bench, folded the pink sheets of his *Financial Times* under his arm and approached her, saying, "Mrs. Davis, my name is Hopkins. I wonder if I might have a word with you."

Ten minutes later, she was walking down the promenade overlooking a broad sweep of the Pacific Ocean while Frank Hopkins spun a story that had at first seemed ridiculous and surreal.

He had said that her old friend, and lover, Alisher Byko was involved—somewhat tangentially—in a political conspiracy which had the potential to have a major negative impact on the entire Western world. MI6 knew she had been corresponding with Byko— had in fact been intercepting their email exchanges— and needed her to go to Uzbekistan to see him.

According to Hopkins, Byko had gone underground and was unreachable due to some internal political conflicts in Uzbekistan. Her going to meet Byko was apparently the only way the man could be drawn out into public. They promised that Byko would not be harmed, that they just needed to talk to him. But Julie's years of NGO work in faraway places had taught her to be suspicious of intelligence agencies.

Bullshit, she had told him. *Do you seriously think I'm that naive?*

Hopkins had persisted, giving his word that he'd told her everything, but she knew he was lying and walked away. He'd chased after her and reluctantly surrendered more. Thousands and thousands of lives were at stake, he told her. British lives. American lives. European lives. Then he showed her documents and photographs and played tapes of conversations. And finally he'd convinced her that Byko was . . .

No! She forced herself to put all of that out of her mind. If she even allowed herself to think about what Hopkins had told her then Quinn would ferret it out. She had to make that into a blank spot in her mind.

She fast-forwarded to her decision. Hopkins had stressed that there was very little time and he insisted that she not discuss it with anyone, not even her husband. Julie had felt terribly guilty as she spent that evening at home—cooking, playing with the children, engaging in small talk with Charlie. Everything had seemed so excruciatingly normal. But even then, she knew that she had to go.

The truth was, from the very moment she and Charlie had left Uzbekistan, she felt ashamed about their hasty retreat. There had been so much left to do. And Byko was a part of that guilt. Maybe it was a silly thought, a self-aggrandizing exaggeration of her own capacity to bend the world to her will, but she began to think that if she'd stayed perhaps she could have restrained Byko, kept him connected to his better self.

Over the years she had never told Charlie how she felt about leaving Uzbekistan. He, after all, was the one who'd been shot. He was the one who'd been so certain that the conservative path they'd chosen was the right one. And yet she couldn't help think-ing that in his heart of hearts, Charlie might just feel the same way she did—that they had traded a chance to make a difference in the world for a bland, crabbed life of safety and comfort.

Here was a chance to make amends.

And if she was brutally honest with herself—as she was now—she had to admit that her own rest-lessness was part of what had driven her to take this on. She had *burned* to do more in the world, to do something bigger, something that *mattered*.

Of course, sitting here on this soaking-wet chair, the only thing that mattered to her now was find-ing a way back home. To see her children and her husband again.

"Julie! Julie!" Quinn's voice intruded into her reverie, as if he was calling to her from the other side of a dark forest. "Earth to Julie!"

She wanted to respond. She knew there was something terrible coming if she didn't.

But Los Angeles was so much nicer. Why had she ever left? What had she been thinking? If she hadn't engaged in that email flirtation with Byko, none of this would ever have happened . . .

She could feel her body shivering. But it seemed disconnected from her mind, almost as though she were watching someone else suffer.

Then she was holding hands with Ollie and Meagan. They were walking through Disneyland, all of them skipping toward a sprawling castle, music growing louder as they got closer. "It's a Small World After All." Meagan's favorite ride.

Ollie and Meagan laughing. Closer and closer, the music swelling.

It's a small world after all, it's a smaaaaaallll, smaaaaaallll world!

It was warm. The sun was bright. She was happy. They were all so happy. Why hadn't Charlie come, too? That would have been nice.

CHAPTER THIRTY-THREE

It took almost five minutes—getting transferred here and there, connecting to various receptionists and skeptical-sounding duty officers at MI6—until finally a man of some apparent authority got on the line. "This is Hopkins."

Charlie gripped the phone. "My name is Charlie Davis. I'm calling about my wife, Julie Davis. If you don't know who she is, find someone who does."

"Go on," the man said.

"She's been kidnapped by Alisher Byko. She's being held in Uzbekistan."

There was a long pause before the man replied. "And you know this how?"

"I assume you're tracing this call, which means you can see I'm sitting on the shoulder of the A217, smack in the middle of the Fergana Valley."

"You know where she is then?"

"I do," Charlie said. "And I also know where Alisher Byko is. But before we go any further, I need to know how she got herself involved in this mess."

"I'm afraid I don't understand what mess you're speaking of."

"Then maybe you're not the guy I should be talking to."

"I don't mean to sound dense, Mr. Davis, but I know you understand the constraints of operational security for a man in my position. So I'll need to know what the 'mess' is that you're speaking of before I can divulge classified information to you."

Charlie took a deep breath. He needed Hopkins's help to rescue Julie, but before he simply downloaded everything he knew to an agent of MI6, he had to find out exactly what all of this was about. Without information, Charlie had no way of gaining leverage on the man, of keeping him honest, of being able to hold his feet to the fire. But he also had to respect the position Hopkins was in. Which meant it was going to require a gradual trade-off of information and reassurance if Charlie was going to get anywhere with him. It would be a delicate dance.

"Look, Mr. Hopkins, I know you or somebody close to you tried to take Byko down three days ago in Samarkand. I don't know why. But I do know that my wife was used as bait."

"I'm going to need to ask you some questions now, Mr. Davis. So I can be sure you're making this call to me of your own volition. Answer me honestly and I'll know that you're not under any kind of coercion. Are we clear?"

"I get it," Charlie said, "but make it fast."

"What is your daughter's birthday?"

"August nineteenth."

"And her middle name?"

"Victoria."

"And who is she named for?"

"My mother."

"And the color of her bedroom?"

Charlie closed his eyes. For a moment, he almost couldn't remember. And then when he did, when he pictured it, pictured Meagan lying in bed reading one of her favorite bedtime stories, he suddenly found himself choked up.

"The walls are yellow and blue," he managed, clearing his throat. "With lots of animals on them."

"I am glad to hear that you're safe."

"Well, that's very kind of you, but Julie's being tortured for information as we speak. So how about cut through the bullshit and tell me what the hell's going on."

"Very well." Charlie could tell that Hopkins was thinking hard, trying to determine the minimum amount of information he could dribble out in order to placate him. "Your wife had, shall we say, a romantic history with Byko. We knew that and sensed a vulnerability on his part. We've been tracking his legitimate communications for several years. We needed to reach him. We saw that your wife had reconnected with him after some years of being out of touch. We asked her to help us establish contact with him. And that is the sum and substance of her connection to my organization."

"So she had never been associated with MI6 before this?"

"Whatever gave you that idea?"

"Byko," Charlie said. "He claims you recruited her at Cambridge."

"You've seen him?" Hopkins asked, the tone in his voice betraying what felt like titillated surprise.

"He thinks you sent her to Uzbekistan to spy on

him, that you assigned her to get close to me—to get me to plant stories in the local press."

"The paranoid ramblings of a deranged lunatic," Hopkins insisted. "If you met with him, then clearly you must have seen how far gone he is."

Charlie wiped away a bead of sweat from his forehead and noticed that his hand was shaking. He hadn't intended to ask Hopkins these questions, but now here he was doing just that. Had he completely lost sight of who his wife was? Had his trust in her utterly evaporated? That he was now doubting every moment of their relationship? That he was allowing Byko to get into his head?

"I understand you don't know me and have no reason to trust me," Hopkins continued. "But does it really make sense that Julie would be some kind of deep-cover operative for British intelligence while living in suburban Los Angeles? I would hazard the argument that it does not. All I can say is that she was never an agent of the British crown. If it's any consolation, she was quite torn about this whole business. On several occasions she expressed to me that her greatest reservation about the undertaking was not the danger—but the fact that she had to lie to you. I'll also say this—I like your wife very much. I suspect I like her for the same reasons as you. She is a very frank and earnest person. An open book, as it were. Honestly, she would have made a wretched agent over the long term. She managed to pull off this one thing because Byko was blinded by his attraction to her. Beyond that, I'm afraid there's little I can do to reassure you. Now if we can move past this point to the matter at hand, Mr. Davis—"

"The matter at hand is that you dragged an innocent woman into your world and then didn't protect her!"

"We believed she would be safe. And I deeply regret what's happened to her."

"You deeply regret—" Charlie cut himself off, seething. "So she did everything you asked, then the operation went south . . . and you sent her home like she was some flight attendant on her weekend off? She's a mother with children. Her name's in the goddamn phone book! It never occured to you that Byko might suspect her? That he might send some-body after her? Couldn't you have called the CIA or FBI and gotten her some protection?"

There was a moment of awkward silence. "I un-derstand your anger, Mr. Davis. All I can tell you is that we had certain operational constraints and no reason to believe her cover had been blown."

"And what is it that Byko's into that made it so damn important for you to recruit a mother of two young children and put her in this position?"

"I'm afraid that is where the line has to be drawn, Mr. Davis. I cannot breach security on the specifics of this matter."

"Then I guess you don't want to know where Byko is."

There was a slight pause before Hopkins an-swered. Charlie could tell the man was about to go with a new tack.

"I'm assuming the real reason for your call is to find out how we can help you save her?"

"Would you even give a shit?" Charlie barked. "Given that she's just a civilian asset you've used up and thrown away?"

"I do very much give a shit, Mr. Davis. And you

are wasting valuable time by not telling me what you know."

"You're right, Mr. Hopkins. The clock's ticking. And Byko's not going to stay at this location for very long. So you'd better come clean with me now."

Hopkins sighed loudly. "You understand this is a matter of grave international security. And I'm going to trust that I can rely on your integrity as a journalist. What I'm about to tell you cannot be repeated. To anyone."

"You have my word," Charlie said.

"Byko is planning a coup against the Karimov government. Whatever the West's reservations about the current regime, they have been a valuable ally. We need them. And we need to convince Byko that now is not the time."

"Bullshit," Charlie snapped. "Julie despises the regime. She would never have risked her life to help that gang of crooks and thugs."

Hopkins said nothing.

"Five seconds, Mr. Hopkins. Do you want Byko or not? Five. Four. Three. I'm hanging up now—"

"Mr. Davis! Wait." Charlie could hear something verging on panic in Hopkins's voice. "What about this? Tell me Byko's location and I swear on my own children if you go to the embassy, I'll speak to you on a secure line and clarify every—"

"Good-bye, Mr. Hopkins."

"Bombs!"

The line was quiet for a moment. Charlie could almost feel Hopkins's regret and desperation as his voice dropped to a whisper. "Dirty bombs."

"Where?" Charlie asked.

"A variety of major cities across the globe."

"Los Angeles?"

"No. Not Los Angeles."

"What cities then?"

"That is where I must draw the line," Hopkins replied heavily. "You know I've already told you far more than I should have."

"And how do you know that he's planning this?"

"We've tracked shipments of strontium-90, uranium-238 and cesium-137 from his uranium mine to these various cities. But we haven't been able to find or penetrate any of the individual terror cells or pin down the exact targets in those cities. That's why we need Byko."

Charlie ran his hand across his face as he tried to make sense of this enormous revelation. And then something occurred to him. Oliver's birthday.

"Jesus Christ, it's happening tomorrow," Charlie said. "The anniversary of the massacre."

"Where is he, Mr. Davis?"

"What about Julie?"

"If she's with Byko, as you say, we'll find her, too. We've got an SAS team on standby right now. They can be wheels up in a matter of minutes. We'll find her and we'll bring her home. I promise you. Meantime, we'll vector in a satellite to the location you identify. That'll allow us to track them."

Charlie didn't want to admit it—as angry as he felt at the man—but there was something about this Hopkins guy that he liked, something that seemed solid, staunch, reliable. He'd interviewed a lot of spies over the years. And he'd found that some—for want of a better way of putting it—lied with purpose and integrity because it was part of doing their job, while others lied because they enjoyed it. Charlie's guess was that Hopkins was the former type of man.

"Okay," Charlie said. "Here's what I've got for you . . ."

Charlie gave Hopkins the location of Byko's compound and waited while Hopkins's team vectored in the satellite.

It took nearly ten minutes before Hopkins came back on the line. "Brilliant. We've got the satellite up."

"Can you see the compound?"

"We can," Hopkins replied. "And what look like a half-dozen armored vehicles parked in some kind of atrium."

"They're still there," Charlie said, exhaling gratefully.

"It appears that way. If they move now, we'll be able to track them."

"So you're sending in a tactical unit?"

"As soon as we're off the phone, I'll scramble the SAS team."

"You'd better not be screwing with me," Charlie warned.

"Mr. Davis, it must be clear to you at this point that our interests are entirely aligned. I have no reason to screw with you."

"Nevertheless," Charlie continued, "if I don't hear something from you in the next six hours, I'll be calling the Associated Press and giving them everything we just talked about."

"You gave me your word," Hopkins replied.

"Yes I did, as I'm sure you gave Julie your word that you could protect her."

"Mr. Davis, this is becoming quite preposterous. I can assure you—"

"I don't need assurance, Mr. Hopkins. I need in-surance. And that's what I've got in my back pocket."

"I understand you loud and clear, Mr. Davis. And you *will* hear from me. But please understand, I can't tell you what Byko is going to do with your wife in the next few hours. All I can promise is that the men we'll send to save her are second to none, and if she's still alive, we'll get her out of there."

"Well, get going then," Charlie ordered.

Without reply, Hopkins was gone and Charlie set the phone down on the seat next to him.

They were professionals. They would do what needed to be done.

It was almost over.

CHAPTER THIRTY-FOUR

Hopkins hung up the phone, his eyes jumping to the huge screen at the front of the War Room. He was so angry he could barely concentrate on what he saw in front of him. He had never really expected that Byko would reach out to Los Angeles to snatch Julie, but he'd known that retribution against her was possible, and he'd asked Bryce to organize a protection detail for her until Byko had been neutralized.

Bryce had categorically refused.

His explanation was that Julie Davis bore dual UK–American citizenship. As an American citizen, she was prohibited by U.S. law from acting as an agent of any foreign power. If he alerted the FBI about her status as an agent for MI6, he would not only risk a diplomatic brouhaha, he might be opening the door to espionage and treason charges against Julie.

Then what about authorizing an MI6 team to protect her? Hopkins had asked.

This request, Bryce had scoffed, was even more foolish. If the team was blown or attracted the attention of American authorities, not only would

Julie be at risk for prosecution, but so would the British agents.

Hopkins had contended rather forcefully that these arguments were unpersuasive, that with three American cities in the crosshairs of Byko's bomb plot, even the territorial Yanks wouldn't be foolish enough to rush about prosecuting agents of allied nations.

Bryce had promptly cut him off at the knees: *No protection for the Davis woman, too much at stake, too much risk, debate over, period.*

Hopkins had suspected that Bryce's real rationale had gone unstated. The discovery of the Byko plot had been entirely MI6's work. Assuming the plot were to be foiled, it would be the intelligence coup of the decade and Bryce didn't want any excuse to spread the glory to foreign agencies—most particularly to the Americans. Moreover, any explanation about Julie Davis's role in the botched Samarkand takedown would raise questions about Bryce's decision making. Which would open the door for the Americans, with their limitless resources, to bludgeon their way into the investigation and ultimately claim the credit that might appertain to it. In that scenario, MI6 would play the role of the pathetic bungler, its incompetence only swept away when the big dogs of the American intelligence community came in to save the day. That was a narrative Bryce would never allow.

Ergo, Julie Davis was expendable.

Hopkins felt a burn of anger and shame. He was the one who'd gone to Los Angeles, he was the one who'd preyed on her ideals, he was the one who'd convinced her to sacrifice, he was the one who'd told her not to confide in her husband. And now the man was calling him from the bowels of Central Asia, having risked his own life to find her.

It was up to Hopkins to do whatever he could to correct the mess.

He picked up the phone, rang Colonel Ian Sturbridge, commander of the Special Air Service in Hereford.

"Hullo, Hopkins," Sturbridge said.

"Go time," Hopkins said. "We've got a fix on Byko. I'm sending you telemetry and satellite as we speak."

"My chap's got it coming in right now."

"Outstanding. We're still gathering intel on the location. We'll brief you in the air."

"Roger that. I'll ring off now. We'll be wheels up in twelve minutes."

Sturbridge was Hopkins's kind of soldier. No hand-holding, no bollocks. And the SAS was the mold from which every group of commandos in the world—the SEALs, the Delta Force, GSG 9, you name it—was descended. If anybody could get Byko and save Julie Davis, it was Sturbridge and his team.

"Get me Bryce," he said to the comms specialist. The young man nodded and within a minute, Hopkins was on the line with Bryce. Hopkins gave him a quick update on Byko, saving the news about Julie Davis's abduction until the end.

"Let's not lose focus," Bryce said tartly, cutting Hopkins off as he speculated about various strategies for finding and saving her. "The Davis woman's safety is rightly a concern. But job one is Byko. Clear?"

Barely more than a few hours ago, Bryce had been

tearing him a new one about the death of Marcus Vaughan. And now, suddenly, the life of an MI6 asset—an innocent civilian no less—was merely an ancillary priority.

"I told you we needed to protect her," Hopkins fumed. "But we abandoned the woman in order to advance your political agenda. If you think I'll sit still this time while we let the woman die—so you can get your peerage—you'd best think again."

There was a long silence. Finally Bryce spoke, his voice mild as milk. "Did I just hear you say what I think I heard you say?"

If Hopkins wanted to commit professional suicide, accusing his boss of trading a woman's life for a title of nobility was certainly a rather fine way of doing the job. But at this point, he didn't care.

"You heard me quite correctly, sir. We're not going to throw this woman to the wolves. Not as long as I'm in this service."

"Nobody said anything about throwing her to the wolves," Bryce replied, actually sounding intimidated. "I was merely reminding you that our number one priority must be to contain Byko."

"That goes without saying, but I would be remiss if I didn't warn you that her husband is well aware of her role in this affair and he will be a liability for all of us if we don't do right by her."

"Her husband . . . ?"

"Is a journalist of some renown. And quite a bit of reach. I've got him under control for now, but he'll need to see results."

Bryce exhaled sourly and Hopkins knew he had won the point.

"We'll need permission for the SAS to make the

hit on Byko," Bryce conceded. "After that disaster last week, we can't allow the Uzbeks to derail this train again. I'll contact the Prime Minister directly. I'm sure a call from the PM to Karimov will sort it out."

"Good. RAF transport should have SAS entering Uzbek airspace at 2100 hours Greenwich Mean Time."

"Excellent. I'll join you in the War Room as soon as I'm off the phone with the PM."

Hopkins hung up and stared at the screen again. There in front of him was the satellite image of Alisher Byko's Fergana Valley compound.

If Byko was in fact still there, then they had him.

They finally had him.

CHAPTER THIRTY-FIVE

What the hell do you mean you can't find them?" Byko yelled into the phone.

The security guard at the other end of the line answered nervously, "We can't get Arman or Victor on the radio and there's no sign of the Escalade, sir."

Byko checked his watch. It had been almost an hour since he'd allowed Charlie to leave with his two men. They should have reached the missile complex by now.

"What about the surveillance cameras?" Byko demanded.

"They don't cover that portion of the road, sir. We thought we would have picked them up on the approach about fifteen minutes ago. That's when we started radioing to them."

"Well have you sent out a patrol?"

"Of course, sir. So far, we've seen nothing, sir, I—"

"What?" Byko barked impatiently. He could hear the crackle of a radio and voices at the other end of the line.

"I'm sorry, sir," his guard said. "Our patrol just

found a piece of the Escalade. It looks like it went off the side of the road and tumbled into the river."

Byko felt a catch in his breath. "Did you find the car?"

"Looks like it sank, sir. We can't tell if anyone made it out."

"Keep looking!" Byko hissed. "And send a patrol to the other side of the river."

He hung up the phone, mind racing.

What was it Charlie had said to him?

"I'm a little in awe of you, Alisher"?

Had Davis played him? Was it possible he'd somehow managed an escape? But he was handcuffed! It couldn't be.

Three minutes later, he got the call. The second patrol had found Arman's body beneath a pile of rubble at the edge of the river.

Byko smashed his phone against the wall, beating it until there was nothing left in his hand. He noted with clinical detachment that his knuckles were bleeding profusely then walked swiftly up the stairs into the communications room and grabbed the ancient phone. It was a hard line connecting him to Quinn's location by a buried cable that had been installed back in the Soviet days. Because it was a simple copper wire buried forty feet belowground, designed to weather a direct nuclear strike, no one on the planet could pluck the signal out of the air, off a satellite, or out of a fiber-optic cable connection running through some NSA outpost in Turkey. It was as secure as secure lines got.

"Get me Quinn!"

Byko waited impatiently a few moments before a voice on the other end of the line greeted him.

"She's not going to give us any more," Quinn said. "Should I go ahead and kill her?"

"Shut up and listen to me," Byko carped. "Davis got away."

"*Away* away? Or is he just running around out in the bushes somewhere?"

"We don't know. We're scouring the area but so far there's no sign of him."

"You know the minute that sneaky son of a bitch gets to a phone, he'll call the American State Department. It'll take Karimov a couple of hours to deploy an air assault, but that's not who you have to worry about. Once State calls the NSA, you've got about seven minutes before somebody vectors in a satellite."

"Bloody hell," Byko said, all too aware that he'd picked up that expression at Cambridge.

"We need to get out of here," Quinn continued. "All of us. Kill the girl, rendezvous at Location Alpha. Everything's prepared. We're less than twenty-four hours from—"

"You say you're done with her?" Byko prodded.

There was a brief pause. Byko could tell that Quinn didn't like being interrupted, but he was paying the man a small fortune and he could scarcely give a shit.

"She was an errand girl," Quinn answered. "Bait. Nothing more."

"And she knows how much . . . ?"

"They told her you were up to no good, but never gave her any of the details."

Byko hesitated. He had a hard time imagining Julie betraying him and putting herself at such risk without something more.

"Don't do anything," Byko said. "I want to talk to her myself one more time."

Byko could hear Quinn's doubt and disapproval in the silence that hung between them, but he felt no need to offer the hired hand any explanations.

"I'll be there in less than an hour," Byko promised. "We'll take the tunnels." He hung up the phone and turned to Homer the tech. "Set the self-destruct protocol."

"Yes, sir." Homer typed rapidly into his keyboard. After a moment a set of red numbers appeared on every screen. In three minutes, all of the computers and video equipment in this room would be destroyed.

"There's quite a lot of explosives involved here, Mr. Byko," the young tech said. "We'd better hurry."

Hasan flashed a look at Byko—eliminate him? Byko shook his head; the kid was still useful. For now.

Thirty seconds later, Byko's personal Esacalade was tearing through a concrete tunnel that would transport them to the other end of the complex.

Even if the CIA or MI6 had a satellite watching the compound, they would have no idea that Byko was escaping underground.

CHAPTER THIRTY-SIX

Hopkins assessed the faces on his bank of screens: the director of the CIA, top men and women from the FBI, Homeland Security, and the NSA alongside reps from the intelligence agencies of Germany, Sweden, France, Japan and Australia. This was the group that had been working together for months to try to avert Byko's plot. Now, they were about to hear something that none of them would have expected.

"I've some remarkable news," Hopkins began. "An asset of our agency has located Byko and we have an SAS team en route to Uzbekistan as we speak. We have TopSat II tasked to Byko's most recent location and every reason to believe he's still there."

These were stoic people by nature, so their murmurs of approval may as well have been whooping and hollering.

"As you know," he continued, "our satellite resources are dwarfed by our American friends. Would it be possible to put a wider-range bird over the location, Eric? It's rather a sprawling facility."

"As soon as you send us the coordinates," said Eric Nielsen, head of the NSA.

"Done," said Hopkins.

"If I might add my two cents . . ." The face of CIA director Patrick Freehold reappeared on the main screen. "I think we all have implicit confidence in the skills of the SAS. But the U.S. has significant assets in the region. I suspect we could task a team from Kanibadam more quickly."

From the very beginning it had been clear that the U.S. resented MI6's leadership on this. But so far they had been unable to bring anything to the party that would dislodge MI6's position at the center of the effort to stop Byko.

"I think not," Hopkins said evenly. "Special Air Service has been preparing for this operation for weeks and we've kept them on standby. Every pump is primed. As I say, they're already airborne."

"I presume," Freehold pursued, "that you have Uzbek approval for the mission?"

"They jumped us through those hoops for the abortive mission last week," Hopkins said breezily. "All we need is the word from Karimov."

"If a call from our President would help . . ."

"Our PM is making that same call as we speak. The matter is very well in hand," Hopkins said, then moved on to a series of other issues, anticipating what the group would need to do once Byko was in custody and—presumably—giving up actionable intelligence about his operation.

Hopkins had been immersed in the call for nearly half an hour when it occurred to him that Bryce was taking an unusually long time to get to the meeting. Normally this was the sort of thing he did not like to delegate and nothing pleased him more than having a rare opportunity to outmaneuver the Americans.

Just as Hopkins began to worry, the red light over the far door blinked on, the door opened and Bryce entered. Hopkins's relief quickly froze into a lump of ice in the pit of his stomach: Bryce's face was ashen.

"Pardon me a moment," Hopkins said to the screen. He made a slashing motion across his throat, signaling for the comms tech to mute the microphones, then crossed the room to intercept his superior.

"We can't bloody reach Karimov," Bryce said.

Hopkins frowned. "What do you mean we can't reach him?"

"He's on a hunting trip or something. Falconry, oryxes, some bloody thing in the mountains near Kyrgyzstan. They claim they don't know his exact location, can't reach him by phone or radio."

Hopkins was appalled. Karimov knew that the Byko situation was at a full boil right now. He should have been waiting by the phone. And now he was *hunting*? With no radio or phone contact? Paranoid dictators never lose contact with their own levers of power. *Never.*

"Bloody hell," Hopkins said. "Do you want to tell them?"

Bryce looked at the silent screen in front of the War Room. "You do it, Frank," he said. "I need to stay in touch with the Foreign Office. We'll keep banging away of course . . ." He swallowed, his mouth twisting sourly. Then he turned abruptly and left the room.

Bryce was never there when it came time to dole out bad news.

Hopkins nodded to the comms tech, then sat back down at the chair in front of the video camera.

"What's the good word?" Freehold asked.

For a moment, Hopkins was so angry he couldn't even speak. But there was only one way to read this.

"I'm afraid that Karimov has fucked us."

CHAPTER THIRTY-SEVEN

Charlie ordered a glass of tea and a sandwich from the harelipped waiter, then sat for a moment in a daze. He was in a town just big enough to have one café—a sort of Uzbek version of a convenience store. The tiny mud-brick building had three tables sitting on the dirt courtyard, a few stacks of canned goods, a pile of wrinkly old apples and a very large number of flies. The town was just a dozen miles from Byko's compound and Charlie had wondered if some of his spies or security force might be in the vicinity. But other than the waiter, Charlie seemed to be alone.

From the moment he'd found out about Julie's kidnapping, Charlie had been trying to find some duly constituted authority which would use its power and reach to help him. Now he finally had. So the only thing to do now was wait and pray.

He took the girl's pink diamond-studded phone out of his pocket and dialed his house. It rang twice before he realized it would be four in the morning there and he would wake everyone. He hung up and thought about them. What they must be going through. Were they even able to sleep? Was Meagan bounding into their bedroom looking for Mommy and Daddy? He hoped that Becca was sleeping upstairs in his and Julie's bed, and that she remembered to leave the hall light on, and the bedroom door open, in case Meagan came looking for her, and that Ollie slept with his Curious George curled up next to him.

He ached to talk to them, to see them, to hold them. But every time he imagined it, the fantasy quickly went sour. Because Julie wasn't alongside him.

Charlie looked around at the miserable little town, trying to shake the sinking feeling that it was all going to shit. The village was a cluster of run-down brick buildings and houses that gave way to cotton fields stretching off in all directions. In the distance, a man in traditional Uzbek garb was urging a donkey cart forward, whipping savagely at the swaybacked donkey with a thin stick. But the donkey seemed uninterested—or incapable—of going any faster, the rain of blows nothing more than an exercise in pointless cruelty.

Charlie didn't know if it was his hunger—he hadn't eaten in a day and a half—or the sight of that man beating the innocent animal, but he suddenly felt light-headed. As if everything was spinning.

And his mind began to taunt him. If everything Hopkins had said was true—that dirty bombs were going to be set off in locations across the world—then far too much was at stake for MI6 to place Julie's life anywhere near the top of their priority list. If an SAS team happened to hit the location where Julie was, they would undoubtedly do their best to save her, but what if Byko had already moved her?

Or if they were in separate locations? Would MI6 really split the SAS team in two? When push came to shove, no matter what Charlie had threatened, would they really beat the bushes to find out where Julie was?

Charlie didn't like the answers to any of these questions and he couldn't help thinking about some of the accusations that had been hurled at him recently. Both Byko and Faruz had made essentially the same point—that Charlie was a self-serving coward who had cut and run when the going got tough, retreating to the easy shelter and security of America.

There were many times, back in Los Angeles, especially in those first couple of years, when Charlie had thought about Palonchi Ursalov and her sons, and all of those demonstrators in the Square, and he'd beaten himself up pretty nicely for giving up on them. But as time went on, he'd been able to push away that guilt, to focus on his new life and his new family. He'd told himself he was entitled to have that life, that God hadn't put him on the earth to liberate Uzbekistan, that it was a kind of hubris to even contemplate taking on all of that.

But now that he was back here, he had to face it. The man who had been standing in his shoes the last six years was a scared man, a reactive man, a man just trying to survive.

Charlie picked up the phone and made a call.

"Garman," he said, "it's me."

"Charlie!" The mercenary sounded enormously relieved—and a bit surprised. "You made it! Damn, I was worried about you."

Charlie gave Garman a quick update about what

had happened at the bathhouse, along with a thumbnail account of his escape and his conversation with Hopkins detailing Julie's role as bait in the blown takedown.

"Holy shit!" Garman said. "That finally makes sense. I had heard that Byko came out of hiding. I couldn't figure why. Of course, the Uzbeks blew it."

"The Uzbeks?"

"The famous Twenty-seventh Air Assault Brigade. The Brits must have had to defer to them. It being their home turf and all."

That made sense and actually made Charlie feel a bit better about the competence of Hopkins and his people.

"Anyway," Charlie said, "the main thing is that MI6 is on the job now." He hesitated for a moment, waiting to see if Garman would comment. "How long do you think it'll take for an SAS team to get to her?"

"Depends where they're deploying from. Let's say they're flying from Hereford on a C-17—that's a cargo jet that cruises at about four hundred and fifty knots—you're talking six hours absolute minimum. If they're coming from Afghanistan, on the other hand, they could be there in a couple of hours. But the real delay is likely to come from the Uzbek bureaucracy."

Charlie thought about it. If there was even a shred of plausibility to Karimov's posture as one of the West's biggest allies in the war on terror, surely he would be waiting by the phone right now, looking to give MI6 all the help he could.

Or . . .

Charlie suddenly had a horrible thought.

"Charlie? Charlie, you still there?"

"Back up a sec. Byko's takedown—you said the Uzbeks screwed it up. What *exactly* happened there?"

"The story I heard was that Byko was at the Café Odillion near the Kukcha Mosque—"

"I know the place. It's been around since the Soviet era."

"Right. So anyway, he's sitting there in broad daylight, apparently with Julie. Next thing you know, two or three companies from the Twenty-seventh are converging on the place. As you can imagine, it's total chaos. They're landing choppers in the street, throwing up checkpoints, sticking guns in everybody's faces, stopping traffic. Everybody's freaking out thinking they're about to get scooped up and tossed in jail. Next thing you know there's a ring of two hundred guys with AKs pointed at the Odillion. They smash the door down, rough up the maître d', chuck everybody on the floor . . . And Byko's gone."

"But that café is at the end of a little cul-de-sac just off the Mannon Uygur. There's a street in front and an alley in the back. Two ways in, two ways out. They could have surrounded that place with twenty secret policemen and a couple of German shepherds. Why would they send two hundred paratroopers in helicopters?"

"Typical totalitarian overkill."

But Charlie had more information than Garman. And he saw the whole picture with crystalline clarity. It was all a show. Karimov *wanted* Byko to get away. It sounded absurd at first—Byko might be the one guy in the entire country Karimov was afraid of—but Karimov was and always had been a master chess player. Over the years, the West's willingness to overlook Uzbek intransigence, inefficiency and graft had worn thin, and as the war on terror wound down, Karimov's usefulness was inevitably waning. But if Byko could pull off his attack (and Karimov could claim that he'd done everything he could to try to stop it), then suddenly Uzbekistan would be catapulted to the front lines of the war on terror redux. Imagine the billions of dollars Karimov could squeeze out of the West in order to "clean up" the extremists within his borders. What a gorgeous piece of geopolitical jujitsu. Not only would Byko be completely marginalized as a player on the Uzbek stage, not only would Karimov practically get buried in Western money and military assistance, but he'd have the perfect excuse to clean house and wipe out any stray enemies whom he hadn't squashed in the past few years.

If all of that was true, and Charlie felt quite certain it was, then Karimov would come up with some way to cock-block the entire MI6 operation.

"They're never going to make it," Charlie said, half to himself.

"What's that?"

"Julie. She's got maybe another couple of hours before she's outlived her usefulness to Byko. SAS is never going to get there in time. If at all."

"You don't know that for sure. Anyway, there's not much you can do about it."

"I'm going to have to go back there and bust her out."

"All due respect, Charlie—"

"Give me some guys who can handle themselves.

I've got eight grand and change as a down payment. Plus, Julie's family's got money—"

"Hold on a second. Okay? Just hold on."

Charlie could feel the rationalizations coming.

"This isn't about money, Charlie. There are practical issues here. I'm a professional. You can't just grab a couple of yahoos with guns and charge into fortified locations full of armed men. These things take meticulous preparation. Floor plans, maps, transpo, special weapons, explosives, guys with very particular skills . . ."

"It isn't just Julie!" Charlie blurted out. He'd been trying to heed Hopkins's warnings about disclosure, but now he had to appeal to Garman's morality. And to hope that he still had some whiff of humanity left in him. "The reason MI6 wants Byko isn't to stop a coup. It's because Byko is the mastermind of a plot to kill hundreds of thousands of people. And not here. I'm talking New York, London, Paris . . ."

This last part Charlie was making up, but given what Hopkins had told him, he thought those cities were a pretty safe bet.

"I don't know all the details," Charlie said. "But it's happening tomorrow, and trust me, it'll make 9/11 look like a walk in the park."

"Jesus Christ," Garman muttered.

"Julie was working for MI6. They recruited her to draw Byko out. She went into it eyes open, knowing what was at risk. Because she had to do something to try to stop it."

This was Charlie's last, best hope. Hooking into Garman's sense of chivalry and shame. After all, how could a man like Garman stand on the sidelines and do nothing when untrained Julie Davis had thrown her pound of flesh into the game? And as Charlie recounted what Julie had done, said it aloud for the first time since uncovering all of her lies, he began to understand her choice. To feel for her. To admire her.

Charlie thought for certain he had gotten through to the mercenary because when he'd finished, Garman was silent. So he pressed on. "Byko and Julie are at the same place. We go in there to get her, we get him, too. You put the screws on him, we save the world."

"Listen, Charlie." Garman sounded anguished. "My wife's Uzbek. My kids are Uzbek. This is my *home* now. You're asking me to put my family on the chopping block for what sounds like a serious no-win proposition. Truly, I wish I could help you. But it's just too little too late at this point . . . I gotta go, Charlie. I'm sorry."

And the line went dead.

Charlie set the phone down slowly. Just ten minutes ago, it had seemed like the cavalry was cresting the hill and everything was going to be okay.

But he saw now that it was nothing but a mirage.

Everything was on him. As it had been from the start.

PART III

DESTINY

CHAPTER THIRTY-EIGHT

As Byko's Escalade sped through the dark tunnel twenty feet below the surface of the ground, his young communications specialist quickly connected his gear to the onboard cameras and monitors that could be viewed from the rear of the vehicle.

Within a matter of minutes, the display was live.

Lipstick cameras had been hung at the various target locations—covertly taped onto telephone poles, set into holes drilled out of mortar joints or wedged beneath flowerpots. The young tech wordlessly handed the remote control to Byko then seated himself on a small fold-out chair built into one of the car doors.

Byko clicked from view to view to view. There was Hanover. There was London. There was Minneapolis. There was New York.

He smiled as the people on each screen scuttled around, full of the importance of their days, rushing from here to there on some little errand or other—pushing a mail cart, delivering flowers, walking to a deposition, chastising subordinates for some minor oversight—unaware that if they were in this same place tomorrow, their lives would be ended.

And Byko saw no sign of surveillance teams posted anywhere, no collections of heavily armed men with German shepherds, no unusual blast barricades or traffic barriers. Everything was still looking good.

"Are you ready, sir?"

Byko glanced at the young tech. "Not quite." He wanted to take in the city scenes a bit more.

The tiny cameras transmitted amazingly clear and vivid pictures. Here was a lovely young woman, her breasts straining at her thin blouse; there a self-important-looking man with a briefcase and a tailored suit; here a woman limping along on a bad leg, stopping to massage her swollen ankle; there a young man who looked as though he might be rushing to make his first day of work.

One might be tempted to pity them . . . if one didn't understand that their destruction would, in the end, lead to a world that was not so full of pain and ugliness and degradation.

"All right then," Byko said, nodding to the technician.

The young man clicked away feverishly on his laptop, arranging for the transmissions.

The connection between Byko and the people he was about to speak to was known as a discontinuous link—a high-tech version of the trick used in old kidnapper movies where two telephones were ducttaped together in a safe house so that the phone company couldn't trace the call. Only, in this case, instead of duct tape, they'd used a specially designed computer in a safe house somewhere in Bangladesh.

Or maybe it was in Karachi. Or perhaps Lithuania. There were twenty-three safe houses around the world, each used only once, randomly chosen by computer, each wired to be destroyed as soon as the phone call was completed.

"Start with London?" the techs asked.

"It doesn't matter," Byko replied.

The tech typed a few commands into his laptop. Then Rasul, the leader of the London cell, appeared on the screen attached to the driver's seat back.

Byko greeted him calmly then asked, "Is everything arranged?"

"It is." Rasul swallowed nervously. "But what about Samarkand? I heard you were almost captured just four days ago. I am very concerned."

Byko laughed pleasantly and waved away Rasul's worries. "Everything isn't what it appears to be. I was never in danger. Not for a minute."

Rasul frowned. "Are you saying—"

"Let's not get distracted. Nothing has changed. The operation is still entirely on track."

"But what about the targets? If they know where you are, they might know where *we* are."

"You are ahead of yourself, my friend. Do you even know the targets yet?"

"I assume someone on the ground does, sir. And it—"

Byko smiled condescendingly. "Only I know the targets. In just a few hours, you will know them, too. But not until the time is right."

"But we won't have enough time to prepare if you still want to do this tomorrow."

Byko gave Rasul a long, hard look, then leaned forward and softened his voice. "We are on the verge of something magnificent. *You* are on the verge of something magnificent. Your courage and resolve have never failed you. They will not fail you now. Have faith, my brother. Tomorrow we shall prevail."

Byko thumbed the remote. The face of Idris, his man in New York, appeared. Byko took one look at him and knew he'd be facing the same withering of will.

It took Byko nearly the entire drive through the tunnel to talk his men down from their various psychological ledges. By the time he was finished, his stomach was churning and he felt fidgety, as if bugs were crawling under his skin—the sensation signaling that he was on the verge of losing control over himself.

Why was it so hard to find decent men?

He did a line of coke off the back of his hand. Better now.

CHAPTER THIRTY-NINE

This was where it had all started—the village of Radgovir. It was here that Charlie had seen the mutilated body of Palonchi Ursalov's boy, it was here that Charlie had written the story which catapulted the destiny of the Uzbek people toward Andijan.

Charlie's initial instinct had been to try to recruit fighters from one of the villages where Julie had worked six years ago. But those villages were all too far from the Fergana Valley to do him any good in the short span of time that he had. So he'd surveyed his map, looking for a village where the people might remember him. As it turned out, Ragdovir was only eleven kilometers from that dumpy café. And it was a place where they would surely never forget him.

Crowded into the mayor's living room was a knot of three dozen men. Hollow cheeked, traditionally dressed in the long shirt dresses of the region, beards down to the middle of their chests, they stared soberly at Charlie, faces blank, bodies unmoving. The room was dark, lit only by kerosene lamps and the light from one tiny window. It smelled of unwashed bodies, cumin and smoke.

On the drive, winding up the foothills of the Tian Shan Mountains, Charlie had rehearsed what he would say over and over again. But now, standing before them, seeing some of their eyes, filled as they were with judgment and suspicion, Charlie realized there were fences to mend before he could even contemplate asking for their assistance.

He would have preferred to speak to them in their native Uzbek but for something as delicate as this he had to go with his superior Russian.

"Many of you remember, I came here six years ago because I wanted to help you. And I made promises that we could do something together to change your country." He scanned the room and cleared his throat. "I'm sure some of you feel I left before completing the job, that I didn't finish what I came here to do. Some of you may not know that I was shot that day in Andijan and I felt I had no choice but to return to my own country. But there has not been a single day that has passed in the last six years when I haven't thought about you people and ached for your suffering." Charlie paused and surveyed the room.

Just then, a young man slipped into the back. At first, Charlie didn't recognize him in the gloomy half darkness, but then he saw his milky left eye: it was Salim. He was nineteen or twenty now, the same age his older brother had been when he was murdered.

Charlie nodded to him, then continued. "My wife never wanted to leave here. If it had been up to her, she would have stayed. Some of you have heard of the work she did in villages much like this one. Because she loves this country and wanted it to become a better place. Last week, she came back here and risked her life to stop a man who will only make things harder for everyone in this country."

He tried to make eye contact with the men in the room. "I need your help now to save her. But I'm not coming here with my hand out. I will pay. I will pay five hundred dollars to any man who comes with me."

A soft rustle spread across the room. Heads turned. Voices murmured. To most of these men, five hundred dollars was more than a year's income.

"And what do you need then?" asked one of the elders.

"My wife was being held at a compound just south of here. If she's still there, she'll be guarded by professionals. But if—"

"What is this compound? Whose compound is it?" This was a toughed-eyed clan chief named Khalil.

"It belongs to Alisher Byko," Charlie said.

At the mention of Byko's name several men got up and headed for the door.

Charlie plowed on. "I understand that Byko is a powerful man, but we will have the advantage of surprise. And he'll have no way to track any of you back to this town."

The murmurs became derisive and the men filtered out of the room en masse.

"Wait a minute!" Charlie barked at them. "Just wait." There was an urgency in his voice that stopped them. "There's something else," he said. "There is more at stake here than just my wife.

Far more at stake." He surveyed the men's faces. "I am not supposed to tell you this, to tell anyone this . . ." He could feel everyone in the room tense. "Alisher Byko is planning a large-scale terrorist attack against the United States and Europe. If he succeeds, not only will hundreds of thousands of people be killed, but you and the rest of your people will pay the price for it. You can only imagine what President Karimov will do once he has an excuse like that to clamp down on 'extremists' in this region. That is why Byko remains at large. Because Karimov wants him to get away with it. Karimov can't wait to have another reason to take away more of your freedoms . . ."

Charlie felt sure this time that he had them. "So I'm asking you now, come with me. Together we will find Byko and bring him to justice. And we will prove to the world that the people of this region are a proud people, a worthy people, a noble people. This is what I was hoping to do when I was here six years ago, but now there is really a chance. To do something for the world and something for your-selves. Please. Come with me."

For a long moment, no one spoke. Charlie could see that many of the men were moved. But then Khalil spoke.

"We have no reason to believe this man. And even if what he says is true, Alisher Byko has his own private army. The women of this village will all end up widows, the children orphans. What he wants . . . is simply not possible. Not for any amount of money." He looked at the men and issued what might as well have been a command. "Now we go."

Charlie's heart sank as one by one the men headed

out and disappeared into the village square. Khalil waited by the door, apparently making sure that no one was fool enough to disobey him. Only when the exodus was nearly complete did Khalil notice that the one-eyed teenager was still here.

"Salim!" Khalil called out sternly. He didn't have to say anything more. The kid rose reluctantly and dragged himself toward the exit. But there were four others who did remain.

"They're grown men," Charlie insisted. "They can do as they please."

Khalil looked them over for a long moment, as if deciding which tack he would take, then spit on the ground and warned Charlie, "If these four never come back, we will all be better off." And with that, Khalil took his leave.

Charlie turned to face the men who'd stayed. They were thin, wiry and disreputable looking with scraggly beards and torn clothes. Clearly the dregs of the town. But they were armed with battered AK-47s and at this point Charlie knew beggars couldn't be choosers.

"All right then," he said and started counting out the money.

"Not five hundred," one of them said in Russian. "Five thousand."

Charlie looked up. The man, apparently the de facto leader, smiled without mirth, revealing all three of the teeth that were left in his mouth. "Apiece."

Charlie shook his head. "Not possible."

"Is possible," said the man. "You want your wife, you want stop these killings . . . is very possible."

A long session of bargaining commenced. Tempers flared, threats were issued, automatic weapons were waved, and once the four men even made a feint toward the door. But Charlie had spent enough time in Uzbekistan to understand that the men had to go through this exercise, to make sure Charlie had left no money on the table.

In the end the terms were made: two thousand dollars cash per man. One thousand now, one thousand upon completion of the mission with the men agreeing to supply their own weapons and transport. Charlie shook hands with each man in turn and suddenly everyone was smiling and laughing, the best of friends.

As they exited the building, Charlie heard furtive footsteps behind them. He whirled, half expecting to be jumped.

It was Salim.

"I'm coming with you," he said.

The hired men laughed, but Salim ignored them, pointing at something on the hillside above the town. "You see that?"

It took Charlie a moment to make out what he was being shown: it was a Coke bottle, perched on a rock. Over a hundred yards away.

Salim lifted his ancient, battered Soviet bolt-action rifle and took careful aim. The rifle went off with a sharp crack and an explosion of foul-smelling smoke. The Coke bottle exploded in a shower of glistening pieces of glass.

"I can help you," Salim said with disarming confidence.

"No," Charlie said, "I can't allow it."

Then something caught Charlie's attention, just beyond Salim. A woman stepping out of the shadows. She was wrapped in a dark burka, only her eyes visible. But even after six years, those eyes were burned into his mind. They belonged to Palonchi Ursalov, Salim's mother.

For a moment no one moved.

There was much Charlie would have liked to say to her, but she simply nodded then turned and walked back into her house.

She'd given her blessing.

"I can help you," the boy said again.

Charlie hesitated, then got into his stolen car.

"Let's go then," he said to the kid. "You ride with me."

CHAPTER FORTY

Quinn was waiting for Byko in the large vaulted parking area at the end of the tunnel. A few small, innocuous buildings aboveground marked the location, which was part of the same former Soviet nuclear complex as the bathhouse Byko had left nearly an hour earlier. The moment Byko stepped out of the Escalade, Quinn launched in.

"I have her primed and ready for you, but I honestly can't imagine what else there is to get out of her."

Byko walked right past Quinn, in no mood to be second-guessed. "I'm telling you she's not a pro," Quinn hounded. "Let's just kill her and get out of here."

Byko marched toward the entrance to what was once the command center of the Russian complex, explaining to Quinn, "I talked to my sources in the government on the way over. No military units are on standby and there's no activity among any of the special police tactical squads."

"That doesn't mean anything. The Americans could be sending in a Delta team from Qarshi as we speak. They're not going to wait around for Karimov to get his act together. Not after what happened in Samarkand."

"I need to talk to her," Byko insisted.

Quinn kept following. "By my count, it's eighty-three minutes since Davis escaped. Figuring it took him half an hour to get to the A217 and another five, ten minutes to get through to one of the intel agencies, our cover was blown forty, forty-five minutes ago. All of this is my way of saying we don't have any more goddamn time."

Byko was sick of the mercenary's insolence. He wordlessly stepped past him, then snapped his fingers at one of his own bodyguards, signaling him to open the huge steel blast door that linked the parking area to the former command center.

Byko blasted through the door, entering a long, grim hallway made of reinforced concrete. At the end of the hallway, he climbed a flight of stairs that fed into a more finished part of the complex, this part resembling the interior of a pleasant but windowless house. Another hallway led to Julie's cell, its heavy steel door flanked by two armed guards. At the sight of Byko, they opened the door.

Julie sat slumped over in the heavy wooden torture chair, shivering hard, her arms and legs attached by Velcro straps. She looked terrible—her face pale and blotchy, her hair uncombed and unwashed, her clothes soaking wet. Byko wasn't sure what Quinn had been doing to her—but he knew waterboarding must have been on the menu.

Julie looked up at him blankly, almost as though she had never seen him before.

"Bring her some bloody soup or something!" Byko shouted out the door. "And a blanket!"

She moaned softly as he gently unfastened her straps, so weak that he had to support her with his own weight to keep her from sliding out of the chair.

When one of the guards entered the room with a bowl of soup and a coarse wool blanket, Byko wrapped her up, then fed her himself, spooning the warm soup into her mouth as if she was a baby. She was so ravenous that Byko suspected she hadn't been fed in days.

Bloody Quinn. He was excellent at his job but Byko was beginning to realize he was also something of a sadist. It was one thing to inflict pain upon your political enemies, it was quite another to take personal pleasure in the agony of an individual. How Julie had been treated here was well beyond what was called for and Byko regretted it. Particularly because it cost him the moral high ground he so dearly coveted.

As he cared for her, Byko began to feel something odd. A tender nostalgia for the halcyon days of their youth and a particular memory of a cold, rainy day at Cambridge. It was mid-December, and Julie had insisted they stay at school for the holidays. Against all of his better judgment, she'd convinced him it would be romantic to stroll the ancient courtyards when everyone else had gone home and they could have the place to themselves. By the second day, Julie had come down with the flu and was bedridden with a 103-degree fever. Byko had cursed his luck: he could have been sunbathing on a yacht in Dubai, but instead he was stuck in a dank dorm room having to play Florence Nightingale. Forced to make the best of the situation, he fixed Julie a bowl of *plov* from his grandmother's old recipe and fed it to her much as he did now. On that day, her soulful brown eyes had conveyed such gratitude. Today, there was barely acknowledgment.

Julie looked up at Byko and met his eyes for the first time since he'd entered the room. For what felt like days, she had been so consumed by drugs and physical pain, she hadn't realized the toll that cold and hunger could take.

But now that she had food in her belly, and some strength had returned, she was able once again to focus. And began to feel a glimmer of hope. Because she could tell by the way Byko was looking at her, the way he had fed her, the way he had stroked her hair, that he still had feelings for her. And this was what she would need to prey on.

"I cannot say that I approve of how you've been treated," he said quietly, "but I'm afraid you left me with no choice, Jules."

Jules. That name. The familiarity, the intimacy. It was what Charlie called her and it made her almost sick to hear Byko utter it now, as if they were at the quad back in Cambridge. But she knew she couldn't afford to let her emotions get the better of her. She needed to play to Byko's ego, to renew some kind of connection. "I understand," she said. "You've been put in a difficult position."

"You know," Byko continued, "Quinn thinks you were a dupe, that MI6 convinced you to lure me to that café without giving you half a reason why. But that just doesn't make sense to me. Given who you are."

"I'm sorry to disappoint you, but who I am is a bored, lonely housewife, Alisher."

"Maybe so, but I don't see you showing up in Samarkand and selling me out without some kind of proof from MI6 that I'm up to no good."

"So you admit that you're up to no good?" she probed.

"That is a matter of interpretation," he answered, appearing oddly defensive. "I am quite sure they would have needed to convince you of as much. If you were to leave your family to come here. If you were to lie to me. And to your husband."

There was no arguing with his logic. He was too smart and continuing to tap dance with him would only backfire. She needed to give him something.

"They told me about the uranium," she admitted. "They told me that you intended for it to be used to make dirty bombs. I didn't believe them. I told them there must be some kind of mistake. So they showed me the manifests. They showed me how they traced the shipments back to your reactor and processing plant."

"And where were the shipments sent to?"

"Cities around the world," she admitted. "They showed me specific ones to Boston and Manchester, but the names of the other cities were blacked out on the document. They needed to convince me, but they refused to give away all of the information."

"And you were convinced."

This was the moment. She needed to make him believe.

"I was convinced there must be a misunderstanding. I told them that the Alisher Byko I knew would never do anything like that."

"And they said what?"

"They showed me a photograph of your sister, of what happened to her."

"And then you started to believe them?"

"No," she said adamantly. "I told them it was impossible. I said, 'Maybe someone from your processing plant had stolen the uranium.' I told them there was no way you yourself could be behind it."

"And yet you came."

"There was no persuading them," she implored. "And I was sure they were going to find you and kill you if I didn't help them."

"Oh," Byko chuckled ironically, "so you did this for me?"

"I thought if I helped them get to you then you'd be able to convince them they were wrong. That you would help them figure out who in your organization had stolen the uranium."

Byko leaned back in his chair and folded his arms.

"And why not just tell me the truth?" he asked.

"Because I would have been committing treason."

"So . . . ," Byko replied, "you were between the proverbial Scylla and Charybdis."

"I was, Alisher. You have to believe me."

She felt his eyes boring through her.

"If I had it to do over again," she said, "I would have just stayed in Los Angeles and minded my own business. Then none of this would be happening."

She could have sworn she saw something—a flicker of compassion—in Byko just then. Surely if he understood anything, he understood the devastation of being ripped away from one's family.

A knock interrupted what might have been a moment of connection. Byko turned and saw

Quinn's face in the door's tiny window. The sadist held his wrist up to the window and tapped his Rolex with one beefy finger.

Byko simply glared at him and Quinn disappeared from view.

When Byko returned his attention to Julie, the softness in his expression was gone.

"So what would you have me do now?" he asked.

"Let me go. Please. I just want to go home to my children."

"If this was the story that you had told me from the beginning, perhaps that might have been a possibility. But now . . . I'm afraid you've lost your credibility."

Julie put her face in her hands, her entire body trembling. "I'm sorry, Alisher. I should have. I should have told you from the beginning, but I was so scared."

"You told me that you loved me," Byko said, staring right past her into space. She couldn't tell if it was a question or merely a mournful statement of fact. But she felt it required a response—and she knew that if she overplayed her hand, he would smell it. Smell it and maybe strangle her right here and now.

"Alisher," she said, trying in vain to get him to look at her. "You know that I have feelings for you. I always have. I even had second thoughts about leaving you all those years ago." She sighed. "But I love Charlie."

She felt a sudden and unexpected upwelling of emotion as she said those words. Things had been so tangled between them over the past couple of years, but now that she was here—staring death in the face—a newfound clarity came to her. It was Charlie. It had always been Charlie.

Byko must have heard the crack in her voice and detected the tear in her eye, because he looked at her again. And his expression grew ice cold. "It's too bad he couldn't have seen you say that," he teased. "I'm sure he would have appreciated it. Unfortunately, for him, the last thing he saw of you was you saying how much you loved me." He paused. "How much you *always* loved me."

Julie wasn't sure she'd heard him correctly.

Byko pointed to the camera on the wall. "We showed him the video."

This wasn't possible. For Charlie to have seen the video, that would mean . . .

"Oh yes!" Byko continued. "He came all the way from Los Angeles to hunt down his beloved. And he had read all of our emails. You can imagine how distraught he was."

"Where is he?" she heard her voice rise in panic. "What did you do with him?"

Byko smiled. "Sadly, that's how he died. Believing you loved another man, believing that you'd lied to him all these years." With that, he rose. "I suppose there's a price to be paid for deceit, Jules."

She felt as if her skin had been ripped off her entire body.

He had killed Charlie?

She lunged at Byko. But he simply planted his palm in the middle of her chest and shoved her back into the chair. And with that, her strength gave out.

Charlie was dead. It began to sink in, like the incontrovertible logic of some mathematical proof. Charlie was dead.

And it was her fault.

She buried her face in her hands and sobbed. Below her, through her interlaced fingers, she could see Byko's leather shoes—handmade Italians, lustrous and black, perfectly polished. They seemed to mock her in their perfection. But she didn't care. She had run out of will, run out of strength, had even run out of fear.

"Kill me," she whispered. "You're going to do it, so just get it over with already. For godsake just do it."

But the glossy black shoes disappeared from her field of vision as he rapped twice on the window with his knuckles.

She looked up to see the heavy steel door grind open.

"Now?" Quinn asked, his voice impatient as he racked his pistol.

She had never imagined she might welcome that sound. But in this perverted moment, she did, the metallic clank of the gun in her ears, the messenger of oblivion. The shame, the grief, the horror, the pain—she simply wanted it all to go away.

CHAPTER FORTY-ONE

The rattletrap van driven by the four men Charlie had hired was leaking oil and belching blue smoke as they caravaned along the A377. His stolen Mercedes could easily have been cruising along at a hundred miles per hour, even on these thump-and-bump Uzbek roads, but he had to cut that speed in half in order to accommodate the shortcomings of the other vehicle. So he found himself checking his watch every four minutes, muttering under his breath and trying to push aside his nightmarish fantasies about what Julie might be going through.

At this speed, Charlie calculated that they'd be at Byko's compound in less than forty minutes, but what then? He knew where the bathhouse was and had a vague idea about where he was headed when he'd managed to capsize the Escalade into the river, but he really had no idea where Julie was being held. And the compound had to be at least a hundred square miles.

So as soon as they passed through the provincial city of Kokand and Charlie had a strong enough cell signal, he put in a call to Garman. It rang four times before going to voice mail. Charlie hung up and tried again—with the same result. He wondered if Garman was too ashamed to pick up the phone. So he borrowed Salim's mobile and tried again.

After two rings, there he was with the blandest of greetings. "Garman."

"It's Charlie."

"Oh hey," Garman replied with far too much enthusiasm. "Good to hear your voice. Where are you?"

"Still in the Valley. And I managed to pick up some local hires. I'm heading back to the base but I'm going to need some help."

"Like I told you, Charlie, I'm really not sure what I can do for you at this point."

"Look, I know that Byko had her in some kind of ultrasecure compound near the bathhouse. They were driving me north on a road that crossed a river, supposedly heading right to her. Do you have any idea where they might have been taking me?"

"That's really remote country. I don't know that area at all."

"The bathhouse was part of an old Soviet missile complex. That mean anything to you?"

"Yeah, yeah, that was Vasilevsky," Garman replied. "I remember Byko bought it after it got decommissioned."

"Well, someone somewhere must have some old maps of the area."

"I could check into it, but I really don't know what that's going to tell you. I mean, you need some pretty specific intel if you're going to be storming the place yourself with a half-dozen amateurs."

"Don't you think I know that?" Charlie snapped.

"Jesus Christ, Garman. I get you have to protect your family, I get you couldn't throw together a unit at the eleventh hour, but now I'm asking you to do whatever you can. From behind your god-damn desk. After I told you Europe and America are going to burn. Do you have a shred of honor left in you at all?"

There was a long pause.

Charlie cursed himself, certain Garman was about to hang up on him.

But when Garman finally spoke, the tone in his voice was suddenly different—he was grave and focused. "You said SAS was supposed to hit the location? That MI6 was putting their satellite on it after you gave them the tip?"

"That's right," Charlie said.

"Look," Garman replied, "this is a long shot, okay? But I know this guy who worked for the contractor that built the British spy satellites. There's absolutely no way to snoop on the imaging—the encryption is totally secure—but he told me once that there was some kind of bug in the telemetry."

"What kind of bug?"

"MI6 has to send TopSat a GPS location to point the camera at. If you could intercept that GPS coordinate, you'd know exactly where the satellite was looking. Presumably by now MI6 has been over every inch of that compound and homed in on their best guess as to where Byko is."

"And if he's already fled the compound, the satellite should be tracking him to wherever he's going."

"That's right. Hopefully for you, that would lead you to Julie."

"Make the call," Charlie said.

. . .

The moment he got off with Garman, Charlie dialed Becca. On the third ring, Charlie heard someone fumble for the phone, then his sister-in-law's English-accented voice, slightly muted, "Careful, sweetie, hold on to the side of the tub! Ollie can help you. Ollie, can you . . ."

Charlie felt a rush of emotion. He had dialed Becca almost reflexively and told himself he was merely calling to get an update on Ollie and Meagan. But hearing them now, splashing around in the tub, falsetto voices chirping, he was faced with a rather grim reality. Considering what he was about to do, this might be the last time he ever spoke to his children. And he realized that was in fact precisely the reason he was calling.

"Hello, is that you, Charlie?"

He did his best to put on an optimistic tone of voice. "Sounds like everybody there's doing okay."

"Yeah. We're good."

"Oh good," Charlie responded, not knowing what else to say.

"Do you have an update for me?" she asked tentatively.

"I know where she is. And I have some help now."

She lowered her voice to an urgent whisper. "Can you tell me what this is all about, Charlie?"

"Now's not the time."

In the background he heard Ollie shout, "Is that Dad?"

"They've been asking about you," Becca said. "Obviously."

"Well put him on."

There was some rattling and rustling, then Ollie spoke, his voice sounding tentative and uncertain. "Hey, Dad."

"Hey, tiger!"

"Where are you?"

"A place called the Fergana Valley. Where your mom and I used to work."

"Isn't that where I was born?"

"That's right, it is."

There was a brief pause, then Ollie said, "The police are here. They're checking around everywhere. In my drawers and closet and everything." Ollie paused, his voice quivering. "They said you might not be coming back."

"Of course I'm coming back!" Charlie said sharply. "I would *never* leave you." In truth, there was absolutely no way he could promise that and Charlie hated himself for lying.

"What about Mom?" Ollie asked. "Did you find her?"

"Not yet. But I will."

He was digging himself an even deeper hole now.

"You swear to God, Dad?"

Deeper still.

"By all the angels in heaven," Charlie said.

"Okay."

"I love you, little man. You know that."

"Yeah."

Charlie wanted to give his son some words of wisdom, something for him to hold on to, in case they never spoke again, but what could he say to a six-year-old that wouldn't scare or confuse him?

"Take care of your little sister," was the best Charlie could come up with.

"I always do," Ollie said and that nearly broke his father's heart.

"Can I talk to Becca again?"

Becca came back on. "Hey."

"The cops are there?"

"I'm sorry. I didn't know what good it would do to upset you."

"You keep those assholes away from the kids. They have no right to talk to them."

"I know. I will."

"They told them I wasn't coming back?"

"They're just trying to get to you."

"Well, it's not going to work. And you can tell them as much."

The line was silent for a moment. Then Becca called his name. There was a strident urgency in the way she said, "Charlie!" and he was pretty sure he didn't want to hear what was coming next. "No matter what happens now, you know I'll be there for Ollie and Meagan, but . . ." Becca's voice broke and her words trailed off. "I don't know what kind of risks you're taking over there, but if there's any danger of you not coming back . . . you know she'd tell you to come home."

Charlie swallowed hard. He knew what it took for Becca to say that. "And I'd tell her to cut the shit."

"All I'm saying is you don't have anything to prove. You know that, don't you?"

"That's not what this is about," he told her.

"Okay," she said softly. "I love you. And I'm sorry I lied to you." Her voice cracked a bit and he heard her crying.

"I love you, too," he told her. "Everything's going to be all right."

"Okay," she said. He could hear how desperately she needed to believe that.

"Put Meagan on, okay?"

Charlie heard more splashing around and childish banter, then Meagan came to the phone. Unlike Ollie, she was chipper and playful. The power of denial, Charlie thought. It started so young. Oh, how he wished he could tap into some of that now. They talked about her preschool and Ollie's habit of stealing her toys. She didn't ask where he was and he didn't volunteer it, she didn't ask if he was coming home soon and he didn't make any uncertain promises. She said Becca had to wash her hair now and he told her that was a good idea. She said she loved him and he tried to keep his voice from cracking as he said he loved her, too. Then he hung up, staring at the red button which had disengaged them.

"End," it said.

He put the phone away and felt Salim looking at him.

"My children," Charlie explained.

Salim half-nodded. "I am very sorry for what happened to your wife. You are one of only people tried to help us. You left before we could say thank you."

"Well, I'm back now," Charlie said ironically, thinking about what Becca had said. That he should come home. That he didn't have anything to prove.

"Tomorrow is birthday of Andijan," Salim continued. "There will be many people there. For the memory of what happened. There will be candles and singing and remembering."

Charlie couldn't imagine the regime sanctioning something like that. "Is there usually an event staged on the anniversary?"

Salim shrugged. "This is first time I have heard of such a thing."

So while mourners were sitting vigil for their lost friends and family members, Byko would be creating more mourning families all across the globe. Charlie still couldn't fathom what had happened to Byko that it would come to this.

"I will go there," Salim said. "Unless you still need my help."

Charlie looked at him. He knew this was the boy's way of trying to connect. To acknowledge Charlie's sacrifice. But he couldn't fight back the urge to warn him: "You shouldn't go there. No matter what."

"The government cannot come again, not to the same place on the same day. With the world watching."

"The world isn't watching, Salim. The world doesn't care."

"The world is getting smaller," Salim replied. "That is why Byko plans what he plans. Yes . . . ?"

It was an unusual insight for a boy who'd spent his entire life in an isolated little border town. Charlie considered Salim's wisdom for a moment, but rejected it. Salim was giving the drug-addled megalomaniac too much credit.

"Byko's suffered," Charlie said. "Now he wants others to feel the same. It's nothing more than that."

Salim nodded. He'd seen his own share of suffering and that seemed to be a concept he could understand. "Then we must stop him," Salim said quietly. "At any cost."

Charlie looked at him. Two days ago, he was

making dinner for Julie and the kids in Santa Monica, waiting for them to come home from Disneyland, wondering if he could find a way to save his job. Now here he was, driving a stolen Mercedes through the oustkirts of Uzbekistan alongside this brave kid with his battered rifle, contemplating what they needed to do to alter history.

He nodded grimly at Salim.

"At any cost."

CHAPTER FORTY-TWO

As far as Hopkins knew, both the Prime Minister and the President of the United States had failed to get through to His Majesty Islam Karimov. And when Hopkins had suggested that they pursue a preemptive strike, going around the Uzbek government the way the U.S. Special Forces had circumvented the Pakistanis in the raid on Osama bin Laden, Bryce simply scoffed at him. Bin Laden had been the most wanted man in the world. Alisher Byko had done nothing yet and all they had on him was circumstantial evidence. It was simply impossible.

So here was Hopkins, staring at the satellite image in the War Room. The bird had been glued to the location that Charlie Davis had given them: the bathhouse, several outbuildings, and a parking lot with five American-made SUVs. But there'd been no sign of movement. No guards patrolling, no vehicles in and out, nothing.

"How long has it been?" he asked the satellite tech.

"Two hours, twenty-six minutes, sir."

It didn't make any sense. Surely Byko had to be

aware that Charlie Davis had escaped. Surely Byko had to know that Charlie would call the Western intelligence agencies. And most surely, that had to make Byko nervous. What then had Byko been doing for the past three hours? Sitting around the bathhouse, taking a steam? Could he be that arrogant?

Hopkins pointed at a small round object on the screen. It was difficult sometimes to make out what things were from the high perspective of the satellite and this one had been puzzling him for a while.

"What is this?" Hopkins asked the image analyst.

The tech was a thin young man whose face seemed to be stuck in a perpetual wince. "Mm. No shadow. That means it's more or less flush with the ground. Two meters in diameter. Possibly some sort of drainage pipe. Mm. No. Wait. Not drainage. Ventilation. It's probably the cap on a ventilation shaft."

Hopkins felt a sudden burst of irritation with himself. "Christ," he said. How had he missed this? If this was what he thought it was—

"Decrease magnification fifty percent," Hopkins said sharply.

The tech's fingers tapped away on the keys of his workstation. The screen blinked and a new image wavered into view, this one displaying a much larger area. Hopkins reoriented himself . . .

There was the bathhouse. There was the ventilation shaft. About two feet higher on the screen, he saw a second small round blob, identical to the ventilation shaft near the bathhouse. According to the scale at the bottom of the screen, roughly three hundred yards separated the two.

"Decrease mag another fifty percent," Hopkins said.

More tapping. Another view. This time a third blob, now no more than a handful of pixels. The distance from the first to the second to the third shaft was identical. And you could draw a straight line right through the lot of them.

A tunnel. There was a bloody tunnel leading due north.

"Maps!" he shouted. "Do we have maps of this facility?"

One of the techs fiddled with her computer. "No sir. The facility predates our satellites." She cleared her throat delicately. "Only the Americans had satellites when this facility was built."

Hopkins quickly dialed Eric Nielsen, his counterpart at the NSA. "Eric, it's Frank Hopkins. Have you got maps of the old Vasilevsky Missile Complex?"

"Mind my asking why, buddy?"

"Do you have them or not?"

"Of course we do. But what are you looking for?"

"As you know, Byko's current location is in the complex. But I think Byko escaped from that location through some kind of tunnel. I want to know where that tunnel leads."

Nielsen was silent for a moment. Finally he said, "Ah. Yes. There is a tunnel leading due north to another location. This map is almost fifty years old. Satellite imagery was in its infancy, so it's pretty crude. But there was a sort of central node about thirty miles north. As best we can tell, the tunnel went all the way there. According to this map, it was the command center for the missile complex."

"Damnit! You need to task a satellite on that location right now! Byko's probably already there. He may even be gone by now."

There was a long pause. "Actually, we've already got a bird on that location."

Hopkins felt his face grow hot. "And when the hell were you planning to tell us about that?"

"Hey, hey, easy, pal. You asked us to check out the whole area. So that seemed like our next logical step."

"Might have been nice if you'd told us."

"Nothing's popped up yet, okay? But we're on it."

How many birds did the Americans have? How many locations were they watching? It was a waste of time even asking. He'd been down this road before with the Americans. The CIA was bad enough. But the NSA? There had been a time when they had employed more than twenty thousand people and had a budget that was literally bigger than the GDP of 90 percent of the countries in Africa, and the Americans wouldn't even publicly admit that it existed.

"Do keep us in mind if you find anything, Eric," Hopkins said acidly. Then he broke the connection and turned to the comms tech. "Put Sturbridge on the line."

A few seconds later, Hopkins was connected to the commander of the SAS. "We may have to change the destination," he said. He gave Sturbridge the GPS coordinates of the command center.

Sturbridge repeated the numbers back to Hopkins, then asked, "Any word on authorization?"

"Not yet," Hopkins said tersely.

"We're twenty minutes from Uzbek air space. What's the holdup?"

"It's a diplomatic issue. You'll be the first to know when it's resolved." Hopkins hung up the phone. It was decision time. The UK had only one satellite in that quadrant of the globe. Should he take the chance and vector to the new location?

"Sir?" The satellite tech looked up expectantly. There was no question what he was asking.

"Do it," Hopkins said.

CHAPTER FORTY-THREE

As Charlie and Salim approached the turnoff that led to Byko's bathhouse, Charlie grabbed for his phone and dialed Garman again. This time, Garman picked up immediately.

"I got hold of my guy," he announced without prelude, "but I still haven't heard back."

"Well, I'm almost at the compound. How about trying him again?"

"He's going to call me as soon as he knows anything, Charlie."

"Try him again."

"Hang on," Garman said, sounding a bit exasperated.

The phone went silent for a moment. The next thirty seconds felt like an eternity. But finally Garman came back on. "I'm assuming you have a GPS in your car?"

"I do," Charlie assured. "Does that mean you have the coordinates?"

"You ready?"

"Hang on a sec," Charlie said and pulled over to the side of the road. "Okay, go ahead."

Garman read them off slowly, "N41 16.00253 E69 12.99875."

Charlie input the digits then repeated them back to Garman.

"You got it," Garman said. "I'd wish you good luck, but I'm not sure luck's gonna have much to do with it."

"Probably not, though I could use all the help I can get," Charlie quipped.

"Well, good luck then," Garman said.

Within a minute or so, a map appeared on the GPS screen. Their destination was nine minutes away. And it appeared to be part of the same compound. Which meant MI6 believed that Byko and company were still there.

Charlie smiled for what seemed like the first time in days and pulled onto the road again, checking his rearview to make sure the van was still following them.

The navigation program, as it turned out, couldn't locate any of the local roads and Charlie was forced to improvise. There was one road—a small dirt track that twisted up into the hills to the north—that appeared the only sensible choice. He took that road and endured its winding, meandering nature as it alternately moved closer to and away from the blinking yellow dot on the small screen.

The nine minutes turned out to be more like sixteen, but at last they were rounding a bend and approaching the small hill that aligned with Garman's coordinates.

Charlie pulled his car to a halt and stared at the wretched little outpost. Could this be it? A couple of corrugated steel sheds and a rusting antenna tower? Even during the Soviet era this must have been a place of no importance. And now it was just a forgotten remnant from the edges of an empire that no longer existed. Two dinky little shacks, no cars, no trucks, no fences or imposing guard towers. Nothing.

Garman's guy had blown it. He'd led them to nowhere.

"This is the place?" Salim asked incredulously.

As the rattletrap van pulled in behind them, Charlie frowned, then backed up the Mercedes so that it was out of view of the sheds, put on the parking brake and took a moment to think. The well-worn dirt road on which he had been driving seemed to simply end, not four hundred yards from the car, and Charlie needed to take a more thorough look. He grabbed the Sig Sauer pistol one of his hired men had given him, shoved the holster onto his belt, then jumped out of the Mercedes and crossed the road.

He found shelter behind an outcropping of rock and pulled out a pair of binoculars. As he scanned the area, he realized that earlier he had been looking at the end of the road from the wrong angle. From his new vantage point, he saw that the road sloped down into some sort of underground parking structure, its entrance disguised to look like a natural feature of the landscape.

This was it. They'd been holding Julie underground. Here. The only question now was whether or not she was still down there.

By the time Charlie got back to the Mercedes, Omar, the leader of the ragtag Ragdovir gang, was out of the van waiting for him. As Charlie explained the situation, the other three joined them.

"I don't like it," Omar said. "We go through those doors, guards might be waiting." He mock machine-gunned with his hands. "Boom, we're all dead."

The other three men nodded.

"We want the rest of our money now," Omar said.

Charlie shook his head. "That wasn't the deal."

Omar grinned. "You don't trust us?"

"You don't trust me?" Charlie countered.

"We don't know if you make it out of this alive," Omar said. "Then we don't get our money."

"The money's on me," Charlie said. "I die, you can take it off me then."

Omar's smile faded. He exchanged glances with the other men and suddenly all four submachine guns were pointing at Charlie's face. Much to his own surprise, Charlie didn't feel frightened. Mostly just pissed off. They were underestimating him and wasting his goddamn time. He was about to tell them this when he heard the sharp clack of a rifle bolt.

He looked to his right and saw Salim, weapon pointing directly at Omar's head.

"After," Salim said.

Omar turned to Charlie. "You got your own personal bodyguard?"

"Why do you think I brought him? Now you want to get to work?"

Omar laughed brightly and motioned for the others to lower their weapons.

"Okay," Omar said. "How we going to do this? You got big plan, Mr. Charlie?"

Charlie weighed the alternatives. They could go

down into the "cave" where the road disappeared. If there were any guards, they were sure to be there. Or they could go to the sheds and see if one of them hid an entrance to the facility. Again, if it did, the shed was likely to be guarded.

Or they could try the ventilation shaft.

"There's a hole in the grill," Charlie explained. "We climb down it, get into the building, catch everybody by surprise."

"Let me see," Omar said, beckoning for Charlie's binoculars.

Charlie handed them over. Omar looked through them for a few seconds, surveying the area, then lowered them skeptically. "There are cameras," he said.

"Salim's going to take them out," Charlie replied.

"The noise will give us away," Omar argued. "And if someone's inside watching, the picture going out will warn them we are coming."

"We leave the cameras operational, they'll see us go into the ventilation shaft. We knock them out, at least they won't know which direction we're coming from."

Omar looked at the other men and reluctantly bent to Charlie's logic.

Charlie took back the binoculars and handed them to Salim. "There's one on that large tree, just above the shed. The other one's—"

"I see it," said Salim. "I'll need to go to the rock."

"We all will," Charlie replied. "In case there's any guards in those sheds."

Charlie looked at his men. There wasn't exactly great enthusiasm for the plan, but at least no one was arguing.

They crossed the road as quietly as possible and settled behind the boulder.

"Now we split up," Charlie said. "Omar, you and Vlad get yourselves behind that bush, you'll have a clear sight line on the first shed from there." He turned to the others. "You two, there's an old tree stump thirty yards to the right that'll put you close enough to the second shed, though you'll probably have to come out from behind it to get off a shot."

The men looked at Omar for final confirmation. He nodded his approval and only then did they follow Charlie's orders.

Meanwhile, Salim settled into a crouch behind the boulder, resting the stock carefully on the hard surface of the rock. He took a careful bead and waited for Charlie's command.

"You got it?" Charlie asked.

Salim nodded. "Are the others in position?"

Charlie surveyed Omar and his men. They appeared to be ready.

Charlie took out his Sig Sauer, clicked off the safety and contemplated what was about to happen. He'd never thought when his old man was teaching him to hunt deer in rural Ohio, or even when he'd shot a few rounds from an M4 carbine with Navy SEALs in eastern Afghanistan, that he would be going into battle against hardened mercenaries and trained soldiers in God-knows-where Central Asia. That he would be holding a weapon in his sweaty right palm, ready to kill. Or be killed.

He'd come face-to-face with his most primal self back at the river when he'd slain the mercenary under a pile of rubble, and again when he'd used that Mercedes like a battering ram to take out the drug dealers, but in both cases he'd been acting on pure instinct—an animal doing what it needed to do to survive.

This was something different. This was premeditated. A choice to enter the battle.

Charlie realized he would have to dispense with the childish revulsion he had felt after that first killing. In fact, he would need to savor and cultivate the rush of power that was his first reaction to the murder. That was the only way he was going to get through this and find a way to save Julie. And there was something crystallizing about that epiphany— the sheer rawness of it—that was oddly freeing.

"Take your shot," Charlie said.

Salim hesitated for a long moment, then squeezed the trigger.

The bullet thudded harmlessly into the shed at least a foot wide of the camera, but the loud crack of the shot echoed and faded, reverberating from one side of the valley to the other.

Salim wiped his forehead and muttered to himself, "Wind. I forgot the wind."

Charlie's eyes darted back and forth between the two sheds. Thus far, no guards had emerged.

Salim took aim again and squeezed off another round. This time the camera exploded in a cloud of shattered glass and broken plastic.

"You got it," Charlie said.

The kid lined up his second shot and was just about to fire when one of Quinn's mercenaries came out of the first shed.

"What you want me to do?" Salim asked.

"Take out the second camera," Charlie instructed.

As Salim took aim, Charlie watched the mercenary lift his rifle and scan the area in front of him. The man's eyes widened just as there was another sharp crack from Salim's rifle.

"Down!" Charlie whispered.

They ducked as the shots ricocheted off the boulder. Then there was a burst of automatic weapon fire from their left. When it was over, Charlie looked up to see that Quinn's man was down. Omar and Vlad had taken him out.

Charlie held up his palm as if to say, "Wait." He wanted to see if there were more guards stationed outside. When none showed, he signaled to both twosomes, "Let's go," and they bounded toward the ventilation shaft, guns ready in case they were running into an ambush.

Charlie reached the shaft first and levered himself underneath the rusting grate. It was a tight fit and his pant leg snagged on the jagged metal. "Hurry!" Salim hissed.

Charlie yanked his leg and a sharp piece of metal raked across his shin. He cursed under his breath, then slid under the grate to find himself at the top of a dark concrete cylinder.

Looking down, all he could see was an inky blackness. But there was enough light at the top to make out a steel ladder embedded in the wall. He grabbed the top rung and swung himself out into the shaft. For an unbearably long moment he hung by his fingers, feet pawing the air until he found purchase on one of the lower rungs.

Heart pounding, Charlie descended into the darkness.

CHAPTER FORTY-FOUR

Charlie could see Salim, Omar and the others moving down the ladder above him. But the farther down the shaft he went, the darker it became and soon he couldn't see anything below him. He knew that he was getting closer and closer to the thrumming fan that propelled air up the shaft as the artificial wind tore relentlessly at his clothes. From the sound of it, the thing was spinning fast enough to chop his feet off. Was there any sort of grill to keep him from sticking his feet into the fan? He looked down again, squinting, hoping perhaps that his eyes might become adjusted to the darkness.

Suddenly, he saw a seam of light directly in front of his face. It was barely more than the width of a hair and he realized it must be a crack around some kind of hatchway. He pressed his eye to the crack and could make out a lightbulb attached to a concrete wall maybe five feet away.

Feeling around with his right hand, he found a rough metal handle on the edge of the door.

He considered his options. Go deeper, hope to find an entrance that afforded him a better view—and hope he didn't get his feet chopped off by the ventilation fan—or take a chance and burst blindly out this door into the hallway.

He opted for the hallway. But there was no way to signal the others in the darkness and yelling would potentially alert Byko's men inside. So he was just going to have to hope the men followed quickly.

He took a deep breath, his pulse hammering in his throat. Then he twisted the handle and yanked the door open. Its rusty hinges screamed and he swung into the hallway, imagining a half-dozen guards training their guns on him as he burst out the door.

Instead, he found himself in a completely empty space. At the far end of the corridor was a large, heavy door with a circular handle like the doors of a submarine. That must have led to the old Soviet command center.

It made sense. This place had been designed to take a hit from a nuclear bomb. If the ventilation duct had passed directly into the main working space, it would have been able to transmit fallout into the shelter. So the air had to pass through some kind of filtration while the access tunnel was shielded by an air lock.

Charlie left the door open, which would flood the shaft with light and alert his troops to his route, but it was a painful ninety seconds as he waited for them all to arrive, and when they did, they were sweating heavily. As their supposedly fearless leader, Charlie hoped he didn't look as nervous as they did.

"Okay, listen," he said. "We'll probably have to split up once we get into this place. You're looking for an Englishwoman with brown hair. If you find her, don't do anything that would harm her. Just call me. Okay?"

Omar swallowed and nodded, apparently on behalf of all of them.

They made their way to the end of the hallway, where Charlie began twisting the big round handle of the "submarine" door. It was about four inches thick and moved with glacial slowness. When it was far enough open, he peered out, seeing a long, empty hallway that went in two directions. He could hear voices, speaking urgently in Uzbek, but he couldn't tell from which direction the sound was coming. Charlie squeezed through the door, followed by the rest of the men. He pointed to Omar, signaling for him to go to the left. Omar nodded and headed that way, the other rogues following close behind him. Charlie started to cry out, to indicate that he and Salim needed one of them to even the odds, but they were already too far away. He and Salim would go to the right. Alone.

They began moving rapidly down the bare concrete hallway. Behind them, Omar and his men disappeared in the other direction. In front of them, Charlie could hear voices. Bathed in sweat, clutching his pistol with both hands, he moved forward, twisting and turning through the maze of tunnels.

The acoustics of the concrete caused strange echoes and dead spots, the sound of the voices getting louder and softer by turns, seemingly unconnected to the distance from the people who were speaking, and Charlie still couldn't make out where the voices were coming from.

Finally, as they continued to move forward, the voices became clearer. There was an urgency to the speaker's tone and Charlie felt certain that the guards must have been discussing the intruders. But then he began to discern the words. It was someone complaining about the hours they'd been working. And there was a soft clinking sound—someone stirring sugar into a glass of tea?

His eyes communicated relief to Salim. Somehow, no one in this bunker was aware that they'd shot out the cameras and killed the guard outside. As they rounded the corner, approaching the room where the voices were coming from, there was suddenly shouting from somewhere in the other direction and a deafening clatter of automatic gunfire.

Before he could even begin to register what was going to happen next, two men burst out of the adjacent room and into the hallway. Charlie fired off twelve quick shots, emptying his chamber without a conscious thought.

The two men fell, one dead before he hit the ground, the other gasping and holding his chest. The surviving man looked up at them imploringly, gasped his last few breaths and passed into the afterlife.

Charlie groped in his pockets for another clip, reloaded and looked at Salim. The kid looked to be in shock. It was one thing to shoot a Coke can or a security camera, another thing to be four feet from a dead man who'd just been shot in the face. Charlie turned his attention to the opposite end of the hallway.

The gunfire had ceased. In fact, the entire bunker was completely, eerily silent.

Then a terrible, high keening of agony and fear pierced the quiet.

Charlie sprinted back down the hallway toward the source of the screaming, Salim on his heels.

There were two more gunshots.

But the screaming didn't cease. It became almost

like a chant: "Ahhhhhh! Ahhhhhh! Ahhhhhh! Ah-hhhhh!"

Closer and closer.

Charlie rounded a corner. And walked into a bloodbath.

Literally. There was blood on the walls, on the ceiling, splashed across beds and chairs. Splinters of wood and chunks of concrete and empty magazines lay everywhere. The air was still heavy with gun smoke.

And only one man was alive. One of Quinn's mercenaries. The screamer. Standing in the middle of the room clutching his face as blood poured through his fingers.

"Ahhhhhh! Ahhhhhh! Ahhhhh!"

The man stumbled around the room, blundering into furniture, his mouth open in horror. Charlie raised his gun and put the zombie out of his misery.

Silence fell as Charlie counted the dead. Six of Byko's guards plus Omar, Vlad and the other two men from the town, all grotesquely shot up.

"I'm sorry, Salim," Charlie said. "I'm sorry about the men from your village."

This seemed to snap Salim out of his funk and he looked down at them without pity. "They were bad men." He bent down and pulled the cash out of their clothes. "Here," he said, offering it to Charlie. "Your money."

Charlie stared at the bloodstained dollars. "You keep it," he said. "Give it to their families."

Salim stared uncomprehendingly at him for a moment, then tucked the money wordlessly into his pants.

"Let's go find your wife."

CHAPTER FORTY-FIVE

The complex was constructed in a rough ladder shape, with two main longitudinal halls and a number of smaller connecting hallways, some of which were straight and some of which contained confusing doglegs and cul-de-sacs. Salim and Charlie started at the eastern edge of the tunnel complex and worked their way west, room by room, hall by hall. The first few hallways consisted mainly of living and eating quarters. Because the staff of the missile command had been far larger than Byko had ever needed, most of the rooms were empty and dank, smelling of mold and neglect.

At the other end of the complex were briefing rooms, offices, control rooms and so on. Some were full of equipment that had been obsolete long before the Cold War was over—tube-driven amplifiers and radio sets, broken oscilloscopes, controls for missiles that had been dismantled decades ago.

Occasionally they found signs of recent use—coffee cups, pens, stocks of tin cans, a microwave oven, an occasional box of ammunition. But no sign of Julie. No sign of Byko. And no sign of anything related to his planned attacks or where he and his men might have gone.

As they worked their way closer to the end of the complex, Charlie began to feel less and less hopeful and then, halfway down the final hallway, they found the small white-painted room. Cameras in all four corners of the ceiling, drain set into the concrete floor, white chair with Velcro straps at the wrists and ankles.

This was where Julie had been held, and interrogated and tortured.

"She was here?" Salim asked.

Charlie picked out a couple of wavy brown hairs from one of the Velcro straps. He thought he could actually smell her.

"I think she is still alive," Salim said matter-of-factly. "If they killed her, there would be blood."

Charlie took in the boy. Six years earlier, Salim's own brother had been killed in a room much like this. But that didn't make the kid an expert. What he didn't know was what the drain on the floor meant. Quinn could have easily drowned Julie in here and dumped her body in any one of the scores of rooms in the complex.

One way or another, Charlie needed to know for sure.

"Let's finish," Charlie said and headed back into the hallway.

It hadn't been obvious until they reached the final corridor, but now that Charlie was here, it seemed clear that this had been the area where Byko's people had spent most of their time. The walls were freshly painted, the lights brighter, and the electrical system appeared to have been newly restored to fit the world of laptops and cell phone chargers. There were also full wastebaskets, uneaten food, discarded clothes, and various other signs that people had recently left in a hurry.

"You start at that end and I'll keep working my way down from this end," Charlie whispered. "And be careful," he warned. "If there's anybody left, they're here somewhere."

Charlie checked two more rooms. There were clear signs of recent use, but nothing that pointed to Julie's presence. He was about to step back into the hallway when he heard a soft, stealthy creak.

Charlie poked his head out and scanned the corridor. Salim was standing at the far end, fingers poised on the handle of a door, trying to pull it open. Apparently the door was locked and Charlie felt certain that the creaky sound did not come from Salim.

That was when Charlie saw—halfway down the corridor—another door slowly opening. Before Charlie could call out, the door burst open and Hasan emerged.

Salim whirled, ready to fight but then he saw the red dot of the laser from Hasan's tricked-out machine gun pointed at his chest. He dropped his rifle, hope draining from his eyes.

Charlie had a shot from where he was—fifty yards down the hall—but the chances of hitting Hasan from that distance were next to impossible.

"Who's with you?" Hasan barked. "How many of you are there?"

Salim's eyes flicked over Hasan's shoulder. Charlie crept closer, a finger to his mouth, shhh.

"Please," Salim said, trying to stall. "Don't hurt me. I'm just a—"

"How many?" Hasan hissed.

Charlie took one step, then another. Then another.

"The rest are dead," Salim said. "They were killed by your men."

Closer. Charlie needed to be ten yards closer.

"Who sent you?"

Three more steps.

One, two . . .

"Who sent you!" Hasan demanded again.

As Salim was about to answer, Charlie's shoe squeaked. In any other circumstance the noise would have been so insignificant as to be unnoticeable. But here, Charlie might as well have set off a firecracker.

Hasan turned.

And Charlie fired. Pressing the trigger as fast as he could.

Hasan roared like a wounded lion, his AK-47 haphazardly spewing bullets as he stumbled toward Charlie, trying to find his balance.

Charlie ducked but kept firing and Hasan collapsed, his rifle falling to the floor.

Charlie was still pointing the pistol at him, squeezing the trigger over and over. But the gun was empty.

Hasan was bleeding profusely from his shoulder and neck, but the fight hadn't gone out of him. "What you gonna do now?" he growled. "You got no bullets left."

"No," Salim said, stepping toward him with his rifle. "But he's got me."

"Where's Julie?" Charlie barked at Hasan.

"They're gone," Hasan said. "You never going to find them now."

Charlie grabbed the AK and pointed it in Hasan's face, finger tightening on the trigger. "Answer now or you're a dead man."

The big man broke into a coughing fit, his face going pale. He grabbed at his bloody neck, trying to staunch the bleeding, but his body gave out, eyes staring blankly at the ceiling.

Even in death there seemed to be defiance in his eyes.

Charlie sat with his back against the wall, holding his head in his hands as Salim worked his way down the hallway, checking the last few doors. His mind felt as empty as the bunker in which he sat—a hollowed-out shell, nothing of any substance left. With Hasan dead, with no evidence here of any kind as to where Byko had taken Julie, this was the end of the line.

For a moment Charlie pictured himself arriving at home, having to tell the kids that he'd gone all this way and come back empty-handed. What would their faces look like? How would they feel? For Ollie, losing his mother would leave a scar that would probably never heal. But what about Meagan? She was young enough that she might forget Julie altogether, her only memories of her mother cobbled together from the photos and home videos they'd taken. Which would be worse? The loss or the absence of any memory at all?

As he was mulling this over, Salim came out of

the last door and shook his head. Charlie looked away, his gaze falling on Hasan's lifeless body.

Then something struck him.

Why was Hasan here? He didn't seem like the hide-out-and-keep-his-head-down type. He was Byko's personal bodyguard, yet he had stayed behind.

Charlie stood and looked into the room from which Hasan had exited. As Salim had already reported, it was basically empty. A table, an iPod trailing a pair of white earphones and an empty bookcase of gray-painted steel. That was it. As innocuous as a room could possibly be. And yet something about it didn't seem right. Charlie found his eye drawn to the bookcase and realized that it was sitting at an odd angle, as though it had been hurriedly shoved into place. He moved toward it and noticed scrape marks on the floor.

The bookcase had been moved.

"Give me a hand, Salim!"

Salim came into the room and together they dragged the heavy bookcase to the side.

Sure enough, they found a door. Charlie yanked it open and walked in.

The room was brightly lit and lined with painted white walls. There were several racks of modern computer servers and several cubicles containing various computers and monitors. Plus a radio and a phone. This was the nerve center of the facility.

And every single piece of equipment in the room was wired with explosives.

Charlie eyed Salim warily. "That's why Hasan was left behind. He was supposed to blow the place."

Salim nodded and stepped forward cautiously.

"Don't touch anything," Charlie warned, looking around for some sort of detonation timer.

What he found was a small black box attached to some wires. A tiny red light burned on the front of the box. But other than that, there was no clear sign of what it did or how it worked.

He felt pretty sure that the explosives couldn't detonate spontaneously. But still . . .

Where was the trigger for the detonator?

And then something else caught his eye. Sitting on a table off to the side of the room—a computer that looked like it was owned by an individual. A sleek Apple, the screen still lit up, a wire connecting it to the big stack of servers.

SHUT DOWN NOW? said an icon in the middle of the screen.

"I think you should get out of here," Charlie told Salim.

"What are you going to do?"

"Just go. To the next corridor."

Salim hesitated but headed out.

Charlie waited two minutes—long enough for Salim to get far away—then moved the mouse over the button that said NO.

He took a deep breath and clicked.

CHAPTER FORTY-SIX

Quinn sat in the back of Byko's Escalade, which was hitched to a flat car thundering through the tunnel from one end of the Vasilevsky Missile Complex to the other. The small train of about half a dozen cars, including a battered old electric engine and a Spartan crew car, ran on narrow-gauge rails of the sort used in mining operations. The flatbed cars had been built to transport both medium-range ballistic missiles and tracked military vehicles, and so served well for transporting the SUVs in Quinn's convoy. But it was so dark inside the tunnels that Quinn could see none of this.

They had left a skeleton crew at the command center to guard the place while Byko's most trusted bodyguard, Hasan, wired the communications equipment to blow. Quinn had managed to convince Byko to leave his own computer at the command center, to be blown up along with the rest of the gear. The more places that information was stored, the greater the possibility of penetration, and as far as Quinn was concerned, Byko was already too exposed.

After eleven months in the man's employ, Byko

remained an enigma to Quinn. How could a man willing to unleash dirty bombs all over the world have such a weakness for this woman? This woman who had lied to him and betrayed him? Who had humiliated him and nearly destroyed him?

And now here she was, sleeping like a baby—they'd been forced to give her a sedative—her head leaning against Byko's shoulder as if they were still lovers.

Quinn supposed that she was attractive in her way, that there was a certain earnest quality in her that might be intoxicating to a man looking for reassurance. But still . . . to drag her along with them now? To what end?

In spite of himself, Quinn had to admit that he admired her spunk and tenacity. She'd endured almost everything he could dish out—the drugs, the waterboarding, the hours of sleep deprivation—and still, when they'd tried to remove her from the bunker, she'd writhed and fought like a wounded animal, cursing them all for killing her husband. Quinn smiled—he thought that was rather a nice touch on Byko's part, lying to her about Charlie's demise.

Byko looked up at Quinn, as if he knew he was being observed, and nudged Julie's head off of him.

"Do you have a signal yet?" Byko asked.

Quinn suspected he was merely trying to change the subject, unspoken though it was, from Julie to Hasan, but he checked his cell phone for effect. "It's not going to work down here. We'll use the hard line when we get to the silo."

"How long?"

"Less than five."

Byko shifted in his seat, glanced again at Julie, then stared out the window into the darkness.

What drove a man like him? How had he progressed from libertine playboy to rabid revolutionary to international terrorist in less than a decade? Quinn supposed the drugs had something to do with it. And the deaths in his family, of course. But there was no way that could be the whole story. People lost their families all the time. Quinn was no psychologist, but he suspected there must have been something megalomaniacal about Byko from a very early age. Maybe it was being surrounded by all of that wealth and power and violence. Maybe it was knowing from the time he was a toddler that he would inherit billions.

Who the hell knows? Quinn thought. *Who the hell cares really?* He was getting his fifty million and soon he'd be sitting on an island in Fiji sipping banana daquiris on a private beach in front of his own goddamn mansion.

The train shuddered, jerked and began to slow with a scream of rarely used brakes as it pulled into a concrete bunker similar to the terminus at the command center.

"We're here," Quinn said.

He bounded out of the car and leaped onto the platform while the train was still moving, heading straight for an old-fashioned Bakelite telephone handset that hung from a concrete pillar near an airlock door. He lifted the handset, consulted the brass plate with its list of Cyrillic numbers and dialed the four-digit extension for the command center.

It rang and rang and rang.

"Nobody's answering," Quinn told Byko as he

hung up. "That probably means it's done. I'll go up top. We can catch a cell signal there."

Quinn headed up a huge concrete ramp, leaving behind workers busy unhitching the vehicles from the train cars. Predictably, Byko stayed with Julie. When Quinn reached the top of the ramp, he found himself standing on a high desert plateau. The sun had just set and a moonless night cloaked the world in darkness.

He took out his secure cell phone. It was a very sophisticated model that generated unique SIM numbers for each call, making it essentially impossible to trace, and then it encrypted each call so that anyone who happened to lock on to the signal would be unable to make any sense of it. He dialed the number for Hasan's sat phone. Unlike cell phones, which depended on proximity to cell towers, a sat phone would work almost anywhere on earth. As long as Hasan was aboveground, he'd be able to reach him.

But again, Hasan didn't answer.

Quinn tried three more times, each time allowing the phone to ring for at least a minute.

As a fallback, Hasan was supposed to leave a message on a one-time-only voice mail box to confirm the job was done. Quinn tried that. But there was nothing there either.

An aching feeling rose slowly in Quinn's chest.

Something had gone wrong.

CHAPTER FORTY-SEVEN

Charlie closed the cover on Byko's computer.

As best he could tell, this machine contained the raw data Byko had used to construct his plans. Manifests, maps, names of men, locations of dead drops, lists of nuclear material weights and types . . .

Putting it all together, Charlie could see the outlines of Byko's plan. The nuclear material had been shipped to nine different cities, then picked up by members of various cells and transported to other cities. The actual target cities.

The final targets seemed to be London, New York, Hanover, Chicago, Tokyo, Minneapolis, Vienna, Sydney and Copenhagen. It seemed an odd list. Hanover but not Berlin. Vienna but not Paris. Minneapolis but not L.A. or D.C.

He supposed that some of it had probably been happenstansical: maybe it had something to do with logistics or communications, or perhaps Byko had only been able to staff his terror cells in certain cities. Both Minneapolis and Hanover had a significant Muslim presence. But Vienna had almost none at all, while Paris had the largest, and perhaps unhappiest, Muslim population in any European city. There was no way to know, really. In any case, he needed to get this information to MI6 as soon as possible.

He didn't have an email address for Hopkins, so he opted to send everything to his old friend Alan Marsh at the British Embassy with instructions to forward it. But when Charlie tried importing the files on to an email, he found that they were all blocked. They had been firewalled so that they could never be duplicated or sent out.

Could he just walk out of the room with the computer? No, he had to think that Hasan might have anticipated that. After all, the computer already had a lump of plastic explosives attached to the rear of the screen. It seemed entirely plausible that the individual charges might have some kind of tamper circuit built into them that would blow the whole room to smithereens when he tried to disconnect the computer from the detonation wire.

Then something struck him. Quickly, he called up all of the files that he'd already examined and began to take photos of them off the computer screen. This would take some time and Charlie felt agitated that the task was diverting him from finding Julie. But in his heart, he felt sure that this was what Julie would have wanted him to do. She'd risked her own life to put a stop to the madness. He had to honor that and follow her down the same path.

Byko felt a wave of panic run through him. If anyone found that computer . . .

He took out his phone and dialed the number for General Tempkin, a powerful general in the Interior Ministry. Aleksi Tempkin was one of the few ethnic Russians who had remained in the country after the split from the Soviets and Byko didn't trust any Russian as far as he could throw him. But the General had been on the payroll for many years and he knew nothing of Byko's plans—which meant he had every reason to believe the big payouts would continue indefinitely.

"You shouldn't be calling me directly," the general greeted him.

Byko was in no mood for this. "Did anyone authorize a raid on the command center at the Vasilevsky Missile Complex?"

"Absolutely not."

"*Any*one? Could the CIA or MI6 have hit it?"

"No. The President has made himself unavailable to the foreigners. No incursions have been authorized."

"You will let me know if you hear otherwise," Byko said firmly.

"Of course," said the General.

Byko hung up the phone and exchanged a glance with Quinn.

"Let's try the command center again," Quinn said. "Maybe Hasan got hung up for some reason."

Byko lifted the hard line himself this time and dialed.

Charlie was snapping off the last few photos of the computer files when the hard line rang again. The first few times Charlie had declined to answer, but now that he was done, he thought there might be an upside. If this was Quinn calling—or better yet Byko—to check on what Hasan was doing, Charlie might just be able to leverage what he'd found here for Julie.

It was a chance but a chance worth taking.

He picked up the phone, but he didn't say a word—he'd wait for whoever was at the other end of the line to reveal himself.

For a long moment, his adversary refused to speak as well.

Then finally, Byko caved. "Hasan?"

"Hasan's dead," Charlie replied. "So are the rest of your men down here. And I've had a pretty good look at your computer. Impressive things you've got planned, Alisher."

There was a long pause. Charlie figured it was Byko trying to regain his composure.

"What do you want, Charlie?"

"I want my wife back," Charlie said. "For that, you can have your computer."

"How do you know I haven't already killed her?"

"I think you would've left her here if you had."

There was another pause. Byko apparently considering the trade.

"And where would you like to meet then? To make the exchange?"

"Somewhere public. I'm thinking the square at Kokand." That was the nearest town of any size.

"Always with the squares," Byko replied. "It seems that is our destiny."

Charlie looked at his watch. "Tonight. Eleven o'clock sharp."

"Agreed," said Byko, almost too affably.

"I'll need to hear her voice, Alisher."

"You don't trust me, Charlie?"

"Put her on."

There was some rustling, then a groggy female voice. "Wha—?"

"Say hello," Byko coaxed.

"Go fuck yourself," Julie said wearily.

Charlie heard Byko laugh, then the sound of his wife being taken away. She sounded out of it, but she was most definitely alive.

"We have a deal then?" Charlie asked.

"We do."

And with that, Byko hung up.

For a moment, Charlie felt a surge of elation. She was alive. She was alive and he would be with her in less than an hour. But then it occurred to him that there was something too easy about all of this. And how could Byko be assured that Charlie wouldn't just call MI6 and relay the information verbally? The answer was—he couldn't.

Charlie looked at Byko's computer. At all of the explosives attached to it.

What if Byko had a backup plan? A detonator switch that could be activated remotely? What if Byko was merely stalling Charlie until Quinn got it ready?

Charlie bolted out of the room.

CHAPTER FORTY-EIGHT

Charlie sprinted through the maze of passageways.

"Salim!" he called. "We have to get out of here! Run! Run toward the air lock!"

The basic layout of the command center was simple enough. But navigating the corridors at a full gallop was easier said than done. Some of the passageways doubled back or shifted direction unaccountably. And—if Charlie was right about what Byko was up to—there was no time for mistakes.

As Charlie turned a corner, Salim darted out of one of the nearby passageways.

"We have to get out of here!" Charlie shouted. "Follow me!"

And then Charlie led him right into a dead end.

"Shit!" Charlie muttered and doubled back through a narrow opening into one of the main corridors. Charlie could see the air-lock door. But it was a long way—half a football field at least.

"Faster!" Charlie shouted.

As they neared the massive door, Charlie felt a shock smash through him, as though he'd been hit with a hammer. Then a great resounding boom.

Charlie kept running, but couldn't help looking back over his shoulder. For a moment or two, there was nothing. Then, at the far end of the corridor, he spotted it. A wave of fire rolling toward them like some inanimate beast.

They were only a few feet from the door and everything seemed to slip into slow motion.

"Hurry, Salim!"

The oncoming fireball roared and crackled like a thousand blowtorches.

Charlie turned the handle on the air-lock door, but it was heavy and tight and slow to open.

They weren't going to make it.

And then suddenly Charlie had the door open.

"Go!" Charlie screamed.

Salim dove past him and crashed to the floor. Charlie followed, fighting to shut the door before the fireball devoured them. The great hinges groaned as the heavy door slowly but inexorably closed. Just inches before the door met the jam, the fireball hit with an all-consuming crash. A thin curtain of flame ripped through the gap, singing the air in front of Charlie's face.

Then the door slammed shut with a deep bell-like clang, and the flame was gone, replaced by a thin pall of smoke that wavered, ghostlike, in the air before finally disappearing into nothingness.

Salim winced and reached for his leg, gasping in pain.

Charlie bent to him. "Let me see."

"It's nothing," Salim snapped, swiping away Charlie's hand.

Charlie assessed the kid. He was brave and stubborn. "Can you walk?"

"Of course I can walk. Where are we going?"

Charlie looked around. They were in a vast, high-ceilinged concrete bunker, the extent of the thing so immense that it dwarfed all human scale. There were lights here and there—but in this vast structure, they were like candles in a forest at night, barely beating back the darkness.

"What is this place?" Salim asked.

"It's a missile silo," Charlie answered and began walking toward the other side.

At the far end of the huge concrete space, he saw two thin lines, their dull sheen barely visible in the murky light.

Moving toward it, he thought he smelled something like diesel and as his eyes started to adjust to the darkness, he realized that those steel lines disappeared into a large hole in the wall.

"It's a tunnel," Charlie said. "They're on a train."

CHAPTER FORTY-NINE

ulie! Julie!"

She was sure it was Charlie's voice, but then again, how could it be . . . ?

Julie felt as though her mind was being dragged from some half-waking, half-sleeping state in which dreams interpenetrated reality, but that voice—Charlie—it had to be a dream.

Because they had killed him.

She forced herself to open her eyes and found that she was slumped on a hard bench inside an immense room, her body aching, her face sore, her wrists raw. At first she imagined she was inside a cathedral, the ceiling was that high, the space that vast. But then she realized the entire structure was built of rough concrete—she was in some kind of underground bunker. It was so large, in fact, that it had room for a small train of flatcars with automobiles chained to their beds.

And then it all flooded back. She was with Byko and his gang of thugs. And this was part of the same network of underground structures that Byko had been hopscotching through all day.

Byko's lieutenant—the sadist—was playing traffic cop in the murky light of the cavernous space, shouting and swearing at his men as they backed a number of large SUVs off the train. Julie winced as the voices and engine noises and ringing chains echoed loudly in the bunker. She had a crashing headache and with the headache came a deeper pain, the pain of regret and guilt. *"Julie! Julie!"* The voice from her dream was still echoing in her head. The dream grew sharper now as she recalled more details—someone holding the phone, someone restraining her, Charlie's voice shouting her name from the tiny speaker. She could hear the desperation in his dream voice, a desperation that was all her doing. *She'd* brought him here, *she'd* caused his pain, *she'd* exposed him to danger. In the end, she'd killed him.

And she wept, wishing she could have died in his place.

Then she spotted Byko. Immediately the weeping ceased and her sadness hardened into outrage. As usual, Byko was impeccably dressed. It seemed a little absurd to her. Here they were at the back of beyond and he looked like he'd just walked out of an Italian tailor's shop, wearing a distinctive white linen suit and white shoes. He was speaking with another man, a man she had never seen before. They were so similar in height and build that she might have mistaken him for Byko except for the fact that the man was dressed in traditional Uzbek garb.

Byko handed the man a suitcase then walked up to the top of the ramp leading to the surface, several of his bodyguards in tow. As he walked out the door, the surface was suddenly flooded with powerful lights.

Julie looked around furtively. For the first time since she'd been captured in L.A., nobody was watching her.

As she stood on tottering legs, she realized that she was wrong. A pair of eyes was tracking her from the open passenger door of one of the Cadillacs. It took her a moment to fill in the detail in the dim light, but then she saw that the watcher was a very attractive young woman staring at her without expression. She was dressed no differently from Julie—jeans and a conservative white blouse—but Julie had spent enough time in this part of the world to recognize the type. Despite her youth and beauty, her face showed her to be without expectations or hope. A prostitute, probably a heroin addict, kept in Byko's orbit as a virtual slave.

Julie met the young woman's gaze and put her finger over her lips. The young woman stared at her for a moment, then looked away with drugged-out incuriosity. Julie peered around and saw a half-open door set into the nearby wall. Maybe she could get to it and slip away unseen.

But before she'd gone twenty feet, she felt a powerful hand close violently around her upper arm. It was one of Quinn's mercenaries.

He propelled her roughly across the concrete in the opposite direction from the door.

"Where are you taking me?" Julie asked, stumbling toward the far side of the bunker.

The mercenary said nothing and soon they reached an old Soviet military truck.

"Don't move," he warned as he yanked back the canvas tarp over the tailgate.

Julie's eye caught Byko again. He was bawling

orders at his guards as the man in traditional dress stepped away from him and began disrobing.

"What are you waiting for?" someone else barked.

Julie looked toward the sound of the voice. It was Quinn, bounding toward her, yelling at her chaperone. "Get her ass in the truck!"

The hulk lifted Julie and threw her over the tailgate into the truck like a rag doll. As she rolled over, wincing from the pain, the canvas tarp descended, leaving her alone in the darkness.

Outside the truck she heard the convoy of Cadillacs and Mercedes drive by, then roar up the ramp to the surface. There was some brief shouting, barely discernible at this distance, then the sound of the convoy fading away.

Why is Byko still keeping me alive? she wondered.

She couldn't begin to imagine. She had begged Byko to kill her—back at the compound—after she'd heard that they'd murdered Charlie.

She realized now how foolishly melodramatic and selfish she had been. If there was anything that was demanded by Charlie's sacrifice, it was that she find a way to get out of this. Death would be too easy, a cop-out. She needed to live. To get back to Meagan and Ollie, to labor every day to make it up to them. To be able to explain to them what had happened, and how heroic their father was. How he had flown across the world, facing down killers whose numbers, arms and resources dwarfed anything that he could bring to bear . . .

Charlie had come for her. And had gone down fighting. She couldn't allow guilt or grief or pain or exhaustion to overwhelm her.

Somehow, some way, she would escape.

CHAPTER FIFTY

"Sir. It's him."

The comms tech pointed at the phone on Frank Hopkins's workstation in the front of the War Room.

Hopkins snatched it up. "Davis?"

"She's still alive!" Davis said, his voice almost rising to a shout. "She's with Byko. They were at the command facility of the Vasilevsky Missile Complex. There are two tunnels leading out of the facility here. One is a road. I'm pretty sure it leads to the bathhouse. No way he's going back there because he knows the location is blown. But there's a second tunnel with a railway track. I think they somehow loaded the cars onto the track and took them somewhere."

Hopkins rubbed his face, letting the burst of information settle into his brain. "Wait a moment, Mr. Davis, just . . . slow down, will you? How do you know all of this?"

Hopkins listened in wonderment as Davis explained that he'd broken into the missile complex with a team of hired guns, that he'd subdued a skeleton crew of Byko's men, that he'd found Byko's computer, rigged with explosives and that he'd managed to get some information off of it before Byko remotely detonated the equipment. Davis closed his story insisting that Byko had gotten away through the tunnels with Julie . . . "I know you must have maps or something," Davis said. "Figure out where that train comes out and you'll have a chance of catching up to him. I'm assuming the SAS is en route as we speak."

"Hold," Hopkins said. He cupped his hand over the receiver and called to his comms tech, "Get Eric Nielsen on the line."

"Let me guess," Davis said. "Karimov's giving you problems?"

"We're in the process of trying to straighten that out." Hopkins cleared his throat. He rebelled at the notion of giving sensitive details of the operation to a civilian. On the other hand Davis had already proved himself to be quite an asset. The comms tech signaled to Hopkins that he had his NSA counterpart on the phone. "Hold the line again, please."

Hopkins quickly explained to Eric Nielsen that they suspected Byko had used some kind of underground train to dodge the birds.

"Jesus," Nielsen said. "There's a narrow-gauge rail underground. It was intended for transporting missiles from one silo to the next."

"Do your maps show any logical place where they'd be able to stop the train, unload the cars and then take off again on surface roads?"

"Give me a second," Nielsen said. Hopkins heard him conduct a hushed conversation with an assistant in the background. Then he came back on the line. "As far as we know, there are only two places that have access to surface roads from the train. There's a terminus at the command center and another at the last stop on the line, Silo Thirty-nine. All the other stops just lead to subterranean silo service bays. No direct contact with surface roads. I can give you the GPS coordinates."

"Can you put a bird on it and route us the visuals? We'll keep TopSat on its current location just in case."

"I'm on it."

Hopkins rang off, then pulled up the line where Davis was holding.

"You said you found Byko's computer?"

"That's right. And I think you might have the wrong target cities . . ."

Davis went on to explain that the information he'd gleaned from the computers implied that Byko had expected Western intelligence agencies to track the nuclear-material shipments. As a result, he'd sent the material to decoy cities. And he'd chosen his decoys well—Berlin, Boston, Stockholm—cities that seemed like perfect targets.

Hopkins shook his head. If what Davis had just told him was true, then MI6 had been barking up the wrong tree for months.

"Mr. Davis, I trust you won't be insulted if I express a certain skepticism about your story."

"I took photographs of all of the files. Give me an email address and you can look at them yourself in three minutes."

Hopkins held his breath for a moment. This bloody scribbler had just built his own private mini-army, attacked a hardened facility, killed off half a

dozen trained operatives, infiltrated Byko's security
apparatus and come away with hard evidence.

He gave the man a secure email address.

Ninety seconds later, Hopkins was leaning over
the shoulder of the comms specialist, surfing through
the information. Not only was Davis correct in his
assessment about the target cities, but there was information here that could lead them to the cells in
each of those cities. Shipping manifests, credit card
statements, bank transfers, an odd cell phone bill or
two—even an operation trying its best to remain
hidden left ghost footprints everywhere. And perhaps it was Byko's obsessiveness, his impulse to mi-
cromanage and control, along with his businessman's
bias toward record keeping, that had led him to cen-
tralize what little information was available about the
comings and goings of his terrorist cells.

Hopkins didn't have exact locations for the cells
or their safe houses, but there were intimations
about their codes and communications patterns and
tangential evidence that would clearly point MI6 in
the right direction.

Hopkins only hoped it wasn't too late. The anniversary of Andijan was tomorrow and tomorrow
began in roughly thirteen hours. The intelligence
agencies would have to be notified that all of the
target cities were wrong—security units in Mel-
bourne would have to be moved to Sydney, Osaka
to Tokyo, Berlin to Hanover. The French would
have to be told to stand down while the Austrians
would have to be alerted. Same with the Swedes and
the Danes now that he knew Stockholm was the
decoy and Copenhagen the real target. And finding
the members of those terrorist cells in such a short

time—with most of them hiding in safe houses, preparing for the attack—would be beyond difficult. They might be able to get to some of them, to stop some of the attacks, but without knowing the actual targets in these nine cities, they were still in deep trouble.

The big screen at the front of the room blinked and a satellite image flashed across it. Hopkins couldn't help but feel a sense of envy at the clarity and detail of the image. The bloody Americans—all their gear was so much better than anything MI6 could afford.

Hopkins stared at the screen, orienting himself. The image appeared to be nothing more than a large empty parking lot. Then he saw several human figures emerging from what must have been a ramp from some underground structure, its entrance half concealed because of the high angle of the bird's view. Even with the superior quality of the American bird, it was impossible to make out faces. But it was clear that several of the men were carrying assault rifles.

Hopkins jumped back on the phone and briefly sketched what he saw to Davis.

Suddenly the analyst stabbed his finger at the screen. "That's him! That's Byko."

The analyst pointed at a white figure at the center of a number of darker-clothed figures. "Notice how he's giving all the orders? Pointing, gesturing. And everyone else is responding to him. Then there's the distinctive dress. This man is wearing a Western-made suit of a light-colored fabric. Everybody else is either wearing black suits or plate carrier vests and baseball caps. The black suits are his personal bodyguards and the guys with the plate carriers and baseball caps are mercenaries commanded by John Quinn."

"Okay," Hopkins said to Charlie on the phone, "it appears you were right. Byko is just leaving Silo Thirty-nine."

"What about Julie?" Davis demanded.

Hopkins gave the analyst a quizzical glance. The analyst, who was listening to Davis on a pair of headphones, shook his head.

"Not yet," Hopkins said.

As they watched, five vehicles nosed out of the exit from the bunker.

The analyst watched closely. "Escalade, Escalade, Toyota Land Cruiser . . . no, sorry, wait, that's a Mercedes G series, another Escalade, another G series . . ." He nodded. "Right, these are the usual vehicles in Byko's convoy. Look how this one rides heavier. That's Byko's personal car. Very heavily armored. It's quite distinctive, as you can see."

Hopkins could see no such thing. But the analyst knew his business.

"Right, now they're getting into the vehicle. They're . . . wait, Byko's walking back down into the bunker. Okay, okay, he's gone now . . ." After a moment the white-clothed figure came back, striding confidently toward one of the SUVs. "Ah! He's back. Now he's in the Escalade."

Another figure emerged from the underground ramp, this one being pushed or perhaps even carried by two larger men.

"Wait! That's a woman. See the hair? Western clothes, slim build . . ." The analyst looked at Hopkins and smiled. "That's Julie Davis."

The woman was quickly transferred to Byko's car and the door slammed shut. Then the convoy began to move.

"We've got her, Mr. Davis," Hopkins said into the phone. "She's going with Byko."

Charlie's heart was vibrating with excitement.

"You see her? You're *sure*?"

"Absolutely," Hopkins said. "Byko's convoy is in motion. Dirt road. Bloody great plume of dust. It's getting too dark to see . . ." Hopkins's voice changed as he issued an order to somebody in the room with him. "Switch to thermal and decrease magnification."

Charlie waited nervously. He could hear a bustle of activity behind Hopkins, bits and snatches of shouted comments and commands.

"Where are they going?" Hopkins asked someone in the room.

Charlie couldn't hear an answer.

"Map, please," Hopkins said.

Charlie heard a muffled shout by a female voice. "He's making a break for it! Holy Christ, he's heading for . . ." But Charlie couldn't make out the destination.

"What's going on?" Charlie asked. "Where's he taking her?"

"They're on the A376," Hopkins said. "They're heading for Tajikistan."

In a flash, Charlie knew where they were going. "There's a town there," he told Hopkins. "An old town just over the border that Byko's father used to own. I think there may even be a landing strip and a couple of planes."

"Yes, yes, we know it," Hopkins replied. "Just east of Kokon on the A386 . . ." He paused, presumably studying a map. "Konibodom."

"That's the one," Charlie said.

"Look, we've got an entire company of SAS lads en route to Uzbekistan. We'll simply re-task them to Tajikistan and set up an ambush. We'll take him down the moment he crosses the border. I can't tell you how grateful we are to you, Mr. Davis. But I really must get back to work. I'll call you the moment we have Julie in hand."

And the line went dead.

Charlie stared at his phone for a long moment. The screen winked off and he gazed into the semi-darkness, feeling oddly numb. The sky was growing black now and the wind bit into his skin. Salim sat on a curb a few feet away, resting his wounded leg, his clothes rattling and rustling in the frigid breeze.

Charlie should have felt encouraged. This was what he'd wanted all along. But when he thought about the reality of a military ambush on Byko's heavily armed contingent . . .

Charlie had seen Byko up close and there was simply no way that he would allow himself to be taken alive. And Quinn, those mercenaries—he just didn't see them throwing up their hands and walking placidly toward a lifetime in prison.

How could Julie avoid getting caught in the cross fire? How would an SAS team possibly protect her?

The answer was . . . they couldn't.

CHAPTER FIFTY-ONE

Charlie drove in silence for almost an hour, first down the dirt road from the command center, then on the highway. He was exhausted and famished and despondent. And Salim seemed to recognize it.

"Would you like me to drive?" the kid asked.

Charlie slowed and pulled off onto the dark shoulder of the road. Uzbek highways were never that busy, but at this time of night there was not a single headlight in view. As Charlie got out of the car and leaned against the trunk, he realized he had been driving aimlessly down the highway, no particular destination in mind. He pulled out his phone, not expecting to find any signal available. To his surprise, the screen showed three bars.

Charlie dialed home. Becca answered.

"Hello?"

"I lost her," Charlie said. "I was so close. But I lost her."

"Oh, Charlie . . ." Becca's voice was thin, distant. "Is she . . . ?"

"No. But it doesn't look good. I know I shouldn't be telling you that, I . . ." He didn't know what to say or why he was saying it to her. "She's the only woman I ever loved."

He could hear Becca crying, then manage to gather herself. "She loves you, Charlie. No matter what happened . . . you know she loves you."

He stared out into the blackness. He supposed he was parked at the edge of a cotton field, but there was no way to know for sure. No moon, no street lamps, not a farmhouse or a car in sight. Just utter darkness. He had never felt so alone, so empty, so defeated.

In the background Charlie heard Meagan's joyful voice. "Daddy! Daddy! Is that Daddy? I wanna talk to Daddy!"

The sound of her voice cut through Charlie's despair. "Put her on," he said.

"Hi!" Meagan shouted.

Charlie wiped his face with the back of his arm and tried to steady his voice. "Hey, sweetheart."

"Are you coming home soon?"

Charlie's heart felt like it would wrench itself out of his chest. "Yeah, sweetie, I am. Real soon."

"We're having a cake tomorrow. For Ollie's birthday."

Ollie's birthday. Jesus, he'd almost forgotten. It seemed like something from another life. "I know. I'm going to try to make it home for that . . . I'm really gonna . . ." Charlie's voice trailed off.

As he stared out into the blackness, something struck him. He stood and looked at Salim, standing there on his one good leg, leaning against the driver's side of the car.

"Daddy?"

"Sweetheart, I gotta go," Charlie said, his voice

suddenly urgent. "I gotta call you back later, okay? I love you. Tell Ollie I love him, too."

"Bye!" Meagan's voice was cheerfully oblivious.

Charlie came around the car, close to Salim. "The rally in Andijan—who organized it?"

Salim shrugged. "Nobody knows. The word just spread."

That was exactly the answer Charlie wanted to hear.

Something had been tugging at his mind. It was what Byko had said to him on the phone a few hours ago.

Always with the squares. It seems that is our destiny.

Charlie reached past Salim and opened the car door. "I'm driving." He hopped in and fired up the motor as Salim circled around and got back in the passenger seat. Charlie thumbed Hopkins's number as he pulled onto the highway again.

"Hopkins!" Charlie could hear a loud engine whine in the background. It sounded as though Hopkins was inside a chopper.

"What is it?" Hopkins had to shout to be heard over the sound of the engine.

"There's going to be a major demonstration in Andijan tomorrow. Commemorating the massacre."

"And?"

"It can't be a coincidence. Byko's going to be there!"

"No, Mr. Davis, he's not. I already told you—"

"Listen! It doesn't make sense. It's been *six years* and there's never been any kind of ceremony. Not so much as a couple of old ladies lighting candles. I'm telling you, Byko organized this demonstration himself. And that's why he's keeping Julie alive. He wants to take her there. To show her. So everything comes full circle in some way."

"Maybe he did organize it, Mr. Davis. Maybe he even intended being there. But now you've been chasing him around the country, his cover's blown—he's going underground."

"And you're sure it was him on the satellite?"

"We're tracking his every move. He's still heading straight for Tajikistan and I'm going to be there personally to supervise the SAS ambush. I promise you, if Julie is there, I'll do everything I can to make sure she walks away safely." The jet engine was rising in pitch. "Now do yourself a favor. Get to the capital, sit tight and wait to hear from us. I have to go now."

The phone clicked.

Salim looked at Charlie as a road sign swam up in front of them.

Tashkent 130 km

Get to the capital, sit tight.

Charlie had a sinking feeling in the pit of his stomach. After all of this, was he really going to check into the Radisson and wait to hear from Hopkins?

He thought of everything that had happened in Andijan six years ago, everything that he'd been through, how much of his life had been structured as a reaction to the tragedy there.

Tashkent: 130 kilometers.

Safety.

No, Charlie heard himself say. *Some things are written.*

One way or another, he had to return to Andijan.

Charlie blew past the exit for Tashkent and pressed his foot to the accelerator. If he drove straight through, they would be at the rally by sunrise.

CHAPTER FIFTY-TWO

Julie sat in the backseat next to Quinn, hands manacled behind her, feet bound to hooks in the floor. There was no way to struggle and nothing to do but try to figure out where they were headed. She gazed out the window, hoping she might be able to see a street sign or something in the landscape that might give her a clue. She could tell they were speeding down a highway, but the rest was a blur.

"Where are we going?" she asked Quinn.

"Where do you think?" he replied.

"It's not like I can do anything to hurt you with that information."

"I don't know," Quinn said. "You're pretty cunning."

"Are we headed for the border?"

"That would be a logical idea."

"Tajikistan or Kazakhstan?"

"Hmmm . . . what makes you think I even know?"

He smiled with that malevolent glint in his eye, toying with her.

The idea of vengeance had always seemed anathema to Julie, a reductive idea that only perpetuated a cycle of violence that still enslaved half the world.

But sitting here now, staring at this horror of a man, she found herself yearning for the chance—one chance—to bludgeon him to death. Or better yet, to within an inch of his life. Then maybe to pour gasoline all over his wounded body and stand over him with a match. Yes, that might be something. To watch him writhe in agony, begging to be spared.

"Penny for your thoughts," Quinn baited.

"Oh," Julie said, "maybe I'll tell you some other time." She opted for another tack. "Alisher! Alisher!"

The tinted window divider lowered and Byko stared at her from the front seat.

"You're not being a very gracious host," she said. "The least you could do is tell me where we're going."

"You haven't asked me why," he said.

"Why what?"

"Why I am doing all of this."

"Well, go ahead then. Enlighten me."

"After you left—after Andijan—all the politicians from the West came out with those sanctimonious faces. You remember . . . ? The 'shock' and 'horror' as they declared: 'There must be progress on human rights in Uzbekistan.' For years they had been saying this while they casually turned a blind eye to the regime. But this time, Karimov was on the defensive. He tells the U.S.: 'You don't like how I do things, sorry, no more military base.' And he kicks them out.

"So what does the almighty USA do? Well, their multinational corporations need our resources, the military needs that base on the Afghan border, so . . . they come groveling back to Karimov. America leads and then here comes England and Germany,

Australia and Japan—and soon they all begin to trade again, as though nothing at all had happened. The gold, the cotton, the oil . . . this is what they care about. Not the people. Only what they can buy and sell. And your media? The humanitarians like your beloved Charlie?" His lips curled into a bitter smile. "Of course, your media forgets about us entirely."

Byko was leaning over the seat, as though by his sheer physical effort he could convince her of his point and she realized that he wasn't really talking to her but to some idea of her, some idealized, invented Julie who had betrayed him.

"So now Karimov knows for sure: he can trade our resources and land for the silence of the West. He can do anything he likes to quiet us—there will be no limits, no consequences for his actions. In fact, America and Britain declare Uzbekistan a 'close ally' in the war on terror. Your security agencies even lend a hand, helping us to root out extremists in our country. 'Extremist,' of course, is a code word for anybody who doesn't do precisely what Karimov tells them to do."

Julie was no stranger to this argument. It was the same thing every liberal-minded person who knew anything about Uzbekistan said. But it didn't exactly give Byko an excuse to blow up thousands of people. And after all of the lying and begging, obfuscating and cajoling she'd done with him, she couldn't take it anymore. So she finally let it rip . . .

"You think you're the only one who's felt pain? You think this is what Daniella would have wanted you to do? Kill thousands of innocent people? You disgrace her name, you disgrace your son's name!"

Byko's eyes burned. "Listen to me!" he said.

"No!" she cried. "I don't want to listen to one more word from you!"

"Listen." His voice dropped to a whisper. "I told you about my sister being tortured . . . how she came home and killed herself . . . ? What I never told you was that the CIA was at Jaslyk. CIA was leading the interrogation."

Julie's eyes met Byko's. Guys like Quinn didn't appear in a vacuum. Guys like Quinn became who they were because the CIA manufactured them. But maybe Byko had just heard some spurious rumor and chose to believe it because it justified his insanity.

"And MI6," he continued, "*your* MI6—well, my dear, it turns out they are the ones who tipped off Karimov about the rally in Andijan six years ago."

"Who told you that?" She flashed a hateful look at Quinn. "Him?"

"You don't believe it? How do you think Karimov had so many soldiers ready?"

Her mind was racing. And it had always needled her. How had so many soldiers and choppers and armored personnel carriers converged on Andijan so quickly? Even if they'd been tipped off by Karimov's secret police, there was only a small military garrison in Andijan. The rest had to have come from someplace miles and miles away. And it wasn't as if the Uzbek military was the most efficient organization in the world. . . .

She looked at Byko and knew he could read what was going through her mind. Her own bearings were vulnerable now. But maybe if she could acknowledge his point of view, meet him halfway, it would give her some credibility to penetrate him.

"Even if it's true, Alisher, it doesn't justify what you're doing."

Byko had turned all the way around in his seat, his left arm gripping the headrest as though he wanted to strangle it, his eyes looking through her into his own private horror. "I saw her body," he whispered. "I saw what they did to my beautiful little sister."

"Then think of her," Julie said. "Think of what she would have wanted. Not this. Not this, Alisher."

For a long moment, he held her gaze. Then the tinted window rose with a soft whine and he disappeared.

CHAPTER FIFTY-THREE

Hopkins stamped in the cold to keep his feet warm. He was standing outside an abandoned farmhouse overlooking the virtually deserted A377 highway, just over the border in Tajikistan. The sun was beginning to paint the horizon, but it had done nothing yet to cut the chill.

Two companies of SAS soldiers were now set up to interdict Alisher Byko's convoy, which had been racing toward the border for the last seven hours. Hopkins had been an infantry officer before joining MI6, but he was making no attempt to give "helpful" tips to the SAS. They were the best in the world at what they did. All he needed to do was tell them to stop the convoy and capture Byko and that's what they would do.

"Eighteen minutes," one of the SAS men said into his microphone.

The convoy was being tracked by satellite—U.S. and UK—just to make sure no one lost them. A sortie of American F-22s lurked over the horizon in case close air support was required. Hopkins was monitoring the convoy on his laptop.

At the window, a half-dozen snipers were busy

stuffing bits of foliage into the mottled fabric of their ghillie suits while a platoon of paras jogged toward the road. A large tractor-trailer was pulled round on the shoulder of the A377. In another two and a half minutes, it would back out onto the road, mimicking a jacknifed truck and cutting off the highway.

Byko's convoy would slow at the sight of it and the SAS lads would pounce.

Gordon Bryce was monitoring the op from the command center at the Puzzle Palace, adding his two cents by radio when necessary. The last time he had given instructions, though, the SAS commander, a Major Rowbotham, had gotten unnecessarily testy, something to the effect that he ought to "bloody well piss off until the professionals have bloody well done their job."

Just as well—he had better things to do than hand-hold some gun-toting prima donna in Uzbekistan. He'd been on the phone almost constantly since two o'clock in the morning, riding point on the dissemination of information to the various parties who were threatened by Byko's plan. In fact, he'd had a rather long conversation with the PM himself, briefing him again on the specifics of the threat.

The information that had come from Charlie Davis had yielded some serious results—arrests in Copenhagen, Vienna, Sydney and London (including a raid on a warehouse in the East End where they'd recovered some of the uranium), but all of the captured men seemed to be at the lower levels of their respective terrorist organizations. By all accounts, the bombers were still out there and the intelligence agencies were no closer to finding them. The one piece of intel that gave everyone hope was this: under interrogation, each captured man had insisted the same thing. That everyone in their organizations was still in the dark about the targets and that Byko was intending to wait until the last possible moment to disseminate those targets to the bombers. Which meant that capturing Byko had the utmost importance. If they could get to Byko before the targets were given out, it seemed clear that there was no backup plan, that the cells would be standing by with no instructions and that the bombings would in fact not occur.

"Put the SO feed on," Bryce said to Wilson, a doughy-faced comms tech.

The young tech flipped some buttons, toggling over to one of the dozens of tiny screens on the wall, and the satellite view of Uzbekistan disappeared.

Now the main screen showed hundreds of uniformed police, tactical officers and plainclothes SO detectives gathered in a warehouse for a briefing. At a lectern stood London's Police Commissioner, Sir Ian Craille, along with the commander of Special Operations and various other police functionaries. The briefing had begun a few minutes earlier and the police commissioner, a long-faced man with white hair, was in midsentence: " . . . suffice it to say that we are to be on the highest alert. All leave is canceled and every available officer will be assigned to protect all the usual sensitive targets. Due to the lack of specificity of our intelligence we must prepare for the possibility that the attack could come from anywhere at any time."

The head of SO, Assistant Commissioner Cressida Bevis, leaned forward and whispered something in Sir Ian's ear.

"Thank you, AC Bevis. As to the issue of the precise nature of the threat—we anticipate dirty bombs packed with high levels of radioactive materials which are capable of inflicting substantial human damage—not to mention untold property damage."

Sir Ian surveyed his audience gravely.

"I must stress that this is more than just a threat. We have hard intelligence that this is going to happen today. It's only a question now of precisely where and when. I trust that each and every officer in this room understands the need for absolute and utter secrecy. If word gets out, the panic will cause untold damage to this great city. Now I can answer a few brief questions before—"

Bryce pulled a finger across his throat, signaling the comms officer to cut the feed from the police briefing. He was satisfied to know that wheels were in motion. According to the latest reports, similar briefings were going out to police in each of the targeted cities. He could only imagine how shocked—and frustrated—the police in those cities must feel.

So now it was all down to the SAS operation to seize Byko.

"How much time?" he demanded.

"They should have a visual in the field within thirty seconds, sir."

"Put it on."

The satellite image appeared: three vehicles blasting down the A377 at high speed. The tech had set the satellite on infrared so that they were seeing heat, not visual spectrum. He could make out three teams of SAS, white splotches against the green-tinged ground.

Bryce hunched over the microphone and shouted, "Prepare for R and S. We'll go on my command."

Stupid bloody prat," one of the SAS men muttered after Bryce's command came over the radio.

Hopkins tried unsuccessfully to stifle a smile. There had been a time when units like the SAS were entirely independent of control from headquarters. But with the advent of modern comms, soldiers often had to do their work with London peering over their shoulders, second-guessing their every move. They made no bones about how much they hated it.

"On my mark," Major Rowbotham said, ignoring Bryce.

Hopkins could hear engines in the distance now—Byko's convoy—and he trained his field glasses on the hill about a half mile away. The location had been carefully chosen so that the convoy would come over the ridge and have very little time to react to the semitrailer "jackknifed" on the road.

The truck had been backed out about a minute earlier, the hood lifted, and some sort of small incendiary device ignited inside the engine compartment so that it appeared to be suffering from a major engine malfunction.

Any vehicle Byko traveled in could be presumed to be fully hardened—steel-plated doors and roof, inch-thick polycarbonate-reinforced windows, Kevlar paneling—but depleted uranium rounds would cut through hardened steel plate as though it were

cheesecloth and there were three sniper teams running .50-caliber Barrett rifles on the hillside overlooking the road, prepared for the ambush.

Hopkins shifted focus slightly on his binoculars
as the first of the three SUVs crested into view.
Almost immediately, all three were braking hard,
their tires squealing on the road.

Rowbotham spoke into the radio. "Go."

Three loud gunshots split the air, echoing back
and forth in the narrow valley. The simultaneous
shots from the sharpshooters were perfectly timed.
The .50s slammed into the SUVs' engines, smashing through the armor plate and into the engine
blocks, blasting a shower of wrecked pistons and
timing gears out the bottoms of all three vehicles.
With that, the vehicles rolled silently to a stop,
steam pouring out of their engine compartments.

Again, the .50s banged, sending another set of
rounds downrange—this time through the windshield of each car. The intent was not to kill anyone
inside, but to send the clear message that any resis-
tance would result in the massacre of everyone in
the cars.

At the sound of the Barretts, two dozen men rose
out of the ground as though spawned from dragon's
teeth. They had been there all along, of course—but
so effectively camouflaged that it had been nearly
impossible to spot them.

Less than half a beat later, a second fire team
burst out from around the truck.

Hopkins imagined how terrifying it must have
been for the occupants of Byko's convoy. One
second, they were bombing down the road, only a
few miles from their destination. The next second,

they were stopped dead, holes punched in their "bulletproof" cars, sixty automatic weapons trained directly on them. It was a classic, perfectly executed L-shaped ambush. Hopkins felt a burst of pride in the men. This op had been dumped in their laps at the last second and they'd executed everything perfectly, leaving Byko only two choices.

Surrender or die.

But thus far no doors had opened, no return shots fired, no one had appeared at all. Rowbotham nodded to Hopkins and they began hiking down the hillside toward the three motionless vehicles. Hopkins would have been well within his brief to have waited at the top of the hill and let the SAS handle all the risky bits. After all, there was still a possibility of gunplay.

But he wanted to be there to see Byko's face.

Thirty feet from the lead car, Hopkins stopped, crossed his arms and shouted into a bullhorn, "Right then, Byko. Out you come!"

For a moment nothing happened. Then the rear door of the second SUV opened slowly.

Sixty rifles swiveled toward the door.

A young woman stepped tentatively out of the car. With her brown hair, blue jeans and white shirt, she looked vaguely like Julie Davis. But this girl couldn't have been more than sixteen.

Another door opened and a tall, dark-haired man in a white linen suit stepped out of the car, hands extended, palms out to show he wasn't armed. He stood slowly, buttoned his beautiful suit, smoothed the front of his coat, took off his sunglasses and smiled.

"You've got me," he said in Russian.

"Christ," muttered Hopkins.

The SAS commander looked at him curiously, brow furrowed.

"That's not Byko," Hopkins said. "It's a double."

CHAPTER FIFTY-FOUR

Charlie felt an odd mix of anxiety, sadness and anticipation as he and Salim drove through the outskirts of Andijan. It was the capital city of the province, but it was a drab, ugly town. The streets were poorly paved, the storefronts were barren, and at this early hour, the sidewalks were nearly deserted. But when they neared the city center, he saw many more people, and by the time they got within half a mile of the Square, the streets were packed and vehicular traffic could no longer move.

Charlie spotted a vacant lot on his right and pulled into it. They'd have to walk from here. He grabbed his Sig Sauer, made sure he had a dozen extra cartridges in his pocket and got out of the car. His cohort did the same, but the instant Salim shut his door and started limping toward the town, Charlie saw how injured he really was.

"What's going on with your leg?" Charlie asked.

"Nothing. I'm fine."

"Let me see it."

"It's okay. There's nothing wrong with—"

"Salim."

Charlie bent down and Salim reluctantly allowed

him to roll up his pants. The edges of the gaping wound were angry and red, with a rim of white showing along the margins of the cut. A clear liquid weeped out the bottom, crusting along the top of his sock.

"This is infected," Charlie told him. "You need to get to a hospital."

"Not when you still need my help."

Charlie looked at the kid—his bravery, his nobility, his largesse.

"You're not going to be any help to me if you can barely walk," Charlie told him. "There used to be a clinic just up the road. I'm going to leave you there."

Salim tried to fight him, but the instant he put any pressure on the leg he nearly collapsed.

Charlie put his arm around him, absorbing the kid's weight, and helped him trudge through the growing crowd. They walked a half-dozen blocks in silence, each of them taking in the scene around them. The mood today was far different than it had been the last time Charlie was here. The placards themselves told the story. Six years ago they were adorned with hopeful slogans. Today, many had photos of friends and family members who'd been killed in the Square.

When they arrived at the clinic, Charlie was grateful to see that it was still there and that it was open today.

"You don't need to take me inside," Salim said. "I am slowing you down as it is."

Charlie took out some money and offered it to Salim.

"I don't want that," Salim snapped, looking insulted.

"It's for the doctor," Charlie said. "Make sure they give you the proper medicine. An antibiotic."

Salim reluctantly took the cash and crumpled it into his pocket, then looked at Charlie incredulously. "How are you going to find your wife?"

"I don't know," Charlie said. "But I know Byko will be here."

"I wish you luck."

Charlie nodded. "I can't even begin to thank you."

"I am the one who should be thanking you," Salim said. "For making us believe that we must fight. That change was possible."

"I'm not sure I was right," Charlie said.

"You were," Salim assured him. "Even if it hasn't happened yet."

Charlie felt himself well up with tears. This kid—this naive, yet worldly kid—reminded him so much of himself at that age.

"You better go," Salim said.

Charlie touched his heart with his palm. *"Assalaam aleikum."*

"Aleikum salaam."

And with that, Salim smiled, limped toward the clinic and disappeared inside.

Charlie watched the closing door for an extra moment, then turned back toward the Square. Now that he was finally here, in Andijan, he felt in his bones that Hopkins was wrong, that Byko and Julie would be here, too. Somewhere.

Julie was trussed up in the rear of Byko's vast presidential suite. The hotel was a holdover from the final days of the Soviet Union—a Stalinist fun house mirror version of a Western luxury hotel. Fancy woodwork, a grand piano, oil paintings on the walls, Belgian chocolates on the pillows. And yet when you homed in on the details, there was something weird and cheap about it all—Bakelite handles on the furniture, worn patches in the silk carpet, hideous pink and green reimaginings of 1970s-era Pop Art.

She glanced surreptitiously at Quinn, who was watching her like a hawk. Then her eyes fell on Byko, who was standing on the balcony overlooking the gathering crowd in Babur Square. Two more bodyguards stood at the doorway outside the room.

Julie considered her odds if she tried to bull her way past Quinn and dive off the balcony into the crowd, but quickly rejected the idea. The fourth floor was too high and there was a pretty good chance she'd die if she fell. If not, she'd certainly break a leg and Byko's guards down below would be on her in no time.

Besides, before she could think of escape, she needed to take one more stab at Byko. She'd seen his vulnerability back there in the car and she still felt there might be an opening, however narrow and elusive, for her to convince him to call off the horrendous enterprise he'd set in motion.

The French doors opened and Byko came in off the balcony.

"How many people are down there?" she asked.

He stared at her for a long moment, as if appraising how to get through to her. "I know you think that what I am doing I do merely for revenge. For my own pain. But it isn't true. I am very well aware that my country is filled with people who've lost far more than me. Today I will speak for them."

"But you don't speak for them, Alisher. If they knew what you were planning, they would be horrified."

"If you ask them, yes, that is what they would say. But in their hearts a part of them will cry out, 'Finally! *Finally* someone has done something to wake up the world.'"

"So you're doing all this for 'your people'? What do you think will happen after all the bombings? The West will rally around Karimov, America and Britain will give him more money to contain the 'extremists,' and he'll have even freer rein to clamp down on the people in the name of fighting terrorism. You must know that."

"Sometimes things need to be pushed to a breaking point," Byko replied. "For there to be real change."

"You still have time to call it off. Please, Alisher. There's still decency inside you. I know there is."

"Decency is not a luxury I can afford," he said. "And there is nothing inside me now but rage."

Charlie thought he was prepared for how strong his feelings would be when he got near the Square, but as soon as he spotted the sculpture of Babur in the distance, he broke out in a cold sweat.

Even from afar, he recognized the precise spot where Byko had clung to his dead son and screamed up at the heavens. From there, his eyes trailed to the patch of stone where he had been gunned down. Then his gaze settled on a young girl. She couldn't have been more than ten and her hair was blond but there was something about her face, her posture, her manner that reminded him of the girl from that day. The one he'd tried to save.

And suddenly, he was back there again, reliving it all.

As the memories overwhelmed him, spots of light swam in front of his eyes and he thought he might faint.

"Sir," someone asked. "Are you all right?"

Charlie found his focus and noticed an elderly man in a beige linen suit standing next to him.

"Are you all right, sir? Do you need something to drink?"

The man offered him a bottle of water, but Charlie straightened and took a deep breath, "I'm fine," he said. "Thank you. I'm fine."

The old man nodded as if he understood everything. "It is hard to come back here," he said. His eyes met Charlie's for an instant and then he headed into the Square.

Charlie took another deep breath, then gazed around, unsure what he was looking for when he felt his phone vibrating in his pocket. He took it out and saw it was Hopkins.

Was it news of Julie? Charlie closed his eyes for a beat, took a deep breath, then answered . . .

"This is Charlie Davis."

"We were wrong," Hopkins admitted. "We were wrong and you were right. Byko's in Andijan and he has Julie with him."

Charlie stiffened. "Where?"

"A safe house outside the city."

"And how do you know all of this?"

"We've captured some of his men. They've coughed up the truth."

"So what do you want from me?"

"We have no way to gain access to the country. Karimov has made himself unavailable and there isn't the political will to send in a covert operation on foreign soil. Even if there were, there simply isn't the time at this point." Hopkins hesitated. "We need you to get to Byko."

"And do what?"

"We believe he's waiting until the last moment to give out the targets to his people. It's possible there may still be time to stop him."

"And what if I'm too late?"

"Then it would be a matter of coercing him to tell you where they are. Either way, it means apprehending him by force."

Charlie nearly laughed. "Oh, is that all?"

Hopkins's voice was gravelly and tired. "I know we've already asked too much of both of you. Believe me, I know that. But you are our only option at this point."

"The men you captured, they say Byko's in a safe house?"

"That part is our deduction."

"Well, it doesn't make sense," Charlie argued. "Byko didn't come all the way here to hole up away from the action. He'll want to be close, maybe even participate in the event."

"At this point, I am willing to defer to your judgment, Mr. Davis."

For the first time, Charlie could hear a defeated tone in Hopkins's voice. He almost felt sorry for the man.

"I'll do what I can," Charlie said. "You can trace my whereabouts by tracking this phone."

He hung up and looked around.

Most of the buildings surrounding the Square belonged to the government. But there were a couple of hotels—the Metropol and the Rossiya. The Metropol was the nicer of the two, a hotel that went back all the way to czarist times. But Charlie vaguely remembered hearing that former Soviet premier Mikhail Brezhnev had visited Andijan once and had stayed at the Rossiya.

According to the story he had heard, the local party bosses had spent millions of rubles to build a massive presidential suite on the fourth floor in preparation for Brezhnev's one-day stay in the city. Charlie seemed to recall a photo of Brezhnev reviewing a parade from the balcony, wooden faced, with his giant cartoon eyebrows and his fur hat. From a security perspective, the huge suite would be the best place for Byko to stay. Plus, it would appeal to Byko's grandiosity, his lunatic sense of historical mission.

Charlie began pushing through the crowd toward the Rossiya, a squat, ugly building that took up an entire city block along the western edge of Babur Square. As he got closer he saw a figure standing on a balcony overlooking the giant expanse of the Square, but from a distance he couldn't quite make out the man.

He walked faster, heart thrumming with anticipation. Because Charlie could scarcely believe his eyes.

Standing there alone—unguarded—was Alisher Byko.

CHAPTER FIFTY-FIVE

Charlie pulled the hood over his jacket to obscure his face from Byko. He was looking straight down at the people in the Square and Charlie felt sure that Byko could actually recognize him in the crowd. But Charlie quickly realized that Byko's head was barely moving, that he didn't seem to be looking around. He couldn't see Byko's eyes from that distance, but he imagined that Byko might not be surveying the crowd at all. That he, too, was back in time, reliving the events of six years ago.

For a split second, Charlie's heart ached for the man. After all, he had lost everything—his wife, his son—while Charlie's wife and son had been spared, had in fact been delivered.

It made Charlie think about the nature of pain and what people do with it. Some are able to rise above it, to survive and heal, while others slip deeper and deeper into anger. He wondered what it was that had sent Byko down this harrowing path.

In any event, there was no saving him now. Now, he and his rage simply needed to be extinguished.

Charlie stuck his hand in his pocket and felt for his trusty Sig Sauer. Could he get off a shot from here? He dropped to a knee as if he needed to tie his shoe and lined up a shot with his finger. Byko must have been sixty yards up. And the balcony wall, plus the railing, created a very difficult angle. This would require a sharpshooter of the highest order. Someone like Salim.

Charlie cursed himself. He should've brought the kid after all. Should he go back for him now? By the time he fetched Salim and brought him here, was there any chance that Byko would still be standing on the balcony in this private reverie?

Charlie seriously doubted it. He would have to find another way. A way into that presidential suite.

A light rain began to fall as Charlie approached the large green awning over the hotel's main entrance. Immediately, Charlie noticed two men standing there. They both wore tiny earpieces and there were bulges under their leather jackets big enough to be submachine guns.

Byko's men, for sure. No way he'd get past them.

Charlie pulled his baseball cap down over his face and circled around the block until he reached the rear of the hotel.

An alleyway led behind the Rossiya to a loading dock.

A door was propped open with a stainless steel trash can and Charlie could see cooks inside the kitchen, making food over large gas stoves.

This was his way in.

Charlie moved quickly, but surreptitiously. When he got twenty feet from the entrance, two men burst out of the door.

Leather jackets. Earpieces.

Charlie froze as Byko's guards fixed directly on him. He knew that if he turned and ran, he'd give himself away. But he couldn't just stand there frozen either. He had to do something. So he tripped intentionally. As he stood, he scooped up a champagne bottle from the ground next to the Dumpster and began singing loudly in Russian, weaving from side to side and waving the empty bottle in front of his face as though conducting an orchestra. Between the rain and the baseball cap and the bottle in front of his face, maybe the guards wouldn't recognize him.

"Get out of here, you shit-eating drunk!" one of them yelled. Charlie "slipped" and fell, crawled a few steps and then stumbled away, Byko's men laughing and hurling abuse at him until he reached the corner. Righting himself, Charlie cursed and hurled the bottle at the wall in frustration. He was running out of options.

He continued to circle the building—but every single entrance was guarded. Worst-case scenario, he would have to try shooting his way into the building, but he knew that would almost certainly be a losing proposition.

Maybe a distraction? A disguise?

No. There had to be another way into the hotel. He surveyed the area and spotted a recently built multistory parking garage behind one wing of the Rossiya. Next to it was a run-down old tenement. And the top floor of the garage was connected to the roof of the hotel.

What if . . .

He stared up for a few seconds, shading his eyes

against the rain with a cupped hand. It was hard to tell from here.

He jogged around to the front of the tenement. The property was surrounded by a rusting chain-link fence. Charlie crawled over it, sprinted through the gaping front door and up the urine-smelling stairway. At the top was another door, this one secured with an old padlock. Charlie kicked the door twice and the rotten wood gave way, the door falling onto the roof of the tenement with a sodden thud.

The rain was coming down much harder as he walked out to the edge of the building and looked down. The top floor of the garage was about six feet from the roof of the tenement and about ten feet down. Surrounding the roof was a low brick wall, maybe three feet high—just high enough that it would be dangerous to jump over. He'd have to perch on the wall and leap with no running start. He felt the surface of the brick. Typical Soviet workmanship—the brick so spongy and friable that he was able to gouge it with his fingernails. And if that wasn't bad enough, a stiff wind was driving the rain right into his face. He'd be jumping against the wind.

He climbed up onto the little wall, balancing on his tiptoes. When he was standing on the roof it had looked like quite a drop, but now, swaying in the windy rain on a four-inch-wide piece of slippery brick, it felt like it was a million miles down.

In the alley below, under an awning, one of the guards flicked his cigarette into the air, then stretched and surveyed the alley with a slow, professional sweep of his head.

Charlie tested his weight, swinging his arms and

readying himself to jump. Something gave way under his foot and he fought to keep himself from falling. He managed to recover his balance, but as he straightened, moving his foot to a more secure part of the wall, a small hunk of brick broke free and fell, tumbling slowly through the air.

The brick hit not ten feet from Byko's guards, letting out a sharp crack that echoed loudly through the alley. The two guards started, one of them frowning curiously, the other reaching under his coat and smoothly sweeping out an MP5 submachine gun.

It was now or never.

Charlie coiled, bent his knees and leaped.

CHAPTER FIFTY-SIX

Julie sat on the piano bench in the palatial living room of the Rossiya Hotel's presidential suite, playing "Chopsticks" on the astonishingly out-of-tune grand piano.

Byko continued to stand on the covered balcony in the rain, looking out at the Square. Quinn sat ten feet from Julie, his feet up, whistling what she thought might be a tune from *West Side Story*. Across the room, the young man with the Homer Simpson shirt was setting up a computer and a video camera.

There was really nothing she could do. Quinn carried a gun and had the reflexes of a cat. Unless there was some kind of distraction that would help her escape, she suspected she didn't have more than an hour or two to live.

It was a very strange feeling. The drugs and the waterboarding had given her something to fight against, something to focus her. But this—sitting around letting the clock tick down on her life, here in what passed for luxury in Uzbekistan—seemed ridiculous and surreal.

The computer tech fussed with the camera, then

the lights, then the camera, then pecked away on the computer again. When his work was complete, the technician moved to the balcony door and told Byko that everything was ready for him.

Byko came in and sat in front of the computer. From Julie's perspective it appeared to be a fancy version of Skype: a camera and several bright lights were pointed at the chair in which Byko sat.

"Security protocols?" Byko asked.

"Totally untraceable, high-prime encryption, parallel packet redundancy, sir. Everything's working perfectly and the recipients are standing by."

Byko looked at his watch, then nodded at the technician.

"Three . . . two . . . one . . . ," the technician said. Then he pointed his finger silently at Byko as he pressed a button on the computer.

On the side of the camera, a tiny red light blinked on. Simultaneously a rectangular window opened on the screen and Byko's image appeared in hi-def, the lights perfectly picking up the lines of his jaw, the intensity of his eyes. He looked like the host of a news talk show on CNN.

Byko stared solemnly into the lens. "The time is near, my brothers, and all has been said that need be said. Thirty minutes after I conclude this transmission, you will be sent the targets and routing plans for your escape. I will go into hiding. You may not hear from me for six months or a year. But I *will* contact you again, and we will see then what still remains to be accomplished. Until then, go with force toward what is right."

Byko nodded at the technician. With that, the red light blinked out and the connection to his far-flung network disconnected. Byko must have felt her gaze on him because he turned suddenly to face her.

"There was so much you could have done in this world," she said grimly.

He assessed her coolly. "To know that you'll be watching me, this will be very satisfying. That it will be the last thing you do before you die—I'll find a way to live with that."

Then he turned and strode out.

As the door slammed shut behind him, she caught a glimpse of the two guards standing in the hallway. That certainly wouldn't be the way out.

Again, she considered making a break for the balcony and jumping into the crowd. It was her only chance at this point. If she could get to the balcony door and throw it open, it would block Quinn for a moment. Once she got out the door and onto the balcony, she'd have a step, maybe a step and a half lead time ahead of him. Throw in the element of surprise and she might just make it to the ledge.

She clenched her fists, focusing, readying herself. Once she started to go, there would be no turning back. Three strides to the door, three strides to the—

Quinn's walkie-talkie crackled loudly, interrupting her train of thought. A voice said, "There's something happening on the roof."

"Like what?" he demanded.

"I don't know," the voice replied. "It's raining like a bitch out here. But I think someone just jumped across it."

CHAPTER FIFTY-SEVEN

Charlie's feet slammed into concrete and for a moment he teetered on the edge, fighting the wind that threatened to blow him over. Just as he was about to fall, he spotted a short stub of rusting conduit sticking up from the concrete, grabbed it and hauled himself onto the roof.

Had the guards on the ground seen him? No way to know. Either way, he needed to move fast. He rolled, sprang to his feet, sprinted across the parking garage and climbed over a low concrete barrier that led to the adjoining roof of the hotel. A brief scan of the roof revealed a door. He tried the handle but it was locked. He kicked hard—several times—each kick sending a wave of shock through his back. Grimacing, he eyed the roof for something to pry open the door. A tool, a knife, a stray piece of metal. But there was nothing around but a broad expanse of wet gravel, a few rolls of tar paper and some conduit that appeared firmly affixed to the roof.

Charlie drew his Sig Sauer and fired into the lock. The noise of the gun, reflecting off the steel door, was terrible. Even with the clamor of the crowd in Babur Square and the din of the storm, there was no doubt that Byko's people would hear it. He grabbed the handle and tried to turn it, but it still wouldn't move. He fired a second time, aiming the 9-millimeter slug at the exact junction of the door and the frame. The second shot did the trick, cracking the bolt in half. He braced one foot on the frame and pulled on the handle. With a scream of metal on metal, the door slowly ripped open.

As he descended the stairs, he heard another door banging open somewhere down below. He knew it couldn't be an accident. Somebody was coming for him.

He gripped the Sig Sauer in two hands as he crept down the stairwell. One step. Another. A third. There were no lights and with each step the space grew darker. Charlie paused. Listened. Below him he heard a soft scrape, a pause, then a creak.

He took another couple of steps. Standing on the wall two minutes ago, he had been terrified. But now, much to his surprise, there was no fear. Instead he felt an almost eager anticipation, as though he were engaged in an extremely high-stakes chess match. He took a few more steps, maintaining a sight picture on his weapon, planning how he would confront whoever was down there hunting him. As soon as his stalker appeared, Charlie would frame him in his front sight and squeeze the trigger.

Three quick shots, then duck back into cover.

Now he could hear breathing. Rapid breathing. Charlie smiled. Whoever was down there was more scared than he was. Or maybe he was just out of breath. Either way, the advantage went to Charlie.

Charlie forced himself to stay completely still,

breathing silently through his nose. The man wasn't more than ten or fifteen feet away.

Front sight. Wait for the target.

Scrape. Scrape. Creak.

A sudden burst of thunder rumbled through the stairwell and a shaft of lightning illuminated the space through a grimy window.

The light projected a shadow against the wall.

Gotcha.

Charlie knew exactly where he was now.

This was the moment.

He leaped around the steel banister, prepared to confront his target. A large man carrying a submachine gun stood poised, barely visible on the edge of the landing, eyes wide, jaw tight with tension.

Charlie fired—three quick bangs—then took cover.

Another flash of lightning illuminated the stairs. But he heard no thunder, only the deafening kickback of the Sig Sauer.

He strained, waiting for the ringing in his ears to subside, but he could tell it might take several minutes. And that was time he didn't have.

He took a chance and peered around the banister, whipping his gun into firing position.

The man was gone.

Charlie took a few stealthy steps down the stairs. It was even darker here than at the landing above. Another step. His ears still ringing. Unable to hear even his own footsteps.

He jumped onto the landing, sweeping the area with his gun. It took his eyes a moment to adjust, but then he saw him.

The man lay on the ground, his hand reaching

feebly for his MP5. Charlie ran down the last few feet and kicked the submachine gun away.

"Where is she?" Charlie hissed.

The man made a wheezing noise, air bubbling from a wound in his chest.

"Where is she?"

The man rolled over and spit blood at Charlie's shoe.

Charlie was in no mood to mess around. He fired into his leg. The man screamed in agony. Charlie pressed the heel of his boot into the wound and ground it with all his weight.

"Where is she?"

"Room 404," the man wheezed. "The presidential suite."

"Where *exactly*?"

"In the main living room."

"How many guards?"

"One inside, two outside."

"And Quinn?"

"He is the one inside."

Charlie noticed a radio attached to the man's belt. He grabbed it and commanded, "Tell them I'm on the third floor. Heading down the hallway from the stairwell. Tell them to cut me off by taking the elevator."

The man stared defiantly into Charlie's eyes. Charlie pushed the barrel of his gun into his crotch. "Do it or I shoot!"

"Okay, okay!"

Charlie put the radio to the man's mouth.

"It's Markov," the man said. "I'm hit. The bastard's on the third floor."

CHAPTER FIFTY-EIGHT

As soon as Markov finished, Charlie grabbed the walkie-talkie and sprinted down the flight of stairs to a large metal door with the number 3 spray-painted on it. He pushed the door open and found himself in a long hallway. At the far end was a small elevator lobby. He shoved a fresh magazine into his pistol, then ran toward it.

There were two elevator doors with small brass dials mounted on the wall. The arrow on the dial of the closest elevator was halfway between the 3 and the 4—moving slowly down. The ringing in Charlie's ears had died down and he could hear the elevator coming. He ducked behind a column just as the elevator dinged. The column was made of glass brick, allowing him a view—albeit a distorted one—of the elevators.

The doors shuddered, then slowly opened.

Charlie jumped out and settled his front sight on the figure emerging from the elevator.

To his horror, it wasn't a big man in a leather coat, but a slim old lady wearing a maid's uniform and pushing a cart full of laundry. Was there anybody behind her? He didn't want to catch her in the cross fire.

The housekeeper spotted him, quickly dropped her eyes to the floor and scurried away. Charlie moved slowly toward the elevator only to find it was empty.

Suddenly, he heard children's voices.

He wheeled and saw a family coming toward him. Father, mother, three children. The father was showing his oldest son a banner. They were headed for the rally in the Square and so caught up in their excitement that they didn't even notice the Sig Sauer in Charlie's hand. The youngest boy ran toward the open door of the now-empty elevator, but reached it just too late. The doors closed.

Ding.

Charlie jumped, startled. The second elevator was coming and this one was surely carrying at least one of Byko's bodyguards.

The family crowded toward the door. As it opened, they suddenly halted, the wife grabbing the arm of her three-year-old son and pulling him backward. From the look on her face, Charlie knew she must have been reacting to something frightening—most likely, a man or men with guns.

Charlie ducked back behind the pillar of glass bricks. All he could see was a mass of shifting colors, people moving in all directions.

He waited a beat, then stepped out from behind the column. The doors were closing on the family. A balding heavyset man in a leather coat was hustling down the hallway, pistol at his side.

Charlie carefully lined up his shot. Just as he was about to squeeze the trigger, a door opened. A door almost precisely halfway between Charlie and his target.

It was a young woman, emerging from her room.

Charlie held his fire, but she saw his gun and let out a bloodcurdling scream.

The bald man wheeled and fired rapidly at Charlie, heedless of the innocent woman in his line of fire. Charlie ducked behind the column as she continued to scream. The bullets were smacking into the glass brick, throwing chunks onto the floor with each impact. Charlie considered shooting back but discarded the idea, afraid he would hit the innocent woman.

The bald man advanced, firing steadily. His barrage quickly smashed a hole in the far side of the brick. Charlie knew that if he didn't do something soon, one of those bullets would crack all the way through and put a hole in his head.

The young woman was huddled against the wall in an almost fetal crouch, hands covering her ears as she whimpered and prayed, trying to take up as little space as possible. Then the housekeeper appeared, poking her head nervously out of another room.

"Get back!" Charlie screamed.

Three more rounds smacked into the column, sending a spray of glass chips in his face.

Charlie stuck the gun out and fired several shots, intentionally aiming for the ceiling so as not to hit the young woman. It was enough to send the bald man lunging for cover.

For a moment, there was something like silence. A brief stalemate.

But Charlie knew reinforcements were bound to

be on the way. As soon as they got here, they'd surround him, cut him off, and he'd be dead meat.

He eyed the abandoned laundry cart left by the housekeeper. It was only eight or ten feet away. Charlie poked his gun out again and fired, hoping to draw a fusillade of bullets in return.

The plan worked. Maybe a little too well. Shards of glass flew off the column, cutting Charlie's arms and face. He closed his eyes, thinking it might be better if he didn't go blind.

And then there was something like silence. Silence and gasping sobs. Underneath those sobs, Charlie heard a clink—the sound of a magazine dropping to the floor. The bald man was reloading.

This was Charlie's only chance.

He dove across the hallway, grabbed the cart's cracked plastic handle and charged toward his foe, using the cart for cover.

The bald man got off two shots and dodged to his left—to avoid being run down.

Charlie redirected the cart, giving himself a clear shot.

For a frozen moment he saw the gleaming bald head just behind his sights. He fired once and the man staggered against the wall, a round hole in his cheek. As his adversary lifted his gun to retaliate, Charlie squeezed the trigger again.

The lumpy figure slid down the wall and hit the floor with a heavy thud.

"Why is this happening?" the traumatized woman stammered.

Charlie scrambled over to her and grabbed her by the shoulders. "Go back to your room. Lock the door and don't come out."

As she scurried away, averting her eyes from the dead man on the floor, Charlie ducked into the room where the housekeeper had disappeared. He found her speaking rapidly into the phone.

"Hang up!" he said. When she hesitated, he raised his gun to her. "Hang up."

She dropped the phone.

"I need you to take me to the fifth floor," he said, "to the room just above the presidential suite."

CHAPTER FIFTY-NINE

wo minutes later, Charlie was walking onto the balcony of room 504 on the top floor of the hotel. The small patio was flanked by two pillars that rose from the larger balcony of the presidential suite below. The scalloped design of the pillars created a ladderlike projection that made it suitable for climbing. If he managed to scale down it, he could come straight into the suite and catch Julie's guards by surprise.

That was the plan anyway.

Charlie holstered his gun and began descending the pillar. The concrete was slippery in the driving rain and sharp gusts of wind clawed at him. Hearing a cry below, he couldn't help glancing down to see if he had been spotted. As it turned out, it was just the call of someone in the Square hailing a friend. But looking down, he felt his head spin and for a moment he froze.

He closed his eyes, took a deep breath and tried to think of Julie's face. After a few seconds, he opened his eyes and began shimmying slowly down the pillar, putting his foot on top of the railing. A few more feet and he would be there. But as he lowered himself, he felt his holster snag on one of the scalloped protrusions from the pillar, tugging and twisting him.

He felt something dislodge from his hip and looked over the edge just in time to see his pistol wheeling toward the ground below and smashing on the flagstones.

He'd lost his gun.

Julie sat on the couch by the piano, her breath rapid and her hands trembling as she listened for a radio update about the gunfire. The rain was pounding hard outside and a bank of televisions on the other side of the suite played international news and finance shows, making it hard to hear the chaotic reports coming over Quinn's radio. She could tell that Byko's guards were still off balance, still searching for the men who'd attacked them from the roof.

It must be MI6. Or the CIA. Or American Special Forces. They'd located Byko somehow and they were coming for him. Finally. She only hoped that if they came in here guns blazing, they'd take some care not to kill her in the cross fire. She looked around the room, searching for a place to dive for cover if and when they came crashing through the door.

Quinn signed off on the radio and sat down about ten feet away, pistol in his lap, arrogantly paring an apple with a small curved knife. The knife looked wickedly sharp and he seemed to delight in the thinness of the slices he was making.

"So they're coming," she said.

He looked at her with amusement.

"What's so funny?" she demanded.

Suddenly, there was a crackle on Quinn's radio and a Russian voice.

"*Eto tuzh,*" the voice said. "*On odnoy.*"

Her heart skipped a beat. Had she heard that correctly?

"It's the husband. And he's alone." That was how she translated it.

The husband? Charlie?

Her heart was racing. But Byko had said . . . had he lied to her? Just to torment her? Why hadn't she thought of that before? Why had she assumed he was telling her the truth?

Another crackle from the radio. "Markov's shot. Nanzer's dead."

And Charlie had killed them? She knew that Charlie had grown up around guns, that his father was a hunter, his uncle a cop, that he had an aggressive, competitive side. But *this*? Gunning down trained mercenaries? For a moment, she dismissed the idea, certain that she had misheard them. But if she *had* heard correctly, who else could they have meant when they said, "the husband"?

She watched Quinn closely, trying to read him. "No," he said in Russian. "Byko doesn't need to know about any of this."

He put down his walkie-talkie and looked at her. "He really does have a soft spot. For both of you."

She looked at him impassively, seeing him perhaps for the first time as a fellow human being. "How can you do this? How can you be a part of this?"

He smiled thinly. "I wonder if Charlie really

thinks he's going to be able to get past all of my guards. I have to confess, it would offer me a certain amount of closure if he did find his way here. I regretted not finishing him off in Los Angeles and now here he is causing all kinds of trouble."

Quinn pared off a slice of apple and crunched it in his mouth.

Suddenly, Julie saw motion behind Quinn. Something outside, something moving on the other side of the French doors. Not something. Some*one*.

A rain-drenched man in a baseball cap.

Standing there in the downpour, Charlie could scarcely believe it. There was Julie. No more than twenty yards away, the only thing standing between them . . . John Quinn.

His eyes found their way to hers and in that brief instant something electric passed between them. Something primitive and essential. An agreement that they would survive this. An agreement that somehow, some way, they would find a way out of this.

A radio crackled and Quinn picked it up.

"There's someone on the balcony," the voice said.

Charlie flattened himself against the wall just to the right of the French doors. It was a blind spot where Quinn couldn't see him.

"What are you talking about?" Quinn barked into the radio. He was holding the knife and the apple and the radio, looking like he needed a third hand.

"We're at the front door. We saw a gun fall from up near the—I think there's somebody up there."

"Up *where*?" Quinn shouted as he moved toward the balcony.

Julie had to do something to distract him.

But Quinn was a quick man. And the instant he saw Julie bolting away, he grabbed her ponytail and yanked her ferociously to the floor.

As Charlie smashed through the door, the world seemed to slow down. He was a good five strides from Quinn and he threw himself across the room as hard as he'd ever run, aiming his right shoulder at a spot in the middle of the man's back.

Quinn, hearing the sound of the door shattering, whirled to meet him, a gun appearing—seemingly from out of nowhere—in his hand.

SLAM!

They smashed into the piano with a thunder of jangling bass notes then slammed to the floor, Quinn's gun slipping from his grasp and disappearing under a cabinet.

Finding himself on top of Quinn, Charlie pounded him in the side of the head.

Not bothering to deflect the blows, Quinn wrapped his arms around Charlie, bucked his hips and threw Charlie onto his back. Pressing Charlie to the floor, Quinn methodically hammered away at him, grunting in satisfaction as Charlie tried to cover his face with his arms. When he tired of punching Charlie's face and arms, he hammered on his ribs. Then, as Charlie dropped his elbows to protect his ribs, Quinn pounded away at Charlie's head again. Charlie tried to grab Quinn or throw him off, but he simply couldn't break through the barrage of expert punches.

As yet another blow sneaked past his guard and clipped him on the temple, Charlie's vision dimmed. He was still conscious, but this couldn't go on much longer.

Julie lay stunned on the floor. In the back of her mind she recalled someone drawing a gun. There had been a loud noise and now there was a lot of grunting and cursing coming from the other side of the room. But her mind felt blank and empty and cold, as though she were a spectator inside an empty, echoing ice rink.

What was happening here? The noise on the other side of the room seemed disconnected from the cottony emptiness of her mind. She lay on the hard floor and stared at the water stain on the ceiling above her. It was a brown stain, darker at the margins than in the center, and vaguely resembled a cartoon character whose name she couldn't quite bring to mind.

Casper the friendly ghost? No. The Michelin Man? No, not him either. Was it—

The grunting and cursing grew louder. She felt a burst of irritation at the interruption. Then, as though her unconcern was peeling away, she began to feel anxious. If her mind could only focus. She sat up slowly and looked at the source of the noise.

Two men. Quinn and Charlie. Quinn sat on Charlie's chest, smiling as he pummeled him into oblivion.

And then it all came rushing back. The container, Quinn, the waterboarding, Charlie's assault on the hotel . . . the fog began to clear. Charlie had come to save her and now he was getting beaten to death for his trouble.

Summoning all her remaining strength, she pushed herself to her feet. On wobbly legs, she grabbed hold of a table to keep from collapsing. The room was spinning.

Thud. Thud. Thud. The steady, awful impact of the blows was the only sound.

Quinn's back was to her, but what could she do? Pull him off of Charlie? She was too small. And she could barely stand.

Then she saw the answer. A thin, slightly curved knife sticking out of an apple. She moved to it slowly, grabbed it like an ice pick and staggered toward the two struggling men on the floor. She knew that if Quinn sensed her behind him, he would snap her neck in two. It didn't matter. Whatever might happen to her, she was not going to let Charlie die here like this.

Julie managed two more strides and as her legs gave out, she launched herself toward Quinn, bringing her arm down in what seemed like a terribly long, terribly slow arc.

Peering through the gap between his elbows, Charlie saw a flash of brown hair, then felt a thump.

Quinn leaned forward and stared intently at Charlie, as though he had something important to say. Then a drop of blood ran slowly down his tongue and fell into the middle of Charlie's chest. Charlie waited for another hammer fist. But Quinn seemed unable—or unwilling—to move.

Charlie seized the moment and rolled him over, putting his hands around Quinn's neck. The mercenary flailed his arms wildly as Charlie squeezed the life out of him. A kind of recognition passed into the killer's eyes as his mouth moved, trying to say something. But no sound passed from his lips. And then the struggle was over.

Quinn's eyes were still open, staring up at Charlie. But Quinn—the essential Quinn, the predatory and unconquerable Quinn—was gone and all that remained was a mild, childlike stare.

Slowly Charlie forced his cramped hands to relax. Exhausted and emptied, he sat back on the floor and found Julie.

She was kneeling five feet away, exhausted and woozy, her hand clutching a small curved knife, its blade slick with blood.

Charlie looked at Quinn again and saw a sheet of blood pooling under his back. He'd been stabbed in the neck.

Julie had saved Charlie's life.

Charlie pulled her to her feet and wrapped his arms around her, a wave of relief and joy running through him.

"You came!" Julie sobbed. "You came!"

"I'm right here," he whispered, never so glad to see her as in this moment.

"He told me you were dead," Julie whispered, "that he'd killed you."

The sound of her soft tears, the smell of her hair, the familiar feeling of her body pressed against his—it seemed as though it had been a million years since it had been like this between them.

As his wife cried softly into his neck, Charlie felt as if he never wanted to let go. But there were still at least four of Byko's guards in the building. Plus the man himself.

"Where's Byko?" he asked her.

"I don't know," she said. "I think he's going to the Square."

The radio on the table crackled. "Quinn! Quinn, come in. Come in, Quinn."

"There's more," Charlie said. "We gotta get out of here."

He reached under the cabinet and grabbed Quinn's Makarov.

"Can you walk?" he asked her.

She nodded, but as she tried to step forward on her own, her legs buckled.

Charlie knew—after everything she'd been through—that she simply did not have the energy for what would now be required of them.

But what was he supposed to do? Carry her? Hide her somewhere and come back for her later?

He looked around the room as if that might provide him the answer. And then his eyes caught sight of something.

Quinn's kit.

Charlie rushed toward it.

"What are you doing?" Julie cried.

He rummaged quickly through the box and found what he was looking for. But when he came toward her with a syringe, she recoiled in panic.

"No! No no no!"

"It's okay, sweetheart. It's me. It's Charlie. It's okay."

Once again, the radio crackled. "Quinn, come in, Quinn."

"This is adrenaline," Charlie told her calmly. "It'll give you what we need to get out of here."

She searched his eyes almost like a child.

"It's me," he told her. "Trust me."

CHAPTER SIXTY

As Charlie and Julie sprinted down the fourth-floor hallway, Charlie heard the *ding* of the elevator.

"This way!" he insisted and pulled her toward the stairwell.

Looking over his shoulder as he opened the door, he saw several men exiting the elevator.

"There!" one shouted.

Charlie bounded through the door as Julie started to run down the stairs.

"No," he said, grabbing her arm. "Up."

They surmounted the stairs and Charlie pushed open the roof door, grabbing Julie's hand. They ran across the roof, through the driving rain, and clambered over onto the parking garage. Within seconds they had pounded through the deep puddles and arrived at the edge that led to the tenement on the other side.

"We have to get to that building," Charlie said.

Julie looked across the alley and hesitated. It was a much easier jump from the hotel to the tenement than it had been from the other direction: there was a gap in the traffic barrier around the parking garage, allowing them to get a running start. And there was a small ledge on the other side extending out toward the hotel, shortening the leap to about four feet. But still, knowing all that she'd been through in the past few days, he still wasn't sure if that shot of adrenaline would be enough.

"Can you make it?" Charlie asked.

They heard shouts behind them. Julie whipped her head around and saw Byko's men coming.

"Got no choice," she said.

She backed up a few steps, sprinted toward the other building, and leaped over the gap. She hit the ledge, rolled and bounced off the wall. She was about to tumble backward when she regained her balance and climbed through the window into the building.

Behind him, Charlie heard a loud yell and a fusillade of shots. He hurled himself across the roof then dove through the half-open window on the other side.

He found himself in a grim hallway that smelled of burned grease, bad plumbing and kerosene. Julie was already on the move. He caught up to her as she pushed open a stairway door and began charging two at a time down the stairs. From Makarov's radio on his belt, Charlie could hear the guards shouting over the airwaves.

"They're in the tenement!" one voice called.

Then another. "We're coming over from the roof. We're in the building behind them now."

Another voice. "They're coming down the stairs."

The first voice. "We'll cut them off from the street!"

Charlie grabbed Julie as they hit the third floor. "Wait. They know we're here."

He pushed open the door and entered the corridor, pulling Julie behind him. Out of nowhere, an old couple emerged from one of the doors.

"Inside!" Charlie shouted, pointing his gun at them. "Now!"

The cowering old couple backed into the room.

"We're not going to hurt you," Charlie said to the old man as he locked the door, "but we need absolute quiet. Understand?"

The old man nodded and Charlie herded the couple into a back room.

"What are we doing?" Julie asked.

"We're going to wait," Charlie said. "We're going to wait for them to come to us."

CHAPTER SIXTY-ONE

Charlie stood by the door, gun drawn, ears straining. He'd turned the radio down but had it next to his ear so he could monitor what his assailants were doing.

"This is the only way out," one of the voices said.

"We checked all the hallways," another voice answered. "Nothing."

"They must be hiding in one of the apartments," the first voice said.

"Farhod, Stas, guard the roof. We'll check all the apartments."

So they were coming.

Charlie took a deep breath. It was the first time since he'd reached Julie that he had a moment to really take her in, to see what she'd been through. She looked wan and exhausted. There was a bruise on her cheekbone, a cut above her left eye. Her wrists and ankles were freshly bandaged, but blood was already seeping through the gauze.

"What did they do to you?" he whispered.

She shook her head and smiled bravely. "Nothing. It's . . ." She looked back at him, her eyes brimming with tears. "I'm so sorry for what I've put you through. For everything."

Charlie felt a wave of tenderness. But before he could respond, the radio crackled. "First floor clear."

A loud bang. Then another. Byko's guards were kicking in doors somewhere on the floor below. *WHAM.* Shouting. *WHAM.* More shouting.

Charlie peeked out the door, scanning the third-floor hallway. It was empty for now, but the shouting and door banging from the floor below was getting louder and he was sure that Byko's thugs would be here soon.

The radio crackled again. "Second floor's clear."

"Head up to the third floor," said another voice.

Charlie could hear footsteps thumping up the stairs at the end of the hallway and left the door open about half an inch—just enough to see out. Through the crack, he saw two armed men burst out of the stairwell. One wore a black coat, the other brown. Someone screamed as the man in black kicked down the first door, while the man in brown covered him from the hallway. They began alternating doors— one covering, one kicking. Once the door was kicked in, they would both enter the apartment.

Charlie turned and put his finger over his lips, signaling to the old people in the bedroom to remain silent. The old man nodded, his eyes pinned on Charlie's gun.

The screams of protest, the threats, the thudding of boot heels and the splintering of doors continued, growing closer and closer and closer. Julie pressed against Charlie, holding his hand. He could feel her rapid breathing against his neck and squeezed her hand silently.

The man in the black coat kicked in another door, then disappeared inside. This would be the last apartment before reaching the one where Charlie and Julie were. But for the first time, the man in the brown coat didn't follow his compatriot into the apartment. Instead, he hesitated in the hallway, head cocked, as though he'd heard something that bothered him. Charlie was sure he hadn't made a noise. Maybe the man had noticed the door was a few millimeters ajar?

From inside the next apartment came loud voices, then several thuds and a groan of pain. Someone was being beaten. The man in the brown coat frowned, muttered something to himself, then disappeared inside.

"Now!" Charlie whispered.

They stepped into the hallway, Charlie holding Julie's hand in his left, Quinn's Makarov in his right. As they began to run toward the far end of the hall, the man in the brown coat stepped back out of the apartment. His eyes widened as he spotted Charlie.

In full sprint, Charlie fired three quick rounds at point-blank range.

The man in brown went down in a heap.

Charlie let go of Julie's hand and allowed her to run ahead as he turned back, still running at three-quarter speed himself so he could lay down cover fire.

The man in black poked his head out the door but the moment he realized Charlie was shooting in his direction, he ducked back inside.

This was just enough to give them a lead. Eight seconds. Maybe ten.

As Julie opened the stairwell door, Charlie could hear the man in black shouting into his radio, "Shots fired! Shots fired! Jasur's down!"

Charlie took the stairs two at a time, still holding on to Julie. As they hit the next landing, the door from the floor below flew open and a man with the crooked nose and scarred face of a boxer plowed out into the stairwell.

Charlie released Julie's hand and speared the boxer with a flying tackle. The boxer grunted and slammed into the wall, but didn't go down. Charlie tripped the stunned thug and gave him a hard shove. The boxer clawed wildly at the wall, trying to arrest his fall, but to no avail. The next thing he knew, the boxer was tumbling ass over elbow down the steep concrete stairs.

Charlie raced after him, Julie in tow.

The boxer hit the next landing hard, squealing in agony. When they caught up to him, Charlie saw the boxer's left leg sticking out at a stomach-turning angle. But with gun in hand, the man was still dangerous.

Before Charlie could react, Julie stomped the boxer in his face, slamming his head into the concrete. The boxer's body relaxed and he slumped backward, unconscious. Julie aimed another kick at his face, then a third.

"Son of a bitch!" she screamed, plowing her foot yet again into his pummeled scowl.

It dawned on Charlie that this face must belong to one of the men who'd helped Quinn torture her. But there was no time for vengeance now. Charlie grabbed her and pulled her away.

"Come on!"

"The motherfucker!"

"I know," he said. "I know."

They hurled themselves down several more flights of stairs and reached the ground floor. But when Charlie shoved at the door, it groaned on its rusting hinges, opened a few inches then stuck, leaving them just barely enough room to get out.

Charlie looked up the stairs. The footsteps were getting louder. And closer.

He urged Julie through the tight gap, then squeezed through himself.

Not a second later, gunshots rang out, splintering pieces of the door.

Charlie grabbed Julie's hand and they rushed toward the Square, pushing their way into the thickest part of the crowd.

"I think we lost them," Julie said.

Charlie nodded. "We need to find Byko."

"What are you talking about?"

"Hopkins. MI6. They think Byko might not have given out the targets yet."

"He hasn't. I don't know why, but he's waiting."

"You're sure?"

"I saw him talking to his people on his computer. He said they would be sent the targets in half an hour. That was maybe twenty minutes ago."

"If I can get to him, Jules . . ."

"His men are out there! They're everywhere!"

"I have to try."

"Charlie." She touched his face gently, voice cracking. "It's over. There's nothing we can do now. Let's just get out of here and go home."

Charlie hesitated. That sounded so good. And so easy. And it was everything he'd wanted since this whole nightmare began. To be home. Safe. With his family.

But what about London and New York, Copenhagen and Vienna, Sydney and Tokyo . . . ?

Those people.

That was why Julie had entered into all of this to begin with. Even if she was willing to give up—out of exhaustion or the belief that it was futile—how could he? When he knew there still might be a chance.

He pulled her by the hand, forcing his way through the crowd. "Come on. I'll get you a taxi at the Metropol and meet you at the embassy in Tashkent."

"No," Julie said.

"Jules—"

"You're not going alone."

They had reached the edge of the Square and the clouds had parted. In the sudden wash of light, everything was visible with crystalline clarity. On the far side of the Square the statue of Sultan Babur thrust upward from the throngs of people. A young man shouted into a public address system from just to the right of the bronze steed. The municipal building where Julie had sought shelter stood unchanged. Same sandstone walls, same green roof, same high windows. It was as though nothing had changed at all in six years, as though they were stepping back into the past.

She took his face in her hands, looking into his eyes.

"I know you think that you left me that day," she said. "That you should have been there with me. But that's just chauvinist bullshit, Charlie. I left you. I left you alone in that Square. And what you went through, what you saw—" Her voice cracked. "Don't bother arguing with me, Charlie. I started this whole mess. If you're doing this, there's no way you're going alone."

Charlie sighed. He knew that expression. She hadn't been broken by three days with Quinn; she wasn't going to be broken now by him.

He paused for a moment and surveyed the scene, trying to work out what he needed to do next—and to figure a way to pull it off without getting Julie hurt.

As he tried to make sense of the confused mass of humanity, he realized that Byko would be standing up on that statue soon. How was Charlie going to work his way through the crowd to get to him? How was he going to evade Byko's bodyguards? And how was he going to stop the dissemination of the targets? It was a madhouse already—teeming and jam packed and he was nowhere near the heart of the action yet. He needed eyes on the scene.

And then he remembered back to that day six years ago. How he had climbed up that pole, how he'd been able to see the whole thing . . .

That was it. This time, Julie would be his eyes.

CHAPTER SIXTY-TWO

Byko was so angry that his entire body felt like it was vibrating.

He stood behind the statue of Babur, shouting derisive instructions to Stas, the senior surviving member of his crew. What was wrong with these cretins? An entire team of Russian special forces veterans against one *journalist*? And the journalist had decimated them?

Well, it hardly mattered, did it? There was nothing that Julie and her meddling husband could do to stop him now. In a few moments he would execute the final part of his masterpiece then go into hiding.

Byko held his right hand in front of his face, willing it to stop shaking. The thought that his plan was now virtually unstoppable began to calm him and the trembling subsided.

In front of him, Uktam searched the crowd with his field glasses, looking for the Davises. Stas and Farhod flanked him, submachine guns hidden under their leather dusters.

Byko forced himself to put Julie and her husband aside, to ready himself for his speech.

It was nearly time.

* * *

As they pushed their way through the crowd, Charlie explained his plan to Julie. She was skeptical at first, thinking that he was merely trying to get her out of harm's way, but she soon realized he'd never pull any of it off without her help.

Now the question was finding binoculars or a camera. The group assembled in this Square was not a wealthy one—and Charlie needed to find someone with decent equipment.

So far, he'd seen lots of cheap cell phones and point-and-shoot cameras, but nothing that would serve his purpose. Finally, Charlie caught sight of a man who could help them. He was pointing a Russian-made Zenit with a long lens in the direction of Babur's statue.

"You got a good look?" Charlie asked the middle-aged man, poking him on the shoulder.

The man lowered his camera and looked at Charlie with annoyance.

Charlie instantly pulled out a wad of cash and waved it at the man.

"I want to buy your camera," Charlie said. "Two thousand U.S., no questions asked. And I'll need your cell phone, too."

The man frowned as he stared at the money. The offer was simply too good to be true. But he hungrily snatched the money, forked over his camera and cell phone and scurried into the crowd as if he'd just stolen something.

Charlie grabbed Julie's hand and led her to the half-dozen large trucks parked on the other side of the Square. On the cabs of those trucks, several young men stood, high above the scene, watching everything.

Charlie handed the camera to Julie and programmed his newly acquired phone with the number of his pink-and-diamond beauty. He tested it and the bimbo's phone rang, chiming out her song of choice.

" 'Baby I Love Your Way,' " Julie noted with a tiny tear in her eye.

"Rather appropriate," Charlie quipped.

She grabbed him and kissed him hard on the mouth.

"I'm not going to say, 'Don't do anything stupid,' " she said. "Just don't get yourself killed after all of this. 'Cause that would really suck."

He kissed her again and held her hard. "There's no way," he said. "Our story doesn't end like that."

She nodded, wanting to believe him. "I love you."

"I love you," he said, then called to one of the kids atop the truck. "Hey! Can you help this lady get up there?"

Salim skirted the crowd, dragging his wounded leg, trying to find a good location.

Charlie was a good man, maybe even a great man, but despite all they'd been through together, he still seemed to think that Salim was just a boy, someone who needed to be protected. Well, he was not the first one to make that mistake. People had been underestimating Salim for a long time.

He stopped and surveyed the Square. He had seen a video once of the rally from six years ago. It had been larger than this one. But not by much.

He looked for a place that was higher than everything else, someplace from which he would have a clear, open view of the Square.

Then he saw it. On the far side of the Square was a big municipal building with a green roof. It had high windows that looked directly down onto the statue of Babur.

Perfect.

Charlie stopped fighting his way through the throngs of people when he got to within twenty yards of Sultan Babur. He had spotted several of Byko's remaining men at the base of the statue.

"I see at least three on the base," Charlie said into the phone.

"There's four," Julie responded. "One's on the western side, in your blind spot."

"I can't see Byko."

"I've got him. He's about to get up on the statue."

Charlie had to get closer. Even if there was a danger of being seen. He was sure Byko was going to send out the targets during his speech.

"I'm moving in," he said.

"There's some kind of barricade around the statue," she replied. "He's got two, wait, no, three guys moving right next to him. Two of them are bodyguards. The other one, it's this guy in a Homer Simpson T-shirt. I saw him back at the hotel. He's some kind of computer geek."

Charlie pulled the pistol out of his waistband, letting it dangle where nobody in the crowd would spot it, then put his shoulder down and bulled his way toward the statue.

"Where's Byko?" Charlie barked.

"East! He's on the east side of the statue."

And Charlie spotted him—eyes intent, body coiled with energy. Charlie considered trying to shoot him from here. But it was pointless. He was too far away. And in a crowd like this, all he'd do was kill an innocent bystander.

Suddenly Byko turned and looked out at the crowd. This time, he seemed to be searching the faces of the people in front of him. Charlie tried to avert his eyes, but it was too late. Byko was staring right at him.

How in God's name did he get here?

Byko whirled and shouted at Farhod, "He's here! Goddamnit, get him!"

He watched Charlie duck into the crowd and disappear from view.

But Byko would not allow that man to get in his way, or to get in his head. There was nothing Charlie Davis could do now.

Byko turned back toward the statue.

A college student had been speaking to the crowd, his mouth so close to the microphone that his cries of outrage and optimism were distorted by the powerful sound system. Byko recognized the innocent ardor in the eyes of the young man as he shouted about democracy and freedom, and supposed there had been a time when his own face had probably looked like that. But platitudes were not enough. Not anymore. The message Byko was about to bring to the stage was going to be darker than this boy's. But it would also be clearer, purer, more mature.

And his people would recognize the hard wisdom in it.

Byko closed his eyes and prepared himself. He had played this moment over and over in his mind. The performance needed to be perfect.

"And now let us hear from the hero of Andijan ...," the young man shouted. " ... Alisher Byko!"

Byko swung himself up onto the statue and looked out at the crowd, remembering the last time he had been here, the hope with which that day had begun—and the tragedy into which it had descended. This time it would be different.

Forget Julie Davis. Forget Charlie Davis. They were irrelevant.

Byko raised his hands and the crowd broke into a long, sustained cheer.

This is my moment.

Julie could see Byko's men—four or five of them—fanning out into the audience, all armed with AK-47s. And they were getting closer and closer to Charlie.

"Where exactly are they?" Charlie asked. "Give it to me on a clock."

Julie looked through the camera. "Two at your three o'clock. One more at eight o'clock. I don't know where—I lost the other one."

She swung the camera wildly, trying to isolate the most important threat, to guide Charlie to safety. But then she lost him altogether.

She panned back and forth anxiously, catching a view of one hard-faced killer, then another. But no Charlie.

* * *

Charlie ducked down to conceal himself, still clutching the gun in his right hand, the phone cradled in his left.

"Where am I going, Jules?"

"I don't know. I lost you. I can't see you."

In the roar of the crowd, Charlie could barely hear her. "I'm twenty yards south of the statue!" he yelled. "I can see the middle of the base right in front of me!"

Suddenly the shouting began to die down.

Charlie peeked up to see Byko standing on the pedestal, holding up his arms, hands extended, as motionless as the statue looming over him. When the crowd finally went silent, Byko slowly lowered his hands. The last time they were here, he had spoken through a crude megaphone. But today, his people had set up a high-quality sound-reinforcement system and his voice blasted through speakers.

"Six years ago, we came together here, in this Square, as a signal of our solidarity. To say to our government that we would no longer stand for its oppression and tyranny . . ."

Angry voices shouted agreement throughout the crowd.

Byko calmed them again. "The government responded that day the same way it always does. And since that day, we have been cowards. Living in a state of retreat and denial. But today, all of that will change. For good."

The crowd roared. Charlie knew they were responding to the easy aphorisms and vague optimism. If they only knew what Byko really had planned . . .

"Today we will finally strike back," Byko continued. "Not with candles or banners, but with force. Today, we will strike back at the West. For this is where our true enemies lie."

Charlie pressed the phone to his mouth. "We're running out of time, Jules. I need a path."

"There's a sort of passageway in the barricade. In the back, behind Byko. Nobody's guarding it now. It comes from the rear of the statue. You might be able to work your way around to there."

"All right," Charlie said, as determined as he'd ever been about anything. "You're going to get me there."

His leg throbbing in agony, Salim limped up to the second floor of the municipal building and rapidly located a perfect sniper location—a small nook just the right size for one man to stand in, more or less invisible from the rest of the lobby. A quick blow with his fist knocked out one pane of glass. He would be visible from the ground, but he didn't care about that. If he was spotted after it was over, so be it. He racked a round into the chamber, braced the rifle carefully on the ledge, then sighted on his target.

It was the traitor. And he was standing on Babur's monument.

Our true enemies," Byko roared, "are those in governments which support and prop up this murderous regime. Our true enemies are in every country which buys our cotton and our oil, our uranium and our gold, knowing that the people who work to produce it toil in abject poverty."

Byko had been speaking for about five minutes and the crowd was still with him. But he sensed their enthusiasm had dimmed a little since he began. They wanted to hear him talk about the regime, about his plans for taking it down and replacing it with something better. He had to convince them that they were missing the point.

"We have lost control of our country. Somewhere out there—in London, in New York, in Washington, D.C.—are little men in little rooms, pushing the buttons, moving the chess pieces of the world around. They consider us their pawns. Pieces which can be sacrificed to satisfy the thirsts and hungers of their kings and queens. And all the while, they themselves are hiding. Refusing to admit what they do, refusing to say what they believe. They obfuscate everything and expect us to swallow it or look the other way. But all of that is about to change. Because I am here, standing before you, before the world, to proudly say, 'Here is what I believe!'"

Salim was no billionaire, no worldly sophisticate with an international education, but he knew who was to blame for his brother's death. It wasn't Americans, it wasn't Englishmen . . . It was the men who had dragged his brother away, beaten him, cut him, broken him—they were Uzbeks. If you wanted to fix this country, it would do no good to point the finger of blame at foreigners.

The enemy was here.

Salim had been just a kid when his brother had

lain there under a white sheet in the courtyard of their home. But he could still remember the sight of him when his mother had pulled the sheet away. A thing like that, you didn't forget. Salim was a quiet boy, and most people didn't realize how much he had thought about what needed to happen in his country. But Salim *had* thought about it. Someday this would be a country where young men weren't dragged off and murdered just because they didn't like the government.

Salim had dreams for his country. And Byko was getting in the way of those dreams, confusing things, distracting the people with foolish tales about who their real enemies were.

The target swam in the bull's-eye of Salim's rifle scope and he settled the crosshairs on the man's chest. Salim took up the slack in the trigger with his index finger as gently as you might stroke the lips of a beautiful girl and gently squeezed the trigger.

But instead of the customary boom and kickback all he heard was a click.

The rifle had jammed.

Charlie crouched as low as he could and moved toward the rear of the statue, ducking in and out of the crowd so he could see.

One of the bodyguards was less than ten feet to his left and Charlie could glimpse his AK-47 through the throngs of people. The guard seemed to know that Charlie was close but couldn't quite find him.

"Keep going!" Julie said. "You're thirty yards out. You're almost there."

To Charlie's left, he saw the crowd part like the Red Sea. The bodyguard was waving his rifle at them. He was heading in the wrong direction but it would only be a few seconds before Charlie was revealed.

Charlie pushed to his right.

"Not that way! Go—" Julie's voice momentarily dissolved into a crackle of static. Charlie looked at the phone. The charge was down to 2 percent and he was losing his signal.

"I've got one of them coming up behind me!" he shouted.

Julie's voice cut through the static of the dying phone. "Another one's coming up right in front of you! Go back, go back, go back!"

Charlie bulled through the middle, heading straight for the statue.

Some of the men in the crowd pushed back at him and Charlie had no choice but to wield his gun. "Out of my way!"

Byko paused, hearing screams behind him. He wheeled, but couldn't see what was happening. Perhaps his men were apprehending Charlie Davis. He turned back to the crowd. They were clearly sensing that he had reached some important turning point in his speech.

"Today, we are reclaiming something. Today, in this small place, we are going to do something that affects the so-called great nations, the so-called powerful. But what makes them great? What makes them powerful? It is only because we are afraid to see through the smoke screen of their power, and challenge them where they live."

He pointed down at Gulbadeen, the young man standing there with his spiky hair and his foolish Homer Simpson T-shirt. Byko might have been angry that the computer technician had so little sense of occasion. But it could be argued that he was the perfect symbol for what Byko was arguing— that this silly doughy boy could unleash a firestorm that might eventually consume the world.

"When this young man presses a button on his screen, word will go out to people like you—all over the world. Within minutes, great actions will be put into place and we will finally have our say!"

Byko nodded to the young man and thrust his fist toward the sky.

As Charlie saw Byko punch the air, he lifted his gun, pointing it toward Homer Simpson, trying to get within range. He had Homer in his crosshairs, about to shoot, when a young woman in front of him shifted ever so slightly, bobbing her head into his line of fire.

"Down!" Charlie shouted.

Everyone in front of him ducked for cover, but as Charlie went to line up his shot again, the young computer tech stabbed the tablet with his finger.

"It is done!" he heard Byko proclaim.

The crowd seemed stunned, unsure how to react.

Charlie wheeled around, looking for Byko's guards, still brandishing his gun to make sure no one jumped him. He put the phone back to his ear. "I didn't do it," he said. "We were too late."

"I know," Julie told him. "Get out of there, Charlie!"

Charlie retreated as quickly as he could, but Byko's thundering continued from the platform. "No longer will our gold form the bars of our prisons. No longer will our oil power the tanks that roll over our broken bodies. No longer will our cotton form the ropes that bind our hands . . ."

Charlie saw Byko extend his arms into the air as though they were handcuffed, as though he was the prisoner.

"Because our enemies are not here. In our own country. Our enemies are in New York and London, Copenhagen and Vienna, Sydney and Tokyo—in every country that buys T-shirts made from the cotton picked by a generation of child slaves. Today, these enemies will pay the price for their hypocrisy. Today, they will pay for it with their *blood*. If money is all they care about, let them choke on it!"

Suddenly it dawned on Charlie. *New York and London, Copenhagen and Vienna, Sydney and Tokyo . . . Chicago and Minneapolis!*

It was the dramatic inevitability that told the story. Today, this Square, the anniversary, Byko on that statue. The money and the greed. That was what Byko meant to punish.

know what the targets are!" Julie heard Charlie say into the phone.

She gripped the camera tightly, could see Byko's men converging toward him.

"Charlie! Look out! They're coming. From every angle!"

She heard him click off and he disappeared from view.

"Charlie! Charlie!"

She whipped the viewfinder left and right. They were coming for him. And they were close.

"Charlie!" she screamed. "Charlie!"

CHAPTER SIXTY-THREE

opkins sat outside the farmhouse as the SAS men packed their gear in preparation for evac. They were still holding Byko's double and the guards who had come along with him. But it was pointless. Byko had outfoxed them.

Hopkins blew out a long breath. Unless Charlie Davis was able to somehow get to Byko, the mayhem and destruction was coming and there was nothing anybody could do about it. He grabbed his phone for what must have been the hundredth time in the last half hour, checking to see if he'd somehow missed a call from the American.

Much to his surprise, the phone vibrated and chirped in his hand.

It was Charlie Davis.

Hopkins hit the answer button and spoke into the phone. "Please tell me something good."

"He's hitting the commodities markets!"

"I don't see—"

"Why Hanover and not Berlin? Why—" Davis's voice cut out for a moment "Vienna and not Paris? Why Minneapolis and not D.C. or L.A.? Every single one of the target cities has a commodities market. A big building with thousands of people in it that also has great symbolic value."

As Charlie shouted into the phone, Byko's thugs were pushing inexorably closer to him. He couldn't see them all, but he could feel their presence, the anxious people in the crowd making way for the armed men.

"What?" Hopkins said. "I can't hear—"

"Commodities! He's hitting the commodities markets. Trust me. Just trust me. He wants to hit us in the pocketbook. And the symbolism. He's—"

Sensing he was getting no response, Charlie checked his screen to see if he was still connected. But the phone had gone entirely dead.

Had Hopkins heard him? Had he believed him?

Charlie dropped the useless phone, clasped the Makarov, and pressed forward, trying to find a seam in the crowd.

On the pedestal Byko refused to stop. "Tomorrow the news will say that we are terrorists, lunatics, fanatics. What they will *not* say is what really happens in this country."

Byko held out his hands toward the crowd, beseeching them to understand his vision. "How we live!" he shouted. "What we suffer! This they will never say . . . but we will *know*."

Salim tried once again to rack the bolt on the old Mosin Nagant. It had always been a little sticky, but not like this. Now it wouldn't even rotate.

Of all the times for his rifle to jam.

Salim could hear the cadence in Byko's voice, the rhythms in his speech, and could tell that the man was winding down, that he had precious few moments left.

He had to get the bolt free, but if he simply jammed it onto the paved ledge, he would most certainly distort the viewfinder. At this distance, Salim couldn't afford to be anything but precise. So he pulled off his shoe and hammered the bolt with the heel. At first, it didn't seem to have any effect. But on the fourth strike, he felt some movement. On the seventh, the bolt began to rotate. On the ninth, it came free.

He yanked back the bolt and ejected the jammed round. It fell to the floor next to Salim's injured foot as he looked into the breach of the gun. The next round looked okay and he slammed the bolt home.

CHAPTER SIXTY-FOUR

Charlie pushed himself through a soft spot in the crowd. But then he saw guns in front of him, AK-47s held aloft in both directions, the guns forcing the terrified crowd to fall back.

When he wheeled around and saw two more, he was cut off. Surrounded.

After everything he'd been through, after all of this time . . . perhaps it *was* written. Perhaps it *was* his destiny to die in this Square. He gazed across the ancient space and spotted Julie standing on the roof of the truck, shouting into the phone.

He wanted so badly to reach out to her, to touch her one last time. But he realized that he'd done what he came here to do. She was going to make it home. And maybe, just maybe, he'd managed to complete her mission.

Byko's men were closing in now, weapons at the ready, apparently unconcerned with opening fire right here in the middle of the crowd.

This was it. Charlie's final moment. Nothing to do now but wait for it . . .

• • •

A single shot rang out, echoing from one side of Babur Square and back.

For a moment, all Julie heard was silence.

Had they gotten to Charlie? She could see Byko's men, but they were looking around in confusion. None of them seemed to know the source of the shot.

Instinctively, she swung the camera toward the focus of the crowd's attention: Byko himself.

His face was fixed in an expression of puzzlement. Then he moved his head as though trying to work a crick out of his neck. She thought Byko was craning to see where the gunfire had come from or perhaps who had been shot.

But then the red spot blossomed on his chest. Blood. Blood forming an oblong splotch on the front of his white shirt. A moment later, Byko fell, clutching at his chest.

And the screaming began.

The crowd had to assume the shooter was one of Karimov's. And where there was one, there would always be more.

As the people started to stampede, Julie saw one of Byko's bodyguards fall. Whether he was intentionally knocked down by someone who assumed he was one of Karimov's internal security thugs, or whether he just lost his footing was impossible to know. Then somebody shouted something and another bodyguard succumbed to the fury of the crowd.

But where was Charlie?

Through the camera, Julie watched the tumult of the mob. People pushing and shouting, trying not to trample each other. It was chaos.

"Hey!" she heard a man shout. "We going!"

It was the driver of the truck.

"No!" she said. "I need to stay here."

She looked back through the camera, searching for Charlie.

And then, she thought she saw something. A glimpse of dirty blond hair.

She racked focus on the camera, trying to hone in on the man stumbling in her direction. As he neared her, forcing his way through the crowd, she finally found his face. His eyes. It was Charlie.

"Jules!"

She lowered the camera and saw his broad smile as he arrived at the truck.

"Jules, jump!" He extended his arms toward her. "Jump!"

It was a long way. But she didn't hesitate.

For a moment she was weightless, airborne, the sound of the screaming and yelling filling her ears. Then, with a hard thump, her feet slammed into the ground and Charlie's arms closed around her.

"Hold on!" Charlie screamed at her.

"I'm not letting go of you!" she yelled. And she knew that she would never let go of him again.

A disconnected part of Alisher Byko's brain told him that he was hit. He was hugging the base of the statue, blood streaming down the granite. But he couldn't feel anything below his navel—nothing but a sort of shifting darkness, groping its way up his spine.

As he rested against the stone, the surging crowd visible out of the corner of his eye, it occurred to him that maybe this was what he had been searching for all this time. Not just relief from his pain, not just a dimunition of the fury and horror that tugged at him every waking moment of every day—but *this*, this dark force he felt taking over his body . . .

Extinction.

He could see his son's beautiful face, as clear as if he were here with Byko still—his silky soft skin, his angelic brown eyes. And Daniella was here, too. Cradling the boy, nursing him from her supple breast. Smiling at Alisher almost sheepishly.

As he peered up at the aching gray sky, he realized that everything he had set in motion was merely the final futile gesture of an overmatched, defeated man. He would see Daniella soon, and his boy. His sister and his father. His mother and his cousins. All of the Bykos who had come before him.

Around him, the people in the Square were shouting and running for their lives, though he was quite certain none of them were in danger. He felt sorry for them. And he began to see that he was no different from them—the nameless, faceless people in this Square. In fact, he was no different from the nameless, faceless victims of the attacks he had put in motion. Because, in fact, they all *had* faces, just like his little boy.

And now he began to see those faces: the boys and girls in Vienna and Copenhagen, the sons and daughters in London and New York, the brothers and sisters in Tokyo and Sydney.

What have I done? Byko thought. *What have I . . .*

·   ·   ·

The surging crowd began to diffuse as Charlie and Julie spilled out of the Square and there was finally room to breathe. After a few more blocks, the crowd thinned out and the screaming abated. There were no more gunshots, no sound of bullhorns or tanks or helicopters.

"Where did the shot come from?" she asked Charlie.

"I don't know," he replied, looking around.

They paused in a doorway and watched the crowd stream past.

"Do you think he's dead?" she asked.

"I hope so," he said, searching her face to make sure she felt the same way.

"Yeah," she said softly and allowed herself to lean against him.

Now that they were safe, Charlie's mind turned to the larger issue. Had Hopkins understood him? Did he believe him? Had his phone died before Hopkins could hear what he'd said?

If he'd gotten through to Hopkins—and Hopkins had believed him—the information would skate around the globe within minutes. Aircraft would leap into the skies, satellites would vector in on targets, rooms would fill with anxious people watching video monitors . . . and at the tip of the spear, vans full of hard men wearing black helmets and carrying submachine guns would plow into the streets.

Charlie could only hope those hard men would reach the targets in time.

CHAPTER SIXTY-FIVE

asul Erekat ran his hand nervously through his short beard and fought the urge to pound on the horn. What was the holdup?

He had left the safe house garage in the London suburb of Slough at six this morning—seemingly in plenty of time to make it to the target. But there had been construction on the M4 and then a major wreck on the bridge over the Thames had resulted in the entire southbound lane being shut down. So he had cut through the East End—only to find that everybody in London had apparently tried the same trick, clogging up every major artery in the city.

And now, just blocks short of the target, traffic had completely locked up, nothing moving as far down the street as he could see. He wasn't even the one assigned to perform this mission. His two assistants, Masun and Sa'ir, were supposed to have delivered the van to the target.

But they had turned out to be cowards. They were both English Muslims of Pakistani extraction, soft and weak from their Western upbringing. For the past two days they had been whispering and carping and making sarcastic remarks at everything Rasul had said. In the end it had become clear to him that either their nerves would fail in the breach or they would simply slip away and disappear.

He had taken Sa'ir, the smaller of the two, into the back room of the flat and garroted him with a piece of twenty-two-gauge speaker wire. Then he had walked into the living room where Masun was watching *Doctor Who* on the tellie.

Rasul had shot him in the back of the head with a suppressed Glock 17 and it had made quite a mess on the television.

Rasul had never killed anyone before and he was surprised that it had been as easy as it was, the whole business over in less than two minutes.

But with both of them dead, the entire mission had fallen on Rasul's shoulders.

It was simple enough. In theory. Drive to the target, park the van, press the big red button in the back, and walk away. The problem was, this was supposed to be a two-man operation. The detonator switch was hidden in the rear of the van in case the van got pulled over and searched. That was why Sa'ir was supposed to drive, while Masun was to sit hidden in the back.

But still . . . Rasul would find a way. Park, throw open the rear door, crawl over the oil-soaked fertilizer, press the red switch, walk briskly away into the gentle southwesterly wind. He'd have two minutes and fifteen seconds, just enough time to escape the blast radius without breaking into a run.

He hadn't admitted it to Masun and Sa'ir, but the raid by British tactical police early that morning on the bomb-making warehouse had unnerved him, too. And now MI6, MI5, Special Operations and every cop on the street was probably looking for him.

He took a deep breath.

Well, whatever was going to happen, it would be over soon.

He was almost there. Two blocks ahead on Cannon Street, he could see the large silver letters spelling out LIFFE. The London International Financial Futures and Options Exchange was a market where commodities such as cotton, oil and metals were bought and sold. Byko had repeatedly made the point—and it was a good one—that money was the lifeblood of the West. Stab her here and her blood would flow into the streets in torrents.

The back of Rasul's white Volvo van contained over a ton of fertilizer and fuel oil, making a bomb big enough to bring the entire building down. But that was not the real purpose of the attack. The small glass jar of nuclear material sitting on top of the fertilizer—that was what would make the mission a success. The cloud of dust would rise hundreds of feet in the air and then drift for blocks and blocks, rendering a three-square-mile area of central London uninhabitable for a century.

Traffic again came to a standstill. And Rasul's sense of foreboding grew. For a moment an idea flitted into his mind: what if he simply climbed out of the van and set off the bomb here? With the traffic stopped, he might have time to run around and flip the switch before he caught anyone's attention. And if the bomb blew two blocks short of the target, who would know?

Byko and Quinn would know, that's who.

It had been made clear, once he had committed

to the mission, that there was no margin for error. Everything was to go according to blueprint or it wasn't to go at all. Quinn had not so subtly indicated to Rasul that he knew exactly where Rasul's father and mother and sister were—that deviation from the plan would not simply result in Rasul being hunted down and killed, but that his entire family would go to the grave with him.

Rasul gripped the wheel, hands shaking. On the sidewalk, he saw a young woman walking toward the Exchange. She was holding hands with a little boy. The boy was dawdling, pulling his mother's hand, wanting to stop and pet a dog that was being held by a tattooed girl with her belly showing in the immodest, whorish fashion of the West.

The traffic started to move in front of him. Almost there.

Still, Rasul hesitated, not pressing the accelerator. Instead he continued to watch the mother and child in their silent tug-of-war as the boy fought to pet the dog.

Rasul suddenly felt a wave of emotion as he looked at the pair. If the boy continued to distract his mother, they would probably reach the Exchange at almost the exact moment that the bomb detonated. His own son had been the same age when he was killed by the American bomb, burned to death in the arms of Rasul's wife—a bomb aimed at an Al Qaeda operative who was briefly visiting Rasul's hometown in Yemen.

Rasul smiled as he looked out at the people on the sidewalk. They would die—the mother, the boy, the tattooed girl with the dog—all of these heedless people. They would pay for what had happened to Rasul's family.

A horn tooted behind him.

Rasul released the brake and drove slowly forward. He continued to watch the mother and son in his mirror, barely paying attention to the road in front of him. As he nosed toward his destination, he realized that his hands weren't shaking anymore. In fact, he felt terribly calm, a sense of utter peace. Nothing could go wrong. A *thousand* MI6 agents couldn't stop him now!

Suddenly the truck in front of him braked hard. He glanced away from the mirror, nearly slamming into the trunk of the larger vehicle. Something was going on up in front of the LIFFE building. But his vision was blocked by the truck and he couldn't quite make it out.

Why was nothing moving? Rasul slammed his fist on the horn.

Again the cars moved, crawling forward. After a moment he saw the source of the problem . . .

Men in blue uniforms, blocking the street. Security guards? Police?

Surely they couldn't know about—

And then, seemingly without warning, there were armed men surrounding his van. Black helmets, bulletproof vests, machine guns.

They knew! They knew and they were here to stop him.

Well, no matter. He could still arm the bomb. He would simply have to crawl to the back of the van, dive over the fertilizer and—

He reached under his seat, took hold of his Glock and fired wildly through the window, hoping to drive the helmeted men back.

Instead there was a loud bang in reply. Then another. Something hit the side of the van. Another bang. Another. It sounded as though hammers were being thrown at the doors. He wasn't hit yet—but he would be soon. As he began crawling toward the back and over the soaked fertilizer, he heard a huge blast and suddenly the back doors flew open.

Six submachine guns were aimed directly at him. "Hands in the air! Hands in the air now!"

But his hands were only three feet from the detonation switch.

He was overwhelmed by a blinding sense of panic and horror. For all his anger, for all his need to avenge the wrong inflicted on him, he had not signed up for a suicide mission. On the other hand, he wasn't interested in spending the rest of his life in a Western prison. And if he gave himself up, what Byko and Quinn would do to his family . . .

He had no choice but to reach for the red button.

CHAPTER SIXTY-SIX

Charlie and Julie settled into their seats on the plane, silently busying themselves with their belongings. Bags, tickets, passports, a week-old copy of *The Economist* . . . everything seemed so ordinary, so familiar, so routine. Julie had bought a toothbrush and a change of clothes inside the Tashkent airport and now they looked like any ordinary pair of Westerners—albeit ones whose bruised and weary faces indicated that they might have recently been in a car wreck.

A small television set played CNN from the nearby bulkhead as they belted themselves into their seats.

"In what was some of the most stunning work by the international intelligence community in recent years," the reporter said, "terrorist suspects were arrested today in cities across the United States, Europe, Australia, and Japan." Images of elite anti-terrorism units flashed across the screen, arresting bewildered-looking suspects in a variety of different locations. "Apparently a coordinated series of so-called dirty bomb attacks was planned for four P.M. Eastern Time today. In what highly placed sources have indicated was a multipronged, coordinated international operation, executed with clockwork precision, all nine terror cells involved in the plot were simultaneously taken down. No bombs were detonated and all of the low-grade nuclear material held by the terrorists was recovered."

The television showed a sequence of shots—men in suits standing at podiums in front of various flags making solemn statements about the superior skill and determination of their respective intelligence services.

"In an unprecedented gesture," the reporter's voice-over continued, "the CIA and MI6 released a joint statement announcing that it was their mutual cooperation and that of their counterparts across the globe which made the sting possible . . ."

A flight attendant poured each of them a glass of water from a chipped plastic pitcher. The engines began to wind up, the cabin lights dimmed and the little television went dark.

When the cabin lights came up again, the flight attendant switched off the TV with a clunky remote control about the size of a paperback book.

Charlie supposed that he ought to be angry that the most powerful intelligence services in the world were crowing about doing something that had actually been accomplished by a pair of amateurs. But he couldn't seem to muster even a shred of exasperation. Right now he was too damn tired to care.

He turned and looked at Julie. Now that everything was over, he had no idea how they would begin again.

•   •   •

Julie knew what Charlie had to be thinking. She had violated his trust and it would be a long road back to regaining it. She looked at him, trying to read how deep the damage went. And when he smiled, her heart nearly broke. Eyes brimming with remorse, she took his hand. "I'm so sorry, Charlie. For lying to you, for not trusting . . . for endangering all of us, I thought I was doing something good, but—"

"You were," Charlie conceded. "Look at what we did."

"I was going to tell you. That night. As soon as I got home from Disneyland. I was going to tell you everything."

Charlie nodded, no doubt wondering what exactly was encompassed in the "everything." As he looked away, Julie grabbed his face, forcing him to look her in the eye. "I never loved him. Not the way I love you."

"I read the emails."

"He reminded me of a time and a place. That was all, Charlie. A time and a place. When we were different."

Charlie sighed and looked at the blank screen. The plane began taxiing up the runway.

He thought about all of the ways in which he had let Julie down over the years, what he must have done to drive her toward Byko, what she'd sacrificed to give him the life that he said he wanted.

"I threw in the towel," he said heavily. "I left you no choice but to throw yours in, too. And then I never asked you how you lived with it because I didn't want to hear the answer."

Julie grabbed his hand and kissed his palm. "No more secrets," she said.

"No more secrets."

The engines wound up to a high whine, then the plane lumbered forward and took off. The air was turbulent—bags rattling in the overhead bins, magazines spilling on the floor. Charlie clasped both of her hands in his. Then, abruptly, everything steadied and the plane began to climb as smoothly as if it were on rails.

CHAPTER SIXTY-SEVEN

Charlie and Julie deboarded the plane at Heathrow and were met at the gate by a small neatly dressed man with a military bearing and a brush mustache of the sort once favored by British Army officers.

"Frank Hopkins," he said, extending his hand toward Charlie. "We'll need to go over a few things, I'm afraid."

"We're going home," Charlie said firmly, taking Julie by the arm, then pushing past him toward the American Airlines gate at the far end of the terminal.

"We have a private plane," Hopkins insisted. "Eleven hours in the air. We can get it all done by the time we touch down. Then you'll never hear from us again."

Charlie stopped, scowling at the man.

"Let's just be done with it," Julie said.

Ten minutes later they were airborne again, climbing out of London in a spacious and well-appointed jet bearing Royal Air Force markings.

"I'll show you some photographs," Hopkins said after they'd reached cruising altitude.

Charlie identified a series of faces, all of them men in Byko's coterie of personal guards.

The mercenary in the Escalade.

"Dead."

The driver crushed by the boulder.

"Dead."

Hasan.

"I shot him," Charlie said. "But his body was burnt in the missile complex when Byko blew it up."

Hopkins paused and looked at Julie curiously. He seemed astonished that some untrained journalist had managed to eliminate all of these hardened killers.

Charlie felt like telling the neatly dressed spy that anybody would have done the same thing if their wife's life had been at stake. But then, he supposed, that probably wasn't true. And sitting here in the comfortable leather chair of the RAF jet, it seemed almost as though it had all been done by someone else.

There were several more before Hopkins handed him the photo of John Quinn.

This time, Charlie glanced at Julie before answering. "That one was a joint effort. I'd give Julie most of the credit there."

Hopkins looked at her with unabashed admiration.

"There were some others, " Julie said. "They were chasing us at the Square. They must have gotten away."

Hopkins nodded, then laid down a picture of a thin boy wearing a gray prison jumpsuit.

"And what about him? The man who shot Byko?"

Charlie stared at the photograph. "It was *Salim*?"

Hopkins frowned curiously. "You know him?"

"He was one of the people who helped me. I never would have made it out of Byko's compound if it wasn't for him."

"As you can see, he was arrested by Karimov's police."

Charlie felt a flash of anger. "Well, you're going to get him out."

Hopkins leaned back in his leather seat. "There are three dozen witnesses who saw him do the shooting. And he hasn't denied it."

"Give me a break!" Charlie said. "Karimov's thrilled to have Byko out of the way. This should be an easy one for you."

Hopkins smiled perfunctorily. "I'll do what I can."

Charlie laughed without humor. "You know, there's a rumor that CIA was there when Byko's sister was being tortured . . . that in fact they may have orchestrated it. And that MI6 tipped off Karimov about the Andijan demonstration six years ago, knowing that Karimov would go in with force. You add that up with John Quinn—a former CIA man—being Byko's operational man . . ." He paused, letting this sink in. "It'd be pretty grim publicity for the security agencies if all that came out."

Hopkins looked at Julie as though asking for her help.

Julie glared at him. "Is it true?"

"I don't think that matters to your husband."

"It matters to me," she said edgily.

"I have absolutely no idea. But we all know that anything is possible," Hopkins admitted.

Charlie took the man in for a beat, appreciating his candor.

Hopkins rose. "I'll have our Foreign Minister make the call himself."

"I know guards inside that prison," Charlie warned. "They'll let me know when Salim is released."

Hopkins regarded Charlie for a long moment, trying to gauge whether he was bluffing.

In fact, he was. But Charlie had a damn good poker face.

And apparently Hopkins couldn't afford the risk. He walked to the far end of the plane, picked up a handset and made the call.

Charlie watched him for a beat, then turned to Julie. "For the record, next time you decide you want to save the world, I think we ought to talk about it first."

Julie smiled and they both allowed themselves to laugh. Then she laid her head on his shoulder. He kissed her hair and she closed her eyes.

Charlie smiled and felt himself melt against her. It would be good to see the kids again. It would also be kind of fun to walk into the homicide bureau of the LAPD and watch Reamer's and Alvarez's faces when he introduced them to the woman they thought he had murdered.

CHAPTER SIXTY-EIGHT

As Charlie pulled into their driveway and came to a stop, Julie burst out of the car before he'd even had a chance to put it in park.

By the time he did, Meagan and Ollie were rushing from the house.

"Mommy!"

Meagan leaped into Julie's arms while Ollie attached himself to her leg. Julie was laughing and crying at the same time, hugging and kissing both children in turn.

For a moment Charlie didn't move, his entire body sagging into the upholstery of the car. It was done. He'd brought her back and saved his family.

As Charlie climbed out of the car to join the homecoming, the front door of the house opened again and Becca appeared. He knew she was taking in the cuts and bruises on his face when she smiled ruefully at him, a silent acknowledgment of what he had endured.

"Am I gonna have a makeup birthday . . . ?" Ollie squealed. "Since you missed my real one?"

Julie wiped her eyes on her sleeve and kissed him on the forehead. "I think that can be arranged!"

"With more presents?" Ollie jumped up and down with excitement.

Julie looked at him with mock sternness. "We'll see."

They ran inside, Ollie sprinting to be first, Meagan tugging Julie's hand. Julie turned and flashed Charlie a broad, thankful smile then disappeared inside.

Charlie looked around the yard. He noted with a mix of fondness and annoyance that the grass needed mowing. Most of his neighbors hired lawn services, but Charlie had always enjoyed doing the work himself. There was something about coming inside for a beer late on a Saturday afternoon, the smell of new-mown grass and sweat clinging to his body that reminded him of his old man. And of Youngstown.

Becca was still standing on the porch, holding the door open for him. He walked slowly toward her, still soaking in what it meant to be home.

When he reached the door, he paused and spoke softly to her. "Thank you. For holding down the fort."

Becca nodded stoically, then allowed herself to break down, clinging to Charlie's neck and silently sobbing. After a few moments, she pulled away from him, seemingly embarrassed by her outburst.

"I made us a good English breakfast," she said.

"Well let's get to it," he replied.

Without another word, she hurried into the kitchen, where she bustled around making final preparations for the meal.

Charlie walked into the dining room, listening to the clatter of plates and pans, the laughter of the children as they competed for Julie's attention, the strains of an old Simon & Garfunkle song that Becca had put on the stereo.

Later that day, after a long and luxuriant nap, Charlie got up and checked his email. The only message he was interested in came from an unidentified mailbox. There was no note, no subject, just an attached video file.

Charlie clicked on the attachment and a short movie popped up.

A painfully thin boy of nineteen looked into the camera. Salim.

Palonchi Ursalov sat silently next to him with her usual unblinking, stoic expression.

"Hello, Charlie," Salim said. "I wanted to thank you. I know there is no way they let me out of jail unless you help. I am home now with my mother. We try to make new life here. Maybe you can send us picture of your wife and family. So we can remember you. Good luck in California!"

Salim grinned and waved joyfully, like an excited boy. There was a brief, somewhat awkward pause as he and his mother continued to stare at the camera. . .

Then the screen went blank.

Charlie quickly downloaded several pictures of Julie and the kids and composed a quick note to Salim: "I'm happy you're home. And thank you for everything. We wouldn't have made it without you. Your friend, Charlie." He fired off the email and closed the laptop, experiencing a satisfaction he hadn't felt in years.

• • •

While Oliver cued up his favorite music video in the den, Julie sat near Meagan on the couch and looked around the house, trying to imagine how it ever could have felt so small. Becca had left a few minutes earlier, after a long hug at the door and a cautionary whisper in Julie's ear: "You have a beautiful family."

This was not something that Julie needed to hear. She'd always known how fortunate she was to have these children, this husband, this life. But why had this never felt like enough for her? Was it because she truly wanted to give something back to the world? Or was it because she felt the need to leave some kind of mark on things? Perhaps a little of both. One way or another, she had gotten her wish.

And now she was home. Within a couple of days she would return to fixing the kids' lunches, running the fund-raising drives at Meagan's preschool and driving Oliver to soccer and baseball practice.

And it all sounded better than she ever could have imagined.

But would it be enough?

She supposed that was something she would need to figure out in the weeks and months ahead, but she knew that no matter how it went, she and Charlie would work it out together. Because they were kindred spirits once again.

Charlie bounded down the steps and could hear Meagan nagging her mother in the den, "I want to see him now!"

"Your father's taking a nap," Julie insisted. "And you're going to let him sleep."

Charlie slowed as he approached the den, hovering in the doorway, wanting just to watch them. Meagan was dancing around in front of Julie, and Ollie was playing with a pair of action figures on the floor. Sitting on the countertop was a homemade birthday cake (blue and white for the Yankees) that Julie must have whipped up while he was napping.

Charlie had never quite been able to wrap his head around the fact that Oliver's birthday and the anniversary of the massacre would, for eternity, fall on the same day.

But it occurred to him—now—after all this time, that this was the nature of life. That the agony and suffering and pain were almost always situated too closely to the joy and love and redemption. That it was man's best hope to make peace with that idea and to somehow go on living. Moving toward the joy and love and redemption no matter the risk, no matter the price.

"Daddy!" Meagan squealed, as she ran toward him and grabbed his leg.

Charlie lifted her into his arms. "Well, it's certainly nice to be wanted."

He came toward Julie, kissed her long and hard.

"Eeeeew!" Meagan cried and squirmed out of his grip.

Charlie leaned down to Ollie and affectionately mussed his boy's hair. "How's it going, tiger?"

"Good," Ollie said without looking up from his Power Rangers.

Charlie's eyes met Julie's. She shrugged and gave him a little smile.

"How are you doing?" he asked.

"Good," she said. "Really good."

He ran his hand gently down her back and moved into the kitchen to inspect the eats.

"Sal called while you were sleeping," Julie said with a hint of suggestion. "He said he needs an answer about Shanghai. Guess he didn't hear about the last few days."

"What are you talking about?" Ollie asked, barely looking up from his toys.

"Just work stuff," Charlie answered as he pulled out his cell phone and scrolled down to Sal's number.

Julie watched him, a look of nervous expectancy in her eyes. He got the impression that she was actually holding her breath.

He waited a beat, made her suffer for as long as he could manage, then cracked a smile. "You okay with me being gone a couple of weeks?"

Julie grinned back. "I think we can work it out."

Charlie dialed Sal. It was a quick, unremarkable conversation—a few dates, a few details and a last benediction from his boss:

"You're doing the right thing, Charlie."

"I know, buddy. I know."

As Charlie set his phone on the table, he felt as though a giant wall between himself and Julie had just melted. A sense of happiness—of rightness—coursed through him.

"Hungry?" she asked.

"Starving!"

"Then have a seat, my lord."

"I think I shall, my queen."

He sat down as she put a loaded, steaming plate in front of him. It was his favorite meal.

"Pepper steak medium rare," she said, "lyonnaise potatoes, creamed spinach, corn on the cob with extra garlic butter."

"Guess we're not too worried about my cholesterol today," Charlie said with a smile.

"We're not worried about anything," Julie replied.

Charlie waited until everyone was seated, then cut himself a forkful of red meat.

He regarded Julie for a long moment, remembering everything he had ever loved and respected about her, from those first moments when they met in Tashkent until this last, crazed adventure.

"Of course, if I'm going to Shanghai, we're gonna have to figure out your next move," he said. "Spunky girl like you, you gotta get back out in the world, huh?"

Julie reached out, resting her hands on Ollie's shoulders as if they were a life raft. And a parting of her lips revealed a grateful, almost knowing smile.

"The world can wait," she said. "For now."